UNFAIR *My* *Lady*

KATHRYNE KENNEDY

sourcebooks
casablanca

Published by Sourcebooks Casablanca, an imprint of
Sourcebooks, Inc.
P.O. Box 4410, Naperville, Illinois 60567-4410
(630) 961-3900
FAX: (630) 961-2168
www.sourcebooks.com

Printed and bound in the United States of America.
QW 10 9 8 7 6 5 4 3 2 1

*To my readers, whose encouragement means
the world to me.*

One

London, 1885

SUMMER WINE LEE PEEKED THROUGH THE DRAPERY covering the second-story window of their rented London town house, hoping to catch a glimpse of the man she intended to hire to change her life forever. She'd sent an invitation to the impoverished Duke of Monchester asking that he meet with her today regarding an urgent business matter, but she wasn't quite sure if he'd come or not.

She started twisting the fringe that adorned the dark green drapes. They'd been in London for over a month, and nothing had happened. No invitations. No visitors. Not even a nod from the elegantly clad English people when they passed her by as she strolled along Curzon Street. Her friend Maria had told her to be patient, that she needed to gather all the information she could before they implemented their plan.

But it was hard to be patient when she felt so lonesome.

Summer sighed. She'd been lonely her entire childhood; why should she start feeling sorry for herself now? Pa had been obsessed with that mine in Arizona, and she'd foolishly thought that he'd spend more time with her when he'd found that vein of silver. That the huge strike would rid him of his obsession for wealth. Instead, he'd uprooted her and Maria from the frontier town of Tombstone and plunked them in New York while he'd continued his obsession in other ways— investing in railroads and banks and property.

Summer glanced around the room at the raised-panel walls, velvet upholstery, and plush rugs, all of it a bit frayed and worn. Everything felt so old in England—unlike the burgeoning newness of New York—and yet neither city had welcomed her. New York society had shunned both her and her friend, until she'd met Monte. She smiled at the thought of her intended, the man she'd come all the way to England for... so that she could become a different person, a real lady, that his family would accept.

She just wished that Pa had come with them, instead of staying in New York. He claimed that his health wouldn't allow him to travel, and he did have a horrible cough from working in the mine all those years, but Summer still had a feeling that he simply didn't want to leave in the middle of business negotiations. The only time she heard from him was when he sent more funds.

But she had her best friend, Maria, she reminded herself. And although she couldn't have brought all her slobbery crew of pets with her on that terrible ocean voyage, she did manage to bring her little Chihuahua, Chi-chi. She wasn't entirely alone.

"Maria, this had better work," Summer muttered to the empty drawing room. For this was her friend's plan, not her own. Summer had wanted to hire one of the American heiresses who had already married into a title, the ones who had gone through money so quickly entertaining Prince Albert that they sponsored young American girls looking for an introduction into society.

"Not good enough," Maria had responded, flipping her long black hair over her shoulder. "Trust me when I tell ya', if ya' want to be a lady, ya' hire a man to teach ya' how to do it. And I finally discovered the perfect fellow, a poor duke with two falling-down castles, who's feared by all in the social circle for his quick wit and nasty tongue… but is also a particular favorite of His Highness."

Neither of them had ever met the duke, yet Maria had been confident and told Summer it was her golden opportunity. So Summer had sent her invitation and didn't know what scared her the most: the idea that the duke might just show up out of curiosity, or that he'd ignore the invitation entirely.

Feet pounded up the stairs. "He's coming!" panted Maria, her green eyes wild with excitement. Summer's stomach flew up into her throat, and she felt her entire body tremble.

"How do you know?"

Maria put her hand over her heart. "'Cause one of the chambermaids seen him before, and I set her up to watch the street."

Summer pressed her nose to the pane of glass, trying to see around the edge of the window to the cobbled street below. Several men strode toward the direction of her house. "Which one is he?"

"The one without a hat," answered Maria before she spun back around.

Summer only heard her steps pounding downstairs, for she couldn't take her eyes off the man who strode toward her home. All the other men wore bowler hats, so he was easy to pick out. Even the feeble rays of England's sun reflected off his blond hair, making it glow a golden yellow. He wore it unfashionably long and bare of the pomade that slicked most other men's hair back. Summer liked it.

The duke had on a long coat of pale blue, narrow trousers, and a deep blue cravat. He carried no umbrella or cane, and as he passed a group of gentlemen going in the opposite direction, she realized that he was also not a particularly tall man. For some reason this made her feel more at ease, so that when the bell jangled, and Maria came in to announce that she had a visitor, Summer felt almost quite calm.

Until he walked into the room.

She had arranged herself on the settee, folded her hands in her lap, and then quickly covered Chi-chi with her skirts, mentally scolding the chambermaid who'd promised to keep the little critter from underfoot. She felt the dog settle down beneath the warmth of her petticoats—none of them had been prepared for the coolness of England even in the summer—and breathed a sigh of relief.

"Are you Miss Lee?" inquired the duke as he ran his eyes from the top of her head to the tips of her kidskin boots. "Miss Summer *Wine* Lee?" The deep richness of his voice made her heart turn over with what she could only assume was terror, and she jumped to her feet, jostling Chi-chi and making her growl. Tarnation, she didn't need her dog to attack this man's ankles, so she quickly sat back down, lifting one slippered foot beneath her skirts to rub the side of the dog's belly.

"How… how do you do?" she stammered, holding out her hand but not attempting to get up again.

His golden brows rose in astonishment, but he came to her anyway as if nothing were amiss, as only a true gentleman would, and took her hand as if to kiss it. But the moment their skin met he froze, staring at her with the bluest eyes she'd ever seen, a mouth so perfect it reminded her of a statue of Apollo, and above that masterpiece a nose that seemed slightly crooked, saving him from being extraordinarily handsome to just boyishly so.

Chi-chi started to growl again and broke the spell that had fallen over them. The duke glanced around looking for the source of the sound, while Summer renewed her belly rub and the little dog quickly quieted again. With more bravado than she felt, she imperiously waved at a chair next to her, and with a frown he took it, his compact frame settling elegantly into the velvet upholstery.

The duke studied her, trying to believe what his eyes told him. He'd met many an American heiress intent on claiming a title and a position in society, but they generally resembled Englishwomen, albeit sometimes prettier and… healthier. But this one looked like some elfin creature that had tumbled out of a fairy tale from his childhood, with her hair and eyes and skin all shades of golden brown. "You have an interesting name. I presume that you're an American?"

Summer's eyes widened. He said it as if it were a curse. "Yes."

"And you have a business proposition for me?"

"Yes." He sounded as if he should be the last person in London she should approach for anything.

"Do you know who I am?"

Tarnation, his voice dripped with arrogance, thought Summer. "Yes."

His eyebrows rose again. "Including my reputation?"

She opened her mouth and closed it again. How confident was she in Maria's information? Was he some kind of rake? Had inviting him into her home already ruined her reputation and spoiled any chances of her social success?

"I... I'm not sure what you mean."

"Then, madam, let me enlighten you." He leaned forward, his masculine presence filling the room, his eyes glittering with anger. "Before you present any proposition to me, you must understand that *I do not like* American women. I abhor this method of purchasing titles. I use every opportunity I can to discredit these social hunters to His Highness, who is a particular friend of mine, as I'm sure you're aware. Why else would you seek me out? As a gentleman I feel it only fair to warn you of this. My truthful comments entertain the prince, which allows me to live in some of the comfort I've been accustomed to, and I would use all information at my disposal to continue to entertain him. Including any proposals you wish to put forth... as well as information about your person."

Summer stared at him in utter astonishment, unprepared for his speech. She'd been rehearsing her own proposition and hadn't considered he might have something to say as well. She could only think to ask, "My person?"

"Quite."

"Such as?"

"Such as the quaint cut of your dress, several years out of date, if I don't miss my guess, and the appalling way your hair continues to escape from your coiffure and flop about your head. And what is wrong with your voice? Unfortunately, I know several American women, and none of them have that twangy accent making them sound even more uncultured than they already are." The duke relaxed back into his chair and crossed his arms over his broad chest. "And oh, please, please enlighten me about this condition of yours that makes your leg twitch."

Maria had told her he wielded his tongue like a sword; Summer just hadn't thought it could cut so deeply. She tried to remember that this was exactly why she wanted his help. With his support she'd be able to conquer society in half the time than with any other sponsor.

He pierced her with his steady gaze, full of arrogance and confidence, waiting for an answer, waiting for her to burst into tears. Summer grinned and lifted her skirts.

The duke's mouth dropped open, those beautiful lips that disguised such a wicked tongue forming a complete "O" of surprise when Chi-chi popped out—five pounds of snarling, snapping fur.

"I was trying to prevent her from biting your ankles, but now I think I'll let her have a go at it."

Unfortunately, the duke wore tall boots, and Chi-chi only managed to scuff the leather up a bit. "Bloody hell, what is it?" he asked as he shook his leg to make the animal let go.

"It's a dog," snapped Maria, who'd obviously been listening at the door. She charged into the room and swept the white bundle of fur up into her arms. "And she don't like ya', and neither do I." She spun and faced Summer. "How can ya' sit and smile at the man? Draw yore knife! Poke him a good one and send him on his way! I'm sorry I ever got this crazy notion to invite him here."

"You have a knife on your person? Is it beneath your skirts as well?" inquired the Duke of Monchester, staring at the ruffles in alarm. He'd never met another woman like her before. Boredom had become an almost constant companion to him, yet the moment he'd walked into her presence, the world had suddenly come alive, this woman somehow making the very air sparkle.

Summer could feel laughter welling up inside. His expression looked so funny! It was a good thing she'd given up carrying her gun around her calf after they'd left Arizona. But she'd never give up the knife her Apache friend Chatto had given her. "Of course."

The duke raised a golden brow. "May I inquire what else might be under there?"

"No, ya' may not," Maria spat, her pale eyes sparkling with anger, her black hair nearly lifting from her head with the force of it as Chi-chi continued to yip and growl and squirm to get out of her arms and find a vulnerable place in the man's clothing. "Ya' ain't no gentleman, and I suggest ya' leave this house at once!"

Summer didn't know what it was, but the duke's attempts to insult her didn't bother her in the least. After all, she was used to this type of man, although he used his prowess differently. And the laughter that kept bubbling up inside her had to be released, first in giggles and then outright guffaws, until the tears ran down her cheeks and she slapped her leg to get it all out.

Maria's eyes narrowed. "I don't see nothing funny a'tall."

"Neither do I," said the almost-gentleman, but his face was alight with humor and a grin kept twitching at his lips, as if he didn't smile very often and his mouth wasn't used to the configuration.

Summer wiped the tears from her eyes. "Don't you see, Maria? He only came to get some amusing gossip. He's got enough ammunition already to completely destroy my hopes for entering polite society. At this point, my only option is to try and buy his silence, along with his sponsorship, if I can."

Maria humphed.

The duke nodded his head at the black-haired beauty, studying her exotic looks. Where had these women come from, anyway? "Who are you?"

"Her friend," spat Maria. "Although I'm sure ya' wouldn't know a thing about friends, now, would ya'?"

"Enough, Maria. Take Chi-chi and go now. Let me see if his lordship's silence can be bought."

He leaned forward. "His Grace, not his lordship, and it will have to be a great deal of money, madam. This little tableau would keep the prince in stitches for a week, at least."

Summer leaned forward as well, startling him enough with the move that he lunged back in his seat. "Your feelings are obvious, sir, but it's my understanding that the prince *does* like American girls. And the more unusual the better. So perhaps I'm doing myself a disservice by hiring you, for I'm sure your tales would only arouse his curiosity." And ruin her chances of being presented to the Queen, she thought silently to herself. And that was her true goal—for surely that conservative woman's acceptance would meet with the approval of New York's own queen of society, the formidable Mrs. Astor.

He digested her words for a moment, then nodded. "I'm willing to listen to your business proposition."

"Good." Summer grinned at him and rang a little bell on the table. Her footman entered with the tea tray, face flushed and eyes averted. Maria had urged Summer to hire him because he seemed to lack the snobbishness of most of his kind, or so she said. Summer felt sure his athletic build and charming face had something to do with it as well.

"Thank you, Charles. That will be all." She had a suspicion Maria had set him up to spy on them, and waited until he'd left the room before she continued. "The proposition I have for you, sir, is a little unusual." She spoke and poured tea at the same time, unaware that she spilled most of the liquid onto the white lace covering the tray, too agitated over smoothing out that "twang" in her voice. She'd taken voice lessons in New York, but she still couldn't achieve that sophisticated smoothness. "I'd like to hire you to introduce me into society."

The duke snatched the cup from her hand before the slopping tea could soil any more lace. "I believe I've already expressed to you my views on this subject. Do you honestly think I'd actually help an American dupe one of my fellow countrymen into giving her their title?"

"Oh, but you misunderstand. I'm not searching for a husband."

Those golden brows rose again in patent disbelief. "Then you are in a class by yourself."

Summer set down her own teacup before she was tempted to toss it into his arrogant face. He obviously didn't believe her. "I'm already engaged with a man back home. A wonderful man, whose family is highly placed in society."

"Aah." He relaxed back into his chair. "And you aren't quite up to their standards, is that it?"

"What makes you think… No, never you mind. Your brain is as quick as your tongue, and I won't set myself up for your insults so easily again." She glowered at him. "Yes, I need to be brought up to their standards. I need to be presented to the Queen. And then I assure you, I'll leave your precious lords alone and head straight back to America."

"To your wonderful American man?" His face fell as if something about that bothered him. Could he actually be upset that she preferred an American over one of his English lords?

"I told you, I don't want a title."

"I'm inclined to believe you, from that silly glaze in your eyes when you mention this American." An odd feeling swelled inside the duke's chest. Now why would it bother him to learn that she already had an intended? He refused to think about it any further. "Does this paragon of virtue have a name?"

"Monte." The girl sighed when she spoke his name.

His teacup clattered as he slapped it down on the table. "How much?"

"How much—oh, money. Well, as I understand it, your estate is rather sadly in disrepair…"

His blue eyes glittered. "That, madam, is none of your business."

His tone suggested that she pry no further into his family matters, so he had to assume that it was her faulty American upbringing that made her blurt out: "But how do you support yourself?"

"You are an ignorant savage, aren't you? Gentlemen don't work, madam. That is what makes them gentlemen."

"You're blunt with your words, sir," she retorted as she jumped up and began to pace the confines of the drawing room. He made it obvious that he scrutinized her every move.

For such an unpolished woman, he thought, *she had remarkable grace*, as if she didn't so much as walk but *flow* across the room. "As you are with your questions. Don't they teach you American girls any manners?"

"I'm not like most American girls."

"That is rather obvious. You pour tea as if you were slopping hogs, yet you pace this room with such grace, I'd swear you were walking on water. How does a woman like you get made, anyway?"

Summer laughed. Didn't he realize how funny the looks on his face were whenever he watched her? But perhaps only she created those puzzling frowns and that's why he wasn't used to being laughed at, the way his brows rose in astonishment when she did so. But he took it well; it even seemed to amuse him that she thought him funny when he wasn't trying to be.

"If you let me hire you," she proposed, "you'd get to find out."

He adjusted his cravat and smoothed back the hair that kept falling elegantly over his ears. His face settled into polite boredom. "I'm not that interested."

"Would, let's say… a third interest in a railroad be enough to get you interested?" Summer had thought long and hard about what to offer him, and the way society in New York was about new money led her to believe the English may have that prejudice as well. Offering him cash might be something that wasn't *done*. The railroad was small, which was why Pa had given it to her, but profitable enough that she thought he wouldn't be able to say no.

Although, any price would be worth gaining her the man she loved. She'd be willing to give away the entire investment, if needed.

The duke frowned, fighting surprise and interest at the same time. He'd supported himself by entertaining the prince and was welcomed into the finest houses as a guest, all on the strength of that relationship. He wondered what it would be like to be independent again, to *not* have to seek out funny stories and humiliate others? Although, he reminded himself, those whom he exposed usually deserved it, but it'd be a relief not to have to depend on anyone else's generosity. And what she proposed wasn't exactly work, so it wouldn't betray his status as a gentleman.

Summer found his face quite easy to read and, as long as she ignored what he said, found him almost pleasant.

"I'd have to see the papers."

She sauntered over to the sideboard, scooped the pile up, and laid them in his lap. He shook his head, as if she'd done something vulgar again, but began to peruse the papers with eagerness while she paced the room. He finally sat back with a sigh and studied her with such intensity, she felt her dander rise. This man didn't need a sword or a gun to threaten anyone. He did it with the look on his face and the cruelty of his words.

"You're going to take a lot of work."

Summer refused to rise to the bait and wondered how a man like him had been made.

"That gown, for example—what is it, cotton? Give it to your maid… better yet, just burn it. And those eyebrows, don't you know what tweezers are for?" His voice lowered. "But your bones are good, I'll give you that, and your eyes…"

He caught her up in his gaze, and Summer couldn't breathe, her foot frozen in midpace. She'd never felt anything like it before, as if he held her captive with just that look and she couldn't have fought away from it even with her knife. The hair rose on the back of her neck and she felt the warning of trouble—like the time she'd shot that claim jumper, as if she were being mortally threatened. And then she mentally cringed at the thought, for she'd promised herself never to think of that man's death again.

The duke kept doing peculiar things to her. She found herself internally chanting Monte's name like a mantra just to break the spell he had over her. "Do your insults mean that you'll sponsor me?"

He shook his head as if emerging from a trance. "Bloody hell, I suppose it does. I'll have to show the papers to my solicitor, of course. But I warn you now, I've never done anything like this, and I do *not* wish anyone to know about it, understood?"

Summer nodded, brown curls flopping around her face, heart skipping with joy. If she could raise herself to this man's standards, Mrs. Astor would be easy.

"And there's some things I don't know about women's fashion, like underwear and so forth." His eyes flashed back to hers, and Summer knew he expected her to be shocked by his words. So, ladies could not discuss underwear? See, he'd already taught her something.

Summer nodded in feigned sympathy. "Of course. I understand you may have to do a little research yourself."

His face fell, as if disappointed by her reaction. He looked at her hopefully again. "No matter. My current mistress is Lady Windolm. The Marchioness of Windolm. I'm sure she'd be able to enlighten me about some of the more delicate matters."

Summer shrugged. "Excellent. But I'd prefer no one else knew of our arrangement as well. Can she be trusted to keep our secret?"

The duke cocked his head at her, shoving back the blond curl that spilled over his left ear. *This crazy woman*, he thought, *doesn't even know that one didn't discuss one's mistress with another woman.* "Madam, weren't you listening? I'm bloody well sleeping with her! If she can keep that a secret—"

"Good," sighed Summer. "I'll look forward to meeting her, then."

He stood, the gentleman in him hearing the tone of dismissal in her voice and automatically reacting to it. He smoothed the front of his blue coat, adjusted his cravat, and stepped toward her. She barely had to tilt up her face to look into his own, which confirmed Summer's first impression of his height. Yet he still didn't seem short to her. His presence negated any such considerations. She noticed that the color of his clothing brought out the blue in his eyes, making them stand out even more.

He took her hand and brought it to his lips, the breath from his words warming the tops of her fingers. "You are a match for me, aren't you?"

Summer snatched her tingling hand back. "What do you mean?"

He shrugged. "One of these days, madam, I *will* shock you."

Just as he turned to leave, Chi-chi came running into the room, Maria hard on her heels. "Give it to me, ya' little varmint!" she cried. The dog dived beneath Summer's skirts. "Don't think that'll save ya'." Maria sank to her knees and began lifting layers of petticoats.

Summer didn't move, afraid she'd step on the little dog. "What's the matter?"

"This is the stealingest dog I ever did know," muttered Maria beneath the lace. "She's got something and won't give it up."

The duke hadn't moved, his eyes widening with each passing moment. Summer thanked God that she'd paid him to be on her side, 'cause it seemed that a day didn't pass in this house without some kind of shenanigans going on, and if he was going to be a frequent visitor, it was best to get him initiated anyway.

"Chi-chi," she admonished. "Give it to Maria."

The dog responded with a muffled growl. Maria leaned back on her bustle and shook her head, black hair flying.

"Chi-chi…" warned Summer.

The teacup-sized dog shot out from beneath her petticoats, circled the room a few times, then hopped into Maria's lap and spat out the thing in her mouth. Maria screamed and stood, tumbling dog and a very dead rat onto the carpeted floor.

"Tarnation, it's only a rat, Maria." Summer picked the thing up by its tail while Chi-chi jumped up and down in excitement. "Here, take it."

"I'll do no such thing," stammered Maria as she backed out the door. "Don't even know how ya' could touch such a nasty thing." Her pale green eyes flicked from her to the duke, and her face reddened in sudden embarrassment. "I forgot he was—oh, tarnation! Ya'll never be accepted—I plumb—"

Summer took the dead animal and wrapped it in a doily from the back of the settee and handed it to Maria. "Here, take this and the dog back downstairs." Maria made a hasty retreat with a whining Chi-chi in her arms. When Summer turned back to the duke and saw the exasperation written on his face, she couldn't help giggling.

"I have shocked you, sir."

"Any other woman would have been screaming right along with Maria."

"Oh, she's just squeamish. There's no reason to be excited about a dead rat."

He stood frozen, as if his feet were rooted to the floor. "It makes me wonder what you've seen—that a dead rat pales in comparison."

Summer gave him back a perfect imitation of his own shrug.

"And," he continued, "it seems that you have more activity beneath your skirts than all the whores in the East End."

Summer suppressed a grin. Wouldn't he be surprised if he knew the hours that she and Maria had spent in the company of "light skirts" back in Tombstone, Arizona. That Maria's own mother had worked in Hafford's Saloon, and after she'd died, the other women had all pitched in to care for Maria. Summer knew that most of the ladies had been forced into the business in order to eat, and had found them to have kinder hearts and more honor than many of the society people she'd met since.

Besides, if Maria's tales were true, once a woman became married and provided an heir and a spare, she was free to pursue any number of dalliances. What was the difference between them and the ladies at the saloon? She couldn't take offense at his remark; rather, she thought it a very witty joke.

His face fell when he observed her reaction, obviously downcast that he hadn't shocked her with his witticism. For some reason he was keeping score on who shocked whom, and he kept losing. Summer found the duke quite easy to read and wondered why he had a reputation that frightened so many people.

Perhaps the prince took his comments seriously and that's what worried others.

The Duke of Monchester sighed and took her hand, making a slight bow and murmuring that it was time he took his leave. But when he turned to walk out the door, he didn't let go of her, and Summer was forced to walk along with him, for a moment feeling that it was the most natural thing in the world for her to be alongside this man hand in hand. As soon as she recognized that feeling, however, she quickly twisted her fingers the way Chatto had taught her, and planted her feet, dismayed that for a brief moment she'd actually forgotten about Monte.

It was just that this stuffy lord made her laugh like she hadn't in ages, that was all.

He looked down at his suddenly empty hand and turned toward her, his mouth parted in astonishment, as if he hadn't realized that he'd been holding on to her, until she was no longer there. Then his lips quirked, and those brilliant blue eyes clouded in confusion. "It seems that I'm actually looking forward to our next meeting."

"I predict," said Summer, "that we shall become great friends."

He shook his head. "As your companion so eloquently pointed out, madam, I have no friends."

He strode out of the room, and the feeble sunlight through the parted draperies seemed suddenly dimmer, the air less buoyant, the very atmosphere lacking the crackle of electricity. Summer sighed and went to find Maria and Chi-chi.

The Duke of Monchester closed the door of her home behind him and shook his head, feeling as if he'd just survived a cyclone—dizzy, giddy, and relieved that he was still in one piece.

Two

SUMMER, MARIA, AND A BORED-LOOKING DUKE STRODE along the walk in front of the building at 7 Rue De La Paix in Paris, gazing through the windows at the elegantly displayed manikins arranged as if they were frozen into tableaus of dressing, having tea, preparing for a ball. Maria trembled in suppressed excitement, but Summer frowned. "Are you sure this is necessary?"

The duke rolled his eyes. "Madam. Any man, woman, or child will tell you that in order not only to look your best but be in the height of fashion, a wardrobe designed by Charles Worth is essential. It remains to be seen, however, if you'll actually warrant the attention of the great man himself. Most women deal only with the vendeuse and a fitter."

Summer couldn't have cared less, but Maria gave an audible sigh as they entered into the carpeted salon, seized by the elegance of draped silk and gilded mirrors and the undeniable feel of haute couture that permeated the room. Within moments Summer found herself in a fitting room, silently tolerating the poking and prodding and standing still for prolonged periods.

She endured by imagining the pride that would soon be on Monte's face when she returned to New York in her new gowns. Surely his relative, Mrs. Astor, could not disapprove of a Worth gown.

When the fitter removed Summer's shoes to measure her feet, her knife popped out of its sheath. The woman threw quite an unnecessary fit, her French loud and fast as she ran from the room. Summer followed, knife in hand, trying to reassure the woman that she had no intention of hurting her with it, forgetting that she'd been stripped to her chemise and drawers.

The duke turned with a grin on his face. He'd expected some kind of commotion and felt proud of himself for being prepared for it. But when he saw the elfin woman in nothing but her lacy drawers, the elegant curve of her figure and the length of her legs revealed beneath the thin material, his face froze. He'd never seen anyone so perfectly exquisite in his life.

He continued to stare until he heard Maria groan with grief. She tried to cover up her friend with one of the draperies adorning the archways, managing to pull the entire sweep of fabric down over their heads.

"What is it, what is it?" demanded a tallish man with a remarkably prominent forehead emerging suddenly from behind another set of silk draperies. "Gisette, calm down. Is this the way to behave in front of the customer?"

A string of agitated French followed his question, so that by the time the duke had managed to unveil Summer's and Maria's heads from the fall of fabric, the tall man raised an inquiring brow at the group of them. "You bring weapons into my establishment?"

Summer's admiration for the duke—rather, His Grace—soared to new heights as he drew himself up and with great dignity stepped over the tangle of cloth and bowed before the taller man. "Allow me to introduce myself. I am the Duke of Monchester, and the woman with the knife is Miss Summer Lee"—and his voice dropped—"an American."

"Aah," answered the man, as if that explained everything. "Gisette, stop your weeping. She is an American, and they are eccentric, no?" He bowed toward the duke and Summer. "Forgive my employee's theatrics, Your Grace, and allow me to introduce myself as well. Charles Worth, the owner of this humble establishment, and an artiste who appreciates the American woman."

And her money, thought Summer, tucking her knife back into the sheath around her calf. But it seemed that wasn't the only reason for his appreciation, for as soon as she returned to finish her fitting and was decently clothed, the man made her walk around the room, studying her with such intensity that Summer felt her skin crawl.

"Astonishing," muttered Worth. "Such grace I have never seen before, as if you walk on air. American women have true appreciation for my genius, you know. They know that the dresses I design for them are to bring out their own individual beauty, not to display their wealth. But you, Miss Lee"—he paused and spun her artfully in a slow circle—"will do true justice to my designs. You will walk in them for me, *oui*?"

Summer nodded in agreement, and then a whirlwind of fabrics and laces and ribbons were held against her skin, beneath her brown curls, and next to her golden brown eyes. It didn't stop at Worth's, for His Grace then took them to smaller shops where she purchased parasols with walking-stick handles; pleated, ostrich, and gauze fans; gloves of fine kid and lace; jeweled ornaments for her hair; jet enameled brooches; and teardrop and hoop earrings.

Summer blinked. She'd have to wire Pa for more money.

Toward the end of the day, the duke packed them all into their hired carriage without complaint. "Most women," he observed, "are difficult to shop with, taking hours to decide on just the right fan. You, however, picked items up almost at random, as long as I approved of them. I am astonished to say that today has been a pleasure."

Summer closed weary eyes, letting her head bounce against the cushioned seat as they hit every rut in the road. She didn't know why he should be so surprised; she'd hired him for just this purpose. Surely he didn't think she would be fool enough to ignore advice she'd paid for?

"I'm plumb sad it's all over with," sighed Maria. "I could shop the rest of my life and never tire of it."

His Grace ignored her friend. Summer felt his gaze focus exclusively on herself. *No doubt mentally criticizing how fatigue made her look a hundred years old*, she thought. She cracked open her eyes a bit and wondered at the ghost of a smile she saw on his lips. "What?"

"I was just remembering," he said, "when you flew out of that room behind that poor girl with your knife in hand. I thought the fitter had done something to offend you, and that—"

"Tarnation!" interrupted Maria, her voice rising as she shouted out the window. "Leave it, ya' hear? Leave it alone right now, ya' mangy pack of children!"

Summer scooted forward and peered out the window; then she met Maria's eyes, remembering the day they'd first become friends in a dusty alley behind Hafford's Saloon. They had both come to the rescue of a little dog being tormented by a pack of mongrels. Their mutual love of stray animals created a bond that made Summer feel as if she finally had a sibling.

They both banged on the carriage wall at the same time. "Driver, stop the carriage!"

The duke's brow rose, but he made no effort either to inquire as to the view out the window, or to prevent the girls from bolting out of the carriage even before it came to a full stop. Summer thought he showed remarkable intelligence. After only a few days in her company, he'd already realized that he'd be better off letting things develop rather than trying to figure them out.

Maria had reached the pack of street urchins first and shoved her way between the group of them to reach a smoldering pile of fur that hung by a rope from a wooden beam. She screeched and hollered with such vehemence that she scared most of the little ones away.

But a teenage boy who already had the body of a man and the beefiness of a tavern brawler didn't seem to be intimidated. His other two partners in devilry weren't much smaller, and after their initial shock at the interruption wore off, they eyed the black-haired screamer with lustful interest. Not about to be outdone, the largest boy reached around behind Maria and ran his hands across her bosom, giving his cohorts a leering grin before prying her arms away from the bundle of fur and locking them behind her back.

Summer crouched and drew her knife. "Let her go."

She felt the duke back her up, noting from the corner of her eye that he reflexively positioned one foot forward and flattened his hands parallel with his chest, one also in front of the other. Strange that he didn't curl his hands into fists.

The boys spoke in French. Summer couldn't be sure if they understood her words, but knew they comprehended the weapon in her hand and the tone of her voice. She saw the big one's eyes flicker in indecision, his gaze traveling from her to the duke and then back to Maria—who just waited with supreme confidence, the look on her friend's face saying that they didn't have a chance, no matter how big they were.

Summer couldn't be sure what caused them to back off, but the big one suddenly pushed Maria at her and they all took tail. The duke relaxed his stance, and Summer went over and cut down the bundle of fur so that it fell into Maria's waiting arms. "Is it still alive?" she asked.

Maria blinked back tears. "Yeah, though I can't even rightly tell what kind of critter it is. Ever see the like?"

His Grace spoke from over her shoulder. "It's a monkey. I've seen a few before. They come from India."

He spoke in harsh pants, and Summer looked at him curiously. "Are you all right?"

"Certainly. It's just the adrenaline, madam. I suppose I'll have to become accustomed to it, traveling in your company."

"What's—"

"Summer, we have to see to the critter. He's losing a lot of blood," snapped Maria. With the ease of much practice, they sliced strands from their petticoats and applied pressure as they gently bore the animal back to their hotel room, calling service for hot water, alcohol, and proper bandages.

The duke chastised the driver for passing through such a disreputable part of the city and then quietly went to his own room. For a moment, he wished he could go with the ladies to care for the abused monkey, then shook his head at the ridiculous notion.

What he *should* do is demand that Miss Lee start acting like a lady. To quit carrying a knife under her skirts and jumping out of carriages. But he was having such a good time…

"The duke's mistress?" hissed Maria. "How can ya' let his mistress come to our house?"

Summer sighed and watched her friend storm into her room, little India on her shoulder. Although it had been several weeks since they'd returned from Paris, the monkey still looked the worse for wear with bald spots from where he'd been burned.

Summer sighed and answered Maria's question. "Don't tell me you've adopted society's snobbish ways already? What's the difference between a mistress and Lotty or Maisy?" She named two of the kindest of their old friends from the saloon.

"'Cause they don't pretend they're something they're not. And this woman's coming here as if she were some kind of lady, when—"

"She is a lady. Her husband is dead. Do you really think she should spend the rest of her life in loneliness, just because she chooses not to have the restraints of another marriage?"

Maria sniffed. "'Course not. But she's sleeping with our duke, now, ain't she?"

"What possible difference could that make?" asked Summer. Ever since the Duke of Monchester had helped them rescue India, in Maria's eyes he could do no wrong. Her friend laughed off his acidic remarks, and not because she thought he was funny like Summer did. And she stared at him with great big moony eyes, which irritated Summer to no end, although she couldn't figure out exactly why.

"Stop referring to the man as 'our duke,'" commanded Summer. "He's not *our* anything. It would serve us well if you'd also remember he's not really our friend, only a hired employee."

Maria sniffed again but condescended to answer the bell when it rang, ushering Lady Windolm into the bedroom of Summer's London town house.

She didn't look anything like Summer had expected. *Pale* would be the best way to describe her. Pale hair, skin, voice, and personality. A soft, gentle woman who would be frightened by a whispered "boo." Summer couldn't imagine her with His Grace—why, he'd eat her alive!

"How do you do?" whispered the pale woman.

"Just fine, Lady Windolm." Summer's voice in comparison boomed in her small chamber, and the woman near jumped out of her skin.

"P-please, call me Elisabeth."

"And I'm Summer. Our—the duke has told you of our arrangement?"

The lady nodded her head and opened a roll of cloth, spilling out an odd assortment of items onto Summer's vanity.

"What's all that for?" asked Summer in amazement.

Elisabeth smiled shyly. "Byron… I mean, His Grace, said to teach you polite manners and to make you beautiful. And although the men frown on anything remotely artificial in a woman's look, we do have our ways. I thought we'd start with appearances first, then with a new sense of self-confidence, we can work on the manners."

Summer grinned. So his first name is Byron, she marveled, and then wondered why that bit of knowledge gave her a warm feeling of secret joy. She quickly said Monte's name to herself three times.

She blinked up at the woman who'd spoken to her of self-confidence. The lady seemed to need a bit of that herself. Summer watched her hand flutter as she picked up a wicked-looking metal device and began to advance on her. "What's that for?"

"The duke said your eyebrows were a bit too, um, shaggy." She colored a becoming shade of rose. "Those were his words, not mine, of course."

"Of course."

She leaned toward Summer, the scent of roses emanating from her as if she bathed in them, and began to carefully pluck a few chosen hairs. "The trick is…"

"Ouch."

"To not thin them too much, so it looks quite natural."

"Ouch."

"And to let your own brow shape prevail. We just want to soften your look a bit."

"Ouch. Again. Tarnation, how often will I have to do this?"

"Oh my. It's very important you see to them every day, so the little hairs growing back won't give away your beauty secret." Elisabeth stepped back and eyed Summer with a critical gaze. "Just a few more, now. Oh perfect. No, no, don't look in the mirror yet. There are a few other things I want to do to you first."

Summer felt a trickle of fear. Did her relationship with Byron bother Elisabeth? Even though it was strictly business, was she the overly jealous type? Would the pale woman take advantage of the situation and make her look like some kind of clown?

"Um, how long have you been… in a relationship with Byron?"

The lady's color rose again. "Oh my, for quite a while. Now this is petroleum jelly: odorless, tasteless, colorless. But it's quite amazing what a touch here and there will do." And with that she stroked a thin layer of the stuff on Summer's lashes.

"Forgive me if I'm being rude, but whatever do you two see in each other? I'd never have thought… the duke is kind of… Well, I have a hard time picturing you two together."

Elisabeth giggled. "He said you were rather peculiar. And for me to try and not to be too shocked by anything said or seen in your home."

Summer opened her mouth to defend herself, and the lady took up a piece of red crepe paper and pushed it against her lips, effectively silencing her and astonishing her at the same time. *Crepe paper?* Tarnation!

"The Duke of Monchester," said Elisabeth, "is a very handsome man. How can you wonder what I see in him?"

"Looks aren't everything. The man I love is very handsome, although quite the opposite of Byron—the duke. Monte has dark hair and eyes, and is the most polite, soft-spoken, cultured…"

Elisabeth waved a hand in dismissal. "Oh yes, the duke mentioned him. He sounds very nice. But you see"—and she lowered her voice even further so that Summer had to lean toward her to hear—"Byron is a very dangerous man."

A thump sounded outside her door, and Summer rolled her eyes. "You might as well come in, Maria."

The black-haired girl entered with a guilty-looking India on her shoulder. "Ya' just don't know how to skulk properly yet," she reassured the monkey. "But don't worry, I'll be teaching ya'." She stared indignantly at Lady Windolm. "And I couldn't hear what ya' said, ya' speak so softly."

Summer sighed while Elisabeth stared in open-mouthed surprise at Maria. "She said that His Grace is a dangerous man."

"Pshaw," said Maria, settling herself at the foot of the four-poster bed. "He's just got a nasty tongue."

Elisabeth snapped her mouth shut and calmly took a round tin and a soft brush from her supplies and lightly brushed a fine powder over Summer's face. "That tongue often as not wags in the prince's ear," she said. "And woe be to anyone who crosses the man, for with one word, that person would be shunned from all polite society to spend the rest of her days in shame and isolation."

Summer and Maria exchanged pointed glances.

"Don't believe me, but I've seen more than one young hopeful's dream of a good match crushed beyond hope, and it's even rumored"—Elisabeth's voice lowered again, and both women, and the monkey, inched forward to hear her words—"that the reason Miss Carlysle took her own life was because of the duke's amusing anecdote about her, one that ruined her chance of gaining the hand of John Strolm, whom she'd set her cap for with all the pent-up passion of love's first touch."

Summer snorted. "Rather melodramatic, don't you think?"

The lady shrugged her satin-clad shoulders. "Well, it's just what I heard, a rumor only. But honestly, just the thought of saying no to Byron… or not giving him exactly what he wants… makes me cringe."

"Tarnation," said Maria. "Are ya' telling us ya' sleep with the man 'cause yore scared of him?"

A frown marred the pale smoothness of Elisabeth's skin. "Why, no, I mean, well… I guess I just never thought about it before."

They all stared in silent fascination until Elisabeth snapped out of her contemplations and began to wipe the powder from Summer's face with a soft cloth. "It's very important that you always do this. Never leave the powder on."

"Then what do I put it on in the first place for?"

"Believe me, it makes a difference. The powder will stay in your pores to reduce any oiliness and smooth out your skin tones and make you paler." Elisabeth wrapped up her cloth, leaving her supplies on Summer's vanity. "Those are for you. Save the powder and crepe paper for balls and evening parties. The jelly you can wear anywhere; just be careful not to put it on too thickly, as it can melt into your eyes."

Summer nodded but eyed the contents of her vanity with distrust.

Elisabeth snatched up a brush and advanced again. "Now, for the hair. The duke said it was rather, um, wild. But I think it becomes you. What you need is a short fringe of hair over your forehead—which fortunately for you is the height of fashion." She snatched up a pair of scissors and snipped so quickly Summer didn't have a chance to protest. "Now," she continued, "when your hair flops down it looks on purpose, and you just have enough"—she yanked and twisted, securing the knot tightly with hair combs— "to put it in a topknot. However, I recommend that during the day you put the knot in back of your head, at the nape of the neck."

Summer sighed. What took this woman seconds to do would take her hours of twisting and comb-sticking.

"I also recommend that you curl your hair at night with twists of flannel cloth. It will soften your appearance." She took Summer's hand and brought her to her feet, turning her finally around toward the mirror. Summer's mouth dropped open. The lady had done such minor things, but they'd made such a difference!

Maria stood and peered over her friend's shoulder. "Lady Windolm, will ya' do me too? Please?"

The next morning the bell rang and the Duke of Monchester pushed past the footman, storming into the drawing room where Summer sat reading *The Habits of Good Society: A Handbook of Etiquette for Ladies and Gentlemen*, one of the many books Lady Windolm had loaned her. She had just been astonished to discover that a gentleman could not speak to a lady unless she spoke to him first, when Byron filled the room with his presence.

"How dare you?" he hissed, the anger emanating from him in waves of almost palpable electricity.

Summer looked up and met his blue eyes, that shiver running through her as usual whenever he came near her, confusing her again with its intensity. He opened his mouth, presumably to continue his tirade about whatever she'd done, then snapped it closed, his eyes widening at the sight of her new appearance. Summer grinned at his reaction, causing him to back up a step, thereby letting her appreciate his own appearance. Although he wore the blue silk cravat again, his gently worn clothes were all black, from his coat down to his neatly polished boots. They made his hair look twice as light with the contrast, and his overall appearance slightly sinister. She liked it.

"Do you approve of what your mistress did to me?"

The duke recovered quickly from his surprise, the glow of appreciation winking out of his eyes to be replaced by his usual hooded gaze. He frowned, as if trying to remember something important, and then his face twisted again in anger. "That's exactly my point, madam. I no longer have a mistress!"

Summer wasn't about to let it go—after all the criticism he'd given her, he could at least acknowledge that she looked sophisticated now. But if his reaction had been anything to go by, she could only joyfully imagine how Monte would react. "Sorry to hear about that. But what do you think about what she did to me?"

He sighed in frustration. "You're passable. Almost. Now, I want you to tell me what you said to Lady Windolm."

Summer shook her brown curls, caught a glimpse of Chi-chi and India whipping past the open door, playing their usual game of tag. "First, you'll admit you're a liar. I could tell by your reaction that I knocked your spots off."

"Spots? What kind of ridiculous American saying is that?" He raked his fingers through his golden hair, causing those constantly falling curls to tumble over his ears. It was most annoying to Summer, who seemed to notice those curls all the time, making her fingers twitch to smooth them back into place.

She balled her hand into a fist. "Spots, you know, from a playing card. Diamonds, hearts… you shoot them off a card nailed to a tree. It means—"

"I get the drift of its meaning. I'll have to excise those ridiculous American sayings from your vocabulary, especially 'tarnation.'" Byron's hand slashed through the air like a knife. "What exactly does that mean anyway? No, wait, don't answer. You will not distract me from my query, madam. I want to know exactly what you said to Lady Windolm."

Summer blinked her large amber eyes at him. "Why, nothing important. You can't possibly think that I had anything to do with your, er, breakup."

"That's exactly what I think…" His voice faltered as India, having finally quit his chase of Chi-chi and hearing his savior's voice, came skipping into the room and launched himself onto Byron's shoulder. He couldn't ignore the loving greeting the monkey gave him, his furry cheek rubbing against his own. So he awkwardly patted the animal, and Summer could see that his anger had diminished since he'd stormed into the room. She released a sigh of relief.

"Lady Windolm said," he continued, narrowing his eyes at her as if she'd purposely set out to weaken his temper and he'd rather have held on to it, "that you and that black-haired vixen friend of yours made her reassess our relationship. Now what exactly does that mean?"

Uh-oh, thought Summer. "We did ask her… that is to say… we just mentioned that she might be, er, afraid of you."

The duke scowled. "Regardless of the provocation, I've never hit a woman in my life."

Summer shook her head, wisps of golden brown curls tickling her cheeks. "No, no. Not afraid of you physically, rather, fearful of your tongue and what might be said if she didn't… give in to your demands."

"My demands?" His face flushed a flattering shade of pink. "You… you… American! It is quite unnecessary for me to make demands, I assure you. I generally find most women quite willing to…"

Summer leaned forward, eager to hear what most women were willing to do with him. She knew about the act of love herself, but only what she'd overheard and seen from the "light skirts" in Tombstone. Surely there had to be more to it than that! And wouldn't she be able to captivate Monte if she just knew how?

But the duke must've seen the interest in her eyes, for he quirked his lips at her and drawled: "I'm supposed to be teaching you how to be a lady, aren't I?"

He's so frustrating, thought Summer. Always trying to shock her sensibilities with his nasty comments, and when he finally says something interesting, he clams up. She sank back into the velvet cushions and crossed her arms over her bodice. "Yes, you are." If he wanted to be persnickety, so could she. "And I just can't imagine a *lady's* feelings being changed by my harmless remark unless Lady Windolm had them to begin with, can you?"

He froze, staring at her as if reassessing her character. He slowly removed India from his shoulder, and the monkey obligingly scampered from the room. With the air of a man hunting a tigress, he lowered himself onto the divan next to her, a bit too close for Summer's comfort, his thigh pushed so tightly against her skirts that she could feel the heat of his body. He draped his arm across the back of the curved cushions and leaned around to face her, their noses barely inches apart, his mouth a slight movement away from her own. Those blue eyes narrowed, and she could see them harden with a dangerous promise that spoke of a strength of character that Summer could only admire.

"Don't pretend you're not frightened of me."

"Oh but I'm not. I just noticed that your mistress might be."

"You are the most frustrating…" His eyes strayed to her lips, and then quickly back up to her golden brown eyes. The depths of feeling this woman aroused in him… yet he still thought it better than being bored. Of which he was with Elisabeth, anyway. Still, the little American chit had no right to alter his life in any way. "Never interfere in my personal life again, do you understand? I am your sponsor, nothing more, and our relationship has no room for anything beyond our arrangement."

Summer was wise enough not to tell him how conceited he sounded. She wasn't exactly frightened of him, but he did make her shiver with something, an excitement that she'd never felt before, and she still wasn't exactly sure if she liked the feeling. It'd be better all around not to annoy him too much.

She shrugged, careful not to allow the gesture to move her body any closer to his. "I told you, I'm already in love with another man. Why would I have any interest in you whatsoever? I just made an observation to your mistress, that's all."

"Do you call that an apology?"

"No, Byron, I call it an explanation."

Then he smiled, that rare curving of the lips that made the world light up and, for some reason, prodded Summer's heart to beat a bit faster. Elisabeth had been right; he was an extremely handsome man, and she guessed he had good reason to think any woman within ten feet of him would be attracted to him. He got up and moved to the chair facing her, the absence of his body heat making her sigh with relief, evoking a realization that her corset was laced too tight. Surely, that was why his nearness had made it difficult to breathe.

"I accept your explanation." The duke adjusted his cravat and the sleeves of his black coat. "As long as it never happens again. Now, I still have a job to do, and we have little time left to do it in."

Summer frowned. "What do you mean?"

"I managed to procure you an invitation to my stepmother's annual ball. She rather launches the season, and first impressions are the most important, so we cannot afford any mistakes. When will your Worth gowns arrive?"

"I was told within the week." Summer avoided his gaze, not wanting him to see the naked terror in her eyes, for the humiliating memory of the only ball she'd ever attended had been burned into her mind. She remembered the way Mrs. Astor had shunned her, how she'd made Monte ashamed of being with her because of the way she talked and dressed. The cream of New York society had whispered insults at her, saying that she was one of the nouveaux riches, a "climber," and had no breeding. At a nod from Mrs. Astor, she'd been suddenly cut off from Monte by a phalanx of giggling women, and she could think of nothing else to do but slink out the door, like some low-down coyote.

Then Maria had come up with her plan. Summer sighed. No matter how much the duke prepared her, she didn't think she had the confidence to pull it off.

"Excellent," said the duke, oblivious to her inner turmoil. "We'll have to study hard in the next two weeks in order to get that painful twang out of your voice. And I will provide you with more books"—and he nodded his head at the stack Elisabeth had already given her—"about how to address your betters. For example, no one calls me by my first name. Close acquaintances may call me 'Monchester.' But only those I'm on intimate terms with, and have given my leave to, may call me 'Byron.' Social equals I am not close to may call me 'the Duke,' but inferiors, such as yourself, refer to me as 'Your Grace.'"

Summer squirmed with embarrassment. Had she addressed him by his first name? She'd tried not to think of him as Byron, but Maria, after being told not to call him "our Duke," had started calling him Byron herself, causing Summer to use it as well.

"In America, it's customary to call someone by their first name. We don't put such importance on titles."

"Well, in England, it's not. I can just imagine you being presented to the Queen and calling her Vickie!" His eyes widened in mock horror.

Summer giggled. "I wouldn't—honestly. I'd probably call her Your Gracious Majesty of the English Throne, or some such nonsense. Whatever came into my head at the moment."

He threw back his head and laughed aloud, catching himself in midguffaw and staring at her in shock, as if he rarely laughed and it had astonished him to hear it.

Summer wondered about his mercurial moods. What had created such an armor-clad man? And why did she seem to have a rare ability to pierce that armor? Or did Elisabeth also make him smile, and that's why he was so angry at her comments to the lady? She felt rather badly now, that she'd caused him to lose someone who made him happy.

She rose with her usual unthinking grace and melted to her knees in front of his chair, like she did with Pa when they needed to talk of something important. She did owe him an apology, as sincere a one as she could give. She took his hand, just like she'd take Pa's, feeling it was the most natural thing in the world to do. "I am very sorry," she whispered, eyes glowing with golden light, "that I caused your breakup with Lady Windolm."

Byron stared at her small hand in his, then into her face. He leaned forward, as if he was drawn to kiss her, and Summer felt it, so startled that she jumped to her feet, the top of her head smacking his chin as the poor man gave a painful grunt. She hadn't meant to give him the wrong impression, just show him the sincerity of her apology. After all that talk of his about nothing personal between them, she thought she could at least treat him as she would a dearest friend.

And she'd gone about it all wrong, just like usual.

He hadn't raised his head, and she wondered if he'd bitten his tongue or something.

"You can't," he gasped, "look at a man like that, nor touch him that way. Do you understand? Especially a man you barely know. He'd have you on your backside in less than…"

Summer backed up, and Byron stood. "You don't know the least little thing about how to deal with people, do you? Were you raised by wolves or something?"

She shook her head and tried not to giggle. Tarnation, he looked like he'd been smacked upside the head by a gun butt. He was awfully appealing when he looked like that. "Of course not. Mostly by an Apache injun and coatimundis."

"What's a coat… Never mind. I don't want to know. Anything about you. We do not have that type of intimacy, and you need to keep your distance from people you don't know. This will be rule number one you must learn. Don't ever touch anyone."

Summer looked at him incredulously. "Ever?"

"You may give a gentleman your hand, when it's properly gloved, only to escort you to the dance floor, and you may touch him only as much as necessary while you're dancing. But that's all."

"No wonder English women are so sad-looking," she blurted. "Touching should be as natural as breathing."

"Not for a lady." The duke sighed and shook his head. "We have a great deal more work to do than I had thought."

Three

SUMMER STOOD AT THE TOP OF THE LANDING WEARING a Worth gown that cost a small fortune, but one that brought out the golden highlights in her hair and eyes, emphasized her tiny waist, and made her bosom look two sizes larger. Gauzy white fabric draped her shoulders and cascaded down her arms, softening the planes of her face and the muscles in her arms. Ringlet curls framed her cheeks and lay down the sides of her topknot. She looked ready; she knew she did. Why then couldn't she take that first step down the stairs?

Maria gave her a swat on the back of her enormous bustle. "Go on," she urged. "I can't wait to see Byron's face when he sees ya'."

"His Grace," snapped Summer with enough irritation that she forgot how nervous she felt. "Would you stop calling him by his first name?"

"Soon as ya' do, so will I."

"Tarnation!"

"You might as well come down now," commanded that deep male voice from the bottom of the landing. "I heard you, and I know you're up there."

"See what you did," whispered Summer as she started down the stairs.

"Well, ya'd have to go down sometime," answered Maria as she absentmindedly patted India's little head from where he perched on her shoulder.

Summer had reached the third-to-last stair. "But only when I felt good and ready."

And then she saw him, and he her, and time froze. He looked stunning, thought Summer, in his black coat and tails, with his snowy white linen ruffled shirt and matching cravat. A huge blue pin anchored his neck cloth, the hue of the stone exactly matching the color of his eyes. A black top hat held his blond hair back from his face, outlining the hard ridges of his jaw and the highness of his cheekbones. She shivered in her new gown.

Maria spread her hands at Summer with a flourish. "What do ya' think, Yore Grace?"

The Duke of Monchester opened his mouth, then closed it again.

"Stunned speechless," she whispered into Summer's ear. "If'n yore heart weren't so set on that Monte fellow, I'd swear you could have yoreself a duke."

Summer flowed down the last three steps and held out her lace-gloved hand. Without a word the duke took it and led her to the door, his eyes never leaving her face. A tingle ran through her hand and up her arm, and heat blossomed where it certainly shouldn't for a man who wasn't her intended.

Summer's feet planted themselves in sudden alarm. "Maria," she gasped. "Come along."

Her friend shrugged her shoulders, all the dangling red beads on the purple gown she wore clicking with the movement. She patted her black coiffure, pushing a few beaded hairpins back into place. "I know I'll be bored to tears among all them snooty men and women," she grumbled as she patted India good-bye and fetched her wrap. "Give me the kitchen any day, with a snort of brew and a handsome footman."

Something in her voice made Summer break her gaze away from His Grace and turn to her friend with a frown of concern. "Maria, we're like sisters. Anything that I have, you can too."

"No, I can't," she answered, green eyes shadowed with that secret sorrow that Summer had noticed often in the years since they'd become friends as young girls, but which Maria never would share with her.

"Why not? You know my money is yours as well."

Maria glanced from the duke back to her. "It ain't the money… Oh, don't worry none about me. I'll just keep my mouth shut and be a proper escort for ya'." And with that said she walked out the door in a swirl of purple and yellow skirts.

His Grace settled Summer's wrap around her shoulders, his fingertips lightly grazing her skin, making her forget anything but his presence as he ushered her out the door and into the waiting brougham. She sat across from Maria, and at first felt grateful that the duke didn't sit beside her friend, that she wouldn't have to try to face the charismatic lure of his gaze. But when he sat next to her, he was so close she could feel the heat of his body, infinitely more titillating than the touch of his hand, and tarnation, she could smell him. Some rapturous scent of spice and human male.

She groaned.

"You'll be fine," he assured her, misinterpreting her discomfort for dread of the upcoming event.

"I'll never remember everything," she replied, not wanting to let him know the real direction of her thoughts. Then as soon as she said it, she panicked, her heart pounding so hard she could see her near-naked bosom vibrate with the force of it. Her mind had gone completely blank! Was she allowed to speak to anyone without an introduction first? Did a gentleman introduce himself to her, or could she say something to him? Could she walk alone if she was going to the water closet? Unaware that she spoke the words aloud, she began to recite from one of the etiquette books she'd tried to memorize. "A good manner is the best letter of recommendation among strangers. Civility, refinement, and gentleness are passports to—"

"You're never going to make it," interrupted the duke.

Maria watched the two of them with a wicked grin on her face.

Summer glared at him. "What? What! What do you mean I won't make it? If I can learn to run up a mountain, wrestle with a knife, and shoot like a—"

"You're falling apart. Bloody hell, what did those knickerbockers do to make you this anxious over a trifling ball?"

"Anxious? I'll have you know that I have nerves of steel. Why, one time back in Tombstone I—"

He took her hand. The warmth of that contact flowed all the way to her toes, which made her even more confused and nervous. He sighed.

"Your gown is quite nice. You almost do it justice."

The litany of etiquette that still spun through Summer's jangled brain came to a screeching halt. She turned to face his handsome profile. "What?"

"Don't misunderstand me. Worth did a superb job of adorning you. However, one can't expect miracles, now, can one?"

Every muscle in Summer's body had stilled. "What do you mean by a miracle?"

The corner of his lip twitched, but he continued to stare rigidly ahead. "One can't expect you to magically transform into a proper Englishwoman, that's all."

Maria choked on a laugh and quickly turned to look out the window.

Summer lazily wiggled her foot, feeling the comfortable pressure of her sheathed knife wrapped around her calf. How dare he? She didn't want to turn into a proper Englishwoman; she just wanted to be a lady so that she'd be accepted by society and allowed to marry Monte. And what did Maria think was so funny, anyway? Her friend continued to be a silent chaperone, which was very uncharacteristic of her.

She glared at Maria and then back at the duke. Who cared what His High-and-Mighty thought about American women anyway? Women who could take care of themselves, shoot and cook their own dinner... women who didn't need the protection of any man? That's probably his problem, that she didn't swoon at his feet and need coddling like some piece of glass that could shatter at any moment. She continued to grumble to herself about the gorgeous, annoying man sitting next to her.

"Miss Lee?"

"What?"

"We have arrived. Allow me to escort you out of the carriage."

With a start Summer realized that they had stopped, that His Grace stood outside the open door, his white-gloved hand held out to her. She could just see the elegant house behind him, with lights ablaze and a red carpeted walkway leading to the cavernous doors. Throngs of poor folk, held in check by uniformed officers, crowded the streets to catch a glimpse of the guests in their finery. As she descended from the carriage she caught sight of a woman in plain brown clothes, her eyes dreamy with delight at all the elegantly dressed ladies as they walked up the steps into the four-story mansion.

Couldn't the woman tell that Summer was just like her? That she was a country girl dressed up and masquerading as a lady? They'd find her out tonight, just like they did in New York. She'd be exposed as a person not fit to wipe their boots. Dadburn it, she couldn't breathe again! And her legs were shaking beneath her ridiculous dress.

Maria alighted from the carriage and glanced around, looking as if this were all some grand joke. Didn't she realize this was serious? Summer wondered, annoyed as Maria gave saucy winks to any man she thought worthy of them.

Summer clutched at the duke's arm, and he glanced down at her, sighing again. "I suppose you'll want to know about my stepmother and the rest of my family you'll be meeting."

She looked at him in surprise. He always refused to answer any of her personal questions, or ask her anything about her own past. They had a strictly business relationship. This sudden capitulation stunned her enough that her knees stopped their shaking and she resumed her normal, graceful walk.

"My stepmother, the Dowager Duchess of Monchester—that's Her Grace, to you—currently resides in this elegant home in Mayfair along with my half brother, the First Marquis Karlton and his American wife, the Marchioness of Karlton. You will address them as Lord and Lady Karlton."

They had entered the entry hall of the mansion he called a house, with its gaslights and candles and flowers all reminiscent of Mrs. Astor's New York mansion. A touch of panic started to curl up Summer's insides again, and she blurted the first thought in her head. "But I thought your family had no money."

"Again, the rudeness of your comments. Remember, madam, just keep your mouth shut and you will do stunningly this evening."

Summer narrowed her eyes but didn't give up. "But why did you agree to sponsor me if you're not poor?"

"It goes without saying that just because I am sadly lacking in funds, it's no reason my stepfamily need be so."

"Huh?"

Evidently, they had been in a receiving line, for suddenly the duke was introducing her and Maria to a very tall, stately woman: the dowager duchess. She smiled at Summer rather condescendingly but nodded at her with regal acceptance. Maria she ignored entirely, sticking her nose in the air after scanning the girl's gown with distaste. Summer sighed, wishing again that her friend would stop insisting on designing her own wardrobe, but Maria stubbornly allowed that she'd be herself, and blast anyone who didn't like it.

Then Byron introduced them to a rather smallish man, whose own brownish gold hair had thinned into a few strands across the top of his head, and she remembered to bow and call him Lord Karlton to his leering face. When they approached his wife, his American wife, thought Summer with relief, she expected a warmer greeting. After all, weren't they from the same country?

"*Brother* dear," said Lady Karlton, "what sort of trouble have you gotten yourself into this time?" She nodded with disdain at Summer and Maria.

"Certainly not the same sort that my brother managed to get into," he replied.

She laughed flirtatiously and eyed him with a lustful gaze that Summer thought surely wasn't appropriate for a sister-in-law. "You had your chance, Monchester, at a real lady. Whatever are you doing with these bumpkins?"

Byron's face froze into that superiorly scornful mask. "Summer's father is a friend of mine, and I promised to take care of her while she's in London. Careful, sister dear, there are a few amusing stories of your own American background that I haven't quite gotten around to sharing with His Highness yet. Perhaps tonight would be a fortuitous time."

Lady Karlton's black eyes glittered. "You'd never disgrace the family, I'm sure." She leaned forward and breathed out her next sentence into his face. "Do you really think the prince will attend tonight? Please say you've put in a good word for us."

"My family loyalty bids me to do so, as always. But you know he goes where a whim takes him."

Lady Karlton straightened up to her full height and took a half step forward, and Summer realized how exceedingly tall she was, unaware that the lady had been slouching as she talked to Byron. She looked down her nose at her stepbrother-in-law, who had to either tilt his head back to look up at her or speak to her tiny bosom. With a scornful grimace, he chose the latter.

"If you will excuse us, sister dear, I believe the Grand March is about to begin." And he took Summer's arm and lined up behind another couple, the orchestra beginning a solemn tune that had them soon following the procession around the ballroom, while Maria settled into a comfortable chair and watched them with a calculating eye.

Summer hugged the duke's arm, amazed that she felt so protected by his nearness and grateful that she'd hired him. She marveled that his family hadn't ignored her, and the thread of panic that had nipped at her heels all night faded away as she took her full first breath since leaving the coach. Her feet slid along the parquet floors as if they had been buttered; she breathed in the mingled scents of perfume and felt, for the first time, as if she might actually belong among these richly clad lords and ladies.

She leaned toward the duke, noticing the stares that kept drifting in their direction, and although that brief encounter with his family sent a million questions tumbling through her head, she asked again the last one he hadn't answered. "Why did you agree to help me if your family ain't—aren't poor?"

His chin lifted a bit higher, holding back a golden curl that had threatened to tumble over his forehead since he'd removed his hat. "Do you see everyone staring at us? Speculating with excitement about my partner?"

Summer nodded.

"You, my dear, still look every bit of an American. No proper Englishwoman would have a sprinkle of freckles across her nose."

Summer knew Monte loved her freckles. He'd kissed every one of them. And why did this man have to notice every little detail about her? "So, I'm American. Including your stepsister, I'm sure there are several here."

"Aah, yes. But not with me. My… repugnance of the American title-hunter is well known, much to the relief of several English heiresses. Therefore, my partnership with you has shocked many of this company, as well as my family. It seems that what one brother did, they fear the other will do as well."

"So your brother married for money? And that's why they aren't poor?"

"Partly."

The procession had ended and the first strains of a *minuet de la cour*, a French version of the waltz, Summer had learned, began to float through the cavernous room. The duke faced her, placed his right arm firmly around her waist, yet properly not holding her too close. His left hand took her right, and he spun her across the floor.

Summer resisted the urge to lead, something she always tried to do, much to her teacher's dismay, and let herself be swept up in the glory of the dance. The duke had refused to give her dancing lessons, had hired someone else instead, so this was the first time they'd held each other in their arms. He was the perfect height for her; she didn't have to crane her neck or lift her hands too high, and he moved beautifully, with a grace that almost matched her own.

"So why doesn't your family help you with your situation?"

He sighed, his breath caressing her ear and causing her to give an involuntary shiver of delight. "You are persistent, aren't you?"

"Pa says I'm a champion nagger."

He laughed, caught himself, and then chuckled again. Summer noticed a few startled glances cast their way. "Very well, then, champion. The property entailed to me consisted of two run-down castles, the lands not earning enough to keep the servants, much less the income to the dowager duchess that I'm entitled to provide her. The income, investments, and other land that was unentailed was all left to my stepbrother—after my father had bled the two estates dry to obtain it."

Summer's head whirled. "Why would your pa do such a thing?"

She felt him stiffen in her arms. "If I knew the answer to that, madam, I would be content with my lot."

"I'm sorry."

"Don't be. There are many of the nobility who are in the same position as I am, saddled with estates that are no longer self-supporting. That's why there's such a ripe marriage market for American heiresses."

"I told you, I don't want to marry any snooty—"

His mouth and arms tightened, and he spun her in quick succession about the room, certainly too fast to match the slow strain of the music. Summer clutched at him to keep herself from falling down with dizziness, and her chest thudded against his, the softness of his cravat sweeping the top of her breasts, the warmth of his chest penetrating through the thickness of her corset. A distant part of her mind told her they were dancing too close for propriety's sake and wondered at what kind of wanton woman she could be that she responded to the slightest touch of his body. She clung to him and half opened her mouth, staring at his own and feeling a pull toward it that was an undeniable physical craving.

The duke stumbled. He'd only meant to teach her a lesson, that he was just as desirable as any American man, but when her eyes turned glassy he couldn't tear his own away, as if she had cast some magic spell over him. And when her lips opened, it seemed the most natural thing in the world for him to tilt his head and taste them, to want to nip at her full bottom lip. Thank heaven that his sister-in-law's brittle laugh was loud enough to break the spell and bring him to his senses. He'd nearly destroyed his reputation! Kissing a title-hunter. In public, no less!

Summer's eyes widened, and she pulled back in confusion when he sneered at her. "Not so hard to imagine yourself married to an Englishman, I gather?"

"You did that on purpose!"

He swept her to the edge of the dance floor. "Certainly, madam. Just as I purposely baited you on the way here."

Summer frowned, taken aback by his remark. This man played so many games, she had trouble keeping up with him. What a challenge! "And why did you want to make me angry in the carriage?"

"You hired me to make you acceptable in society. Having a breakdown before we get to a ball will not produce the results you paid me for."

Summer grinned. He was right! She'd been so angry at him that she'd forgotten all about her nervousness. And when they'd been in that receiving line, he'd actually offered her personal information about himself that had again distracted her. Why did he have such a reputation for callousness? He seemed an exceptionally considerate man. She didn't pay him to comfort her, regardless of what he said.

The music ended as he led her off the dance floor. She stepped lightly and grinned at him. "Thank you."

He raised a brow and shrugged, trying to ignore that kernel of feeling that grew in his chest as he gazed at her glowing face, the sparkle in those rich brown eyes.

"But that other thing you did…" Her grin had turned upside down. "You don't have to prove to me that Englishmen are every bit as desirable as American men; it doesn't matter what country anyone is from.

It's just that I'm already spoken for, and he happens to be an American. And I don't care about titles."

The duke stared at her a moment, shocked that he almost believed her. He turned and muttered something about bringing her a glass of refreshment, and weaved his way through the crowd, barely acknowledging the deferential nods of his peers. The bloody woman kept being so ridiculously honest and outspoken of her thoughts, he grumbled to himself. How could he keep a professional distance from her if she kept sharing her most intimate feelings with him? He tried not to blame her, guessing enough of her background to know she hadn't been taught even the most basic rules of society, but he still needed to figure out a way to keep his distance.

In his distraction he bumped against another man, making the red punch in the other's hand slosh over expensive kid gloves. He barely muttered an apology, still obsessed with the thoughts of his American heiress. The child didn't even realize that although he'd tried to seduce a kiss from her, he'd certainly had no intention of actually following it through. How had she managed to make him respond that way? He'd had the most skilled courtesans, and the most innocent of marriage-hunting English ladies, offer up their lips to him and he'd always been in control.

"I said," wavered a young man's voice, "that you owe me an apology, sir."

The duke scowled as his eyes reluctantly focused on the red face of John Strolm. Just what he did *not* need tonight, bumping into the boy who thought he'd killed his intended. "I believe I already made my apology, sir."

"If that is so, sir, I certainly didn't hear it!" The boy's voice cracked on the last word, and a rustling of petticoats as people turned to stare could be heard as silence descended throughout the room. Byron could see the boy become aware of the attention, his eyes aglitter with satisfaction as if he'd planned this little scene. Well, he probably had.

Byron sighed. "Then allow me again, sir, to express my apologies over your soiled gloves. Although sadly out of fashion, I'm sure they were the best you had. I'd be happy to pay for their replacement."

The duke paused, while Mr. Strolm pondered that for a moment. The boy's face turned an unbecoming shade of purple as he realized that the apology had been an insult.

I shouldn't have done that, thought Byron, *but some people just make it too easy*. And then he felt her behind him, could smell that fresh-from-the-outdoors scent that she managed to maintain even in a smoky ballroom, and wished she'd stayed away. He intended to make her reputation, not ruin it, and if the foolish boy said something about the rumors that he obviously believed to be true, he could no longer dismiss them as idle gossip to be laughed off.

The boy's chest puffed up, and his words spilled out before Byron had a chance to call him outside. "I, sir, am not afraid of your venomous tongue as those in the rest of this room are! Say what you will of my unfashionable clothes, my coarse manner—the cut of my hair, even—to His Royal Highness. What worse could you do to me than to kill my intended?"

Gasps of horror filled the room. Byron mentally shrugged. The boy had done it now, yet still he berated himself for giving him the chance. If he hadn't been so distracted by that woman... and bloody hell, he felt her brush his backside and stole a quick glance behind him. She'd pulled her knife and had the point of it hidden up her sleeve, the grip curled inside her hand. Was she mad? Worse, did she think he needed physical protection?

He looked up at John Strolm, and like every man in the room, the boy topped him by a couple of inches. But he'd learned in his youth how to take care of himself and felt insulted that the woman didn't think he could.

The American would ruin any chance she had of being accepted in polite society if he didn't end this situation now, sure that she'd pounce into the fray if it came to blows. The duke felt oddly pleased at the thought, regardless of how ridiculous it seemed.

He lifted his chin and let the superiority of his rank settle over his features. "Am I to understand, sir, that you believe I pushed the lovely Miss Carlysle out her bedroom window?"

"I most certainly—that's not my—you know well enough that if it hadn't been for the story you told to His Royal Highness, she'd never have taken her own life!"

"No, boy. I don't know that, and neither do you."

The duke knew John hadn't heard a word he'd said, for his mouth kept opening and closing like a fish, and he might as well let the boy say what he wanted before Summer could intervene; he could feel her tightening up like a drawn bow behind him. He lifted a brow, folded his arms, and waited.

The aristocracy waited with him, their faces revealing an eager delight at the delicious gossip this would cause on the morrow.

"I'm sure whatever story you told the prince was a lie!" sputtered the boy at last.

"Although only slightly amusing, I assure you it was the truth. I also assure you that you don't want the story told publicly, for although we all knew Miss Carlysle to have been a lovely girl, she also had a reputation for being... highly spirited as well. What caused her to leap from that window shall remain a mystery, and you should neither blame me... or yourself, for that matter. Good evening, sir."

The duke knew he'd gotten to the heart of the matter, that the boy might be blaming himself for the deed, for as soon as he said the words, John's shoulders began to shake, and the need not to disgrace himself by bursting into tears gave Byron enough time to grasp Summer's hand and make a hasty exit from the room.

The boy's grief made him angry, because the Carlysle girl certainly didn't deserve such devotion. The story Byron had told had been true, for he'd been there himself, and he had enough information from friends that it probably hadn't been the first time she'd pulled such a stunt.

Someone had been alert enough to have called ahead for the coachman, for the rented brougham sat waiting at the bottom of the stairs, the door already open. Probably his stepmother making sure that he left as soon as possible. Although outwardly kind to a fault, in small ways she viewed him as an inferior, and he knew it, as if he shouldn't have the privilege to even wipe his brother's feet, much less carry the title of duke. She probably felt relieved at his confrontation with Strolm, that it hastened his departure from her home.

As he assisted Summer into the carriage, he realized she no longer held her knife, and hoped it wasn't left behind in somebody's back.

"What about Maria?" she asked.

Byron's voice vibrated with anger. "I'll send the coach back for her." He settled into the seat across from her and flicked his hair off his forehead. "Either you solemnly swear never to pull that knife again in public, or I terminate our business arrangement."

Summer stared at him in wonder. They'd just been through a trying experience, one that he'd certainly caused by some dreadful story, and he had the nerve to reprimand her for poor behavior. That boy had been big. Didn't the man realize he didn't stand a chance in a fair fight with him? But she had to admit, if she'd had to use her knife and they saw her, she'd never be welcome in anyone else's home. Although she still felt pretty sure she could've discouraged the boy with a few nicks here and there without being seen, the duke was probably right.

She let out a long sigh as the carriage bounced over the cobblestones. "I swear I won't use my knife in public, if you tell me what that girl did."

He might not have answered, but she'd spoken as if she believed him, when others obviously didn't.

He stopped scowling at her. "It happened several months ago, at a house party thrown by one of your American heiresses—"

"They're not my—"

"Do you want to hear the story or not?"

Her perfect little teeth clamped together with an audible snap, and he nodded with satisfaction. "Lord Churchill and his American wife, Jennie, had rented a summer house, and perhaps because of this, the room assignments hadn't been properly... arranged."

Summer nodded, a bit bewildered. But she recognized the gleam in his eye and knew that he was hoping to shock her. She fought a grin and pretended to understand.

He wasn't fooled, and he seemed to take great satisfaction in explaining further. "In polite society, if a woman is married, and the match is not quite to her satisfaction, well, once she gives birth to an heir and a spare, it's quite acceptable for her to take a lover."

Summer nodded.

"Or lovers. As in, more than one."

She nodded again. Maria had already told her all this; when would he stop repeating himself and get on with the story?

He must've seen the frustration in her face, sighed with disappointment, and continued. "Somehow the room cards had gotten switched on a few doors, and in the middle of the night, I heard a loud thump and squeal from the room next to mine. Ordinarily I would have ignored it, of course, but the squeal didn't sound like a happy one, and I thought as a gentleman I should at least try to investigate."

"Good for you."

Byron shook his head. She sounded sincere. The child didn't recognize sarcasm when she heard it. He'd opened his mouth to continue when the carriage made a sharp turn and slapped him up against the window. He frowned, something niggling at the back of his mind, but the jostle hadn't bothered Summer. She continued to watch him with eager fascination, and he couldn't refuse that look of entreaty for long.

"The door stood half open, and on the floor"—he choked on a laugh, but refused to give in to it—"lay old Lord Roster, naked and wrinkled as a pig's skin, with Miss Carlysle perched atop him, equally naked, mind you, covered in mounds of white cream, with a pack of his house dogs gleefully wagging their tails as they licked up the cream from whatever part of the couple's bodies they could reach. She screamed at me to help her"—this time he coughed on the choke before he could continue—"because she'd thought it was my room, you see, and there'd be no cream left for us if I didn't call the dogs off." He had to cough again.

"I don't see what's so funny."

"Don't you? She wasn't worried about being found in a compromising situation—she was worried about the cream!"

Summer nodded, but she still missed the humor of it. "But why would she kill herself over something like that?"

"I don't believe she did. I believe she was just a bit unbalanced. Still, married women, madam, are allowed their indiscretions. Young, single maidens are either trying to trap a man into marriage, or excessively loose. Either way, it doomed her reputation. And as it took me and several servants to haul those dogs off her, the story would eventually have spread to His Highness anyway."

The carriage gave another jolt, this time flinging Summer from her seat and into his lap. For a moment the warmth of her, the silky feel of her hair across his cheek, the summertime flowery smell of her, overwhelmed his senses so that his mind went blank, and all he could do was gather her up and cradle her in his arms and just experience the sheer delight of it.

"Let me go," she whispered, her mind muddled by the feel of his strong arms about her. She had to remind herself of her engagement, that she owed loyalty to another man, not this one.

The carriage had come to a full stop, bringing Byron to his senses, that niggling in his mind turning into real concern as he glanced out the window. The cheerful gleam of city gaslights had been replaced by the fog-shrouded light of the moon, its weak glow outlining broken-down buildings constructed of scrap wood and tarpaper instead of neatly tailored mansions. Why had the coachman driven through this part of London? There'd be no reason to bring them through the East End...

The carriage door flew open. "Just take it easy, guvnor," said the coachman, only his livery recognizable to Byron, for the man wearing it had a voice and face he'd never seen before. "You and the lady, step from the coach nice and easy, hear? Then maybe nobody gets hurt."

Four

"WHAT IS IT?" ASKED SUMMER, THE COOL AIR FROM the open door clearing her mind from the obsessive thoughts of the man across from her.

"That isn't the coachman I hired," he whispered. "Just do what he says, and you'll be fine… and remember what I said about that knife."

Too late, thought Summer, the feel of it in her hand as reassuring as the confident manner of her escort. He preceded her from the carriage, in an effort to protect her she knew, for when she followed him out he kept his body in front of hers, between her and the coachman. Did he think she needed protecting? She grinned.

"See here," said the coachman, his voice low and menacing. "Just hol' very still, and my partner here will make yer pockets a bit lighter now, eh?" He carelessly waved a pistol at them, the glint of metal causing the duke to stiffen like a pillar of stone.

Another man appeared from the shadows, a dark shape that walked with a slight limp and shuffled over to Byron's side, patting his hands over the duke's clothing, the smell of him making Summer grimace with distaste. Her eyes skimmed the empty street. She noticed the way the footsteps of the limping man echoed in the silence.

She watched as Byron allowed the man to touch him, and then alarms went off in her head as she saw that the thief did a cursory search, taking only a watch and the stickpin in the duke's cravat. If they were robbers, surely they'd be interested in what he carried in his pockets as well?

"Now, the woman," said the coachman, aiming the muzzle of the gun on Byron. "And no funny moves now."

"Don't touch her," he growled as the limping man reached out for her, his voice so low with threat that he stopped the man in his tracks. "She'll hand you any items on her person. But you don't lay a filthy hand on her."

"Seems you're forgettin' who's got the gun, guvnor."

"No, I do not. But if your partner attempts to touch her, you might have to use it, wouldn't you? And the crime of murder is something I'm willing to wager that you wouldn't want to risk."

Summer shifted sideways, so that Byron now only partially blocked her view of the coachman. She realized that he was attempting to talk their way out of this. And if this had been a real robbery, he probably would've succeeded. But something about this smelled wrong to her.

The coachman snorted, his face splitting into a grin that managed to make him even uglier. "And what makes you think that, guvnor?"

Summer knew, even before the man pulled the trigger, that he intended to kill Byron. She'd seen it in the eyes of a man before. With a speed she didn't know she possessed, she pushed the duke and threw her knife straight at the coachman, causing his shot to go wild.

If only the blasted duke hadn't been stiffened into a stone, the coachman's shot would've missed him entirely; instead she heard the puff of a bullet penetrating skin. And if the *blasted* duke had moved when she'd shoved him, her knife would've flown true; instead it missed the coachman, and she heard it rattle on the cobblestones behind him.

And then things started to happen very fast. Summer yanked the arm of the limping man up and around, heard a satisfying crack and a grunt of pain. She turned to face the coachman, amazed that Byron hadn't fallen down after he'd been shot, truly astonished now to see him flip his body over to the coachman, spin like a top with his leg in the air at a seemingly impossible angle, and kick the gun from the other man's hands.

Then she felt a blow across her face, hard enough to spin her sideways and knock her to the cobblestones, and skinned her hands as she landed. So she hadn't broken the limping man's arm, as she'd thought. Summer tried to shake off the sparkling lights that spotted her vision, tried to get up and help Byron, for now it was two against one.

To her amazement the duke didn't need any assistance from anyone. Both men stood a head taller, both men converged on him at once, but Byron spun like a dervish, kicked and hand-chopped with an accurate precision that caused the most damage to his opponents at the least expense of energy to himself.

He could've taken on a dozen more men. Summer sighed in pure admiration.

Within seconds, both men lay flat on the ground.

Byron rushed to her side. "How badly are you hurt?"

"Where'd you learn to fight like that?"

Byron grasped her beneath the arms and pulled her to her feet. "What? Don't you have enough sense, madam, to go into hysterics, or to at least be insensible from the blow you were given?"

His face swam for a moment but quickly steadied. "No, really, how'd you learn to do that?"

He studied her intently for a second, nodded in assurance that she seemed fine. "The bobbies aren't likely to be about this neighborhood, and the filth are only unconscious, so I suggest we leave before they wake, agreed?"

Summer nodded. She'd agree to about anything he said just now. This ghastly feeling of hero worship when she gazed at him had her giddy with the feel of it. Before he could say anything to stop her, she wobbled down the street and recovered her knife, scooping up the gun that lay not far from it, and at Byron's glare of rage from where he sat in the coachman's seat, hastily scrambled into the carriage. She'd barely closed the door before the duke slapped the reins on the horse's backs and had them barreling through the streets.

She felt her cheek and realized she'd have a nasty bruise from this night, and thought that the man could no longer complain about disasters happening to him while in her company. For she'd had quite an exciting evening, all at the fault of the Duke of Monchester, and really, all he'd ever suffered from her company had been a scuffed boot from a tiny dog.

Sooner than she'd expected, the carriage stopped in front of her own town house, and Byron ducked through the door and sat beside her. He searched her face, brought a hand to her swollen cheek, brushing it so softly that she didn't even flinch.

"If you didn't look so dreadful," he said, "I'd verbally thrash you for what you did back there."

Summer couldn't believe it. "What *I* did?"

He sighed, his hand straying to a lock of hair that had fallen across her cheek, twining it around his finger. "What in her majesty's name made you throw your knife?"

"Aah." She relaxed her shoulders. Excellent fighter, but not very good at discerning a situation. "They meant to kill you."

"Pardon?"

"They meant to murder you. That sham about robbing us was exactly that, a sham. Now who would want to kill you and make it look like a robbery? That's the question you should be asking."

He gave a gentle tug at her curl and leaned away from her, those muscular arms folded across his broad chest, and she noticed for the first time the dark stain spreading across his shoulder. "What makes you think it wasn't a robbery?"

"You're hurt," she murmured, and that giddy hero-worship thing swept over her again. "Let's go inside so I can tend to it."

"The bullet barely grazed my skin. Answer me first."

Oh, he could fix her with that gaze, scarcely allowing her to breathe. "The look in the coachman's eyes."

One golden brow rose. "You could see his eyes from four feet away, in the fog?"

"Yes, if you know what to look for."

"And what made you look for it?"

She shrugged, finding it hard to verbalize what was mostly just a feeling. "The limping man didn't check your pockets. Now what honest thief wouldn't check a man's pockets for money?"

He threw back his head and laughed, the sound of it making her own lips curl upward. "I don't know any thieves—honest or otherwise. But I'll take your word for it that you do. I can't say that I agree with your assessment of the situation, but for now we'll just agree to disagree, yes?"

Summer nodded and laid her hand on top of his. What kind of man would say such a thing? Any other man, including Monte—who she'd gotten into several interesting arguments with—would've made her agree with him or told her that she was wrong. Tarnation, it was bad enough that she felt so physically attracted to him, but if his real character kept peeking out from behind that wall he'd built for the aristocracy, she'd be in great danger of breaking her vow to Monte.

She squeezed his hand. He jerked back as if she'd struck him, then leaned toward her like he had a string attached to her body and felt automatically pulled back. Summer grinned. "Tell me how you learned to fight like that."

He sighed, his breath warm across her face. "We're back to that again. I told you, no personal questions; this is supposed to be a strictly business relationship."

"You saved my life tonight. I think it's safe to say we went beyond your invisible guidelines."

He pondered that a moment. His eyes guiltily sought out the bruise on her cheek; then he shrugged. "We'll make a deal. I'll answer one of your personal questions, and you answer one of mine. And only one. That way we're trading information, and not having an intimate conversation."

Summer nodded. Whatever worked for him. "It's a deal."

She could tell he liked the way she said that, as if it still kept them on a firm business footing. Although she also noticed that he hadn't moved his hand out from under hers, and had actually turned his wrist and laced his fingers through her own.

"In case you hadn't noticed," he began, "my height is a bit below average. Therefore, by necessity, I had to learn to fight very young… or get used to being beaten up. Fortunately for me, we had a Chinese gardener." He stopped for a moment, his face melting into a rare expression, one of respect and a softness that Summer hadn't seen him display toward his own family. Then his features hardened again, back to that aloof mask, so quickly that she wasn't sure if she'd only imagined that expression. "He'd been a priest in China and had studied a discipline called kung fu, not so much a way of fighting as a way of living… it's hard for me to explain to someone else. But even though he was our servant, I always called him 'Master.'"

"Would you teach me?"

"Certainly not. Now, I've answered your question, you answer mine." His fingers had been stroking back and forth across her own; Summer couldn't quite remember when he'd started to do it, only aware that now they'd progressed to her upper arm, past the lace of her gloves, to her bare skin. She suppressed a shiver, not wanting to call attention to what he did, afraid that would make him stop, and it felt too divine for her to let that happen.

"What's your question?" breathed Summer, feeling the strength in his fingers, watching his arm muscles bulge through his jacket, reminding her of the way he'd fought. The hidden dangers in this man took her breath away.

"You've proved to me that you know how to use that knife you carry around. Who taught you to use it—your father? And why would he do such a thing?"

Summer blinked. Didn't he know how dangerous it could be to carry a weapon that you didn't know how to use? "I told you before, I was raised by coatimundis and an injun."

"I thought you were joking."

"Tarnation, why would I joke about a thing like that? Oh, never mind. It's the Apache injuns that taught me to fight, well, one in particular, and the coatis taught me to smell out a situation, which is why I knew that man would shoot you."

His fingers had progressed to her shoulder, lifting up the fall of billowy fabric, and traced circles across her skin. It took all of Summer's self-control not to move. "Why is it," he asked, "that whenever you answer a question, it only creates a hundred more in my mind?"

"I… I don't know. I think it's because the life I've lived has been so different from yours."

His hand crept to the side of her neck. "Has it? Why would an Indian teach you to fight, unless you had the need to defend yourself? The same as a kind Chinaman once did for me?" His fingers stroked the soft skin at the base of her throat. "We may be more alike than you think. Than I ever would have thought." His hand curved around the back of her neck, hot, demanding. Summer couldn't have resisted that pull if she'd tried.

"Chatto taught me to fight because…"

The pressure on the back of her neck increased, pulling her closer to him. "Who's Chatto?"

Summer's head started to spin, her face so close to his that she pulled his breath into her very own lungs. "He's the… the injun. Who taught me to use my knife… who gave it to me."

"Aah." His lips touched hers. Soft heat spread down to her toes. He forced her head sideways and spread her lips wider with the pressure of his own. She lay locked between his mouth and the hand at the back of her neck, grateful for the support, for surely she'd have collapsed by now, turned into a quivering mass of need. She groaned, and he took advantage of the opening, plunging his tongue into her mouth, once, twice, until she felt a hot surge of warmth between her legs, a pulse as if something there tried to reach for him, to be caressed and fondled just as skillfully and surely as he did her mouth.

Summer never knew a kiss could be like this. A thing of such passion that it consumed her entire body, and made her want, need… that other thing. The one thing she'd sought from Monte... that he couldn't give her, not like this man could.

How she knew this, she wasn't sure, but her body did, infusing her with strength, so that she fought against his tongue to plunge her own into his mouth. He groaned and pulled her tighter, pushing her backward on the seat, his body half over her own, his other hand—the one that wasn't busy burying itself in the hair at the back of her neck—caressed the top of her breasts with a kneading motion that pulled them farther out of her bodice, until the tips of her nipples were finally freed to be lightly pinched and tugged, until the wave of heat between her legs erupted into a liquid warmth.

She should be appalled, she knew. No one had ever touched her breasts before, had handled her in such an intimate way, not even Monte.

Monte.

Summer couldn't believe what she was doing. She'd already given one man her word of undying love, and at the mere touch of a kiss, she was ready to betray him. With a man who didn't even like her!

She turned her face away, fought to catch her breath and still the clamoring need in her body. "We can't do this."

"The hell we can't." His mouth, deprived of her lips, sought her breasts.

Summer couldn't let that skillful mouth take over where his hands had been... "I'm an American!"

"Who gives a damn?"

"You did five minutes ago."

"Stupidly prejudiced."

Summer felt his tongue graze her nipple with liquid heat. *She had to say anything*, she thought, *anything to stop him*. She couldn't believe that she'd ever complained that her passion always overwhelmed that of a man. Not his. Never his. She'd met her match; no, more than her match, and it terrified her.

What had they been talking about before? "Chatto," she chattered. "He taught me to use a knife, gave me my first kiss. Thought I'd be his warrior woman—and I almost did! My coatis, so like big dogs that I named them Whiner and Fighter, they raised me too. Don't you see, no matter how much you teach me, I'll always be an uncultured…"

He nuzzled her neck, every muscle in his body taut, refusing to pull away from her. But she could tell that he finally listened.

"I'll never be able to marry you. I can never be a duchess and make you a good wife. I'll be lucky if I can become a lady…"

"Marriage?" The duke shot off her so quickly, he bumped his head against the roof of the brougham. "Who the bloody hell said anything about marriage? And you had me convinced you weren't a title-hunter. Hah! You're just like the rest of them, trying to trap a man into marriage, just so people will have to call you duchess!"

Summer tried not to grin. So, she'd hit on the magic word, had she? The one word that could turn this man's lust cold? She'd have to remember that.

She sat up and pushed her breasts back down into her bodice and took a good calming breath. She'd have to take a bath tonight, she decided, to cool the things this man had done to her body. She'd discovered that although the piped water might be considered warm here, it never filled her bath with anything approaching that temperature. Who would've thought she'd ever be grateful for that chilly water?

"Please be calm, Your Grace. If you recall, I'm already engaged. You just needed to be reminded of the consequences of your actions."

He froze, his face a comical mixture of chagrin and confusion. Summer tried to smother her laughter, but really, she had to release some of the tension he'd created. He looked offended at first, then smiled down at her. *Really, an astonishingly remarkable man*, thought Summer, *that he didn't mind being laughed at.*

The duke bowed out of the carriage and held out his hand to her. Summer took it, hoping that her fingers wouldn't still tingle when he touched them, that whatever reaction her body kept having toward him would go away, but of course it didn't, so she twisted out of his grasp.

And they both became very stiff and formal as he escorted her to the door.

"Thank you, Your Grace, for a most… interesting evening. Are you sure you won't come in so that I can see to your wound?"

Byron felt oddly relieved, and only slightly disappointed, that they were back on formal ground. He could again treat her as a business acquaintance, and he wanted to keep it that way. "As I said, it's only a scratch. And the pleasure was all mine, madam." And then she had to go and spoil it.

"I still don't think it was funny," she told him as he walked away. "That story about Miss Carlysle. I thought it sounded fascinating. The cream, that is."

Visions of those breasts he'd bared in the carriage, covered in sweet, silky cream, danced through Byron's head, and his trousers tightened rather uncomfortably. Why hadn't the sight of Miss Carlysle covered in the stuff affected him this way? He ran to the waiting carriage.

Summer tilted her head beneath her jaunty riding hat and saw the flutter of feathers that adorned the crown from the corner of her eye, and ignored them. If Mr. Worth thought the golden feathers brought out the glints in her eye, then she'd wear the silly things. She faced Maria across the ornate bed of her newly rented room inside the charming inn that Byron had secured for them while they attended the races. She folded her arms across the bodice of her golden silk dress. "You're going with me."

Maria's green eyes flashed fire from beneath her coal black lashes. "I don't belong with all those fancy people and ya' know it."

"You're afraid."

"No, I ain't!"

Summer smothered a grin. "Then go get in one of my new dresses, that one with green trim, and I'll tell His Grace to wait for you."

"And what's wrong with this dress?"

Summer eyed the bold colors and excess of orna-ments. In New York she'd let Maria choose both their dresses, and remembered how they'd been laughed at whenever they appeared in public. Since then, she'd come to understand the subtleties of good taste, but Maria stubbornly continued to wear her own flamboyant wardrobe.

"Tarnation, Maria. It's a Worth gown! How could you possibly not want to wear it?"

Maria sniffed, then spun with a flurry of purple and red skirts, raising her hand to the little monkey on her shoulder so he wouldn't be dislodged, and stormed into her connecting room, mumbling under her breath about how some people just wouldn't take "no" for an answer.

By the time the duke arrived, they were both ready to go to the races. Summer hadn't believed she'd have to wear such an ornate gown to see a horse race, remembering the ones in Tombstone that consisted of shouting bets, drunken riders, and enough cloudy dirt to ruin any dress. But the Ascot, Summer had been informed, was always the high point of the season, and debutantes went to show off their beauty and dresses, not to actually watch the race.

Still, she hoped she'd get a chance to see some horses.

They rode the short distance from the country inn to the races in an open carriage, Summer enjoying the sunshine and fresh air after weeks of living in smoggy London. But not her two companions. Maria still sulked in her elegant gown of green satin-trimmed chintz, and the duke… she stole another glance at him. He wore a dark blue coat and trousers, so dark they appeared black at first, with another pale blue cravat that matched the color of his eyes in the sun, paled to such a light shade that they startled her every time she looked into them. Which she determinedly tried not to.

Summer didn't understand how it had happened, that kiss after the ball, except perhaps that they'd been through a harrowing experience, and she'd had that hero-worship thing after seeing him fight, and he'd only just succumbed to a man's inclinations. But neither of them could look at each other without a coloring of their cheeks, and if Maria hadn't been so annoyed, she'd surely have noticed.

When they reached the moorland and she laid eyes on the race pavilion filled with ladies dressed in such finery it looked like a cluster of fluttering butterflies, her insides started to do the same. His Grace told her he expected His Royal Highness to attend, that he rarely missed the races, and that she'd be introduced to the great man. Her acceptance into society hinged on this singular meeting, and with her feeling all jittery around Byron, the level of panic in her chest threatened to close her throat up. She knew if she didn't settle something between them now, she'd never be able to survive the day.

The coachman slowed the horses and joined the line of other carriages.

Summer leaned forward to speak to Byron where he sat opposite her. "We needn't feel uncomfortable with each other, you know. How's your injury?"

Byron finally looked at her, his jaw unclenching only a bit. "I told you it's just a scratch."

Summer tried again. "Surely what happened between us was just a natural reaction to the events of that night."

"I shouldn't have let it go so far."

"It wasn't your fault." Summer felt Maria shift beside her—the instant perkiness of her body as her friend concentrated on their words, the sulky attitude disappearing as surely as mist in sunshine.

"Probably not," agreed the duke with an arrogant jut of his chin. "If you hadn't reacted so, uh, strongly."

Summer squelched a spurt of annoyance.

"Reacted?" piped in Maria. "To what?"

They both ignored her.

"Now you see why it's so important I get married," said Summer. The duke lifted a brow. "Well, isn't that the point of marriage? So you can... you know?"

He threw back his head and laughed, drawing startled looks from the occupants of other carriages nearby. "To some, I suppose it is."

"You can what? What?" Maria's voice rose. "What happened?"

Summer sighed. "Nothing. Right, Your Grace? Nothing at all happened."

"Nothing," he agreed, nodding his head, looking as if he was trying his ghastly hardest not to stare at the tops of her breasts. He licked his lips.

Summer shivered, her eyes drawn by the sight of that pale pink, to his mouth that she'd warned herself sternly not to look at, for she'd dreamed of it with such sweet torture that she knew she couldn't stand to look at it without reacting. Such remarkably full lips for a man, the bottom one with a slight cleft that only showed when he wasn't angry or defensive, when his face relaxed with desire. Like when he'd kissed her with such skillful gentleness, and then he'd lowered his head, and she could feel again the heat grazing her neck, lower, to cover her...

Maria cursed, a quite remarkable string of profanity spilling out of her mouth like an overfilled bucket. "Don't tell me nothing happened. Look at the two of ya', drooling over each other like a couple of dogs in heat. If yore my friend, Summer Wine Lee, ya'll tell me what happened, or I swear I'm never coming to one of these—"

"Shh, enough." Too many heads turned in their direction. "I'll tell you everything, I swear."

Byron grunted.

"But nothing really happened. We just got caught up in the danger of being robbed."

Maria goggled. "Ya' was robbed? And ya' didn't tell me?"

Summer laid a hand on her friend's arm and lowered her voice. "You've been spending a lot of time," she whispered the last three words, "in the kitchen."

"Oh." Maria blew up to ruffle the fringe of hair on her forehead and grinned wickedly. The duke raised his brows in inquiry, but she ignored him. "I guess I have. But it's no reason we shouldn't be talking to each other. Well now, maybe it's best I came today after all."

The coachman opened the door and lowered the steps, and His Grace assisted each of the ladies to the grass, giving Summer a nod of encouragement, a silent acknowledgment that they were wise to erase their memories of the other night.

Then he looked at Maria with a speculative wrinkle of his brow. "The kitchen?"

"The table's cool as ice on the backside," the saucy wench replied, without batting an eye.

Byron covered his grin with a fist. He might as well give up trying to shock either of these women; whenever he tried, he only managed to be undone himself. *Oh, His Highness will have a grand time with these two*, he thought with a chuckle.

Five

THE DUKE LED SUMMER AND HER COMPANION TO THE Royal Enclosure and held their chairs for them until they were seated. He sat down and touched Summer's arm, and she tried not to flinch at the electrical charge that resulted from that contact. "Switch seats with me," he whispered.

"Why?"

"So you can sit next to the prince."

Her stomach rolled over in a sickening lurch. "No, I can't. Not right next to him! Tarnation, whatever would I say?"

"Anything other than that foolish American slang."

Summer felt him watching her, to see if her anger over the cut would push her fear aside. He gave a grunt of dissatisfaction and tried another tack. "I spoke to the carriage shop about the coachman they hired."

Summer stopped gawking at all the beautiful women and let Maria continue the job for her, the sudden wash of concern for the duke and his enemies swallowing all other considerations. No matter what he said, she knew that the coachman had intended to kill him; she'd seen it before, in the eyes of that claim jumper, the one she'd had to... No. Why did that memory keep haunting her when she'd promised herself to forget it?

"And?" she prodded.

His Grace smiled. "His regular coachman returned to work the next day, covered in bruises. He said someone jumped him while he was going to the... essential, then dragged him into some bushes and he didn't wake until late morning. He can't identify the men who beat him, as they attacked him from behind, and didn't want to call the bobbies, afraid that he'd be accused himself of stealing the carriage." They both nodded. "But his conscience got the better of him, and he finally showed up at the shop to confess the entire occurrence."

Summer leaned toward him, unaware that the feathers on her hat swept over the top of his head like an embrace. "I told you. This seems very well planned for just a robbery. Why not just stop the carriage on the road? Why take the risk of jumping the man in so public a spot and then masquerading as the coachman?"

"Don't keep coming to hasty conclusions."

Summer realized her gaze had strayed to his mouth, and she focused again on his eyes. "Because," she continued, answering her own questions, "then the real coachman wouldn't be there as witness to the murder."

She noticed Byron's gaze had strayed to the swell of her bosom, and he guiltily looked back up into her eyes. "You have a vivid imagination. And the sunlight makes your eyes turn the color of amber."

He looked as shocked as she felt by his compliment, so Summer chose to ignore it. "I'm telling you, that man had murder on his mind." Summer tried to put annoyance in her voice and failed. Looking into his eyes had been a mistake, the pale blue drawing her in and making her dreamy with the lure of them. Tarnation, maybe she should focus on his nose; surely that would be safe?

"If that's the case, how do you know that I was his planned victim?"

"'Cause he was pointing the gun at you."

"I beg your pardon," interrupted a deep male voice. "I hate to intrude on such an… *intimate* moment."

The amused face of His Royal Highness looked down on them.

"Forgive me, Your Highness, I didn't see you standing there," said the Duke of Monchester. "Allow me to introduce Miss Summer Lee."

"A pleasure," replied Prince Albert Edward.

Byron watched his friend look speculatively at Summer and him. He could guess what His Royal Highness was thinking. After all, Byron was famous for his hatred of the title-hunting heiresses from overseas—although to be fair, he always included England's pretty title-hunters as well. He was sure that the prince found it delightful to find him in the company of an American, especially in a conversation that could be misconstrued as intimate. Since the prince's current mistress happened to be an American, and Byron hadn't been very tolerant of the relationship, he felt sure that His Highness would have great pleasure in today's meeting.

Summer smiled shakily at the prince, evidently overcome not only by his large size, but the sheer presence of him as well. Albert beamed back at her, occasionally glancing at Byron with a chuckle, before homing in on her again.

"Am I right in guessing you're another of those lovely Americans?"

"Yes, your…" The girl looked like she didn't know what to call him. "Your Majesty."

The prince laughed, his belly jiggling beneath the exquisite cut of his suit. Hundreds of pairs of eyes turned in their direction, noting the attention he gave to the girl in the gold dress. "Not yet, my dear. Your Highness will do. Tell me, Miss Summer, how long have you been in my country?"

"Not long…"

"How did you ever meet the duke?"

"He's helping me, that is… he's an old friend of the family, and when I went abroad—" She frowned, looking at Byron for help, as if she didn't feel comfortable with her words.

The big man turned and cast a baleful eye on the duke. "Is that right? You *know* an American family?"

Byron shrugged. "I went over to do some hunting, like everybody else, and ran into her father. If I hadn't known him, do you think I'd squire around an American girl, considering my reputation?"

Prince Albert laughed again, as if he was enjoying himself quite thoroughly. "Let me see, what was that you said to my dear American friend, Jennie?"

Summer started to feel uncomfortable and squirmed in her chair. The way the prince had said the woman's name made Summer think she might be his mistress.

"Ah yes." The prince looked around and lowered his voice to a whisper. "The higher the title, the wider they'll spread their legs."

Summer's eyes widened. Yes, this Jennie was the prince's mistress, and she couldn't believe that Byron's tongue was wicked enough to say such a thing in front of his royal friend. And it occurred to her that perhaps the duke believed it of her, as well. Maybe that's why he'd kissed her, thinking she'd also be attracted to his title.

The crowd murmured as the first race began, a thunder of pounding hooves and shaking ground. She felt Byron shift in his chair. "She told you about that, did she?"

Prince Albert seemed to ignore Byron and the race. Instead, it appeared to Summer that she had captured his full attention. "Yes, she did. What think you, madam—is it true?"

Summer couldn't believe they were having this conversation. She thought royalty was supposed to behave, well, *royally*. But then again, she could tell he and Byron had been friends for a long time, shared a comfortable familiarity, as if they baited each other like this often. Well, she wasn't about to be the middleman. She looked to Maria for help, but for once her friend seemed speechless.

Byron narrowed his eyes at the prince. "I know what you're doing, and it won't work."

"Why not?"

"Because the girl and I would have to care about each other in order for your words to hurt. Trust me… I wouldn't marry her if she were the last woman on earth."

The duke's words hung in the air like a heavy weight, threatening to drop down on his head like a guillotine. Byron fought the urge to duck. The moment he'd said it, he wished he could take it back. Of course he'd never marry her, but after seeing the stricken look on her face, he realized he shouldn't have said such a disparaging comment in front of the prince.

He noticed that His Highness gave a satisfied smile and sat back as if anticipating fireworks.

Summer's hand drifted down her skirts toward the knife strapped to her calf. He glared at her motions, and she smiled. "I thought you said you were stupidly prejudiced?" she asked softly.

"That was in the heat of the moment."

Prince Albert grinned even more broadly.

"My lord duke," interrupted a familiar voice. "How wonderful to see you here!"

The prince's smile changed to a frown of annoyance. Byron looked up at the same time Summer did at the smiling faces of his family—the Dowager Duchess of Monchester and Lord and Lady Karlton.

The duke scowled. He'd specifically told them that neither he nor the prince would be here, so hadn't expected to see them; actually, he preferred to see them as little as possible. And now the dowager duchess would be annoyed with him because he'd lied. But his main intention had been to give Summer a chance for a little time with the prince, without the demanding interruptions of his family. He sighed and rose to greet them.

"Your Grace," gushed the dowager duchess. "My boy, what a pleasure to see you again so soon! Shame on you for making us think you wouldn't be here, when you know how *important* it is to me that our family gets together as often as possible."

Summer watched in disbelief. Was this the same woman who'd greeted her stepson with such restrained civility at the ball?

"And Your Royal Highness, what an honor to see you as well." The duchess's regal air vanished as she spoke with the prince. Summer winced at the woman's groveling.

Lord Karlton slapped Byron on the back and held his arm on his shoulder, reminding him of the time they'd gone to the Ascot as youths and sneaked into the horse's stalls. Byron didn't seem to find the memory as hilarious as his stepbrother did, quickly turning to Lady Karlton as she greeted him with a hug. "Brother dear, you're looking as handsome as ever! Is that a new coat?"

Summer saw Byron's lips thin and contemplated giving him a bonus so he could purchase some new clothes; what had he done with the money he'd already received anyway? She squashed that curiosity, as he'd certainly consider it none of her business and be insulted that she had even asked. Just another thing she'd never know or understand, like how his family had treated him with such restrained courtesy at the ball and now gushed over their good fortune at seeing him again. Was it because he was with the prince? Would they even acknowledge his existence if His Highness weren't his friend? Summer tried not to judge, because she'd only met them twice, but they certainly acted peculiar.

"And you, Sammy dear, how are you enjoying our fine weather?" asked Lady Karlton.

"Her name is Summer," growled Byron.

Lady Karlton tittered. Her husband, First Marquis of Karlton, picked up Summer's hand and kissed it. "Such a pleasure to see you again."

Summer couldn't help it; he gave her the willies. She snatched her hand out of his, noticed with disgust that he'd slobbered on her new lace gloves, and resisted the urge to rub it off on her skirts. She couldn't understand how two brothers could be such opposites, or how she could react so strongly to them as well. Byron's eyes of flinty blue had the power to draw her into his soul, yet his brother's eyes, with such a softer hue, repulsed her.

Lord Karlton huffed, recovered quickly, then smiled and turned his attention to the Prince of Wales. The dowager duchess hadn't even bothered to pretend an interest in Summer; she'd immediately narrowed in on the prince and had him engaged in a conversation that centered on the best length of coat to wear in the morning... short or long?

"Short, of course," answered the prince. "I thought everyone knew that a short coat must be worn with a silk hat in the morning!" He snapped at the woman, obviously annoyed at the interruption.

The dowager duchess didn't seem to notice. "That's what I told him, Your Highness. But he still insists on wearing the long."

Prince Albert frowned. "Madam, I believe the next race is about to begin..."

"Oh, of course. Please excuse me." And the dowager duchess half curtsied to him, nodding her head at Lord and Lady Karlton to follow, continuing to nod regally at the prince's retinue as she passed in front of their seats.

Before she left, Summer overheard Lady Karlton when she bent down and whispered into the duke's ear. "The old bat didn't even give me a chance to greet HRH. Really, Your Grace, you must arrange an opportunity for me to exchange a few words with him. After all, what's family for?"

Summer stared from the elegant lady, covered in brocade silk and dripping with jewels, to the woman's husband, attired in the latest fashion, with a golden fob and diamonds on his fingers, to Byron and his simply cut clothing, slightly worn at the hems and shoulders. Each time she'd met them they'd asked His Grace for favors, yet they showed off their wealth to him with a superiority that they either failed to acknowledge or didn't see.

"Did ya' see the black?" asked Maria, finding her voice quickly and loudly. "Did ya' see the way he pelted across the finish line? I knew that pony'd win! Where do ya' place the bets around here, anyway?"

A shocked silence descended on all those within hearing distance. Lady Karlton snickered again as she walked away.

"I don't think ladies can wager," began Summer.

"Only gentlemen can," said the duke.

Prince Albert leaned over, his eyes sparkling with renewed interest. "And who have we here?"

Summer smiled, her lips wobbling a bit when she heard Byron groan, but she held the grin anyway.

"This is my companion, Maria Sanchez, from Tombstone, Arizona."

"An interesting name to call a place," said the prince. "What's your background, my dear?"

It seemed that every ear within eavesdropping distance leaned toward the two American girls, waiting with bated breath for the answer. Summer wished another race would start.

Maria glanced from the prince to the duke, a wicked smile on her lips. Then she looked at Summer, who gave her a worried frown. Her friend sighed. "My mother and father passed on when I was very young, sir. I raised myself in a mining town and then met Summer, and we've been together since."

The prince chuckled. "Do you mean to say that you both come from a Western town... like that Annie Oakley woman?"

"I seen those billboards advertising that Wild West show and can't say as I'm like her," answered Maria. "But Summer here, now she can really shoot!"

"Is that so?" Both the prince and the duke turned and stared at Summer.

"I should have known," muttered the duke.

"I find it vastly entertaining that you didn't," barked the prince. "Who knows what other talents she possesses, eh, Monchester?" He jabbed the shorter man with his elbow. "Well, we must have a demonstration of her talent, musn't we, old man? Bring her round to Sandringham for the party next weekend... and her informative companion as well."

His voice rang with command. The duke responded with a nod of his head. "As Your Highness wishes."

Yet another group of aristocracy came over to give their regards to the prince, and Summer felt a weight lift as the attention of the great man focused elsewhere.

"Why did you sound so reluctant to accept the invitation?" she whispered to the duke. "Didn't you tell me that an invitation to the prince's country house would ensure my social success?"

"As a guest, my dear. Not as the entertainment."

Summer snapped open her fan and began to vigorously wave it in her face. She turned to speak with Maria, but her friend was already absorbed in a conversation with a rather nice-looking older gentleman, who nodded and grinned in fascination at whatever her friend was saying. Summer sighed and turned back to the racetrack. Maria seemed to be having a grand time, and it made Summer feel even more disappointed. She'd thought that when she'd meet the prince it would be, well, romantic almost. That he'd clasp her hand and speak with such elegance that she'd swoon. Instead, he seemed like any other man, and they'd had an astonishing conversation, and now Byron told her she'd be a freak attraction in the prince's home.

Nothing had gone the way she'd thought it would. And she kept hearing the duke's words, that he wouldn't marry her if she were the last…

"By the way," she whispered, "I wouldn't marry you if you were the last man on earth! Why, compared to Monte, you're uncouth, crude, and just downright ornery. So there!" Summer slammed back in her chair. Well, that didn't quite come out the way she would've liked. Tarnation, she'd sounded just like a child.

Prince Albert stifled a laugh when Byron abruptly stood and bowed to him, asking for his leave to depart. Summer had noticed that the prince had only been half listening to Sir Michael's obviously rehearsed speech on the plight of the landless gentry. That he'd had his attention fixed on her and the duke. For some reason he seemed unusually interested in their conversation and now looked as if he'd like to tease the duke for his anger. But he gave them leave to depart with a smile and a wave, making Byron promise to bring Summer to Sandringham.

"Maria," said Summer. "The duke wants to leave now."

"What? I'm just starting to have fun!" Maria pouted quite prettily at the man she sat next to, and patted his arm. "Summer, meet Hugh, uh, Lord Balkett of something-or-other."

The elder man mumbled something in her ear. "Oh yes. Lord of Hanover, a baron. He says he'll escort me home if ya'll let me stay. Can I?"

Summer glanced at Byron, but he just shrugged. "I'm not sure it's proper…"

"Tarnation, yore starting to sound like His Grace. Yore the one who made me come…" Again, the elder man mumbled something to Maria that Summer couldn't hear. "There now, His Lordship says Byr… uh, the duke there can vow… vouch for his reputation."

The duke bowed to the man in acknowledgment, and Summer nodded. That meant she'd have to drive home alone with His Grace, but she couldn't be selfish and drag Maria away just because of that. Dadburn it.

Byron led her through the throng of people in stony silence, those who knew him clearing out of his way at the look on his face. *Bloody hell*, he thought, *why did she have to be so unusual?* Every time he turned around he found out something newly disturbing about her. Oh, he'd hoped Prince Albert would find her amusing, and that eventually she'd get invited to Sandringham, but this sudden profound interest by the prince had him concerned that he'd treat Summer as an oddity, instead of as the lady she needed to be.

He glanced at the girl beside him, the way she flowed across the packed dirt, barely scuffing up the dust. How would he ever get her accepted into proper society if all these hidden talents of hers kept being revealed? Oh, he knew some women could shoot a rifle as well as any man, but they had the common sense not to flaunt it. And he'd just been congratulating himself on teaching her not to use a knife; now he had to worry about firearms!

He escorted her into the carriage, tossing a suspicious look at the coachman to make sure he was the same one he'd hired. Once inside, Byron sat staring out the window as they returned to the inn, trying to analyze his feelings. He knew he wasn't this upset over the fact that she could use a gun. It had to be something else. But he refused to admit that he might be angry about her declaration that she'd never marry him. He couldn't remember the last time he'd been this annoyed over mere words, and he knew that her marriage comment was just tit for tat, and entirely true. After all, she was an engaged woman. So why did it bother him?

He turned and found that she'd been staring out her own window in stony silence as well. "You *are* engaged, aren't you?"

"What?"

"You and this Monte fellow have an *official* engagement, correct?"

Her face flushed, and she batted a hat feather out of her face. "I don't see how that's any concern of yours."

"I think it might, considering that you hired me to sponsor you so that you could marry him."

Summer swatted at the feather again and decided she'd had just about enough of Mr. Worth's accessory, and began pulling out the hatpins that secured it to her head. "That's personal, remember? We don't discuss personal things." She was still so annoyed at him that she didn't even use the opportunity to barter one of her own questions out of him.

Byron watched her struggle with the hat for a moment, trying to find all the pins. That golden brown hair of hers started to tumble in a mess around her face, reminding him of the first time he'd laid eyes on her. "I'll trade you the answer by helping to remove your hat."

Summer sighed. The man just couldn't help turning a conversation into a bargaining tool. "I'm perfectly capable of getting the stupid thing off myself." Unable to find all the pins, she ripped out a few chunks of hair, but did manage to remove it. "You need to hurry up and fulfill your side of the bargain. I'm sick and tired of fancy hats and dresses and, worst of all, corsets. I want to go home."

And she tossed the hat at him.

His astonished face almost made her forget her temper and giggle at him, but she'd just discovered that she missed her mountain and the desert, that when she spoke of home, that's where she meant. Not New York, where Monte waited for her. Tarnation, this man put her all out of sorts.

He tossed the hat back at her, catching her square across the bosom.

"Isn't home with your intended? If he's a society man, I see a future filled with dresses and fancy hats. What do you want to wear anyway… trousers?"

Summer opened her mouth to tell him about the joys of walking in buckskin, when he held up his hand.

"No, please don't. I've had enough of your revelations for one day. Just answer my question, are you, or are you not, officially engaged?"

She liked the way he looked when he got annoyed, his mouth thinning into a hard line, the blue of his eyes turning to ice, his jaw clenched to rock-hardness. He looked delightfully dangerous, and she tilted her head in thought. Had Monte ever looked this way? And decided that no, he didn't have the temper of this man.

She tossed the hat back at him, hitting him squarely in the crotch. He could just find out that she could be as stubborn as he when it came to revealing personal information. Why, he could sit there all day and scowl at her. "You don't scare me."

"You, unfortunately, made that very apparent the first day we met." The carriage hit cobblestone, and he knew they only had a short time before they reached the inn, and for some reason, he had to have the answer to his question. Now, what could he possibly… "You can ask me a question, then. I'll answer it."

Summer lifted a brow in imitation of his own habit, but the hair whipping around her face spoiled the effect. He acted as if he bestowed a gift on the lowly by telling her about himself. "I'm no longer interested in anything about you."

Byron ripped the feathers from her hat, one by one. His stomach had given a little lurch there when she'd said that, and he knew he'd be really angry if he thought she meant it. But the girl had the curiosity of a cat; she was just being stubborn. He scowled. There had to be something he could threaten her with… "I'll kiss you."

"What?"

"Either you answer me, or I get to kiss you. That's the bargain. You choose."

Summer opened her mouth to tell him what he could do with his kiss, but his face got harder, and her eyes strayed to his lips, and she remembered how easily her body had given in to him. She had her knife, but she wouldn't fight him off, she knew it. The moment he touched her she'd turn all rubbery, and… "Tarnation, we never officially announced an engagement. He asked me to marry him, his relatives wouldn't have anything to do with me, so I set off for London to make myself acceptable. That's all."

Byron grinned. He'd started to hope that he'd have to kiss her, but for some reason her answer made him feel just as good. He helped her from the carriage when they reached the inn and escorted her inside.

Summer slammed the door to her room in his face.

Well, he didn't have time to worry about her snit now; he had to figure out some way to avoid her being a sideshow to the prince's houseguests. But how, when His Highness seemed so bent on flaunting the

American's wild ways? He rubbed his nose, checking if any flecks of paint from her door had become embedded in his skin. The Duke of Monchester ignored the questioning eyes of the coachman as he scrambled into the carriage.

Six

"ARE YA' SURE HUGH WILL BE THERE?" ASKED MARIA for the umpteenth time. They hit yet another rut in the road on this long journey to Norfolk, and she steadied India on her shoulder when the monkey squeaked in dismay. Chi-chi took advantage of the distraction and scrambled down from the seat, latching onto Byron's pant leg the moment she hit the floor.

The Duke of Monchester groaned. "Will you please stop calling him by his first name?"

Maria tossed her hair. "I can't help it if I can't get used to y'all's silly rules about what to call who."

"Well, you'd better get used to it," he threatened, while gently disengaging the little rat-dog from the hem of his trousers. "We're almost there, and you'd best remember to address the man as Lord Balkett." He handed Chi-chi back to Summer with a scowl. "Did you have to bring along your menagerie?"

She tucked the sweet little dog into the deep pocket of her skirts and smiled, continuing to ignore the both of them. Really, Byron had shown enormous restraint already, for he'd only responded to Maria's constant complaints on this very last day of the journey. Since Maria had met Lord Balkett, her adoration of Byron had cooled, and Summer almost wished her friend would go back to idolizing the duke. Almost.

"I'm sure Hugh will be there," mumbled Maria.

"Good grief, woman. It's Lord Balkett!" Byron ran strong fingers through his already tousled hair. He glared at Summer. "I agreed to teach you how to be a lady, not your gypsy friend here."

"Pshaw! I ain't a gypsy. I'm part Mexican and part... something else."

His brow rose in that superior way he had. "You don't know what else you are?"

"Listen, Mister. Just 'cause ya' can track yore ancestors all the way back to the Stone Age don't make ya' any better'n..."

Summer turned to Maria and whispered, "I know it's been a long journey, but... enough."

Maria's mouth pursed, and she threw a hateful look at Byron. "He's just so stuffy," she whispered back. "Someone needs to loosen him up."

"I like him just the way he is. Now leave the man alone."

Maria shrugged. "I will, if he will."

Byron watched the two of them with amazement. "Don't you two know it's rude to whisper when another is present?"

Summer smiled at him. Not an ordinary one, mind you, but the kind that lit up her face and made her look like a mischievous elf. Byron couldn't help grinning back and wondered what he'd been so irritated at her friend about. Ah yes. Summer had still been mad at him when they'd started this trip and had blatantly ignored him the entire time. Maria had whined about Hugh until he'd thought he'd gleefully strangle her, and the monkey kept shoulder-hopping, and that little dog had turned the hems of both legs of his trousers wet with slobber.

And all it took was one smile from her to make all his irritations fade away, and he realized that her eyes looked a dark gold, and that her amber gown brought out the highlights in her hair, and her companions couldn't be that annoying, not with her presence filling the carriage.

It was unnerving what her smile could do to him, thought Byron. He'd best get her accepted into society and back onto a ship to New York before he was in danger of... he didn't know what. Just that within that smile laid his own doom.

"Landsakes," gasped Maria as the imposing structure of Sandringham came into view. "The man said it was a house, but it ain't... It's a castle!"

Summer's eyes unlocked from Byron's, and she gaped out the window along with her friend. Maria spoke truly; it looked like a castle. Three stories high, with peaks over the top windows, balustrades, and a domed section... She didn't know the words to describe the architecture she saw, just that it stood grand and ornamental.

"Don't worry," murmured Byron. "They're very relaxed here, unlike the protocol at Windsor Castle or Buckingham Palace."

Summer swallowed and nodded, frowning at her little monkey and dog. Whatever had possessed her to bring them along? They'd be miserable if forced to stay with the servants in their rooms, and yet what if Chi-chi tried to play hide-and-seek under ladies' gowns and India went scavenging for food? A summer home just hadn't sounded so grand.

Fortunately, due to their tardiness, they were shown directly to their adjoining rooms, and India froze like a statue on Maria's shoulder and Chi-chi barely stuck her nose out of her pocket. Maria had just finished instructing the servants in the unpacking (although Summer thought they'd have finished in half the time without Maria's help) when the bell for dinner sounded, and then followed a flurry of activity to dress in the best gowns they'd brought.

Maria opened the door and peeked down the hallway. "Do ya' remember which way we came in?"

"I'm hoping they either send someone for us or His Grace will remember to fetch us. I'm not moving from this room until they do, or we'll get lost in these mazes of hallways and never find our way out."

Both girls looked at each other and shivered, remembering shared horror stories from their youth, while the servants giggled behind their hands. The very young one, Meg, had already offered to keep India and Chi-chi with her for the evening, while the older servant had just shaken her head, lips pinched in a frown, obviously disapproving of her prince's choice of guests.

The duke did come to fetch them for dinner, his eyes never leaving Summer's face as he escorted them to the drawing room. He admired the way the light made her hair glow, the way it cast shadows across her generously exposed bosom and shimmered in the folds of her cloth-of-gold gown. He kept noticing little things about her more and more often.

At some point the Baron of Hanover joined their group. Byron could vaguely hear Maria and the man's whispered conversation, the plucky girl intimidated enough by her surroundings to lower her voice to the pitch of a lady, for which he felt exceedingly grateful. It allowed him to gaze on the perfection of the tiny woman in front of him without distraction.

"Your Grace," inquired Summer. "What's wrong? Shouldn't you be introducing me to everyone?"

Byron nodded distractedly.

"Not that I'm anxious to talk to strangers. I grew up with only myself for company, and I'm afraid I rather got used to it."

Byron nodded again. He hadn't been alone with her since they'd left London and for some reason he didn't relish sharing her with anyone at present. Having her full attention directed at him alone, being allowed to gaze at her lips and fantasize about what he'd like to do to them without having to hide his thoughts, sent a shiver of joy through him. He couldn't imagine what it'd be like to allow himself to do this for the rest of his life. Probably kill him before his time... but he thought it might be a pleasant way to die.

After glancing nervously around the room, Summer made the mistake of looking into the duke's eyes. They'd gone all unfocused again, drawing her in and allowing her to see into his soul. He wanted to kiss her, she thought, and felt her legs go weak. Right here in the drawing room of the prince's house, he thought about kissing her, she knew it. And also knew she'd willingly let him if he tried. She'd never understand why so many of the aristocracy were terrified of him, for although his words could be vicious, his eyes allowed one to see the kindness of his soul. Or could it be that only she could see it?

"Your Grace," said a soft voice. "How nice to see you again."

They both started, Summer recovering first and turning to see the most lovely woman she'd ever met staring at them with barely disguised jealousy. The woman smiled, a mere baring of her even white teeth, and appraised Summer from beneath her elegantly slanted nose. Summer gawked, like the graceless bumpkin she felt herself to be. Fine blonde hair swept artfully away from a face with skin the color of new-fallen snow, a mouth full and tinged the faintest rose pouted prettily at her, eyes of dark lavender glittered with hostile intent. "I apologize if I've interrupted…"

Byron shook himself like a dog, trying to throw off the spell of Summer's attention, trying to shake the feeling of his brain being buried in sand while he fumbled for the woman's name. Ah yes. "Good evening, Lady Banfour. May I introduce Miss Summer Lee?"

The lavender eyes blinked hostility away and left behind only a gracious interest toward the duke. She barely glanced at Summer again. "How do you do? So this is the American I've been hearing so much about. Tell me, Your Grace, is it true she can do tricks?"

Byron stiffened. "Tricks?"

The lady laughed. "Oh, pardon me. I don't know what else to call them. I've heard she travels with a monkey and a rather large rat, and can shoot and ride like a cowboy… or isn't that what they're called?"

"Cowgirl," blurted Summer, caught off guard by the woman's lethal tone. Goodness, the woman's looks certainly didn't match her personality.

The duke stared at the woman for several seconds, not saying a word, until the English rose began to squirm. "Summer doesn't do tricks," he finally said. "She doesn't have to resort to them, unlike some women who criticize others so that they can feel as if their own stature is elevated by doing so."

The woman's mouth opened, then closed. Tears sprang into the lavender eyes, and with a mutter she turned and fled.

Summer brushed her fingertips lightly across the sleeve of his coat. "That was very bad of you. Now I know where you got your reputation for a wicked tongue."

Byron froze, feeling that light touch burn through the fabric of his sleeve. "If she can't accept a rebuke, she shouldn't have allowed herself to be in a position to deserve one."

"Oh, I'm not complaining. I just wish I could think of such remarks myself; then I wouldn't feel so frightened when I'm around all these elegant people."

The Duke of Monchester threw back his head and laughed, a hearty sound that drew all eyes in the room to them and made Summer feel a surge of happiness, and realize with surprise that every time she made him laugh, it caused her to be ridiculously happy.

Prince Albert entered the room at this opportune time and made directly for them, ignoring the bows and curtsies that created a wave before him. He held out his arm to Summer. "Allow me the pleasure of showing you in to dinner."

She nodded her head and gently laid her hand on his arm, every person in the room noting her graceful walk as he led her into a cavernous dining room, a glittering table down the length of it, elegantly dressed footmen behind every chair. The rest of the aristocracy proceeded in order of rank behind them, Byron stifling a smile as he realized that had His Royal Highness not taken Summer by the arm, she'd have been last to enter the room. He had placed the woman ahead of titled nobles, a higher tribute than Byron could have hoped for.

Fortunately, his own rank allowed him to be seated not far from Summer, and the duke could barely concentrate on the chatter of Lady Banfour, who had, as usual, managed to get herself seated beside him. He strained to overhear the conversation between Summer and His Highness but only managed to catch the laughter of the prince at something she said.

Summer tried to concentrate on not slopping food down her chin or otherwise disgracing herself, half-aware that the prince asked her an awful lot of questions about her and the duke. Some of them made him laugh, and afterward she wished she could remember all that she'd told him. But this time His Royal Highness behaved as she'd always thought he might: kind and sophisticated and with absolute charm, even formally apologizing for the absence of his wife, Princess Alexandra, because of a minor ailment. Summer felt dazed.

A startled oath from far down that long table enabled her to forget her nervousness and break the spell of the man next to her. It sounded like Maria, and sure enough she could still hear her friend's shouting over the eruption that had started at the end of the table and was flowing toward her and the prince as a wave of bobbing heads, spilled glasses, and startled oaths.

Halfway toward them, Summer could make out the tiny form of India, scampering over china and crystal and snatching an occasional tidbit here and there. Lord Balkett, who'd somehow managed to be seated next to Maria, had a firm grip on her friend's arm, and when India realized he was no longer being chased, he slowed down, wiggling his eyebrows at many of the guests, managing to turn the oaths into surprised laughs of delight.

"What is it?" asked the elderly lord next to Summer.

"I say, isn't that a monkey?" commented someone else.

"Look there, what's it doing now?"

India had completely gotten over his fright and now employed one of his finest begging tricks. He scampered over to his victim, pointed at an inviting morsel on their plate, clasped his hands together, and shook them as if in fervent prayer. The victim laughed in delight and handed over the tidbit.

Summer realized that if India kept it up, he'd have a bellyache by the time he reached her end of the table.

"Would you excuse me, Your Highness?" she asked as she swiftly rose and headed for the monkey. "Come here, you scamp," she commanded. Maria he might ignore, but never Summer. Although India didn't look contrite as he hopped to her shoulder. He just continued to munch at the handful of grapes he'd managed to get, a look of supreme satisfaction on his furry face.

"Yours, I presume?" inquired Prince Albert.

"I… I'm dreadfully sorry, Your Highness. A servant girl was supposed to be minding him… ."

He waved a pudgy hand. "Quite all right, I assure you."

"Yes," gasped the elderly lord who'd spoken earlier, wiping tears from his eyes. "We haven't had this much fun at a dinner in years! Lady Bischof, if I recall, also hired a monkey as entertainment for the evening. Well worth the price, I believe."

Summer smiled with gratitude at the gentleman, whose face flushed a beet red in reaction. She could vaguely hear the woman with the purple eyes, Lady Banfour, complaining to the Duke of Monchester that they'd all be exposed to diseases and insects from the creature, and Byron muttering something about being ridiculous. But an older woman sitting next to the lady began to scratch earnestly at her arms, and although Summer knew India had no pests, she also knew about the power of suggestion.

"If you'll excuse me, Your Highness? I believe I'll take India back to our rooms."

"Of course, of course. The supper table is hardly a place for the creature, but you must promise to bring him out when we're finished. It would amuse me."

A command. Summer nodded and backed away, trying to ignore the whispered conversations and one particularly smirking mouth, the artful pout of the Lady Banfour. Halfway across the room, she felt a guiding hand on her elbow and looked into the pale blue eyes of the duke.

"I thought that the servant girl Meg had him in control," she started to explain.

They passed Maria, who glared at India. Summer felt the little critter shiver.

Byron patted India's head reassuringly. "One will never be bored when you're around," he commented, as if she needn't explain anything.

His eyes got all soft again, and Summer had a difficult time tearing her own away. "Me or the monkey?"

"You." He chuckled.

Summer grinned. "You're not angry."

"Certainly not."

Summer nudged up against him, their shoulders meeting for just a moment. "You're in trouble, Your Grace."

"How so?" His voice had a breathless quality to it.

"You're getting dangerously used to me."

His laughter drifted behind them as they left the room.

The next day Summer stood outside on the meticulously groomed grounds of the Sandringham estate and breathed in the country air, trying to shut out the conversations of the lords and ladies around her. So much green, here in England, that it almost hurt her eyes, made her long to take off by herself and explore the woods beyond. She sighed.

"Not homesick, I hope?" inquired Prince Albert.

Summer thought for a moment and to her surprise realized that she wasn't. "No, Your Highness. On the contrary, the country seems to fill me with happiness."

"Excellent, as I feel it possible that you might not be returning home."

"Whatever do you mean?"

The prince gestured to where the Duke of Monchester, his face frozen in that mask of disdain, stood with the Lady Banfour. "That poor lady has been after my friend for years, and some even thought, due to his increasingly strained financial situation, she'd have some success."

Summer nodded. She'd learned that the prince loved to gossip and favored those who indulged him.

"A good match by all accounts," he continued, "for she's rich and he's titled. Yet I've never seen him drop the charade he plays with us all, except when he's with you."

"Charade?"

"Ah, the coldhearted lord who holds no other opinions but his own to be of importance, who cares naught for the world…" Prince Albert's voice lowered. "Just as the world cares nothing for him."

"Why would he feel that way?"

"I'm betting that the woman who can make him laugh like a boy again will figure that out."

Summer shook her head, the tiny curls that framed her face bouncing with the movement. "If you refer to myself, Your Highness, I fear I'm doomed to disappoint you. As I've told His Grace repeatedly, there's a man in New York I'm promised to, and as soon as I…"

Albert's eyes lit with interest. "What? As soon as you what?"

"As soon as I finish my tour, I will return to be with him. I seek no title."

Albert frowned in disappointment, as if he'd thought that Summer might confide in him and was disappointed that she hadn't. He turned his attention to Byron and raised his voice. "Monchester, didn't you say your American friend here can shoot?"

Byron glanced at them, his face alighting on Summer's, and that mask slipped just a bit. "If I recall, the lady herself told us so."

Lady Banfour frowned from Summer to the two men; then her delicate face lit up like a candle. "Do your talents extend to the bow, Miss Summer?"

Summer noticed the woman straighten, realizing that she'd been consciously slouching while she'd been talking to Byron. She never noticed his stature, except when other people called her attention to it. Lady Banfour stood almost as tall as Byron's sister-in-law, while Summer was just a bit shorter than Byron himself. Really, she mused, an excellent height for her. She never had to crane her neck while speaking to him. And she never had to crouch either.

"I haven't used one in a long time," she answered.

Lady Banfour batted her eyes at the duke. "Now, we'll have none of that, will we, Your Grace? Let us off to the archery grounds, where we can judge for ourselves the extent of Miss Summer's skill."

The prince grinned with delight, the duke shrugged with indifference, so off they went, trailed by a group of finely dressed men and women. Summer looked around for Maria, noting again that her friend had disappeared with the handsome Baron of Hanover. *The man must be twice her age*, she thought. Maria couldn't really have any romantic interest in him, could she? Yet her friend seemed to come alive when she spoke with the older man, and oddly enough seemed to be the only one capable of deciphering the lord's muttering—besides, of course, the gentleman's sister.

What would happen if Maria decided to marry this man? Summer would have to return to New York by herself, and they might never see each other again. She tried to squelch the loneliness that welled up at the thought of that, for if it made Maria happy, that was all that mattered. Yet she couldn't help wondering what kind of curse she lay under, that all the people she loved in her life always left her.

When they reached the archery grounds, Lady Banfour picked up several bows and tested their pull with an expert air, and chose the one she deemed best, allowing Summer to choose from the others.

Summer's hand hesitated over the selection as she glanced at those around her from beneath her lashes. No frowns of disapproval came their way, and she sighed with relief. So this was one skill she'd learned that was socially acceptable. With growing delight she tested each bow, surprised at the ease of the pull, choosing one of the stiffest because it felt similar to the one Chatto had taught her to use. She noticed that although an Apache bow was excellently crafted, these were even finer, with a string that didn't look like animal gut and a grip designed for a smaller hand.

A weapon designed for a woman.

Lady Banfour had patiently waited and, at the sudden grin of almost predatory delight on her competitor's face, blanched a bit. Then, with a tilt of her chin, Lady Banfour faced the target, sighted, and let fly.

Summer admired the lady's skill, as point after point hit near the bull's-eye of the target. The woman finished her fifth shot amid a round of applause, and flushing with triumph, she bowed to the onlookers and gestured Summer to take her place. She took up a stance next to the Duke of Monchester, who offered excessive praise to the woman. Or so it seemed to Summer.

She sighted and let fly her five arrows in rapid succession, causing the audience to gasp in surprise. But her injun boy had taught her how to shoot rapidly, for if the first shot missed, the next had better be in the bow or dinner would get away.

A mutter grew from the crowd. All the arrows had landed so close together that no one could determine a winner from this distance. Two gentlemen appointed themselves the judges and hastened over to compare the shots.

Summer's arrows had been fletched with brown feathers, Lady Banfour's with black.

The men ran back to the crowd with their news. "The black wins! By only a hairsbreadth closer to the bull's-eye! Finest shooting we've ever seen."

Lady Banfour preened, suddenly surrounded by an adoring crowd. The Duke of Monchester left her side and laid his hand on Summer's arm, the heat of it feeling like a brand. "She's been archery champion for three years running. It's why she challenged you at all."

Summer sighed. "It's been a long time since I've used a bow and arrow, and a different design than this as well. But she is a superb shot, and I admire her skill."

"Do you? And it doesn't bother you to lose?"

She looked into his eyes. Ah, yes, he baited her. Had it become a habit with him then, to try and make people angry, proving himself more in control? "Not to someone who possesses a greater skill than mine. It's a challenge."

He smoothed back the golden hair that had tumbled over his ears. "Lady Banfour doesn't make you jealous?"

"Why should she?"

"For no other reason than she's apparently overly jealous of you."

Summer studied the laughing woman, her head tilted back, accepting the homage of the well-wishers. "I don't know why," she whispered with surprise. "She has everything I don't. Beauty, poise, social acceptance. What could I have that she'd be jealous of?"

One golden eyebrow rose. "What, indeed?"

"I say," shouted one of the judges over the conversation. "Did you see the heads of the browns in the target?"

The other man nodded. "Most amazing thing I've ever seen. They were buried past the shaft."

"You don't say?" queried the Prince of Wales, loud enough to distract everyone's attention to the new conversation.

"Truly, Your Royal Highness. Come and look. I've never known a woman to bury an arrow that deeply before, much less five in a row. Matter of fact, a man would be hard-pressed to match it."

Summer watched as the entire assembly trooped over to the target, each taking a turn at marveling over her arrows, leaving Lady Banfour alone. Summer took the opportunity to finally offer her own congratulations, noting the disgruntled look of the duke and the smirk of the prince.

"American women don't have a monopoly on physical skills, you know," replied Lady Banfour in response to Summer's praise.

"I never said they did," she replied, "and if you have heard so, it's only because we've been forced to acquire them."

Lady Banfour's artfully shaped lips narrowed into unflattering lines. She cast a fearful glance at the duke and lowered her voice when she spoke again. "Because you were raised like a savage."

Summer sighed. This woman hated her, and she had a feeling she knew why. Surely, two adult, civilized people could talk out their differences? "I have seen so-called savages treat a stranger with more respect than the most renowned woman in New York society. But I don't think that's what's bothering you." She glanced over at the duke. "Rest assured, I have no designs on him. I'm already promised to a man in America."

Lady Banfour inelegantly snickered. "What cunning you have! I never would've thought of such a grand scheme to snag a man as that, keeping him off his guard while you entice him in."

Summer's mouth fell open. She'd never understand some people and the games they played! Her hand inched toward her knife. Tarnation, she'd never use it here, it had just become a habit over the years to reach for its comfort when she felt threatened, but the duke didn't realize that, for as soon as he saw her gesture he came striding over, staring back and forth at the two women.

Prince Albert began to laugh with genuine delight.

"I say, young miss," asked an admiring voice, "however did you learn to shoot like that?" Summer backed up in surprise. The crowd had returned and surrounded her, each one of them jostling for a position at her side. While she tried to answer all the questions they asked, she noticed that Lady Banfour had been pushed to the background, and actually felt the glare of jealousy the other woman gave her before she stomped back to the castle.

Seven

SUMMER STOOD IN THE CHILL DAWN OF ANOTHER morning at Sandringham with a grin of delight on her face, while the horses and dogs assembled for the hunt. She'd thought ladies weren't allowed to do anything, yet here in England she'd been able to shoot a weapon, and now she'd be able to go on a hunt! And the best part of all was...

"Let me guess," drawled the duke. "The look of pure joy on your face is because you're wearing riding breeches beneath your skirt, isn't it?"

Summer turned with surprise. "How'd you know?"

"Whether I want to or not, I seem to be getting to know you. And if you recall, I picked out your riding habit." Byron leaned over and whispered in her ear, "And your underclothes as well."

She suddenly became aware of the feel of the silk drawers between her legs and felt an instant throb of heat there. She should've been thoroughly disgruntled that the man could so easily arouse such a response from her, but she laughed instead, 'cause she knew he was trying to shock her again, and he wore a grin on his face that made him look like a naughty schoolboy. He really was fun to be around... why ever had Maria told her that Englishmen, especially the titled, tended to be stuffy? Monte had been stuffy, of course, given the position he had to maintain, but Byron already had the position, so he didn't have to do a thing to maintain it.

The nose of a large horse interposed itself between them, and they both looked up into familiar lavender eyes. "Are you coming, Your Grace? The hunt is about to begin."

Lady Banfour sat her mount well... *as she did most all things well*, thought Byron. The lady's interest in him had certainly intensified since the last time he'd seen her. Because she'd heard of his break with Lady Windolm, or could it be some other reason? Did his arrangement with Summer have tongues wagging? He shrugged, for it hardly mattered, considering he had no interest in the American, really, other than a mild physical attraction.

He watched Summer walk over to the horse the groom had brought for her. Oh, bloody hell, maybe a *major* physical attraction.

She turned to him with a frown of concern on her face, and he felt his legs hurrying over to her without a conscious decision of his own. "What's wrong?"

"It's the saddle." She cocked her head at him, so she could see him clearly beneath the brim of the tilted hat she wore. He prided himself on his choice of that jaunty piece of headgear, the softness of the suede, the exquisite gold decoration against her face that brought out the color of her eyes.

"Your Grace."

"Hmm? Oh yes, the saddle. What's wrong with it?"

"It only has one stirrup."

He stared at her in astonishment. "It's supposed to have one. Only men's saddles have two…" The duke dug the heel of his hand against his forehead.

Summer grimaced. "Maria's afraid of horses, so we never went riding in New York. And in Tombstone they had normal saddles. With two stirrups."

The duke shook his head. What an odd upbringing this girl had, certainly far stranger than any other American girl he'd ever met. "Well, you needn't go on the hunt. We're out of season and likely not to run down a fox anyway. Many women prefer to stay indoors with a cup of tea."

Summer made a face. It held such a genuine mixture of disgust and disdain that he couldn't help the laugh that escaped. The girl had the power to do that to him.

"It's highly irregular but not unheard of. It's just considered a tad risqué in the higher circles." He glanced over at Lady Banfour, then at Prince Albert, who'd started to stare at their whispered conversation with amused interest. "Can't you just try the sidesaddle?"

Summer stared at the ridiculous thing. "There's no guarantee that I wouldn't wind up on my backside in the dirt, and that bothers me more than any ridiculous notions of modesty. I can't ride properly—"

"You there, groomsman. Fetch the lady another saddle. With two stirrups."

"Ummm," started Summer.

"Good grief, madam. What is it now?" They had started to attract even more attention, as the rest of the group had already mounted and were struggling to hold horses that were anxious for a good run. The hounds kept circling the huntsman with whines of anticipation and an occasional snap at each other.

"I'm really just used to no saddle at all."

"No saddle… they'll think you're the savage you're rumored to be."

Summer's face fell, and he couldn't stand the utter look of dejection upon it. "You're the one who wants to be accepted by society—oh, bloody hell. Groomsman, remove the saddle." The duke's handsome face flushed red, but he calmly gestured at the remaining pad. "Is this permissible?"

Summer nodded enthusiastically, and her smile of happiness almost relieved him of his temper. But he couldn't help thinking that he'd have a devil of a time explaining this one. Couldn't the girl do anything normally?

Evidently not, for as soon as the horse lay bare of anything but pad and bridle, she proceeded to rub her hands all over the animal, grasping the horse's head and near hugging it fully with her body. Byron stood transfixed for several moments, watching those graceful movements, upbraiding himself for mentally imagining his own body beneath those delicate hands, wishing that he could for just one moment be that stupid horse!

"What are you doing?" he finally managed to ask.

Summer turned and stared at his handsome face. How could a man be so beautiful and yet so ignorant at the same time? "I'm introducing myself to her."

The groomsman nodded his head, as if finally meeting another sensible person, and gestured at a young boy to hand over the reins to the duke's mount. But Byron had started forward, to the anticipated task of helping Summer into the saddle, for the field had started to move, following the huntsman and dogs out to the chosen covert. He stopped dead in his tracks as Summer vaulted on top of the horse, a horse that stood at least fifteen hands high, and seemed to become one with it, blending her body with the animal's as if they were a single unit.

He took his reins without a glance, climbing into his own saddle, feeling clumsy and awkward after seeing that girl's graceful vault, he who had always prided himself on his horsemanship. He felt distinctly out of sorts and quickly left Summer behind. When Lady Banfour pulled up alongside him, he didn't try to avoid her, hoping that Summer would notice how attracted the woman was to him.

"How can you associate yourself with that American?" hissed Lady Banfour. "Look at the way she's riding that horse. Why, she'll make you a laughingstock." At the look on his face, she quickly changed tactics, lowering her voice to a husky timbre. "Why you would take up with this American remains a mystery to everyone, but I can see that you are intent on championing her."

He impaled her with those ice blue eyes, and she swallowed. "But if you would like any help, you have only to ask."

Byron stopped scowling. Had he misjudged the Lady Banfour? Could he dare include her in their plan? "You could assist me by pointing out that Miss Lee's peculiarities are... eccentricities. That she is a lady, and indeed, to my eyes she always will be, regardless of her escapades."

Those lavender eyes widened. "She's had escapades? I hope nothing as shocking as what she's exposed us to on this visit."

He'd never kept this many outrageous stories to himself before, but the inclination to reveal all of Summer's adventures to this woman passed quickly. He'd been hired to make the girl acceptable, not to expose her, no matter how much Lady Banfour panted at the opportunity for gossip. He would just have to wait until the girl returned to America, and the first person he'd tell would be the prince anyway. It would keep him housed as a guest in the palace for at least a year.

"Just help ease the girl into the pattern of our society, so that she can be presented to the Queen, and I would be grateful."

She leaned toward him, guiding her horse closer to his own, so that their heads nearly touched. "And in what way would you be willing to show your gratitude?"

Byron shrugged. He knew what the lady wanted. And she was, after all, the epitome of the perfect Englishwoman, and although the money from his arrangement with Summer had helped, he still needed much, much more. Of which Lady Banfour had plenty. What did it matter, after all, who he married? He'd never be able to separate his person from his title, so he might as well take advantage of it.

And he felt tired of this game he played, making fools of the people around him, amusing them so that he'd be invited to stay at their well-maintained estates, just to live in the manner he felt entitled to. He realized that he wanted to live in his own estates again, to be respected for what he could accomplish with his ingenuity, not the harshness of his tongue.

He wondered what Summer's reaction would be if he announced his engagement tonight. Was he seriously toying with the ridiculous idea of marriage just to see if it'd make her as jealous of Lady Banfour as he was of this Monte fellow?

Had he completely lost all his senses?

A sudden shout announced that the hounds had flushed out the fox, and the field surged forward, both their horses following the pursuit, making any further conversation impossible. Byron felt satisfied to just let the lady's question go unanswered. Let her hope of it what she would.

He urged his mount into a gallop and surged ahead of Lady Banfour, splashing through streams and speeding across endless stretches of grassy fields, ducking beneath low-lying branches and surging over fences and more than one gully. The thrill of the chase electrified him, and he reveled in the great skill it took to keep up with the rest of the field.

A long stretch of open meadow lay before them, and Byron tapped his heels against the horse's flanks, letting him have his head as they fairly flew over the heather. Movement from the corner of his eye caught his attention, and he glanced over at Lady Banfour, who'd been whipping her horse mercilessly in order to keep up with him. Summer surged from behind and leaned over at a dangerous angle to snatch the whip from the lady's hand. He thought at first that she meant to use it for herself, for she'd refused the whip as well as the saddle, but he could see that she had no trouble urging her horse along with just the pressure of her knees, or whatever she did to make the animal respond like that. Summer's horse was given to ladies because she was of mild temperament, preferring to tarry behind the rest of the field and let the other horses lead. He didn't know how she was making the animal respond like that.

"Give that back," shouted Lady Banfour.

Summer shouted something back at her, but he couldn't make it out, as his attention began to focus on the saddle beneath him. It had started to shift toward the left, and he adjusted his weight to center it again. Had the groomsman forgotten to tighten it properly?

Summer threw the whip away with an angry gesture, and deprived of the inducement of pain, Lady Banfour's horse started to lag behind.

Then Summer's eyes met his, he could feel them across the distance that separated them, and he could see that she sensed something was wrong. She closed the gap that separated them.

The saddle shifted to the right this time, and Byron tried to compensate again, but it felt as if the entire thing had come loose and only the firmness of his seat kept it in place. He resisted the urge to panic and pull back on the reins, and instead gently pulled the horse's head to the left, trying to guide it out of the path of the riders behind them.

"What is it?" shouted Šummer, keeping her mount alongside his.

Byron realized that the riders behind them continued to follow him, instead of the distant figure of the prince. Perhaps they thought he knew a shortcut that avoided most of the furrows in this stretch of land—he didn't know, but the saddle had started to creep back onto the horse's rump and he didn't have time to shout explanations to them.

"Saddle's loose," he finally replied. He had mere seconds to act and wasn't sure if the woman next to him was actually as good a rider as she looked. Or if he wanted to gamble his life on that.

But she was quick, this American girl, and shouted back at him, "I'm ready." And pulled her horse close enough that her leg touched his own.

The duke lifted both his legs, trying to gain some leverage with his left as he slid his right over the slightly lower rump of Summer's horse. His own mount snorted and fought the reins, frightened by the closeness of Summer's horse, and tried to veer away. Byron couldn't decide whether to risk the loose saddle or shift his weight all the way to the other horse. His legs stretched farther apart than they'd been physically designed to do, and he grunted against the pull of his muscles, waiting for them to rip as his bottom hung suspended in midair. For a horrible second he thought he hadn't made it, half on and off both mounts, knowing that if he fell between them, his spine would crack and the horses following would trample him to death.

Then the daring girl grasped his arm and pulled him the rest of the way over and behind her, with him instinctively kicking off his own horse to give her the leverage to do it. As his bottom landed firmly behind her, any trace of annoyance he'd still harbored over her fuss about how she wanted to ride her horse evaporated.

His empty saddle flew off his horse, barely missing the rider behind it, and they galloped on amid the startled screams of those behind them.

"Shall we stop?" called Summer over her shoulder.

Byron had his arms around her tiny waist, his groin smashed up against her bottom, his face nestled in the fragrant locks of her hair, his lips mere inches from the soft skin of her neck. "Not on your life!"

Summer grinned and leaned forward, urging the mare to lengthen her stride with the Apache words that Chatto had taught her, a sudden stab of longing for her long-lost friend melting away when the man behind her squeezed her waist and grazed his lips across the nape of her neck. The scoundrel.

Summer grinned wider, finally slowing her mount when they approached a line of forest, ducking low-lying limbs and maneuvering through bushes and around fallen logs. The hounds had ceased yapping and now growled with fierce intensity, so that when they entered a clearing and joined the ring of onlookers she could actually hear the dog's teeth snapping. A metallic whiff of blood drifted to her nose.

Her horse heaved beneath her while the huntsman rescued the tail of what must have been a very small fox, and handed it to the prince. Summer couldn't help the look of disgust on her face. This was it? A romp through the countryside, so they could watch dogs tear apart some poor creature?

The duke had acquired an uncanny ability to read the lady's mind. He could feel her vibration of disgust through her rigid spine. "The sport is in the chase and keeping up with the hounds. Have patience with our traditions."

Prince Albert circled around to Summer and ceremoniously handed her the bloody trophy of the fox's bushy tail. "In memory of your first hunt, Miss Lee."

She tried to smile graciously, while Lady Banfour glared at her again. It seemed she'd just been bestowed a great honor, one that the other lady wished for.

Summer tried to think of something appropriate to say, managed a humble "thank you," before being rescued from further comment by the exclamations of the other guests.

"I say, Monchester, how long did the two of you practice that stunt?"

Byron breathed a sigh of relief. The American girl had managed to keep her opinions to herself for a change, and although she held the bush as if it would bite her, she did continue to hold it. "What stunt?"

"Oh, come now. Surely you're not going to tell me that you two didn't practice that switching-horse maneuver? I say, it puts me in mind of that traveling Wild West show. Buffalo, something?"

"What's this?" inquired the prince, his beaming face dissolving into a frown of confusion.

"The duke's saddle flew right off," said another man. "Only missed me by a hairsbreadth."

"Miss Lee here," added a young woman, "pulled him onto her own horse. 'Tis fortunate that she sits her mount so well."

This caused a flurry of comments on the benefits of riding astride without a saddle.

"Are you saying that a saddle from one of my own stables had not been tightened properly by my head groomsman?"

Byron frowned. "It's what I assumed, Your Highness, until the entire saddle came out from under me."

The prince scowled. "Take us to where this happened. You, Cromsbey. I want you to ascertain why the saddle became loose."

The man's eyes widened and he bowed, and once at the site, he made a thorough inspection of the equipment. He shook his head and looked up at the prince. "It's been cut clean through, Your Highness. See here, where the girth meets the straps? The fibers show the small amount that hadn't been cut, so that the saddle was held on by a mere thread, and one good gallop would've torn it the rest of the way."

The prince's face flushed red with rage. "I'll get to the bottom of this, Monchester. No guest of mine shall fear for his safety!"

Lord Cromsbey blanched, his self-important grin at the honor of being singled out for the inspection fading to a frown of regret.

Byron felt the small shiver that rippled through the girl in front of him. The thought that someone must've deliberately tried to hurt him had probably upset her. He suppressed a grin of delight. "We'll follow you shortly, Your Highness. I fear Miss Lee needs a few moments to compose herself."

The prince nodded tersely and galloped away, his retinue tagging along behind.

"Summer, are you all right?" He could hear a sob escape her, and when she turned, those amber eyes were brilliant with unshed tears.

Byron smiled condescendingly and hugged her closer, resisting the desire to kiss the lips that were so close to his own. "It's all right."

"No, it's not."

"I'm unharmed, thanks to our mutual good sense. It's just the reaction finally sinking in."

She pulled back and wrinkled her brow at him. The horse shifted and swished her tail at a fly, the thunder of retreating hooves faded behind them, leaving only the songs of the birds and the soughing of the wind in the trees. A secluded, romantic spot for him to soothe her fears. In any way he deemed fitting.

"What are you talking about?" she snapped.

Byron removed his hand from her cheek, unaware that it had strayed there. "Those unshed tears…"

She held the bloody fox's tail in front of his face. "Didn't you say it was out of season?"

He snapped his head back. "What?"

"Babies! I just realized that she must've had little ones and now, because of our sport, they're left with no mother."

"The fox. Your tears are for the fox?"

Summer gritted her teeth. Was the man being deliberately dense? "For the babies."

"I see."

His face fell, and Summer watched that dreamy look in his eyes fade. His lips twisted in that cynical expression he habitually wore, and the thought that he'd been about to kiss her died with a thump that had her wondering at the feeling of coldness it left inside of her.

"What did you think was wrong?" she asked.

"It occurred to me that you might've been upset that someone had tried to... Never mind."

"Kill you?"

Those golden brows rose. Summer waved her hand. "Tarnation, Byron, I already told you someone wanted you dead. Why do you think I've been watching after you?"

He choked. "Me? You've been watching after me?" He felt so surprised, he forgot to correct her for using his first name and tried very hard to feel insulted. Instead, that same elation that had risen when he thought she'd been crying in fear for him filled up his soul again. A single tear escaped from beneath her lashes, connecting two light freckles on the side of her nose, and he didn't even try to stop the urge to catch it with his finger.

Byron suddenly wanted to kiss every freckle that adorned her face. He wanted that tear to be for him, and then wondered why he wished for such a foolish thing. Certainly no one had ever cried for him, not the father who'd raised him with cold tolerance, nor the governess who had near starved him for misbehavior, nor the stepmother who kindly ignored him. He shrugged. If his mother had lived, perhaps she would've shed a tear for him... Not that he needed tear-shedding, he told himself. It's the rest of the aristocracy that needed it, he'd made sure of that!

He forced himself to snap out of such self-pitying melancholy and eyed the bushy fox's tail she now clutched to her bosom. "We don't even know that it was a female. Do you remember where the covert was?"

Her eyes widened beneath her bonnet, and she nodded. He thought she looked like a little child, and he was the parent promising to make it all better. How did one stay detached from someone who had no guile or artifice? She was such a contrast of resourcefulness and innocence that she confounded him at every turn.

"Well, I daresay we could ask the huntsman where the holes he stopped up are, and a thorough digging might uncover the den."

Summer squealed and twisted all the way around to throw her arms around him. He froze, fighting the urge to crush her with his own embrace, to run his hands up to the back of that soft neck he'd been staring at during their ride, to feel with his fingertips the downy softness of the tiny hairs that grew there. He tried desperately not to delight in the feel of the smoothness of her cheek.

Summer felt his rigidity and quickly pulled back, a look of horror on her face. "I'm so sorry, Your Grace, I didn't mean…"

He flipped back the golden lock of hair from his forehead. "It's quite all right, I assure you. In this instance I'll ignore it due to the unusual circumstances of the day." His voice clipped with businesslike efficiency. "Come now, off we go."

Summer blinked, spun back around, and spoke to her horse. With a snort the mare turned and lurched off at an incredible pace, causing His Grace to clutch at Summer's corseted waist for balance. They caught up to the huntsman as he and his hounds reached the covert.

"Good man," shouted Byron over the yips of the dogs. "Would you show the lady where you stopped up the fox holes?"

The huntsman doffed his hat, his mouth twisting at the unusual request, and with a sigh that spoke of years of being subjected to the odd whims of the nobility, shushed his dogs to the ground. They belly-flopped to the grass, tongues lolling, seemingly grateful for the unexpected respite.

The duke dismounted, a bit clumsily without the aid of the stirrup, wincing at the pain in his inner thighs from torn muscles. Summer slid gracefully to the ground, skirts settling around her riding trousers while she waved the bushy tail in the man's face. "Was it a vixen, sir? Did she have cubs?"

The huntsman slowly nodded his head. "Is that what you be seeking?"

She nodded.

He started across the covert, signaling the hounds to stay. "Pardon me for sayin', yer ladyship…"

"Go on," urged Summer.

"It was a vixen right enough, two cubs in the den, if I recall. Usually feed 'em to the hounds—better'n letting them starve to death, and it gets my dogs more worked up for the chase—but didn't have the time this morn, what with Mangy deliverin' the pups and all."

His voice trailed off at Summer's gasp of outrage.

The huntsman turned. "Beggin' yer pardon, for speakin' too bluntly." He glanced at Byron with a worried frown. "Seems I spend too much time with my hounds."

The duke grunted with exasperation. "Just take us to the cubs, man. Before the lady expires on the spot."

The huntsman turned and sprinted, finally squatting over a mound of fresh dirt, looking up with surprise that the lady and gentleman had kept pace with him, trying to hide his astonishment as they knelt and began to soil their gloves with digging.

"Do you think they're still alive?"

"Most assuredly."

The huntsman added his efforts to theirs, so that they soon revealed an earthen cave with a nest of two reddish brown balls of fur. Summer stripped off her soiled gloves and picked both critters up, delighted when they showed signs of life, squeaking at their interrupted nap. They turned and began to nuzzle her fingers.

"They must be fed," she muttered.

The huntsman opened his mouth, glanced at the duke, and snapped it shut again.

Summer handed them to Byron so quickly that he didn't have a chance to protest—as he most certainly would have done—called to her horse, and leaped onto her back when she came. The huntsman's mouth dropped open and stayed suspended.

"Hand them to me," she commanded.

The duke did so with relief, afraid he was going to drop the cubs, then gestured for the huntsman to give him a hand up to mount, and groaned when she handed the fragile things back to him. She glanced from his face to his cupped hands and bit at her lower lip.

The Duke of Monchester rolled his eyes. "They're not going to starve to death in a few hours, nor do you need to gallop dramatically back to the house. Take it at a walk, and I promise I won't drop them." He mentally repeated that last promise. *I will not drop them. I will not…*

Summer rubbed the horse's neck, spoke a few Apache words, and the mare snorted with relief as she broke into her usual stride, a walk slow enough that she managed to snatch mouthfuls of tall grass along the way.

Summer sighed. The duke's muscular legs were snuggled up behind her own, the wind smelled full of late-blooming flowers and musky loam, and the sun warmed the back of her neck like one of the duke's— Monte's kisses. She swayed with the horse's walk and wondered why she had such a difficult time conjuring up Monte's face. They hadn't been in England that long, but the man's features were becoming blurry and indistinct whenever she tried to recall them. The duke's face kept superimposing itself over her attempts to recall her intended. Could it be possible that she was falling in love with Byron?

Summer took a quick glance over her shoulder. Byron's head was bent over the bundles in his hands, his full lips were moving as he repeated something to himself, his face frowning in total concentration. He carried the two baby foxes as if they were the most precious of burdens—creatures he'd called "vermin"—just to make her happy. Their business arrangement didn't extend to her own personal happiness, yet time after time, he'd made it obvious that it was important to him.

Is this love? wondered Summer. *This joyful sensibility whenever I'm around him, this physical draw to his body?* But she'd experienced that feeling with several men, just not as strong. Was she fickle, drawn to whatever man just happened along her path? Or just so pathetically needy that she took whatever was offered her?

She shook her head and dismissed all those confusing thoughts when they reached the palace stables. She decided to be content with the knowledge that she just didn't know what she wanted, that perhaps she never had.

Eight

At dinner that evening, Summer again sat next to the prince, and this time she had the added pleasure of the Duke of Monchester sitting directly across from her. She might've been able to relax if Prince Albert's calculating eyes hadn't been shifting back and forth between her and Byron. As it was, with His Highness's earlier words hinting that the duke may actually be interested in her outside of their business relationship, and her own conflicting emotions, she barely managed to eat anything at all.

When a retainer came over and had a whispered conversation with Prince Albert, Summer took advantage of his distraction to speak across the table to the duke, over a bowl of multicolored flowers and through a candelabra of shining silver, unaware that her posture made her bosom bulge even farther out of the low neckline of her gown.

Byron, however, made notice and smiled in appreciation, hard-pressed at first to pay attention to her words.

"Chi-chi has adopted the babies."

The duke blinked. "The what?"

"The baby foxes. Chi-chi has adopted them. We're feeding them goat's milk."

"Oh. Good for you, I mean, them. Worth is a genius, you know. That dress suits you."

It was Summer's turn to blink. She looked down at herself, the layers upon layers of ruffles flowing across her shoulders and down the length of her skirt, the soft yellow of the fabric blending it all into a concoction of muted simplicity. Did he really care more about the dress than those precious foxes?

Byron reluctantly dragged his eyes back to her face. "Have you thought about what you're going to do with them?"

"With what?"

"The vermin—I mean, the baby foxes you rescued. They will grow up to be adults, you know, and wreak havoc in your house."

Summer grinned, her eyes sparkling. "Then they'll fit right in, don't you agree?"

The Duke of Monchester threw back his head and laughed, Summer smiling innocently, while those within hearing distance stared.

"What's so funny, Monchester?" inquired the prince, his attention fixing on the couple. "And what's this I hear from my huntsman about Miss Lee bringing vermin into my home?"

Summer's eyes grew round. She'd been found out! She looked to Byron for help. What would the nobility say about her now? Although, if it came down to it, she'd take the babies and leave, rather than have them thrown to the dogs for supper.

Byron tilted his chin and carefully set down his fork. "Miss Lee's sensibilities toward animals are rather... too sympathetic for her own good. She has an uncanny ability to pick up the oddest of orphans and welcome them into her home. Rather a charming habit, don't you think?"

Prince Albert sat through this explanation with a look of stunned disbelief. At the last few words, he choked. "Do you mean to say you supported her in this endeavor?"

The Duke of Monchester shrugged.

Prince Albert began to chuckle. "The coldest man in court rescued baby foxes?"

Byron's face froze. Is that what they considered him, the coldest of men? Had that been his intended goal, years ago, when he'd decided since the world had no warmth for him, he'd return the favor? And he realized that if he'd heard himself referred to in that way before he'd met Summer, he'd have been giddy with pride. Now, he could only wonder in dismay if she also thought that he had no heart.

"I beg your pardon, Your Highness," said Summer, taking a deep breath. "But since I've come to England, I've been quite confused by everyone's opinion of His Grace's character."

Albert leaned forward, grinning widely. "How so, my dear?"

She swallowed as she noticed that every ear within range had tuned in to their words, and those not within hearing distance were elbowing their neighbors for a report as she spoke. Well, tarnation, Byron always supported her in ways beyond their business arrangement, and it was about time she set some people straight on his own character.

"Why, they say he's a cold man. That he's to be feared for his cutting remarks and witty stories."

Albert nodded encouragingly. Byron closed his eyes and groaned.

Summer squirmed. "Well, I find his remarks to be truthful, although blunt sometimes. And excessively funny. And, and he's always been most thoughtful and patient."

Albert started to chortle.

"And he helped rescue India," she hurried on, "and it was his idea that allowed us to find the fox cubs, and he never scolds my animals... and he defended me against thieves! Would a cold, uncaring man do any of those things?" Summer started to get annoyed. The prince kept laughing harder at every word she said!

The Duke of Monchester had become more rigid with every word out of Summer's mouth. He *would* be a laughingstock by the time she got done with him!

And yet... he couldn't help feeling pleased. He couldn't remember the last time anyone had ever defended him. He stared into that pretty, elfin face and pondered. The only time he could ever recall was when he'd come home from private school during a break, with his eyes blackened again, and his father had beat him for letting others "unman" him. His father believed that his son would learn to defend himself in order to avoid his own beatings. But fortunately at the age of ten, a Chinese gardener had accidentally entered the room during one of his lessons in manhood and stood up to his own father, very calmly telling Byron to leave the room. He couldn't hear the entire conversation, but from that day forward his father never beat him again. And the gardener had become his master and began to teach him the kung fu.

Byron smoothed back his hair. Why did this Summer Wine Lee dredge up memories of his past that he'd managed to forget?

The prince's laughter had faded to gentle hiccups, and he wiped at his eyes with an embroidered kerchief. "Forgive my laughter, Miss Lee. You speak so sincerely that I fear we shall all be compelled from this moment forward to reassess our opinions of His Grace's character as well." He turned and grinned at Monchester, who groaned again.

"And you, my friend, may wish to consider who might want to do you harm," continued Prince Albert, suddenly becoming serious. "I have made a thorough investigation of the saddle incident and discovered that a new man hired in the stables recently has disappeared from the premises."

Byron sighed with relief at the change of subject. "I have considered it, Your Highness. And I've severely annoyed many people, but I can think of no one who would wish me serious harm."

Summer glanced at him in surprise. So, he had thought about what she'd said after all! He hadn't treated her concerns as if they were some wild flight of fancy.

"Not even a certain John Strolm?" inquired Albert. "Ah, don't look at me with such surprise; I have other advisors than yourself."

"I considered him," replied Byron. "But he doesn't have the courage."

"He could hire someone," suggested Summer. "Those thieves were certainly hired men."

Albert nodded. "I like the way you think, my dear. Yet I find this all most upsetting. Too many royalty have been assassinated for my peace of mind." He gave a great sigh. "Well, we shall get to the bottom of this. I have a vested interest in the security of my home, as well."

And Summer caught a glimpse of the man behind the facade of good humor, parties, and mistresses. A look at the man who would one day be king and carry the full weight of England on his shoulders. He was suddenly everything that she'd imagined him to be, but with the added charm of only being human, after all.

When Byron escorted her to her room after dinner, he declined her offer to peek in on the health of the foxes, and Summer wondered if he was very mad at her for discussing his character so openly. She stayed to watch him cross the hall into his own room, without a backward glance, or even a "good night," and sighed with dismay. It seemed she couldn't do anything right.

Summer opened the door to her room to find Maria bouncing on her four-poster bed, those pale green eyes twinkling with excitement.

"It's about time ya' got here," she said, her unbound black hair looking like wings from her motions. "Yore not gonna believe the news I have for ya'."

Summer sighed. "Well, I can't speak to you with my head bobbing up and down. Do stop bouncing, Maria."

The girl stilled, much to the dismay of India, who'd been enjoying the ride. The monkey squeaked and began to climb the velvet draperies, using them like vines to swing around the canopy of the bed.

"What's the matter, Summer?"

She shrugged and began to unpin her golden brown hair. "Just tired, I guess. And confused about everything. But forget about me, I want to hear your news."

Maria studied her for a minute, frowned, then brightened. "Ya'll have to figure out yore own heart, I figure. But I never thought I might have to worry about mine."

"India, stop that, you're making me dizzy. Maria, whatever do you mean?"

"Summer," sighed her friend as she leaned forward. "I have my very own golden opportunity."

"You?" A bolt of fear swept through her body. Now why on earth would Maria's announcement have that affect on her? "Tarnation, I can barely breathe in this corset. Can you help me out?"

Maria shrugged and started on the tiny buttons down the back of Summer's dress. "Sure, but yore gonna have to hire yoreself a real maid for a change. At least for the next few weeks."

"Whatever do you mean?"

"This corset *must* be laced tight," replied Maria. "Yore voice is all breathless and quivery. Means I'll be going for my own visit to a country house. Hugh, I mean, Lord Balkett, has invited me to stay a few weeks with him… and before ya' go getting all lady-fied, his sister will be our chaperone."

Summer stepped out of her dress and grunted while Maria yanked out her corset lacings. "But—oof—why?

You can't possibly—oof—be considering a serious—ugh—relationship with that old man... Aah..." The corset fell away, and Summer inhaled deeply.

"And why not?" asked Maria, sounding a bit hurt.

"Because you know I'll provide you a sufficient enough dowry that you could marry any man you want."

Maria sniffed and tossed the corset on the bed. "Hugh don't care about money; he's made enough in investments that he can marry for love alone. And he loves me."

Summer couldn't breathe again, even though she'd shed that corset. How had this happened? Those two had only met each other a few times, and although she could understand how Lord Balkett would fall for Maria, she couldn't understand her friend falling for him. "What about the footman?"

"Charles? Ya' know he was just for fun."

"But, Maria, what am I going to do without you? If you marry this man, you'll be staying in England, and I'll be going back to New York. We may never see each other again!"

"Ah, now we get to the real reason. Summer, dear friend, do ya' think I'd leave ya' if it weren't a true golden opportunity?"

Summer floundered for something to say. Anything that would stop her from losing another of her family. "But he's so old," she finally managed.

Maria tossed her black hair. "That's what makes him perfect. He don't want any children."

"And what's wrong with children?"

"I can't have any."

Summer pulled the knife from its sheath and began to rub the handle. Maria gathered India into her arms and began to croon to the monkey. India's eyes glazed over, and a grin of bliss spread across his hairy face.

"How do you know such a thing is true? Have you seen a doctor?"

Maria shrugged. "Don't need to. And I don't want to talk about it. Just know that it's the truth. And that Hugh don't care, which makes him mighty appealing to me. And I didn't say I was in love with him, anyways... I'm just considering his proposal, that's all."

He proposed already? wondered Summer in panic. *Blast his hide!* She stared at Maria as she flipped her knife from one hand to the other. So, her friend did have some dark secret, something that she'd always suspected but only seen a few times, an occasional clouding over of her friend's normally life-filled green eyes. But they were shining now, and although she wanted to demand that her friend *not* take this first step that might result in their separation forever, well, even though Maria might listen to her, what right had she to make that light fade from her friend's eyes?

"Meg seems to get along real well with the animals," suggested Maria, referring to their young chambermaid. "And I think she'd be interested in being elevated to a lady's maid, even if for a short time. Ya' might want me to ask her."

Summer slid her knife back in its sheath and nodded.

"Now listen, Summer Wine Lee. If I didn't think the Duke of Monchester was gonna look out after ya', I wouldn't think of going. But he will, and there's more there than yore willing to see, just 'cause ya' think you owe some kinda' loyalty to this Monte fellow. And I'm not saying it's wrong... just that sometimes things change." And Maria ducked through the adjoining door of their rooms, as if afraid that Summer might change her mind about her leaving, or that she might herself.

I don't mind change, thought Summer, as the door closed behind Maria with a slam. *I just mind losing the people I love.* She knew she should follow Maria, try to find out why she thought she couldn't have children, for they were soul sisters, weren't they? And they shouldn't have secrets from each other! But she couldn't breathe, and the gaslights kept dimming at the sides of her vision, like a tunnel of darkness was about to enclose her. And she realized that for a long time, Maria had been her only family, that as much as Pa loved her he'd never been with her, always trying to make money, as if somehow that would make Ma's choice to marry him, to cut herself off from her rich family, the right thing to do.

But Ma had died when Summer was little, and Pa continued his quest for wealth, telling her that what he'd wanted for Ma, he now wanted for her. For the first time, Summer wondered if Pa really only wanted it for himself.

Why had she never thought about any of this before?

Why did Ma have to die?

The sound of a soft whimper and the slight tug on her chemise made her look down. "Chi-chi?"

The dog whined again and pulled harder on her undergarment.

"What is it, girl?"

Summer followed the little dog over to the basket in the corner of her room. The two baby foxes lay sleeping, snuggled up to each other for warmth. Chi-chi nosed them, gave them a few licks, and raised woeful eyes up at Summer.

"Yes, you've been a good mama to them, haven't you?"

Chi-chi growled and nosed the cubs again.

Summer crouched and reached out a shaking hand to stroke the little critters. One of the babies wiggled at her touch. The other lay stiff beneath the pads of her fingertips. "Oh no."

Summer picked up the small bundle with both hands. The baby fox's eyes were frozen and unseeing, the body stiff as old bread; a little pink tongue dangled from the open mouth. Summer choked on a sob. Chi-chi stood on hind legs and whimpered, licked the soft hair, and entreated Summer with her eyes to do something. To bring back this little piece of life.

"I can't, Chi… Once they leave you, there's nothing you can do."

The dog growled at her, then crawled into the basket, licking feverishly at the remaining pup, pricking her ears at the plaintive mew that resulted, then curling her body protectively around her baby.

"Chi-chi?"

The dog turned her head away.

Tears rained down Summer's face, unheeded. "Tarnation, it ain't my fault! Some people—critters— just ain't strong enough to live without their mothers!" She was talking with that "twang" to her voice that Maria refused to give up, but she didn't care. Her eyes had turned to the lifeless thing in her hands, and she couldn't take them away. Her brain quit functioning, and that wall of blackness that had threatened her earlier began to close around her in earnest.

Summer stood, and her feet began to move. At first she thought they'd take her to Maria, but instead they headed to her door, which she opened and stepped through—unconcerned that she had on nothing but her shift and boots—walked her down the hallway, and stopped in front of the Duke of Monchester's door.

Summer didn't even wonder why she stood there. She tried the knob, and when it turned, she stepped into his room.

Byron had just removed his dinner jacket, had started unbuttoning his white linen shirt when he heard the door to his room open. He blinked at the apparition before him, thinking he'd indulged in too much after-dinner brandy, for the angel standing in his doorway looked just like Summer, as he'd sometimes fantasized, in nothing but her shift, the outline of her legs and the thrust of her breasts showing through the thin material. His groin squeezed in familiar pleasure-pain when his gaze was drawn to the dark triangle of hair where her legs met, and the outline of her boots. Boots?

"Summer?"

She advanced on him like a sleepwalker, her hands held out before her.

"Are you awake?"

She didn't answer, but as she neared, he could see that her eyes were open, glassy with the tears that streamed down her face. His heart skipped a beat, and adrenaline rushed through him. He'd kill whoever had done this to her.

"What's wrong?"

She still wouldn't talk, although her lower lip trembled, and like a child showing a hurt to its mother, she lifted her hands to reveal what lay in them. A bundle of red fur… one of the fox cubs, and dead as a doornail. Good grief, the woman had gotten him all out of sorts over dead vermin!

"Fellow didn't make it?"

Summer shook her head in such dejected agony that he sighed. How many times had he seen one of these animals ripped apart by the hounds and hadn't batted an eye? But this girl had made the creature special, had made its life seem a precious thing. He remembered the care in which he'd carried them home under her watchful eye.

She was taking this unusually hard. He wondered if there was more to this, then shrugged. He'd not likely figure her out if he lived to be a hundred. But he thought back to the pets he'd cared for when he was a lad, and knew just what to do.

The duke threw his jacket back on and led her from the room. She allowed him to lead her like a real sleepwalker; let him throw a cloak over her shoulder, take her through the maze of hallways, down two flights of stairs and out to the gardens. They'd been lucky and hadn't run into anyone, and he breathed a bit more easily, unsure how he'd explain an excursion into the garden in the middle of the night with this young American. He glanced at the bundle in her hand. It wasn't bloody likely that anyone would believe the truth.

"Where the red roses bloom, I think."

Her eyes glowed in the moonlight and gazed at him with absolute trust. Byron tugged at his cravat and led her on, through the maze of hedgerows, past the tinkling pond, through the herb garden redolent with sweet lavender and pungent rosemary, under the trellis, and into the rose garden.

"Which one?"

She pointed at a bush heavily laden with blossoms, the roses just blooming, their fragrance overwhelming the night air. He crouched and swept the dead layer of leaves aside to reveal the solid earth, and wished that he'd thought to bring a spade. A knife thunked in the dirt next to him, blade first through the soil, and he prided himself on the fact that he hadn't flinched, amazed that she'd risk the blade on this gritty soil. He chopped and dug until he had a hole deeper than necessary, rose and removed his favorite handkerchief from his pocket—one of the few left that his own mother had embroidered with the family crest.

He unfolded it, Summer reluctantly laid the fox's body in it, and he wrapped it up as if it were a delicate work of art. He put the bundle in the hole, slowly scraped the earth back over it, and patted it gently when he'd finished. He cleaned her knife and handed it back to her, ready to return to the house, but she stood rooted to the spot, continuing to stare at him expectantly.

Now what? he wondered. With a groan, he remembered the ceremonies from his youth again. He placed his hand over his heart, from the corner of his eye saw Summer do the same, and whispered into the darkness of the night, "You were a good friend. May God see your soul safely into heaven. Amen."

He glanced over at the American. Her tears had finally stopped, and the beginnings of a smile played along her lips. Byron gave a sigh of relief and began to lead her back to the house. "Quickly now, before someone sees us. And if you ever tell anyone else about this, I will firmly deny it."

She sniffed, and he was gratified to see a smile flash out.

They went through the same back door they'd left, only this time the butler stood there to open it for them. A sleepy-eyed cook and two kitchen maids peered at them as they passed the previously empty kitchen, and no fewer than seven chambermaids watched them as they climbed steps and passed through hallways.

The Duke of Monchester cursed under his breath. They'd been seen leaving the house, and word had spread like wildfire. How would he do his job and make her respectable to society now, after completely ruining her reputation? He should have taken the dead animal, told her he'd bury it, and made her go back to her room.

He stole a glance at her glowing face. But then he wouldn't have had the pleasure of watching as he erased her sadness. And she wouldn't have been as content as she was now, for he'd remembered the feeling of losing his own dogs, and the drama and satisfaction of putting the animals to rest. She'd brought all of that back to him, and he accepted it for the gift he felt it to be.

But it came with a price. He sighed again. There was only one way he could think of to save her reputation, and he'd already considered marrying, hadn't he?

She'd changed his mind on that score at least. Maybe it was fitting that she be the one he marry. After all, her fortune would be just as useful as the Lady Banfour's.

Byron felt surprised to discover, now that he'd thought it out with perfect logic, that he didn't mind the idea of marrying this American girl at all.

He reached past her to open the door to her room, breathing in the scent of roses that still clung to her unbound hair, brushing her arm with his own, setting his nerves afire. Had his lust for her made the idea of marriage more palatable?

She walked past the threshold, her back still to him, and let the cloak around her shoulders fall to the floor, revealing the curve of her waist and the roundness of her bottom through the thin material of her chemise. He groaned, muttered a "good night," and started to close the door.

"Don't leave me all alone."

His hand tightened on the doorknob, threatening to tear it from its pins. What did she want from him… Comfort? He'd spent years honing his words to be witty and hurtful; he knew of only one way to bring pleasure to a woman, and he'd be a cad to take advantage of her vulnerability. If she'd just said, "don't go" or "please stay," he would've had a ready refusal. But her words, and the way she spoke them, as if she'd been abandoned all her life and couldn't bear it if he did so as well… He shook his head. "I'll be right across the hall if you should need anything," he managed to say.

Her head bowed, he heard the rip of cloth, and the thin chemise fell from her shoulders, past her golden brown hair, revealing the curve of her back, slowing its progress as it slithered over the mounds of her bottom, and then with a rush that made him gasp, it sank to the floor in a puddle around her boots.

Only a cad would take advantage of her, he reminded himself. But he couldn't prevent the thought that if he'd already decided to marry her because he'd compromised her reputation, why not do the deed for which he was thought to be guilty?

He tried, one more time, to close the door.

Summer spun, her hair flipping over her shoulders and cascading across her breasts, her hands at her hips, her legs splayed wide in her high-heeled boots, making her nakedness somehow even more exciting.

If it weren't for those *bloody* boots, he might've had a chance.

Nine

Her chin tilted. "Don't you dare leave me."

A demand. His brow lifted, and he quirked a grin. "I wouldn't think of it."

Her eyes widened in surprise and then she lowered her head in her hands and her shoulders began to heave with her sobs, and before he knew it, he'd slammed the door behind him and gathered her into his arms, all that glorious, soft, warm skin in his arms, and laid her on the bed. He pulled her hands away from her face and kissed them, the backs and the palms, then each and every finger, until he saw the tears dry up for the second time tonight and felt her body shiver in response to his attentions.

Would he ever forget the feeling of power that coursed through him when he realized that he was responsible for drying up her tears? Oh, admittedly, he was very good at causing women to cry; he'd reduced more than one conceited debutante into a blubbering mess with his cutting remarks. He'd just had no idea that doing the reverse would result in such pleasure.

He took each hand and laid it next to her head, letting his sight travel over the length of her, to the sweet curve of her neck, to the pink tips of her breasts, across the flatness of her stomach to the dark golden curls between her thighs, down the length of her legs to the soles of her boots. She was perfect, and if his eyes had the power, he would've burned her with his gaze.

Summer did burn; she could feel it along every nerve in her body. Just watching him look at her made any other feeling she'd ever had in her life pale in comparison.

And he hadn't left her.

Byron lowered his head and touched her lips with his own. Gently, carefully, he explored her mouth, his entire being focused on that connection, the rest of the world fading away to insignificance. Her arms curled around his neck, and he groaned, amazed with himself, for he'd always kept in control, had always considered himself the seducer. Although his body continued to guide him from long practice, he had to fight himself from getting lost in her.

He followed with his tongue where his gaze had traveled earlier and discovered new places that his eyes hadn't reached: the back of her ear, the underside of her breast, the inside of her thighs.

Summer shuddered. She'd never even imagined the feeling of a man's tongue caressing her entire body, tasting her as if she were the finest of desserts. What had she done? She needed him, now, yes, but what of her word to Monte? Just because she felt so alone, was it right to use the duke just to banish that feeling? She should stop him, oh tarnation, she should stop him now before she no longer had the strength to do so.

He'd placed his hands against her inner thighs and gently nudged her legs apart, his tongue still moving, seeking the part of her that throbbed in time to the strokes of that wet, warm weapon.

"Marriage," she whispered. Well, she thought, it had worked once before.

He didn't even twitch. "Mmm hmm," he responded, his hands sliding up to the center of her, gentle fingers running through her curly, dark hair, spreading apart the petals that protected that nub of desire, which responded to the rush of cool air upon it with a contraction of ecstasy. Her legs spread farther apart of their own volition, and she heard him chuckle and murmur, "I knew it, I knew it," and he shifted those hot, strong hands to the backs of her thighs and pushed upward until her knees met her ears.

Summer hadn't known she was capable of such a position, hadn't known that men and women did this sort of thing. She'd spied on a saloon girl once, on a dare from Maria, and knew that the sexual act consisted of a man's bare buttocks pumping briefly atop a woman's body. Like a starving man gulping down a hot meal, then sitting back with a satisfied burp. That's what she'd always thought she'd be able to look forward to when she married. Not this intimate discovery of herself, nor the indescribable pleasure this man's hands and tongue were giving her.

What in tarnation was the duke doing? Didn't he know the way things were done?

Then his tongue took a long, slow lick from her wet opening up to the top of her nub, and she could no longer think about anything at all but the feeling that prodded her to spread her legs open even farther, like the bloom of a flower welcoming the penetrating heat of the sun.

Byron lifted his head and stared at her with something akin to awe. "Like your name," he said, his voice tinged with delight. "You taste just like summer wine."

He dipped his head and took another slow, sweeping lick. Looked up at her again. "I love the taste of you, woman."

Summer couldn't stand it anymore; she bucked beneath his hands, trying to reach his mouth, that lovely tongue. Why did he keep stopping? Why did he torture her?

The Duke of Monchester grinned at her wickedly, knowing what she wanted, even if she didn't. She seemed so innocent, acting on instinct alone, and he drank in the sight of her face, her eyes wide with wonder, her full bottom lip slightly open, and her panting with a need she couldn't define. He knew she'd be a passionate, wild thing. He'd fantasized about teaching her the many ways of love. But now they'd have years to explore all the ways they could pleasure each other, and if he could just manage to keep himself in control, from not ripping off his clothes and taking her with the violent need his soul kept demanding from him, he'd make her first experience with a real man one she'd never forget.

"Be still," he commanded.

Summer stopped struggling, afraid he'd stop altogether, wanting more of him in whatever way he chose to give.

He dipped his head again. Summer gasped with relief. Another stroke, and another, but slowly, so slowly that she wanted to scream with the tension that racked her body, that made her strain toward relief. She tossed her head in agony, and he only chuckled, the heartless man. He knew what he was doing to her, knew that soon he'd have her begging and crying out his name.

"Byron." She couldn't help it. "Byron, please."

The Duke of Monchester looked up at her flushed face again and frowned. She sounded genuinely distressed. "I can give you partial relief now," he gently told her. "Or give you pleasure in more ways than one. What will you have of me?"

That last question made her adore him. "I want it all."

He grinned with rakish satisfaction and nodded. "I thought so."

When he stroked her with his tongue again, she fought not to cry out. When he lightly penetrated her opening with it as well, she forced herself not to grab his head, and instead clutched at the bedding and twisted it in her fists. His hands continued to hold her legs open, but they began to slide down as he lapped at her, until she could feel his thumbs stroking the cheeks of her bottom.

Summer groaned. Her entire lower body pulsated with a need that she could never have imagined. "Please, please," she begged again.

Byron's voice sounded gruff yet gentle. "There's more."

More? Summer thought, her eyes closed in concentration. She couldn't take any more, truly...

And then he shifted his body, she could feel the fine weave of his dinner jacket and the flutter of his cravat over her sensitized skin. His tongue stopped doing its magic, and Summer cried out in distress but forced herself not to move as a sudden hot warmth enfolded her nipple. Shafts of new pleasure streaked through her body as he suckled first one and then the other of her breasts, adding to the mounting pressure between her legs. His hands moved between her thighs, keeping the tension alive and adding more pleasure as his fingers plunged inside of her, slowly slipping in and out. She breathed in the spicy scent of his hair and the musky smell of his own desire and knew she was about to tumble over the edge.

"Byron," she screamed as her body exploded from the inside out.

He realized that he loved the sound of his first name coming from her lips. That because of his station only a few people had called him anything but Monchester, and her insistence on calling him Byron made him feel that she didn't care that he was a duke. That she valued him for himself and not his title.

"You're beautiful," he replied while he watched her face, watched her eyes open and stare into his own with unabashed wonder as spasm after spasm shook her body.

Byron rose and untied his neck cloth, stripped off his jacket, and carefully laid them across the back of a chair. He turned and waited for Summer to come to her senses, waited for those dark eyes to focus on his every movement. He slowly unbuttoned his waistcoat, the cuffs and collar of his linen shirt, smiling when her breathing began to pick up at the sight of his bare chest.

He's perfect, thought Summer as he stood proudly naked before her, letting her study his every feature with arrogant confidence. Oh yes, he stood only slightly taller than herself—what she supposed was short for a man—but perfectly proportioned none-theless. His biceps and thighs bulged with muscle, and she wondered what he did to keep in such excellent shape, how he managed to have a ridged abdomen and, as he bent over to pick up his trousers and drape them over the chair with the rest of his clothes, such a full-muscled bottom. Summer's body started to tighten again.

He came closer to the bed, and she saw his swollen member and tried not to choke. She'd never fit him inside her, and what had ever possessed her to start something with him she couldn't finish?

She held up a shaking hand, and he hesitated. "We can't."

The duke raised an arrogant brow. "Pardon me?"

"I mean I can't"—she took a deep breath—"make love to you."

He carefully sat next to her on the bed and stroked her wild hair away from her face. Of course, she didn't know that he'd decided to marry her, and he admired her for trying to retain her honor. Not that she had a choice, of course. "I've already made love to you, my American girl. What we do now is rather anticlimactic, don't you think?"

Summer blinked. He looked so beautiful in gaslight. "Yes, no. I mean, I gave my word to another man. I have to uphold that vow until and unless he releases me."

His hands started sliding down her arms. "Too late," he murmured.

"No it's not. I haven't betrayed him completely."

His hands had reached her breasts, and she couldn't help the impulse that caused her to push up against them. A fire started kindling between her legs again, and she tried to squash it down. She'd needed him, and he'd been there for her. He had just misunderstood.

Byron had started to tell her that she needn't worry, he'd marry her and make it all right, when she said the most astonishing thing.

"I know you need me now," she whispered. "And I promise I'll give you as much pleasure... in the same way you did for me."

Both his eyebrows rose. What an absolutely inviting proposition. The girl had no experience. Did she really think she could bring him to the same heights of pleasure that he had her? Well, he wouldn't stop her from trying. He could explain about the marriage later.

She moved over and crouched, rather like a tiger ready to spring, the toes of her boots digging into the bedcovers, her brown-gold hair spread wildly around her elfin face. He'd forgotten about the boots, felt himself harden even further, and winced.

"Lie down," Summer suggested, her cheeks burning with embarrassment. She reached out and touched him without thinking, surprised that as soon as she did her shyness vanished, and he no longer seemed like a stranger, just the wonderful man who had buried her fox cub with such kind consideration. The sensitive man who knew the secret pleasure places of her body better than she did herself.

He stared up at her, his eyes glinting in the gaslight, all skin and muscle peppered with a golden down of hair, and Summer realized with a shiver of delight that he was all hers. Tarnation, she could touch him anywhere she wanted to, gaze at him with unconcealed longing, and fulfill this burning need.

She reached out a shaking hand and stroked the hair off his forehead, let her fingers curl in the thick richness of that golden mane, and then stroked his cheek, immersing herself in the softness of his skin, the scratch of stubble along his jaw, the strength of his chin. He turned his head into her hand, and the warm pressure of his lips made her crave them, and she lowered her mouth to his.

She sucked and nibbled until he groaned and curled his hand behind her own head, pulling her into a fevered kiss, his tongue slipping into her mouth, reminding her of the pleasure he'd given with that weapon, causing a rush of wetness between her legs. Summer turned her head to break away, realizing that he attempted to take control of her again, wanting it to be her turn, and trailed her tongue to his ear, licking the lobe and sighing, making him shiver.

She followed the same path he'd taken down her earlier, breathing in the male scent of him, taking extra care to lave his own small nipples until they hardened as hers had done. She parted a path through the hair of his chest to the soft skin beneath, feeling the hardness of his abdomen, then the strength of his hip bone, going around that swollen part of him to his inner thighs, using her hands as he had, urging his legs apart. Loving the salty taste of him on her tongue.

Byron swallowed the urge to tell her that men didn't spread their legs like a woman, for even though his sore muscles screamed at the stretch, he found himself liking it, his heart racing with an excitement that he'd never felt before. Was she going to do *exactly* what he'd done to her? His groin tightened and throbbed with anticipation.

She spread him wide, her hot little hands on each side of his throbbing shaft, his knees bent to the sides to accommodate the position of his thighs. She looked up at him, her eyes glazed and feral, and he held his breath. Her head dipped, and she stroked her tongue from beneath and then over his rounded fullness, across the length of his shaft, to the tip of his small opening that she gently penetrated with her tongue. Then she dipped her head again, taking another long, slow stroke. And then another.

Her hair tickled across his thighs and hips with each movement she made. He clenched his fists and beat them against the bed, but still couldn't stop himself from bucking against the gentle pressure of her tongue.

Summer lifted her head and stared into his eyes. "Be still," she commanded with a smile. "Or do you want me to stop?"

He froze.

She lowered her head again; another long, slow stroke.

"Don't you want it all?" she murmured.

Byron found himself nodding with silly, boyish eagerness.

He heard her chortle, and then those small hands pushed at the back of his thighs, raising them as he'd raised hers. He could do nothing but comply to her every wish. His feet lay flat against the bed, his legs opened at an improbable angle, his knees pointing at opposite walls. Bloody hell, the woman would surely kill him.

She continued the sweet torture of her tongue, a final sweep bringing him to the brink of his own internal explosion. Byron closed his eyes, his entire body tuned to the feel of her tongue and hands and silky hair.

She shifted. Warmth enclosed one of his nipples, and she suckled, shocking him with the realization that her actions aroused him even further in an entirely new way, for he'd never thought to have a woman pay them this kind of attention. One of her hands continued to stroke his shaft, and he growled with a force that shook the walls as his body convulsed in waves of sheer all-consuming ecstasy.

He'd never thought a woman could give him as much as he could give her. Never thought he'd find his equal in the bedroom. He felt like a bloody arrogant fool.

He distantly heard a knock on the inside connecting door, watched with a drunken detachment as Summer yanked up some bedclothes to cover herself when the door opened, and Maria poked her head around the corner, her green eyes wide with concern that quickly evaporated when she saw him. She sauntered into the room, brazenly scanning his body from head to toe. He couldn't have moved a finger to save his soul, so contented himself with rolling his eyeballs around to her and giving a wink.

Maria winked back. "Not bad," she said, hands on hips. Then she looked over at Summer. "Thought I heard a noise. I told ya' he'd take care of ya'."

"You don't know what you're talking about," snapped Summer. "Nothing happened."

"And I'm the Queen of England."

Byron snorted.

"You're not helping," said Summer, rising from the bed with a sheet wrapped around her like a toga. She grabbed his clothes from the chair and tossed them at him. "It's time for you to go."

He raised a brow. "Bloody hell, woman, give me a moment to recover."

Summer looked back and forth from Maria to Byron. "This is not funny. Maria, nothing happened that will… jeopardize my vow to Monte. And don't come into my room again unless I tell you to."

Maria crossed her arms across her ample chest. "Your Majesty."

"What?"

"Yore gonna have to call me Yore Majesty if ya' want me to believe that ya' didn't do nothing to this poor man. Wouldn't surprise me none if he rolled right over and started snoring."

The duke wished he could. He'd never felt so supremely drained in his life. But he looked at

Summer's flashing eyes, watched her hand start inching toward her leg, and sighed. They'd have to discuss this later, when his brain started working again, and she wasn't in such a temper. He got up and started to dress under the appreciable gaze of both ladies.

He left the room without a backward glance.

"Now look what ya' did," said Maria. "Got him all mad at ya' again just when he was discovering how much he loves ya'."

Summer stomped her foot in sheer frustration. "He does not love me like that. I... I just needed him tonight, and he was there for me, like any good friend."

"Good friends don't do what ya' two were doing."

"How many times do I have to tell you—oh, never mind. Just go back to bed, Maria. You need your sleep. Aren't you leaving me, um, leaving to visit Lord Balkett tomorrow?"

She tossed her black hair. "We're leaving early, so don't worry about getting up with me. Ya'll need the extra sleep more than I will."

Summer pounced on the bed and buried her head beneath a pillow, but it didn't block out the sound of her friend's voice.

"Still got yore boots on," she said. "I'll have to try that look myself sometime." Maria left the room, closing the door behind her, mercifully cutting off the sound of her gentle laughter.

Maria had been right, for the next morning Summer woke to find that she'd slept so soundly, her friend had already gone. She sighed and stared at the ceiling, realizing for the first time that she was very far from home. She rolled over and buried her face in a pillow and smelled the lingering scent of him. The events of the night flashed through her mind, and the resultant throb between her legs told her it had been real. Tarnation, what had she done? Her face flushed when she remembered what she and the duke had done to each other. For each other.

Summer groaned. Technically, she was still a virgin, yet she knew that she'd betrayed her intended, because she *had* been making love to Byron. With every stroke of her tongue and kiss of her mouth, she'd expressed her desire for him. And been disloyal to another man who really did love her. How could she be making love with one man, while still engaged to another? She wasn't like her mother, dadburn it! She'd never betray someone she'd sworn to love by leaving them.

She'd just have to stop these feelings she had for the duke. Thank goodness she hadn't done anything that she couldn't undo.

Then India leaped on the bed and started picking through her hair, and the baby fox whined, and Chi-chi yipped at her for the baby's milk, and she called for Maria. Summer shook her head with annoyance and rang the bellpull for one of the servants.

Meg entered the room, already carrying a bottle of goat's milk for the fox, and completely ignoring Summer, she went over to feed them. "Where's the other one, Miss?"

The small mewling cries stopped and were replaced by the humming of the young girl.

Summer sighed. Maria was right; the girl would be perfect for her.

"He... he didn't make it through the night."

The girl looked at her with wise eyes and nodded. "I'm right sorry."

Summer felt tears welling up and turned to splash water on her face from the basin. "Do you want to name that one?"

"Me, Miss? Oh, could I?"

"Mmm hmm."

Meg wrinkled her plain face in a frown. "How about 'Rosey'?"

Summer blinked water from her eyes and stared at the innocent face of the girl. Did she know about the rosebush where they'd buried the other baby, or was it just a coincidence? She shrugged. "That's a fine name. Rosey it is. And if he's full now, I need help dressing."

Summer chose a riding habit from the armoire and grinned. "It's my last day at Sandringham, and I need to make a good impression. We're going hunting for birds today. What about this chocolate-colored one? With pants."

"I'm sure that'll be fine, Miss. Will the duke be joining you?"

Summer started again. Had she heard another hint of wisdom in the girl's voice? Tarnation, she'd have to stop jumping at every little thing. She had nothing to feel guilty about. Well, not much, anyway. She dressed hurriedly, since she'd already overslept and didn't want to be left behind to drink tea, and had a breathless Meg escort her down to the courtyard at almost a run, skipping the breakfast that the other guests had already finished.

The duke had been waiting for her, slapping his tall polished boots with a riding crop, and froze when she came around the corner. God, she looked lovely this morning, her cheeks flushed pink and her golden brown hair already escaping the confines of her hat, the strands shining like liquid silk in the sun. And it'd felt that way, too, he remembered, as it slid down his body last night. Byron shifted where he stood.

Summer met his eyes and felt sucked into them, unable to look away, unable to stop the flood of visions that overwhelmed her. His desire for her was tangible, a living thing that wrapped around her body and drew her closer to him without a single thought of resistance. The intimacy they'd shared had given her a taste of what it felt like to be in his arms and made her want even more.

The other guests in the courtyard stilled, staring at the couple who stood like frozen statues, until Prince Albert coughed, and they mounted their horses, but not, Byron noticed, some of the older, more staid guests. The ones who lived by the Queen's strict standards of conduct—no matter that they socialized with his son and his circle.

They didn't dare say a word against her, thought the duke, not while he was present. He broke the magic of Summer's gaze and turned a baleful eye on the crowd, reminding them of his reputation for wielding his tongue like a sword, letting them know with a sardonic lift of his brow that he wouldn't hesitate to use it to counter any rude remarks directed at Summer.

Lady Banfour quickly averted her gaze, pretending to be absorbed in petting her black horse, who snorted and shivered at the unexpected attention.

He handed Summer the reins of her unsaddled horse, watched her leap up unassisted, and they rode with the others across the fields of Sandringham, barely saying a word to each other until they reached an area where a group of servants waited.

"What are they doing?" asked Summer, startled from her new shyness around him by the actions of the servants. It helped if she didn't look directly into his eyes.

"They're the beaters," replied the duke, as the men began to form a line in front of the riders. "They'll beat the bushes and draw up the birds for us to shoot."

"Well, that makes it easy."

Byron gestured at a liveried servant who'd ridden out with them. "This is our loader. When your shells are empty, hand the gun back to him, and he'll replace it with a newly loaded one."

The loader handed her a shotgun. Summer stared at it in consternation. "Well, now. This makes it too easy."

The duke glanced around and lowered his voice. "Be grateful they don't have the nets. They trap the birds as they fly up, allowing those less skilled to bag a greater number."

Summer tried to keep a smile plastered to her face. "This is slaughter, not sport. Tarnation, it's worse than the foxhunt."

Byron rolled his eyes. "Will it make you feel better to know that many of the poor will benefit by having fresh game on their table tonight?"

"Not much. Besides, I'm used to shooting with a rifle anyway. Can't I use one instead of this thing?"

"You know you'd blow the bird apart," he chided.

"Not if you shoot the head off. And then you don't have to go picking buckshot out of your kill."

Byron gaped. "Are you telling me you've only hunted with a rifle?"

Summer shrugged. "Pa had a pistol and a rifle, and we could barely afford the ammunition for those. So if I wanted dinner, I had to make sure I hit my mark every time."

The unwelcome voice of Lady Banfour interrupted them. "Are you telling His Grace that you can hit a bird from every shot of a rifle?"

Summer cringed. She hadn't said any such thing; she'd just been telling Byron about her childhood, and now the woman made it sound like she'd been bragging. "Fortunately, it's been a long time since I've had to shoot for my supper. I don't know if I could do it now."

"Hmph!" she replied, as if she'd known Summer had been exaggerating.

"I say," cut in the foppish man who always seemed to be popping up at Lady Banfour's side. Summer still couldn't get all their names straight, they were all Lord something-or-other. "What say we put up a wager on how many birds Miss Lee can shoot with a round of six?"

And before Summer knew it, bets were being laid, a rifle procured, and she was again at the center of attention.

How does she manage to do it? thought the duke. *Every time we go somewhere, she winds up doing or saying*

*something that sets her apart from the other ladies. And
instead of her conforming to gentle society, she just manages
to change their attitudes about her.* It was going to take
a miracle to get her presented to the Queen, and
it confirmed his decision that only marriage to him
would bring it about.

Summer accepted the rifle, relieved that it looked
very similar to the one she'd used in her youth, and a
few of the beaters swept a path through the tall grass,
startling a flock of pheasants up into the air.

One, two, she mentally counted. Three, four—oh,
missed—six. Still, Summer felt satisfied, for she knew
they were all clean kills.

The beaters brought back her birds. Byron grinned.
He'd bet on her missing only one and took in the
largest payoff. Prince Albert had bet that she wouldn't
miss any, and the few men who had pulled her arrows
from the target the other day had bet she'd hit at least
half. The rest had used their good sense and bet that
she wouldn't bring down any at all.

The Duke of Monchester realized that he'd lost
his own good sense where this American girl was
concerned. She'd said she was out of practice, so he
figured she'd miss just one. He didn't feel guilty in
using the advantage he had over the others; he knew
how good she was with a knife, and that exaggerating
or lying just wasn't in her nature. At this point, if the
woman told him she could walk on air, he'd wager
she could.

When the beaters started in earnest, and the rest
of the hunters took up their shotguns, Summer's skill
seemed to cause an enthusiasm that brought down the

largest number of birds the duke had ever seen bagged at a party. He must have shot over two dozen himself before the roar of the guns had stopped.

The group laughed and shouted as they returned back to the palace for lunch, congratulating each other on the number of birds that they'd killed. Wagers started up again on the total for the day by type, and the duke was tempted to bet on the number of partridge with Lord Ripon, when he suddenly realized that Summer wasn't with them.

Summer still sat on her horse, staring with dazed horror at the field before her, her own cold shotgun clutched in her hand. Oh, she wanted to fit in with these people, to belong for Monte's sake, but she couldn't manage to shoot with the rest of them. It still felt like slaughter, no matter how she tried to justify it in her mind. She'd killed for food or warmth or defense. This concept of killing for sport was still as foreign to her as the lords and ladies themselves.

The beaters had taken a well-deserved rest, lounging beneath the shade of an old oak and passing a flask of brew around. Summer could still see movement in the grass before her.

Byron rode up beside her. "What is it now?" he gently asked, wondering if some creature dear to her had been caught in the crossfire, for she had the same look on her face as the night the little fox had died. Except that now it was combined with something resembling disgust.

When she turned to look at him, he blanched, and a feeling unlike anything he'd ever known pierced him through the heart.

Summer stared at him in loathing. "They will be eaten, won't they?"

"I already told you. The birds will feed a lot of hungry people tonight."

She nodded with resignation and slipped off her horse, heading for the still-moving grasses. Byron resisted the urge to throw his hands up in the air with exasperation. What was wrong with the woman that she would look at him that way? How dare she? By Jove, he was a duke, and she was nothing but...

"Summer," he sighed, dismounting and following her.

She stopped at a patch of moving grass, bent down, and he could hear the soft snap of bones. She rose, scanned the grass again, and headed toward another moving patch.

He followed. "The beaters will do it," he said.

Summer turned and glared at him again. "When? They're suffering now, Monchester."

Another ghastly feeling swept through him at the use of his title name. He'd gotten accustomed to her using the intimacy of his first name. He scanned the grass, spied a moving spot, and headed for it. A pheasant flapped its wings, trying to rise again and again. *She was right*, he thought. The bird was in pain and maddened with fear. He reached down and wrung its neck, moving on to the next patch.

Why did she always have to expose him to these kind of things, he wondered with annoyance. He'd never given half a thought to the birds he'd left behind, and he'd been to hundreds of shooting parties. For that matter, he'd never given a thought to whether a fox had left behind any cubs. And the woman had him out at night, burying one! And instead of enjoying a delicious lunch and bragging with his fellows, he was tromping through a field wringing bird's necks.

Frustrating woman!

He turned and stomped over to the lounging beaters. They quickly lowered resentful eyes and doffed their hats at the lord.

"The lady wants their necks wrung now," commanded the duke. One of the men had the audacity to grumble under his breath. Ordinarily, Byron wouldn't blame him. They'd always been entitled to a break after the shooting. But the big oaf, like so many others, had judged him by his height and not his station. Nor his reputation.

"Can't you see what she's doing?" he growled, taking out his frustration on the larger man with a voice laced with such contempt that the huge man winced. "You can lie there and call yourself a man, while a woman does your work? When you tell your children about all the birds killed today, will you also describe to them how you let them lie bleeding and squawking in agony while you got foxed on drink?"

There, thought Byron. *I feel much better now.*

The men rose as one and fled into the field. He stalked Summer, grabbed her arm, and swung her around. Her golden eyes were glassy with horror, and instead of scolding her to let the men do the grisly job, as he'd thought to, he gathered her into his arms and let her soak the front of his shirt.

Ten

BYRON PATTED HER BACK, TRYING NOT TO BE AWARE of the feel of her breasts against his chest. Trying to stay annoyed with her. How could she be so strong and yet so weak? Didn't she know how contrary that was? Either you had a heart of stone or wore it on your sleeve for all to injure.

Byron kept his arm around her and led her out of the field. It was bad enough that he desired her in his bed more than any other woman he'd ever known. Why did she have to awaken long-banished feelings within him as well? Ever since they'd buried her fox and he'd remembered the grief of his childhood over his own mongrel dog, he'd been unable to make the feeling go back to where it had hidden. It had leaped alive again at the pain in her face over the suffering of mere birds.

In his childhood he'd had to work to harden himself to the stoning of street dogs, the little tortures that the village children inflicted on stray cats. For when he'd told his father about the cruelty, the man had looked at him as if he were dung, and told him not to be such a sissy, and that was probably why he kept getting beaten up. So he'd learned, and although he could never bring himself to join in on the "fun" of stoning street dogs, he'd still managed to watch without any feeling at all.

Byron frowned at the girl encircled by his arm. He'd thought the awakening of old feelings a gift, but now he wondered if she might be cursing him as well. He'd worked doggedly to become the man he was, and he couldn't let her break him down.

When they reached the horses, Summer flung her arms around his neck and kissed his breath away. "Sorry, I don't know what's wrong with me lately," she whispered. "I don't often cry. And thank you for your help." She then leaped onto her horse, leading them through a stand of forest.

Byron put his foot in his stirrup and threw his leg over his own saddle and followed. Well, he thought, maybe a *little* chipping away at his heart wouldn't be so bad. "Do you want to announce our engagement at luncheon or after dinner?"

The girl turned and looked at him as if he'd just announced that the sky had fallen. Could it be possible that she didn't understand the honor his proposal bestowed on her?

"What?" Summer couldn't believe what she'd heard. Wasn't this the same man who had said he wouldn't marry her if she were the last person on earth?

"It's necessary," he continued, starting to frown at her. "You hired me to make you socially acceptable to society, and I take my business arrangements very seriously. Ruining your reputation is not an acceptable business result."

Summer ducked a low-lying limb. "How have you ruined my reputation?"

Byron's frown smoothed out. So that was it; she just didn't understand about last night. "Didn't you wonder about all the servants at their previously abandoned posts when we returned to the house last night? Do you honestly think anyone would believe that we sneaked out into the garden to bury a fox?"

Summer laid her head down against her horse's warm neck. So the servant girl Meg *had* known about her and Byron. All the servants knew. And Maria had pointed out to her long ago that what they knew, everyone else did as well. How was she ever going to get presented to the Queen now? Would word of this reach Monte, all the way in America?

But what bothered her most was the duke's manner of stating his proposal. "So," she managed, "you would marry me so that you can fulfill our business arrangement?"

"Certainly," he replied, tilting his chin into the air. "I fulfill my obligations."

Her head shot up, and her mount tossed her own head in alarm, setting off Byron's more spirited stallion. "And what about mine?"

The trees had given way to another field of grass spotted with clumps of wild lavender, and both horses fought the reins as Summer and Byron led them into it.

"Yours?" he asked, pulling on the reigns to bring his horse out of a half rear.

"Yes, my obligation to Monte, the man I've given my word to return to—and marry. Do you think a woman has no honor?"

Byron fought the horse. It was unlike his mount to get skittish over an open meadow. Perhaps the tall grass tickling the stallion's underbelly bothered him. "You sound like a suffragette. I should have known... what with your inclination to wear pants and carry a knife."

"If you mean that I believe a woman has to uphold her honor as firmly as a man, then call me what you like. But I gave my vow, and I'll keep it. I'd never abandon someone that way." She leaned down and spoke a few words in Apache, trying to calm her own mare. Maybe the animals were responding to the angry voices of their riders, because they kept getting more agitated the angrier she and the duke became, and the farther they rode into the meadow.

"But your American man won't have you, anyway. Don't you see you'll never get presented to the Queen unless you marry me?"

"That's kind of backward logic, isn't it? If I marry you, it doesn't matter if I get presented." Summer took a deep breath of the scented lavender and tried to keep the anger from her voice. He acted as if he hadn't insulted her by saying that his offer of marriage was to fulfill a business obligation, and that she should be grateful for such a nasty proposal. She couldn't imagine any woman being happy over such a proposal—well, maybe the Lady Banfour. But what she expected from a marriage was different than what the nobility seemed to.

Or was it? "Tell me, Monchester. After you spent all my money, and I gave birth to an heir and a spare, would you expect me to go my own way?"

A vision of her face bathed in gaslight, the sound of his name on her lips while he brought her pleasure, made him almost groan aloud. No, he'd never let anyone else touch her but him, regardless of what the rest of his circle allowed their wives to do.

"No," he answered, his attention again centering on his crazy horse. The stallion continued to snort and prance.

Summer felt relieved by his answer, but of course, it didn't change anything anyway. She'd just been curious. "If I break my vow to Monte, how could you ever be sure I wouldn't break my marriage vows as well?"

Byron had had enough of this frustrating woman, and the cantankerous horse he sat. He pulled sharply on the reins and growled, "Woman, don't you understand you're turning down a *duke*?"

"You'll have to figure out another way to fulfill our business arrangement. I told you, I don't care about…" Summer had lowered her head again to comfort her horse with a hug, when she heard the single shot of a gun seconds before the sound of the bullet whined over her head.

"Bloody…" Byron looked back toward the wooded forest they'd emerged from.

"Get down," snapped Summer, sliding off her horse and flopping into the tall grass. The man just stared at her as if she'd gone mad. How could he be so sensitive and agreeable in the bedchamber, she wondered, and be so ridiculously bull-headed and thick out of it?

"No one would dare shoot at a duke!" he yelled. "Why, the consequences…"

Another report of gunfire, and he clutched at his shoulder, a look of stunned surprise spreading across his handsome face as he slowly toppled from his saddle. His stallion reared and screamed in terror, trying to bolt, but Byron's leg had caught in the stirrup, and the horse had the sense not to drag his unconscious rider.

Summer's mare had already hightailed it back into the woods, and she didn't even try to stop her, too busy trying to wrest the duke's leg out of the stirrup. She refused to consider that he wasn't alive. He'd just passed out from the shock of realizing that someone had the temerity to shoot at a duke. If the stallion would only hold still for one second, instead of jumping around in panic. She tried every Apache word she knew to calm the horse, and then a few curse words she'd picked up from miners, keeping low to the ground in case of more gunfire while she stalked the animal.

She caught hold of Byron's leg and yanked, pulled his foot from his boot and fell backward into the grass, his body half on top of hers. The pounding of the stallion's hooves faded away while she lay there catching her breath, ears straining for any further sound of a gun's report. The wind swished through the tall grass around her, thrushes started to resume their chirping, and grasshoppers whirred through the air.

The duke's eyes snapped open. "What happened?" he croaked.

Summer's heart leaped with relief and then settled into annoyance. He was lucky to be alive, the stubborn man, after not listening to her to get down, thinking that he was impervious to harm. "Shh. I'm not sure if they're gone yet."

"Who?" He sat up, then lay back with a groan, clutching at his shoulder.

"Whoever shot you," she whispered. Summer continued to listen to the world around them and tried not to flinch when he groaned. A little pain would serve him right, after scaring her to death.

"No one would dare… Is that what's wrong with my bloody shoulder?"

"Tarnation, I think they're gone. What did you say to those beaters, anyway?"

He rolled off her and groaned again. "They wouldn't dare!"

"I'm only joking," said Summer. "I'm sure the same person who tried to murder you before is just trying to again."

She said it with such conviction that Byron half believed her. He pulled his hand away from his shoulder, stared at the blood covering his palm, and quickly put it back. "This is an odd time to make a joke, madam. Shouldn't you be administering to my shoulder instead?"

Summer sighed. "I'm just not sure if it's safe. But you're right, you're losing a lot of blood. I figure the only way to find out if they're gone is to show myself." And she began to stand up, but before she could rise above the level of the grass, the duke cursed and with his good shoulder pushed her sideways and down.

His face lay inches from her own, his breath puffing across her mouth. "Enough of your brave theatrics, my girl. You will stay down until I say so, understand?"

His eyes glittered, and the force of his personality made Summer nod in agreement. Whatever annoyance she still felt faded away, and she shivered from the terror that filled her at the thought of him dying. It would've been easier if she'd continued to stay mad at him.

With a grimace the duke rose, swayed for a moment, and began to whistle for his horse. He cursed and sat back down with a thud. "Beast's probably halfway to the stables by now. But if the gunman were still here, he just missed a good target. So do you think it's bloody safe enough to see to my shoulder?"

Summer nodded, sat up, and pulled out her knife.

"Bloody… You're not thinking of digging out the bullet, are you?"

She blinked at him in astonishment. "You've got some funny notions about me."

"As if they're not warranted."

Summer slid her knife through her petticoats. "Never thought I'd be grateful to have these," she muttered.

"Never thought I'd be grateful for your knife."

"Oh, it comes in handy more often than you'd think," she replied with grave seriousness.

Byron smothered a smile. "Indeed."

"Mmm hmm." She leaned over. "Let me see now."

He reluctantly pulled his hand away from his wound. She slid the knife again through his coat and shirt, and he tried not to groan at the thought of having them replaced, while she continued to saw off the sleeves. "Save the pieces," he muttered.

Summer bared his entire shoulder, used the torn petticoats to sop up the blood, and estimated the damage. She'd only had experience with a gun wound once in her life, and since she'd been the victim, she'd hardly been in a position to examine it.

"Well," she declared. "It looks like the bullet went all the way through."

Byron swallowed. "How do you know?"

"There's a hole in the back of you."

"Aah. Shouldn't you do something about the blood?"

Summer frowned. "If we let it flow, it'll clean the wound."

"If it gets any cleaner, madam, I won't have any blood left."

She nodded, wadded up pieces of petticoat, and pushed them against his shoulder. "Hold this here." Summer leaned behind him and pushed against the torn skin on the other side. She wrapped strips of cloth around his arm and up over his shoulder, hoping it wasn't too tight. "You're very calm about this. Sarcastic, but calm."

The duke grinned, his teeth clenching with every tug of the bandage. "Do you think I'm some sort of dandy? I'll have you know I gave myself in service to my country, like any other hot-blooded, idiotic youth. I've seen my share of wounds."

"Am I doing all right, then?"

He eyed the bandage, watched her tie it off, and nodded. "Very well done, madam."

Summer ignored the feeling of satisfaction that his praise gave her, and gathered up the pieces of his coat and shirt and stuffed them into his pocket. She retrieved his boot and helped him pull it on. "Can you walk?"

"Do you see the horses?"

She sat up and scanned the field. "No."

"Then I suppose I can." He rose with a groan, his face turned white for a moment, and then he took a few steps. Summer picked up his good arm, wrapped it around her shoulder, and tried to take some of his weight.

"I don't need you to carry me," he snapped. "Just steady me a bit."

"Sorry."

He stopped for a moment, breathing heavily. "I beg your pardon. You've done nothing but help me and don't deserve to be snapped at."

Summer grinned. "Hurts, don't it?"

"Like hell."

It seemed like ages before they finally staggered into the courtyard just as an elegant barouche pulled away, and Byron groaned when he saw his half brother and sister-in-law turn from the entrance to the prince's house to stare at them.

Lord and Lady Karlton exchanged a swift look, and then the lady screamed for a physician, while the lord rushed over to support Byron, who by this time had been leaning heavily on Summer.

"What happened?" asked Lord Karlton, spittle flying in his excitement.

"Hunting accident," gasped the duke.

He gave Summer a sharp look, and she nodded. *Excellent girl,* he thought. *Best to wait and find out who's trying to kill me before we raise any suspicions.* He thought she might be capable of reading his mind and wondered at the thought. Despite their obvious differences in breeding and manners, they shared a surprising degree of common sensibility. In bed, and out.

The thought of lying in bed was the only thing that managed to get him up the staircases and into it. Lord and Lady Karlton hovered, while the prince's own physician checked him over. "Fine job of wrapping you up," he declared. "Your companion may have saved your life."

"Wouldn't be the first time," mumbled Byron.

Lady Karlton hissed something about "that American" to her husband.

"Your Grace," continued Dr. Terris, "I've given you a sleeping potion for the pain and will leave a small bottle of it by your bedside, but I suggest you not depend too heavily upon it."

Byron nodded his head dreamily, his eyes straying to the open door. Where was Summer anyway? She'd left the room as soon as the physician had arrived, and as the drug took effect, his impatience for her return rose in proportion to the befuddling of his mind.

Then she appeared, in a white filmy gown covered with tiny red roses, her eyes dark with concern. He sighed with contentment. She looked worried. He tried to open his mouth to reassure her, but a string of nonsense poured out, as if he'd lost all control of his tongue. Lord Karlton escorted the physician out of the room, hustling Summer out as well, and when Byron opened his mouth again to protest, his half brother poured another dose of the vile medicine down his throat.

He looked up into the hard, glittering eyes of Lady Karlton. "Looks like we came just in time," she said, wiping his lips with a silk handkerchief. "Goodness knows what that woman would have managed to do to you given another day."

Byron lifted a brow at her. Or tried to, but his facial muscles weren't working at all well. The blessed numbness of the pain in his shoulder had spread to the rest of his body. He tried to glare instead. "Wha' shoo mean?"

"Ahh, good. You can still speak." The lady pulled up a chair and thrust her face into his own. "Don't you think it's interesting that all these accidents started happening to you after you met this Summer Lee?"

Byron tried to wrap his brain around her words, to consider the impact of them and the motive behind them, and failed at both.

His silence was all that the lady needed to continue. "Isn't it true that until she entered your life you'd never considered marriage? That you would have been perfectly content to live out your life as a bachelor?"

His eyes must've said what he could not, for with a nod of superior understanding at her own correct interpretation of his feelings, she rushed on. "Just what I thought. But consider this. The quickest way for a social climber to get to the top of the ladder is through marriage and a title. But when one is already in love with another... Well, wouldn't it be interesting if the duke she married was known for his... proclivity for accidents, and suffered another shortly after the marriage. Thereby obtaining the title, and then the freedom to pursue another?"

Byron closed his eyes. What an absolutely preposterous notion.

"Ahh, Byron," Jane whispered. "You should have married me, you know." He felt the cold touch of her hand smoothing back his hair and tried to swat the unwelcome touch away, but only managed to flop his good arm once or twice. He felt a rush of air as the door to his room opened, felt her move away from his bedside. "Just consider what I've said," she continued. "I'm still your sister, after all, and you know how much your family cares about you."

"What's that?" asked Lord Karlton. "Oh yes. Quite right, Lady Karlton, to remind him of that fact. He seemed to have forgotten it, when he didn't include us in the prince's invitation for this lovely weekend party. But we found out in the nick of time, yes? One day is better than none at all!"

"Lord Karlton," replied his wife. "Surely, you don't think our dear brother will be fit to travel anytime soon? It seems that our visit may be much longer than we had thought."

Silence followed as Byron fell into a well of ever-increasing darkness. The sound of laughter smothered by sloppy kisses made him feel relieved as the blackness became complete and absolute.

A few weeks later, Summer and Meg sat in the shade of enormous rosebushes in the gardens at Sandringham, laughing at the antics of the baby fox, and the nudges that Chi-chi kept giving the little critter every time it tried to stray a bit too far from her. The chill of approaching fall had Summer wrapped in her warmest shawl and Meg staring at her chattering teeth with wonder.

"If you think this is cold, Miss, just wait till the winter."

"I'm sure I'll get used to it," replied Summer. "But after living in the desert for so long, the blood tends to get a bit thin."

Meg nodded wisely, and Summer sighed, certain that the girl had no idea what she was talking about. Every time she mentioned her past, the girl frowned as if she were being told a whopper but didn't have the gumption to call her a liar. Yet they'd become close these last few weeks, what with Byron shut up in his room, guarded beyond all reason by the Lord and Lady Karlton, and with most of the guests already departed. But Meg insisted on keeping her status as a servant around Summer, and even though she could be good company, and had agreed to accept the position as her lady's maid, she'd never be a substitute for her dear friend. If it weren't for the weekly letters from Maria, Summer would've fetched her from the old man's estates by now. But Maria sounded inordinately happy, and she didn't have the heart to call her back.

A shadow fell over them, and Meg gasped. Summer grinned. It was about time he came out of that room.

Byron's heart squeezed when that elfin face looked up at him. How he'd missed her! If he didn't feel so angry about her not coming to see him, he might've softened under that melting smile.

"The prince has announced his intention to leave," he said without preamble. "Therefore, Lord and Lady Karlton now deem it fit for me to travel as well. I assume you're prepared to return to London?"

Summer frowned. He had that nasty tone in his voice and that wall of disdain built solidly around him again. Where had the man she'd bantered with gone to? She couldn't figure out why he'd put up his guard again.

"How's your shoulder?" she asked, while Meg stared back and forth between the two of them with something akin to horror.

"If you had come to visit me, madam, you'd likely know." He broke eye contact and stared at the spent blossoms of the rosebush, both brows raised and his nose in the air.

So that was it, thought Summer. "I tried to see you, Your Grace, but they wouldn't let me in your room. They said it wasn't proper." She choked back a laugh and stood, making him meet her eyes again, and grinned with impish charm. But he still continued to scowl at her.

"If you had done the intelligent thing and agreed to marry me, you could have seen me at any time."

Summer sighed. He wasn't going to budge, the stubborn Englishman! "Well, now. I'm glad to see you're all right, anyways. But do you really feel well enough to travel back to London?"

Byron shrugged and winced at the pain still in his shoulder. "It doesn't matter. I must get you back to London and then on a ship to New York as soon as possible."

Summer's heart sank at the thought of returning to America. "What do you mean? I haven't been presented to the Queen yet! What about our business arrangement?"

"I'm sorry to say, madam, that if you refuse to marry me, I cannot meet the terms of our arrangement."

Meg, who'd been watching the discussion between the two of them with her mouth open, gasped. When they both glared at the girl, she scooped up the animals and scurried back to the house.

Now look what you've done, thought Summer. *Who knows what that poor child is blabbing to all the servants, as if they didn't already know too much of my business.*

"How dare you try to worm your way out of our agreement!" she snapped. "You can't just send me packing without at least trying to get me presented."

"I have already approached the prince, and he sent a missive to Her Majesty. I received word several days ago of her refusal, based on what one of her closest confidants said about your—our—conduct. Therefore, I see no reason for you to continue to pay me, and I will turn over my interest in your railroad since I failed to uphold my end of the bargain."

Summer felt as if her world had fallen apart. How was she ever going to be accepted by Monte's family now? This had been her only plan, and she hadn't considered failure. "I refuse to accept it back. I insist you continue to use your influence to make me acceptable."

His blue eyes softened, and they roamed over the contours of her lips, to the lobes of her ears, and back to the compelling lure of her brown eyes. "Don't you see, Summer, that you chose the wrong man for the job? Consider, please, that I haven't changed you one whit."

Summer opened her mouth to argue. Hadn't he clothed her, taught her, molded her into a lady? She knew she had more polish now than before she'd hired him. "How dare you make me feel as if I've failed to become a lady!"

He held up a hand. "That is not my intention. You will return to New York in the guise of a sophisticated lady, have no doubt of your success in that regard. But understand that I only managed to mold our society to fit you, not the other way around."

She stomped her foot. How could he say such a thing! Why, every time she did something inappropriate, he…

"I think you're beginning to understand," he said, watching the conflicting emotions roll across her delicate features. "Instead of curbing your natural inclinations, as I should have, and forcing you to act properly, I just explained away your… actions. Made them acceptable to my circle. I fear that when you return to New York, nothing will have changed but your appearance."

Her shoulders slumped. "And if I'm not presented to the Queen, I'll never have a chance with Monte."

"I can only say that I don't like to admit failure, and can't for the life of me figure out how I've bungled this so badly."

Summer knew it was partly her fault, for who had invited him into her bed, after all? Who had dragged him out into the night for the sake of a dead fox and caused the rumors that now tainted her? But she couldn't help feeling that he'd given up too easily, that for some reason he wanted to fail.

"I'll think of another way to be with Monte," she finally said.

He bowed, informing her that they would leave on the morrow, and returned to the house without another word. He had the most ghastly feelings clamoring for attention—relief that she didn't want to marry him, for it proved that his sister-in-law's scenario of Summer causing his accidents to be completely wrong; disgust at himself for failing at a business arrangement; and anger at the girl for insisting to pursue this Monte fellow. Especially after the incredible night that they'd shared.

He couldn't dispel an aching sense of loss. It might be because he'd been robbed of all the delightful fantasies he'd conjured of the nights they'd have together after they were married. But it concerned him that it might be more than that. That the aching hollowness beginning inside of him was because she was leaving, and that it would continue to grow until all the years of work he'd done to achieve the harmony of not caring for anyone would be shattered.

And worst of all was a dreadful anticipation that when she returned home, he'd be alone again.

Eleven

BYRON SMOOTHED THE HAIR BACK OVER HIS EARS. Who'd have thought that he'd miss that wench Maria? The carriage ride had been excruciatingly boring so far, what with the servant Meg refusing to say a word, much less meet his eyes, and Summer just as quiet, always frowning out the window as if she contemplated her life through the English scenery.

Even the dog had been well behaved, not once chewing at his trouser legs, too busy licking the baby fox, and the monkey only occasionally chattered a dejected squeak. The duke looked forward to arriving at Lord Balkett's and having a good row with Summer's friend. He passed the time by considering which insult would set her off the easiest.

By the time dusk had fallen, they'd left the wooded countryside and traveled the narrow path that wound its way along the seaside cliffs of the ocean. The wind carried the salty flavor of the water and the sound of the waves crashing against the crags, and had lulled Byron half asleep.

"When I leave," asked Summer, "who's going to look out after you?"

"I beg your pardon?"

"You've already had two attempts on your life, and if I hadn't been with you, I daresay you wouldn't be alive."

Byron could not believe the audacity of the chit! As if he couldn't take care of himself. She doesn't speak to him for hours, and when she does, she insults him? "That's even more reason for you to leave. I won't have to fear for your safety any longer while you're in my company." And since she reminded him, the duke stuck his head out the window for the umpteenth time that day, making sure that the escort of guards the prince had commanded them to take still followed behind them.

"But what about the money?" she insisted. "What will you live on if you give me back your interest in the railroad?"

He sat back with a sigh. They hadn't lost their escort. "The same thing I lived on before I met you."

Summer leaned forward, the fading light softening the planes of her face, making her eyes seem too large for that elfin face. "But weren't you tired of it, living off other people? If you weren't so stubborn about giving up on me, you could still have the interest."

Byron frowned at her. "I could try for years, madam, and I still don't think you'd ever get your presentation." He watched her study him, as if trying to think of another reason why she shouldn't leave. A shred of excitement twisted his belly. Could it be that she really didn't want to go? Was it possible that she was trying to come up with excuses to stay with him? Or was he being a fool?

He folded his arms across his chest and closed his eyes. She'd made it very clear that she wanted this Monte fellow, and the only way she'd get him was if she got her presentation. She only wanted to make that happen—it had nothing to do with any regret she might have at leaving him.

She just couldn't accept failure.

And he was astonished at himself that he did.

The carriage started to speed up on a road that he knew wasn't prudent for speed. His eyes flew open, and he poked his head out the window again, pulling it in with a curse as he realized that his face had come within inches of a jagged rock. He tried again and looked down a fall of cliff, the surf white and pounding below. The idiot coachman drove at the edge of the road.

"I will never again travel in a carriage that I don't drive myself." He reached between the ladies and lifted the cloth that covered the small window in the back of the coach, completely prepared for the sight of the empty road behind them.

"What is it?" asked Summer as the carriage began to bounce wildly.

Meg blinked open sleepy eyes and watched her mistress with alarm.

"Our escort has disappeared," replied the duke.

Summer snatched up Chi-chi and Rosey and stuffed them in her pockets. "Not another fake robbery!"

"Worse, I think." Byron took India from his shoulder, wincing from the pain of his injury, and stuffed the monkey in the front of his waistcoat until only his furry face stuck out. The duke continued watching the road behind them, not surprised when a group of riders came around the bend, their ragged clothes and shaggy mounts so unlike that of the prince's elegant guard.

"Ragged or not, they seemed to have won the fight."

Meg began to whimper, and Summer shushed her. "Fight?"

Byron watched the men advance. *There's only four,* he thought with a sigh of relief, astonished at himself that he'd raised their odds of survival because he could count on Summer. "Our escort, madam. I'm sure they didn't leave us of their own accord." He pulled a pistol from beneath his coat and flung open all the curtains, so he would have a clear view of the men as they came pounding up beside them, only one at a time because of the narrow road.

The first blighter had the audacity to leer through the window at Summer and Meg with a gap-toothed smile. Byron raised his pistol and fired, effectively removing that smile and a bit of other things as well. His heart started to pound, and he tried not to be too amazed at himself. It'd been a long time since he'd shot at a man, since he'd given up his commission and swore he'd never shoot at another human being again.

Meg screamed, then fainted across Summer's lap. "Nice shot," shouted Summer, her eyes round with admiration, that knife of hers already in her fist. "So you believe me now?"

"That someone's trying to kill me? I'm not a fool, madam."

She nodded, and he cursed that she'd distracted him. Another man had reached the coachman's seat and tried to haul himself up onto it. Byron couldn't fire through the open side window and hesitated to shoot through the glass that overlooked the coachman's seat, afraid that flying shards might strike Summer. He thought the chap wouldn't make it, what with the carriage lurching wildly and the coachman kicking out at the man. But he did.

"I'll be damned," muttered Byron as he reached over and threw open the carriage door. He reached out with his good arm and started to drag himself out.

Summer grabbed his frock coat. "Are you loco? What d'you think you're doing?"

"I'm going to help the coachman…"

A shot went off, and they both ducked.

"You're going to try and what? Swing yourself over to his seat? With an injured arm?"

"Precisely."

And he ducked toward the door just as the carriage swayed too close to the boulders that lined the road. When they hit the door, it slammed shut, knocking him sideways onto the floor. The coach lurched and rocked so that it took him several moments to crawl back onto the seat.

Another rider had overtaken the carriage, and he'd taken a lesson from the man before him, for he had his own pistol trained on the occupants.

"Stay down," shouted Byron, trying to keep his arm steady as he aimed.

A shot exploded in his ears, but it hadn't come from the rider or his own pistol. Byron looked over his shoulder at the glass that separated him from the coachman. A crimson wave covered the surface, and he could no longer see through it. He glanced back to the horseman, who grinned at him with yellowed teeth and waved his pistol in farewell.

The coach lurched, and Byron turned and met Summer's eyes. They both knew the moment the horses went over the cliff, when the floor beneath their feet slanted, and all the jostling and bouncing stopped, as if time froze for an eternal moment before gravity claimed its due. He realized that he'd failed to protect her, that she was indeed the only thing he cared enough about to protect with his own life. He leaned forward to kiss her, angry that there wasn't enough time, when he felt himself falling away from her as the carriage tilted straight down. But he held out his arms to her, so that when they hit solid ground she fell into them, and he shielded both hers and Meg's bodies with his own.

Blackness enfolded Summer, and she knew that she dreamed, but she couldn't wake up. She was five years old again, and she could feel the weight of the earth over her head and hear Pa screaming Ma's name. She ran through the tunnel of Pa's mine, the dust-laden air making her cough, the shards of broken rock hurting her feet. But she couldn't stop, 'cause she knew her ma had been buried in the cave-in, that Pa couldn't lift all the rocks off her himself. That they needed Summer's help.

'Cause Ma couldn't leave her. She'd told Summer that people who love each other never leave. But if Ma got buried under tons of rock, she couldn't find her way back to Summer, now could she?

Then the earth shook, and she could feel Pa's arms around her as he scooped her up and carried her out of the mine. Summer screamed at him to let her go, that they had to go back down and find Ma. That Ma wouldn't leave them. But Pa wouldn't listen, and he screamed at her that Ma was already gone, and the rocks kept falling down, and she thought that the earth would smother them both.

"We can't leave her," Summer gasped, but her voice had changed. It no longer had the high squeak of a little girl, and she awoke fully to the sound of the duke's reassuring voice.

"Shhh, be quiet now. You've been unconscious."

She opened her eyes to complete darkness, and still felt the weight of the earth covering her, and tried to move. Tarnation, it hurt, and Byron responded with a groan of pain. She became aware of the heat of his body beneath hers, and down around her legs the weight of another. Meg.

Her pockets wiggled, but the two critters stayed as silent as Meg.

The duke's head lay right next to her own, his lips so close to her ear she could feel them moving when he spoke. "Don't move either—not yet. The carriage didn't fall far, we must've landed on an outcropping or ledge. Don't know how sturdy it is… don't want to fall all the way down to the ocean. Understand?"

Summer whined. She felt the tiny, furred fingers of India stroke her cheek, and then the light weight of him jump across her back and disappear as she heard him scramble above her.

"We just need to wait a little longer, to make sure that those men have left; then we'll see what's what."

"Can't breathe," she whispered.

"I think when we came down we started a landslide,

and it covered us. That's why it's so dark. But don't worry, we're still getting fresh air from somewhere."

"No," she replied. "We're going to be smothered. Just like Ma." Summer trembled and jerked, fighting the urge to jump up, to move, to push the rocks and dirt off and away.

"Summer, Summer," came his soothing whisper. "Where's the girl who fought off highwaymen with me? Where's the woman who faced a gang of Paris bullies with only her knife?"

She gritted her teeth, wouldn't answer him. How could he understand this terror that made her heart beat so fast she'd thought she'd die? How could he expect her to just lie here for even another minute, when her body told her to fight, to run?

"Who can't you leave?" he asked. "Summer, talk to me. What were you dreaming about when you were unconscious?"

The fear crept into her belly and made it boil. She swallowed against the bile that rose in her throat. "I... I can't do this. Must get out, Byron. Must get out of here."

"We will," he promised.

"Too dark, too..."

"Focus on my voice, you hear me. It's just fear, Summer, that's all. Why are you so afraid? Tell me, what were you dreaming about?"

A bit of warmth trickled through her fear. He had such a lovely voice, deep and compelling, when he wasn't using it to mock people.

"Who can't you leave? Meg? She hasn't woke up yet, and we might have to leave her behind to go get help. But we'll come back for her."

Summer's blind eyes rolled down to where the weight of Meg's body had her legs pinned. She could feel the girl breathing and gave a sigh of relief. And suddenly she felt ashamed of herself, that she'd not given Meg a thought before this, that she'd been so overcome by the panic that had gripped her, she hadn't given a thought to anyone but herself. She took a deep breath, reached into her pocket, and patted Chi-chi and Rosey.

"That's my girl," murmured Byron. "Talk to me, Summer, but softly, just in case. Tell me about your dream."

"It wasn't a dream," she replied. "It was a memory… of when my ma left me, when she died."

"How did she die?"

He spoke in such soothing tones, the rise and fall of his body beneath hers combining to lull her. "Cave-in," she softly said. "I was little, and I haven't thought of it in years, but suddenly I was there again, when the rock came down, and Pa left her there, all alone, when I told him we couldn't do that. When someone loves you, you don't just walk away."

She felt him sigh, as if she'd answered more questions for him than he'd asked. "But sometimes you have to."

Summer felt as if she'd just lost her mother again, that memory-dream had been so real. "And then Pa got worse, started another tunnel, always obsessed with finding gold. Said that he'd buy Ma all the things she'd given up for him."

"What had she given up?"

"Her rich family disowned her when she married my pa. Even after she died, he still kept looking for the gold, saying that now he did it for me... but I never cared about that, all I wanted was him. I felt so lonely after she left."

"But then he found the gold."

Summer realized that she was breathing easier. "No, silver. And I thought that he'd spend more time with me after that, but he just wanted to make more money, to prove to those Tarkingtons that he was worthy of their daughter."

"Do you feel better now?"

Summer blinked in the darkness. He'd taken away her fear, and she hadn't even known it. "Yes."

"Good, because whether those men have gone or not, I've got to move." He kissed her ear, and she shivered, but this time with pleasure. "Both of my legs have gone numb, and if I don't get them moving, I'm afraid they're going to stay that way."

Summer's heart gave a little twist. He'd lain there and comforted her fears, while in pain himself. Who was the Duke of Monchester, really? The man who all of society feared for his cutting remarks, or the one who had used that same voice to soothe her?

She shifted and rolled on the side that didn't hold her critters, then caught her breath as the carriage slid a bit downward. She felt the ache of myriad bruises on her body, the dreadful pounding of her skull, and lifted a shaky hand to gingerly prod at the large bump beneath the hair on the side of her head.

Byron's voice sounded sardonic and laced with pain. "We'd better take this slow. The bottom of the carriage is parallel with the cliff, so move away from my voice until you feel the wood of it against your back."

If only she could see, thought Summer. Even though it had to be nighttime by now, outside she'd have moonlight or starlight to break this wall of black, she could stretch out her arms and run, she could breathe…

Her panting filled the tiny, enclosed space.

"Don't do it, Summer," warned Byron. "Any sudden moves, and this carriage could slide the rest of the way down the cliff. Now, just listen to the sound of my voice, do what I tell you, and don't think at all."

"All right." She closed her eyes, took a deep breath, tried to calm the pounding of her heart. His voice, tarnation, she'd never hear his voice again without remembering the way it reached out to her and wrapped her in a comforting embrace and gave her back some of her courage. She'd never felt anything like this before in her life and didn't know how to deal with it. "I'm not very good at being afraid."

The duke choked on a laugh. "No one ever is. I'm going to try to move now, and no matter what you hear, keep your back pressed to the carriage floor."

Summer plastered her backside to the wood behind her, lifted her arms above her head, and felt the polished surface of it beneath her fingertips. She heard him move, the absence of her sight making the sounds extraordinarily loud, the pain in his grunts making her wince with sympathy.

"So far, so good. Carriage didn't shift that time. I'm going to push Meg over to you, so give her a pull, will you? Seems like my wounded shoulder is as numb as my legs."

She reached down and pulled Meg's inert body toward her, felt him pushing as well, and then sensed his nearness, and smelled the heavenly musky scent of him. She put out a hand, felt the heat of his chest and the weave of his linen shirt, and wrapped her fingers around his neck, beneath the softness of his hair.

"Ah, Summer," he whispered, his own hand reaching out to caress her cheek. "We'll get out of here, I promise. We have unfinished business, you and I."

She wondered at his words but couldn't focus on anything but getting out of this coffin. "How? How do we get out, Byron?"

"You're lighter than I am, so while Meg and I anchor the back, you need to go forward to the left side window, that's where I felt some air coming in, and try to dig out the dirt that's covering it. Can you do that?"

Summer swallowed. "I'm going to have to, aren't I?" She reluctantly let go of him and concentrated on only his voice as he talked her through her task.

"That's my girl. Now go slowly, good, feel along the wall, where dirt has tumbled in. Dig at it, good, spread it behind you. Keep going, Summer, the pile of earth can't be very thick there, not if air can get in."

"Tarnation!"

"What's wrong?"

Summer felt the furry hand of India, and her knife in the monkey's grip. "He found my knife! Thank you, India." The critter squeaked and crawled on her shoulder. With the blade in her hand Summer felt better, made more of a dent in that wall of dirt, until she heard a small slide and felt a cool blast of salt-laden air, and saw the blessed light of a full moon shining through the sudden opening. India scrambled through it before she could blink.

"It's going to be a tight squeeze, getting through this window. Especially with your broad shoulders." She felt his smile and realized what she'd said, and shrugged. Right now she didn't care about his vanity. All she cared about was getting out. She stuffed her knife in its sheath and scrambled right after India, tearing her gown and quite a bit of skin, until she stood in the blessed outdoors, the wind in her face wiping away any residual fear, the moonlight in her eyes making her blink with joy. Byron had been right, the carriage lay on a rather large ledge, the torn traces dangling over the side, the poor horses nowhere in sight. Summer resisted the urge to look down at the rocky cliffs below and instead looked up, scanning the area for any trace of the men who had tried to kill them.

She heard the carriage shift, frowned with alarm when it tilted forward, startled to be grateful that most of it lay buried beneath a landslide of rock and dirt, anchoring it in place. She watched as Byron put first one shoulder and then the other through the tight opening, cursing the entire time, then helped lower him out the window, trying to bear his weight.

He must be made of pure muscle, she thought, for he only topped her by a couple of inches, yet certainly weighed a ton. When they both sat on the ledge, they leaned against each other and just breathed.

Byron tilted his head up and pushed the hair out of his eyes. "It'll be fascinating to see if my shoulder will manage to get me up that."

Summer grinned at him. "No need. India has already been up and back. Seems the ledge wraps around this hill. With any luck, it'll be wide enough for people as well."

"You're smiling, madam."

"I'm glad to be out of that coffin, sir." And ignoring the rule he'd taught her about never touching a gentleman, she leaned over and kissed him full on the mouth. "Thank you for saving my life."

"Seems like you took care of yourself, as usual."

"I would've plunged the carriage straight down the cliff with my panic, and you know it."

"Mmm." He stared at her, and she felt as if he tried to see into her soul, tried to brand her with his gaze. There was something different about him, an intensity that she'd never felt before, that made her remember with absolute clarity the night he'd offered her comfort and she'd taken it so willingly.

"Stop it," she blurted. "We have to get Meg help. If she wakes up all alone in there…"

He blinked and his gaze shuttered. She felt the loss of his attention as if it were a tangible thing, and jumped when he clasped her hand, a physical demand that she stay connected to him. He held on to her and refused any attempts she made to twist out of his grasp. They climbed up the ledge, which did prove just barely wide enough to accommodate their feet, if one didn't mind one's toes dangling over the edge, and staggered onto the road, neither one any longer quite sure who supported whom. For the first time Summer felt the weight of the critters in her pocket, and the one on her shoulder, as a burden.

By the time the sun rose, Summer felt delirious with fatigue, and when a hay wagon pulled up beside them and the man driving it doffed his hat to the duke and spoke to him as if he knew him, she only felt a slight hint of surprised curiosity. She obediently clambered onto the fragrant hay when Byron told her to, and drifted off to sleep. She woke briefly when the man and Byron laid Meg in the hay beside her, and then once again when they reached a tumble-down castle that looked nasty enough to be haunted.

"Yours?" she murmured as she was ushered inside and then carried up the stairs to a surprisingly elegant bed.

"Afraid so. Welcome to Cliffs Castle."

Summer felt all the aches in her body relax, and she melted into the clean sheets, barely felt it when Chi-chi and Rosey crawled from her pocket and snuggled at her side, when India wrapped his arm around her neck and buried his face in her hair. She fought to keep one eye open. "How's Meg?"

"She's fine. I've put her in the small adjoining room."

Summer sighed. "Tell your ghosts not to wake me, then."

A cold, wet nose jabbed Summer's ear, and when she tried to roll over, Chi-chi growled. "It's a good thing you're so cute," she mumbled. "Otherwise you'd be in serious trouble." The dog yipped, turned in a circle, and looked at India for assistance. The monkey gave a remarkably human grin and poked his finger up Summer's nose.

"All right," she mumbled again, then sat up and looked with wonder around the spacious room—at the elaborately carved mantel of the fireplace, the raised-panel walls, the ornate tapestries of mythical creatures, the vases, and highly polished wooden furniture. The castle she remembered from last night should've had spiderwebs throughout and dusty beds. She looked down at her sheets and realized that the only dirt in this room was what she'd brought with her. Summer wrinkled her nose, felt the tangled mess of her hair, and crawled out of bed.

Chi-chi circled again. "I know, me too," she told the dog, and quickly looked for a water closet, sighed, and peeked under the brocade coverlet of the bedspread. Sure enough, a chamber pot. She walked over to the shutters and threw them open, sunlight making her squint, and saw the woods surrounding the house, a twinkle of water through the trees, and smiled.

A connecting door revealed the softly snoring Meg, her head bandaged but otherwise looking quite healthy after her ordeal, and she sighed with relief. She then spied her luggage and figured that being a duke, the man would think of everything. Grabbing up soap, a change of clothes, and her critters, Summer crept out of the room. The hallways looked more like what she'd expected, with blank spots on the walls where missing portraits used to hang and faded spots on the floor where rugs had been removed. The stairs squeaked quite satisfactorily when she ambled down them, as did the door when she opened it onto the broken cobblestones of the courtyard.

She hadn't seen a single soul in the house, nor outside of it, and broke into a run toward that line of forest, stretching out all the sore muscles and kinks from their adventure yesterday.

"Probably should've thanked the ghosts for not waking me," she panted to her critters after they'd all relieved themselves behind different bushes. "Do you suppose that's all that lives in there?" She waved a hand at the monstrous castle, with its peaks and turrets, sagging shutters, and overgrown vines. She shuddered at the sight and turned with a smile. "But I like these woods… very much."

She stuffed Chi-chi and Rosey in her pocket, put India on her shoulder, and began to trek through the trees, marveling at the colors of their leaves, all golds and reds with the fall. In Arizona there wasn't such an obvious change of seasons, and the sparse forests consisted of only spindly trees with the occasional evergreen. She marveled at the bounty of this land, even while she shivered from the dratted cold. The temperature of England's early fall felt like winter in the desert.

Summer unerringly found the water, following the stream to where it widened into a pond in an open clearing. A large, smooth boulder sat at the edge of the water, its surface warm from the sun, and she spread out her change of clothes, stripped off her torn and dirty ones, and grabbed the soap. Chi-chi and Rosey sniffed around with manic delight, and the dog made sure the fox stayed near with nose-nudges and the occasional nip. India scampered up the rock, looked over the edge at the water, and scampered back to Summer.

"You first," she told him, shivering in the chill air, just imagining how frigid that water would really be.

India chattered at her and went to the edge again. "What's the matter, little man, are you scared?"

As if he'd understood the taunt, the monkey jumped off the rock, hit the water, and seconds later shot out of it again, screaming loud enough to wake the ghosts in the duke's castle.

Summer laughed until her sides hurt. Tarnation, that was the funniest thing she'd ever seen—the look on India's face when he shot out of the water!

India spread himself out on the warm rock and looked at her accusingly. Well, now it was her turn, and Summer had never been one to just stick in a toe. She hopped onto the rock, tried to ignore the nasty gleam in the monkey's eyes, and jumped off.

The shock of the icy water stopped her heart. For a moment she couldn't move, and then she swam with all her might, made it to the shore, and turned into one giant goose bump. "I n-now know the meaning of c-cold," she told her friends and tried to pretend that she didn't notice India laughing at her. With a deep breath, she plunged back in the water and washed away all the dirt and grime, realizing that the water wasn't so bad, once her skin had gone numb.

She waded back to the shore, slightly blue but marvelously clean, holding out her arms to the sun, feeling that for the first time in a long while, she was at peace. At home.

And felt his eyes on her, the heat of his gaze chasing away the cold until she felt flushed with fever. She didn't think Byron had meant to sneak up on her. In fact, when their eyes met, he looked more startled than she. His mouth was open as if he'd tried to call out but had unaccountably lost the power of speech. Summer's gaze flickered toward his breeches, and she realized that she wanted him. Not the playing around they'd done, but him, inside of her, a part of her. If only they didn't keep having to save each other's lives, to depend on one another, to build a trust, then maybe she wouldn't have this desire for him. How could she want to keep her promise to Monte and yearn for this man at the same time?

What was she going to do?

Twelve

AS USUAL, HE TOOK CARE OF IT FOR HER.

"I've come to say good-bye," he managed to growl, his blue eyes widening with surprise, as if he couldn't believe what he'd just said.

"What do you mean—where are you going?"

His eyes stayed riveted to her breasts. "I am only human, madam, and cannot stand here talking to you with an ounce of reason if you don't cover yourself."

Summer wanted to apologize but didn't. She'd spent half her life bathing in streams, and he'd invaded her privacy, after all. She took a step, with every intention of getting her clothes, but realized that she'd just managed to move closer to him. Because of his eyes. At her movement he'd looked into her own, that blue stare making her legs go weak. Reminding her of the night that he'd comforted her, making her remember that they'd shared an intimacy that had created a burning need for consummation, as if she'd tasted chocolate but hadn't been allowed to eat any of it. Would she always feel this sense of incompleteness? This horrible emptiness of something undone?

He took a step toward her. "Can't you even bathe in a tub like a normal woman? Instead of outside, in the sunshine… where every pore of your skin sparkles with light… where you look like some kind of forest nymph…" The duke choked, then closed the distance between them even more.

"Don't leave," she whispered, unsure of what she meant. Don't leave her now, or not ever? Is that why she wanted him to continue as her sponsor, so that she would be near him? Why did she want him so badly that it hurt? Perhaps if she finished this thing between them, it would go away, and she wouldn't feel so blamed empty at the thought of never seeing him again.

"I'll only be gone for a short time," he whispered, his mouth somehow now at her ear, his arms folded around her shoulders. "Cook and Bernard will take care of you while I'm away to Scotland Yard. They'll keep you safe while I try to discover who hates me enough to want me dead."

Summer should've felt shocked at herself, feeling more naked held against his fully clothed body. But the throbbing between her legs warred with her modesty and won. "I want to go with you."

"No, you'll stay away from me, surrounded by people I trust. I won't put your life in danger again."

She reached her arms inside his unbuttoned coat, ran them up his back, and squeezed, trying to mold her body against his own. "I can't stay away from you," she whispered, the warmth of him making her shiver. And that's why she wouldn't let him go, not yet. She just couldn't go back to Monte with this aching desire for another man; it was time she did something about it. She couldn't be sure that she'd ever have the opportunity again.

He groaned, the stiffness in his muscles melting away as his entire body sought to wrap around her own, make her a part of him. His lips skipped across her cheek and found hers, pushing her head back while he plunged his tongue into her mouth, the sweet, raspy feel of it making her curl her own tongue around his, making her suck on it until she felt the hardness in his trousers like a burning brand.

Her fingers fumbled at the buttons of his waistcoat. His tore at his neck cloth, popping out the emerald stickpin, which fell unheeded onto the leafy forest floor. The duke shrugged out of his coat, draped it over her shoulders, making her feel as if he'd wrapped her in a cocoon of privacy.

She'd managed to open his waistcoat and shirt; her hands roaming the bare expanse of his chest had slid the clothing so that it lay slightly behind his shoulders, revealing the new bandage covering the injured one. The front of her skin lay bare to his own, with only his trousers and boots in the way, the cloth behind both of them making her feel as if they were in a tent of fine wool.

Summer wrapped her hand around the back of his neck and pulled his head down to her breasts, threw her head back when he greedily latched onto them, sucking until she could feel the draw of it between her legs, the rush of spasms that buckled her knees. One of his hands supported her back, and the other cradled her bottom, his tongue and mouth now nipping at her breasts until she thought she'd go mad.

She swept her hands over the bulge in his trousers, and he sucked in his breath. Summer knew what he looked like, had tasted and caressed him until his image had been branded forever in her mind, but she didn't truly know what he would feel like inside of her. What that soft, throbbing hardness would feel like pushing into her, becoming a part of her.

Her fingers traced through the golden hair on his chest, tugged and pulled at his nipples in demand. He growled and pulled up his head to her neck, sucking hard on her skin until she cried out his name to the trees and the earth and the sky. His fingers squeezed her bottom, and he pulled her hard against him and upward, until only her toes touched the leafy ground. She could hear her coarse hair scraping against the front of his trousers as she wrapped her arms around his neck and rubbed herself against him.

"Wrap your legs around me," he commanded.

She squirmed at the tone and sound of his voice. "But... your shoulder," she breathed, concerned for him, with only him. There was nothing in this world but her and the duke; the rest had faded to insignificance.

He didn't answer. His hand at her bottom bounced her up, and her legs wrapped around his hips reflexively. *Tarnation*, she thought, he hadn't even needed to tell her what to do, her body seemed to take cues from him without any conscious volition of her own.

He took his eyes off her for a minute and glanced around, a quirk at his lips as he headed for the smooth boulder at the edge of the pond, carrying her as if she weighed no more than India. She took advantage of his distraction to nip at his earlobe, nuzzle his hair, suck the salt off the skin of his neck.

Her eyes flew open, unaware that she'd even had them shut, when she felt the smooth hardness of the sloping boulder against the back of his coat that had—somehow—managed to stay slung over her shoulders. Summer leaned back, making a cold space between them that caused her to shiver until she looked into his face. She'd never seen an expression like his before, couldn't quite decide what to call it. His eyes were glazed with a dreamy, intense quality, his face flushed and his lips slightly parted as his breath rasped in and out while his gaze flickered over her, both his hands holding her hips against the support of the boulder. The rock curved out a bit, where he'd sat her bottom, and he pushed himself a bit farther away so he could see her mound of curls, the petals between her thighs.

His stare could melt stone, she thought. And make her long for him without a touch. But she needed his touch, couldn't stand the way she squirmed and bucked at him with nothing but the heat of his gaze for reward.

Summer lay on the slanted shelf and begged him to do more than look at her.

He smiled, his eyes quickly slipping back to stare into her own while he held her up with one hand while the other began to explore between her legs, making her catch her breath and try to pull him toward her. But he stubbornly resisted while clever fingers parted her petals, slipped in and out of her wetness, raked through her coarse, curly hair.

"Please, Byron."

His smiled widened, and he unbuttoned the front of his trousers with one hand, revealing that swollen, beautiful part of him, and she licked her lips, remembering the way he'd tasted, the way he'd felt. How could she ever have thought she'd never finish what they'd started?

She tried to wiggle down the rock, impale herself onto him.

He wouldn't let her.

His free hand moved back to her opening, plunged a finger inside as a promise, and then he stroked her nub, up and down, making her tense with the growing pleasure of her release. His other hand slid around her thigh and cupped her bottom again, cushioning her from the rock and lowering her until she could feel the round tip of him against her opening, holding her there against her struggles to enfold all of him inside of her.

Summer held on to the back of his neck and looked into his light blue eyes, felt herself being drawn into them, into his very soul, while his hand continued to stroke and her opening throbbed wider in invitation.

"You're mine," he said, bringing her to the brink of her climax and then slowing his strokes, keeping her suspended there. "You'll have to marry me now."

A trickle of actual thought filtered past the overwhelming sensation of her own body, and Summer opened her mouth to explain, to tell him that she'd only finished what they'd started. That she didn't want to be bound to him even more, that she'd realized this was the only way she could be free of him.

But he lowered her onto him, just enough for her to feel the promise of his heat before he pulled out again, while his hand resumed stroking her nub, and the words she'd tried to utter turned into moans of ecstasy as she began to explode. He lowered her again, this time farther down his shaft, penetrating her deeper before pulling out, while the first tremor of her climax shook her. On the second one he lowered her again, and then again, until the pain she felt when he entered her fully was overwhelmed by the pleasure that still radiated from her center.

And when he grasped her hips with both hands and began using his shaft to stroke her deeply inside, she felt another sensation growing and building. Not as piercing as the pleasure she'd just experienced, but more consuming in its intensity and greed, for she'd let go of his neck and grasped his bottom, pulling him against her, reaching for a fulfillment that centered not just on herself this time, but him as well.

Summer wanted something from him but had no idea what it was. She climbed another peak but had no idea what would happen when she fell over it.

He slid both his hands to her bottom and pushed her tight against him, until she could feel her nub rubbing against the heat of his groin, felt a lingering tremor of pleasure course through her as he stroked her entire body against his own, faster and faster until he threw back his head with a groan and exploded deep inside of her.

And then Summer knew what she'd sought, for as soon as she felt his own pleasure, she fell off that peak, arching her back with the heavy throb of satisfaction that came from somewhere deep inside.

He stared at her, those blue eyes boring into her own, his golden hair curling over his sculpted cheekbones, and smiled. "Tarnation," he whispered.

She smiled back, ran her fingers through the light sprinkle of hair on his chest, and sighed with wicked delight. Furry little fingers yanked on her hair, and she looked up into the inquiring eyes of her monkey.

"Go away," snapped Byron.

India chittered at him, and Summer laughed as she disentangled herself from Byron and his jacket. She scampered up the rock to stare down at him. "Care for a swim?"

He'd already hooded his eyes, that mask of superior indifference settling over his features. "I told you I have to leave."

Summer stood and stretched out her back, arching her breasts toward the sun. She heard him swallow. Didn't he understand that they'd never be together again? "Don't let it end, not yet," she pleaded and dived off the edge of the boulder. Since she was ready this time, the water wasn't such a shock. She surfaced and managed to smile at him only by gritting her teeth.

He shrugged and discarded the few items of clothing still sagging around his ankles, and clambered up the rock as well, standing with hands on hips. "I used to swim here, when I was a boy. How's the water?"

"F-fine," she stammered.

He cocked a brow at her in disbelief. Summer stared at what a fine sight he made in the sunshine, all hard ridges and soft hair, his stance proudly arrogant. Her body began to warm, and when next she spoke it was the truth. "It's getting warm in here."

He threw back his head and laughed, his shaft already half-swollen from her scrutiny of him, and Summer thought he looked glorious. He took two steps and dived, surfaced with a gasp, and started to swim toward her with deadly purpose.

"You're a wicked wench."

Summer backstroked. "It's not that cold."

"I am shriveled to the point of pain, madam."

Summer's toes touched the bottom of the pond, and she stilled. Could cold water hurt a man that way? "Then get out!"

He choked on a laugh, and his annoyance at her little trick faded. "Does that mean you care about my, umm, health, my dear?"

"Well, of course. Not that it matters, anymore. I mean, it'd just be a shame because…" She started walking out of the water, still backing away from him. His frown of playful anger had turned quite serious.

"What do you mean it doesn't matter?"

Summer couldn't believe this; did he still not understand? "Because it's not like we'll ever be together again."

"Why not?" His eyes glittered dangerously as he stalked her, the water evaporating from his body as if it were being cooked off.

"Because I have to go back to New York. Nothing's changed."

"Hasn't it? Didn't I tell you we'd have to get married, or weren't you listening?"

Summer grabbed for her chemise and scurried into it. "Isn't it the woman who's supposed to be trapping the man into marriage about now?"

"So what was all this?" His arms swept around the clearing at their scattered clothes, his jacket still draped over that shelf in the boulder.

"It was inevitable, that's all. We just finished something that needed to be finished, in order for us to move on."

"Move on?" He smoothed the hair back off his face, staring at her as if he'd never seen her before. His face clouded with confusion as he slowly pulled on his clothes, but by the time he tied his neck cloth on, he had recovered himself. "You're not only a savage but a whore as well."

Summer buttoned the front of her bodice, knowing that he had a right to be angry and expecting his wicked tongue to lash out at her. But he spoke with such calm detachment that his words managed to hurt her, and she hadn't expected that. "The blood on your jacket testifies to what I am, sir."

He lowered his head, his eyes flashing, his hands fisted. "You're a fool to honor the proposal of this Monte person when he doesn't want you the way you are."

"And you're a fool to propose to a woman just because of your honor."

They both panted a bit, their heads lowered at each other like charging bulls, the air crackling with the electricity of their anger. Chi-chi charged his ankle, her little teeth burying themselves into the skin, and India jumped onto his shoulder and started pulling his hair.

"Call them off before someone gets hurt."

Summer gathered up her critters, who whined and moaned at her while the Duke of Monchester pulled on his boots. She tried to apologize for the way her animals had acted, but he waved it off.

"They had every right. I should not have said what I did, nor acted the way I have." He took a deep breath. "You've always been honest with me, in your thoughts and actions. You just don't know that you're mine yet, and I regret my lack of patience with your stupidity."

Summer's mouth dropped open. She couldn't even respond to his statement. He turned his back and walked away, yelling at her over his shoulder, "And wear a bathing costume in the future. For your own protection, I have men watching the grounds while I'm gone."

Summer resisted the urge to ask him not to go again, while she watched him disappear through the trees. She tried not to admire the predatory grace of his walk, or stare at his wonderfully round bottom, to remember the way it felt in her hands. "Stop it," she whispered sternly to herself. "We're finished." Wasn't that the whole point of their encounter today, to end this longing for him? Or did it go deeper than that?

Summer winced. It didn't matter, anyway. She'd made a promise to another man, and it would take more than one steamy afternoon to break it.

Summer spent the rest of the morning in the woods. She only returned to the dilapidated castle because she had nothing with which to make a fire, and it had been too many years since she'd had to eat raw food gleaned from the countryside for her to consider it. When she reached the side of the building, she followed the sounds of a sweetly singing voice and peeked around the corner of an open door.

A plump woman with a red nose and sparkling green eyes turned and clutched at her chest. "Ugh, child, you scared me to death. What are you doing skulking in the doorway?"

Summer resisted the urge to deny that she skulked, and stepped into the room, breathing in the smells of the dried herbs hanging from the rafters, the delicious aroma of baking bread, and the mouthwatering smell of stew atop the black kettle stove. She liked this room and the sweet voice of this woman.

"So, you must be Summer Wine Lee? Quite a name you've got there. Why would anyone call a child such a thing?" Summer opened her mouth to reply, but the woman just continued to chatter on. "And His Grace said you had a monkey too; now what would that eat, I wonder?" She stared in consternation at India, where he sat perched on Summer's shoulder. "Dogs, now, I know what to feed them. Even if one's a fox-dog."

Chi-chi stuck her head out of Summer's pocket, and Summer dug both the critters out, letting them scurry across the floor to accept the ham bone the woman held out to them. It was bigger than both of them, but they managed to carry it over to a safe corner with their heads held high, tails wagging deliriously.

Cook continued to talk away while she scooped out a bowl of stew for Summer, cutting off a chunk of fresh-baked bread and slathering it with lots of butter. Summer took a bite and closed her eyes with sincere appreciation, and then didn't mind listening to the woman's sweet voice while she ate her fill.

"How's about an apple, monkey-boy? Ah, that's what to feed you, hmm? Don't choke it down; it'll like to get stuck. Now, Miss Lee, if you please, when you're finished eating I can show you around the old place, although there's not much to see anymore, not since that old man went and sold off all that poor boy's inheritance. Wasn't safe if it weren't nailed down." She wiped pudgy hands on her apron and tucked a stray hair of gray back into her bun. "His Grace said I was to treat you as if you was mistress of the place, so I imagine you two will be getting married soon."

Summer choked on a bit of beef, and Cook slapped her on the back. "I apologize, Miss. Been out here in the country so long that I forget how to act proper with my betters. Just been me and that old buzzard, and I get so lonesome I can't stop talking when I see a new face."

"Old buzzard?" Summer inquired.

The woman colored a vibrant shade of red. "Oh, I meant Bernard, my husband and the glorified butler here. I'm sure you're shocked at my way of speaking, and I promise to do better, Miss. And now that you're here, I'll fix up the dining room so's you don't have to eat in the kitchen."

Summer washed down the last of her luncheon with a final swallow of warm milk. "I like it here," she said as her eyes roamed the homey kitchen. "Please don't go to any trouble for me. I won't be here long."

Cook's green eyes widened, and she cocked her head at Summer. "But His Grace said that until he caught whoever's been trying to kill him… My word, such wickedness! Now who would want to harm that boy, I ask you? Doesn't have a mean bone in his body; why, when he was a child he was always bringing home all sorts of forest animals that needed fixing up. Always thought he'd be a physician, but well, with the money all gone, he couldn't afford the schooling anymore, much less to do the traveling his heart had always been set on."

Summer tried to hide a grin. She thought that if Byron had known how much of his life would be revealed to her by this one woman, he'd never have brought her here to stay. It seemed that all the questions she'd ever had about His Grace were about to be answered.

"I really can't stay," insisted Summer. "I have to get back to London, whether His Grace gives me leave or not."

Cook frowned. "Your companion, Meg, won't be fit to travel for some time, Miss. Quite a nasty bump on her head."

Poor Meg, thought Summer. After all the girl had been through, she couldn't leave her alone among strangers to recover. She'd have to wait until her maid felt well enough to travel, even though her every instinct told her to leave this man's home as quickly as she could. To forget about the duke and go back to London to pursue the reason she had come to England in the first place.

But she couldn't leave Meg. So, in the meantime… "I'd like to see the rest of this place… as long as there aren't any ghosts to worry about."

Cook startled and stopped her monologue for a moment—although she didn't close her mouth—before starting up again. "Ghosts? Goodness, the only one that's ever passed on here is the duke's blessed mother, and saints don't haunt, now, do they? Such ideas! I suppose it's because you're an American. His Grace did say to overlook any peculiar things you might do. Have you ever seen an honest-to-goodness Indian?"

Summer's head had started to spin. "Of course."

"Is it true they scalp people? Never could believe that myself. Do you remember where your room was? Well, His Grace's room, I mean. But he said to let you stay there and not bother making up another one. It's the rheumatism, you see, so I only keep up the rooms that me and Buzz—ah, Bernard—use."

She waddled out the door, and Summer had to hurry to scoop up her critters to follow. India burped in her ear. Chi-chi and Rosey whined for the bone, but soon both dog and fox were asleep in her pocket, lulled by the rhythm of her walk. And walk they did. Summer tried to imagine how many miles of corridors and drafty hallways they traveled, but her mind couldn't wrap around the idea of an indoors being this big. Besides, it took most of her concentration to keep track of Cook's constant change of subjects. And to keep the woman's ramblings focused on the one person she most cared to hear about.

Cook opened double doors onto a huge, cavernous room. Summer could just make out the pattern of a starburst inlaid in the wooden floor when she swiped her foot through the dust. Gaping holes in the ceiling showed where chandeliers had hung; the remains of a rickety stage and shredded velvet draperies confirmed that this once had been a very grand ballroom.

India hopped from her shoulder and made tiny tracks along the dirty floor. The silk-lined walls lay in peeling tatters, showing the outlines of where enormous paintings must have hung. "Why did he do it? Strip the house bare, I mean?"

Cook clutched at her chest and shook her head sadly. "As to why the old duke stripped Cliffs Castle, and the estate in Ireland as well, is a mystery to many. But I have my suspicions, yes I do."

India hopped back onto Summer's shoulder, leaving smudges of dirt all over her dress. Cook eyed the little monkey. "It won't piss anywhere, will it?"

Summer shook her head while India blinked with an almost human expression of outrage. "India's very smart; he knows better than to relieve himself inside."

Cook shut the doors with a resounding thud and started down another spider-infested corridor. "This is the music room, or was; nothing much to see in there now. Unless you want to, I'd rather not go into all the rooms. Makes me sad to see them now, when I remember how elegant they were in my youth."

Summer shrugged. Truly, after one empty, dusty room, she'd about seen them all. "About your suspicions, Mrs. Cook…"

They rounded the corner and went up another flight of stairs, Cook panting so hard that she couldn't speak. Summer tried again. "It's a shame what his father did, taking all the pictures and furniture, isn't it? Did he leave anything at all?"

Cook wheezed. They reached the top of the landing, went down another hallway, and this time Cook opened the doors. Summer walked into a room that seemed frozen in time. A beautiful dressing table had a brush lying on it that still had golden strands of hair embedded in the bristles, as if it had just been used before it had been set down. Bottles of intricately blown glass contained dried bits of color in their bottoms; a gold case of powder lay open, the puff resting against it, with flecks of the white stuff still on it. She could just make it out beneath the dust. When she walked over to the faded, silk-draped bed, and saw the impression of a head still on the pillows and the tousled bedcovers looking as if they'd just been thrown aside, she shivered.

"This was her room," said Cook, making Summer about jump out of her skin. "This is what I've been waiting to show you, because even the second duchess didn't dare come in here to take anything."

"I thought you said there weren't any ghosts here," breathed Summer.

The old woman shook her head. "I told you, she's a saint."

"Who?"

"Why, the late duke's first wife, His Grace's mother, of course." Cook sat on a bench carved into the shape of a lotus flower and caught her breath. "While she lived this old castle was full of warmth and light, and the old duke still cared for his son."

Summer wandered around the room and noticed how different it was from all the other rooms she'd seen in London. Of course, they all looked old to her. After the newness of America, England reeked of history and age. But this room also felt… exotic, somehow.

India had been eyeing Cook for some time, and finally bounded off Summer's shoulder and hopped onto the bench next to the older woman, who froze in apparent fear. The monkey leered, and Summer tried not to smile when he jumped onto Cook's shoulder and started picking through the gray hair.

"Wha-what's it doing?"

"Looking for lice," replied Summer.

Cook's back snapped stiff as a ramrod. "Well, I never! Get him off me, Miss Lee. I don't have any bugs."

Summer picked up a piece of carved stone in the shape of a demonic lion. "Oh, don't be insulted. Monkeys groom each other as a way to show affection. It means he likes you."

Cook sniffed but continued to sit as stiff as a board while India managed to start undoing her tightly wrapped hair bun. "When the first duchess died," she continued, "the old duke sent His Grace off to school, and the house was a sad place then. But peaceful, until she came."

"The second duchess?" prompted Summer, wiping at an elaborately designed vase, revealing slant-eyed people playing odd-looking instruments among blossoming trees.

"Yes, the second wife. She's the one that poisoned the old duke's son against the boy, I'm sure of it." Cook's posture had started to slouch, her hair tumbling around her face in wild tangles, India's little fingers still intent on their search. "She's the one kept crying about how her own son wouldn't have nothing as second-born, since he wouldn't inherit the lands and title. And when the old duke got sick, she's the one that kept His Grace in school, telling her husband that the boy didn't care to come see him, and look how doting her own little Colin Charles was."

"Do you mean Lord Karlton, the duke's half brother?"

"No other. Such a spineless piece of work I never did see, but considering the mother... He talks sweetly, mind you, but behind that smiling face lies a cunning little brain, twice as crafty as the mother, 'cause with him you can't tell he's doing it. But he poisoned the old duke's mind against his firstborn, just as surely as the mother did." Cook took a handkerchief from her pocket and swiped angrily at the tears in her eyes. "Made him sell off everything he could from the estates and leave it in trust to Colin Charles. If it weren't for the law, he'd have disinherited his own firstborn!"

Summer frowned at the old woman's vehemence and worried when she clutched at her chest. She walked over and took her hand. "I can tell you love Byron; maybe that's why you feel so resentful of his stepmother and brother?"

Those green eyes widened. "What'd you call him? Goodness, His Grace would scowl something fierce if he ever heard you call him by his given name. Don't you know that's not done?"

"Remember, Mrs. Cook, I'm an American."

Her eyes were now half-closed. "That's right, I forgot. My, that feels good, little monkey-boy. And Miss Lee, it's just plain Cook."

Summer tried not to roll her eyes. The word "American" seemed to excuse anything. "Cook, do you think Lord Karlton, or the dowager duchess, would go so far as to, well, kill him for the title?"

Cook's eyes shot open, and she rocked to her feet, India still wrapped in her hair. "My goodness, I never did think of that when His Grace told me about all the trouble he's been having." She clutched at her chest again, and Summer winced. That gesture was really starting to scare her.

The old woman stared at the portrait of Byron's mother. "But I don't think Lord Karlton would have the stomach for it; why, when he was a boy, he'd take one look at His Grace's injured animals and go running for the chamber pot. And as far as the dowager duchess goes, if she could've done it, she would have years ago, when he was a child."

Summer patted her shoulder. "Please, don't concern yourself about it. I'm sure it's just someone he's insulted once too often."

Oddly enough, this seemed to reassure her, and she stuffed her handkerchief back in her pocket and stepped to the far side of the room, being careful not to jar India from her shoulder. She pointed at a yellowed map hung on the wall, tiny pins with flags sticking to them puncturing hundreds of areas on the surface. "See all these places they pinned? Mother and son would talk about how when he became a man, he'd travel the world and bring her home presents from every land he explored. She felt too sickly to travel herself. People just don't understand His Grace, all the dreams he had, and how they shattered when his mother died." She sighed and ushered Summer out of the room. "Why anyone would want to harm him is beyond me. Oh, I admit he has a lethal tongue. But it's not his fault if people don't like to hear the truth about themselves."

Summer thought about her conversation with him earlier and shifted uncomfortably. India hopped back on her shoulder, and Cook's hands flew to her tangled hair, trying to smooth it back into her neat bun. "Let's go back to the kitchen, shall we?"

Summer nodded. She'd had enough dust and old memories for one day. And she was beginning to feel oddly protective toward the child who Cook described, and couldn't risk that feeling transferring over to the man himself.

Thirteen

SUMMER FOLLOWED COOK BACK TO THE KITCHEN, AND she sipped English tea while Cook fixed a tray to take up to Meg. After Summer made sure her maid was properly fed and had fallen back to sleep, she returned to the kitchen and insisted that she be allowed to eat at the same table with Cook and her husband.

When the meal was completely lain out, Bernard walked into the room. He had a completely bald scalp, with large freckles adorning the top of it, a paunchy belly, and kind brown eyes. He barely spoke a word, for just as soon as he managed a few sentences, his wife would finish the thought for him. And he seemed quite happy with that arrangement.

"How's the building coming along?" asked Cook as soon as she had introduced her husband to Summer.

The man nodded politely at Summer, acknowledging the presence of a monkey, fox, and dog with aplomb. He hung his cap on a hook and grunted in reply to his wife's question.

"Good to hear. Where's the boy? I suppose he'll be coming along soon?" Summer opened her mouth to ask about the boy, assuming it was their son, when Cook continued on. Summer pressed her lips together and then grinned conspiratorially at Bernard, who winked and set to his dinner with an appreciation for the skill of his wife. "That child, he spends more time in those woods than he does with folks. It'll make him peculiar, it will. Bernard, tomorrow you should take Miss Lee to the village, show her the building that His Grace is having built."

He nodded, his head lowered to the stew, and Summer thought she could trace the pattern of a halo in the freckles adorning his bald pate.

"Did I tell you, Miss Lee, what His Grace is trying to do? Although, heaven knows where he'd be getting the money."

More answers, Summer thought in glee. Now she'd find out what he'd done with the money he'd earned, for he certainly hadn't spent it on new clothes or castle renovations.

"I don't know how he lives himself, when he sends all he can to us." Cook tasted her bowl of stew and nodded in satisfaction. "He has grand plans, does His Grace. But you know they say it takes money to make money, and I'm afraid he's taken on too big of a job, trying to restore the fortunes of this old estate. More bread, Bernard?" The man nodded, and she rose to get it for him. "Since we get a pittance for any grain we grow, His Grace has decided to raise sheep; can you imagine? And not just to raise them, but process and weave the wool. Isn't that right, Bernard?"

He accepted the bread and her words with a nod.

"His Grace says that with all this industrili... industrialization, the gentry will want clothing made by hand. Says it's hard to tell the social positions apart these days, what with machines to make lace and dresses as good as any dressmaker. So he'll get the villagers trained in weaving and sell handmade scarves and skirts, and heaven knows what all!"

Summer tried not to gape at the woman. And Byron said he didn't work! She'd always felt a bit disdainful about his insistence that gentlemen didn't work, for Americans believed in the honest value of it, and using your brains and sweat to get ahead in the world. And here he was, trying to make a going concern out of his estate, when so many other landowners just bled their estates dry to keep them in style.

Her head spun from everything she'd learned of him today, and she just couldn't piece together this man and the one she'd come to know.

The next morning Summer followed a silent Bernard down an overgrown road, her pups in her pocket and India on her shoulder, loving the way the trees crowded over their path and how wild the woods grew.

Bernard took her to the outskirts of the village, to a collection of buildings where some were still just frameworks. She listened in admiration while Bernard explained about sheep shearing, and wool carding, and old-fashioned loom weaving, convinced that Byron's plan had a good chance of succeeding, but that he needed much more money invested in it.

He didn't have near enough sheep for the number of empty looms set up, and now that he'd decided to cancel their business arrangement, how was he going to get the capital he needed? Summer decided she'd wire Pa; he was always looking for a good investment. And it had nothing to do with the idea that if Byron and Pa were in business together, she'd be able to keep tabs on how the duke was doing when she returned to New York. What did she care, anyway, when she'd be so busy with a new marriage to Monte?

After a picnic lunch under a giant oak tree, she asked Bernard to take her to the Wilder home, remembering Cook's orders for her to deliver the sweets she'd baked for the little ones. It seemed Mr. Wilder had taken off to parts unknown and that the poor mother had all she could do to take care of eleven children.

Their home didn't look large enough to accommodate two children, much less the horde she saw grouped in a circle in front of the door, but Summer still felt a twinge of envy. Chatto had been the closest thing she'd had to a sibling until Maria, and the loneliness of her childhood made her long to be a part of such a large family. Monte had said he only wanted a few children, that even with a governess and a nanny, they could be an awful nuisance, and Summer hadn't thought much about it. But seeing this curly-headed, dirty-faced crew, she wondered what it'd be like to have a large family after all.

She'd expected the children to be as fascinated by her pets as the rest of the villagers had, but they only gave her and India a quick glance before returning their attention back to something in the center of their circle.

"What is it, Bernard?" she asked the much taller man.

A tall, red-haired youth managed to bellow louder than the others, drowning out Bernard's reply. "I'm tellin' you, bastard boy, to put the cat outta its misery!"

Summer wiggled through the group of children just in time to catch the other boy's reply. He stood over a mangled piece of fur, hands fisted at his sides, blond hair and pale face even dirtier than the other children. "He's mine, James Wilder. And you're going to have to get past me in order to touch him."

James took a step forward. He stood a good head taller than the other boy and had the soft beard of a young man. "I beat you up before, and I don't mind doin' it again."

Bernard hadn't said a word, as if he felt it best for children to work out their own problems and wasn't about to start interfering now.

Summer disagreed and inched toward the blond boy, trying to get a look at the animal that he stood so protectively over. The children started murmuring, "Fight, fight," and she could see the boy take a deep breath and brace himself for a blow.

"What's wrong with the critter?" asked Summer, pointing at the bundle of fur.

Startled pairs of eyes fixed on her, as if stunned to find her in their midst, and the redhead, who stood taller than Summer herself, drew back his arm. "Where'd you come from?"

Summer knew what the young man meant, for she'd fox-walked into the middle of their group, and they'd been so intent on their prey they hadn't noticed her. But she grinned at him and purposely misunderstood. "America."

The blond blinked his light blue eyes at her. Now, why did they seem so familiar?

She heard Bernard give a cough of laughter, and while the group of children digested that information, she bent down to examine the bundle, India hanging on to her collar and tilting his head with a whine of sympathy. A tomcat, a tough one at that, with half an ear already missing and bald spots from scars of previous battles. Mercifully, it looked unconscious. Summer sucked in her breath as she unwrapped the makeshift bandage around the cat's back end. Both of its hind legs had been crushed. She looked up at the animal's protector. "What's your name?"

The boy twisted his lips in another familiar gesture. "Didn't you hear what James called me?"

She stared at him and shifted where she crouched. "My name's Summer Wine Lee."

He gave a bark of laughter. "Your name's almost as stupid as mine. Lionel Plunk, ma'am, at your service."

This was too loco, thought Summer. The boy didn't talk like the others; he had a cultured accent with the same disdainful twist to his words that Byron always used. And what had the redhead called him... bastard boy? Well, she had no time to ponder it now. The cat's legs had been fully crushed, so there wasn't any further loss of blood, but they'd have to fix him up soon if he had any chance of surviving.

"Well, Lionel. Carry him back to the castle for me, and I'll see what I can do for him."

James, unfortunately, had found his voice again. "There's nothin' you can do for them legs, and if you fix him up, how can he even walk? Like I already told bast… uh, Plunk, my lady, it would be more merciful just to kill it now." Although his tone had changed from arrogant bully to one of cajolery, as if patronizing the sentimental feelings of the weaker sex, his eyes still glittered with the knowledge that he was the superior person. That only his way of thinking could be the right one, because he'd proven it time and again with the strength of his fists. Summer had seen it before in many men, young and old.

Her dander went up. Did he think because she was a woman, he could scare her? Maybe it was time this young man was taught a lesson in underestimating people. With one move she had her knife in her hand, the blade flashing in the sunshine. "Tell me, James, if I hacked off both your legs right now, would you consider it a mercy if I went ahead and let you die too?"

India hissed at him from her shoulder, and that was the final impetus the children needed. The yard cleared of everyone but James, who backed up slowly, as if facing a wild boar, and then turned to follow the cloud of dust left by the rest of the pounding bare feet.

Bernard coughed again. "Wasn't that a bit… extreme, Miss?"

Summer sighed and slid her knife back in its sheath, while Lionel shivered beside her, apparently terrified by the madwoman but still refusing to abandon his pet. "I expect it was, but tarnation, he won't ever argue with me again now, will he?"

"I rather expect not, Miss."

The boy had picked up his cat and looked like he had every intention of following on the heels of the rest of the children.

Summer spoke as fast as she could. "I have a three-legged dog named Lefty. Got his leg cut off by a cart's wheel, and he fixed up just fine." She grabbed the boy's ragged sleeve and began to tow him in the direction of the castle. "He hops around quite well; you'd never guess he wasn't born with three legs. Though he can't keep up with my other dog, Sweetie. But he's the size of a pony, and even I can't keep up with him half the time."

She continued to talk all the way home, the boy listening with what appeared to be horrified fascination. "Had to leave them in New York, though, and only managed to bring Chi-chi along." She opened her pocket, and the dog's black nose peeked out, followed by the even-blacker one of the fox. "Oh, that one's not a dog. He's a fox that the duke helped me rescue."

"The Duke... of Monchester?" asked Lionel.

"Oh, none other."

The boy's eyes flicked to the monkey on her shoulder.

"Oh, he didn't come from America either. Maria and the duke rescued him in Paris."

"My father helped to rescue a fox and a monkey?"

Summer stumbled, something she rarely did, and looked up at Bernard for confirmation. No wonder the child had looked so familiar! Byron had a son. But why did he wear rags and run around without any supervision? Weren't children of the aristocracy supposed to be dressed in miniature adult clothes and learning lessons all day? That's what she'd heard, anyway. But it seemed that the child was allowed to run as wild as she had.

They had reached the castle, and she scared Cook and Meg witless by charging into the kitchen and sweeping dishes from the table, motioning the boy to put the cat in the middle of the clean white cloth. She continued snapping out orders for boiling water, and clean bandages, and the tiniest, sharpest paring knife, along with needle and thread. Cook scurried about and did her bidding without a word.

Bernard propped himself in a corner and folded his arms, his expression one of unsurprised admiration as he watched Summer and the boy bend over the animal on the table. Meg cowered beside him, content just to keep out of the way.

"Are you sure you know what you're doing?" Lionel asked as she thoroughly cleaned the animal's torso, then poured brandy on it for good measure.

"Is there anyone else who can doctor the critter?"

"There's a physician in Wallings, but even if I could get Hunter there, he won't doctor an animal."

"Well, then, looks like you don't have any choice but to trust me, do you?"

Lionel nodded and stared at the serrated knife in her hand. "I couldn't kill him, you know." His voice choked, and a grubby hand reached out to stroke the yellow-striped head of the cat. "He's my best friend."

Summer's heart turned over in her chest, and her eyes met his, and they stared at each other for the longest time. She felt his kindred spirit. There'd been times when her only friends had been animals, when they were all that had stood between herself and loneliness.

"Maybe it's better if you don't watch." As soon as she said the words, she knew he'd refuse, and quickly spoke again. "But then again, how will you help another critter unless you learn from what I do?"

She started cutting with the knife, glanced at the boy when he cringed, shook himself, then set his lips in lines of determination. Summer copied his motions herself, for she'd learned what little she knew from Chatto, and then she and Maria had just done the best they could. It was true that they'd saved Lefty, but that dog's leg had already been severed from his body; they'd just stitched him up and prayed for the best.

She'd never had to cut… She hoped she was doing the right thing.

Sweat beaded on her forehead, and Cook wiped it away. She hadn't even been aware of the woman standing on the other side of her, and mumbled her thanks. She could hear Lionel swallow when she handed Cook the piece she'd cut away, and her fingers flew without thought as they cleaned and pinched and started to sew. Meg let out a stifled cry, holding on to her bandaged head as she flew out of the room.

Summer could feel the boy jump beside her. "Tell me about Hunter," she ordered.

The boy swallowed again. "He's the best mouser in the village, but still, when we met he was skinnier than a stick. Found him licking the fish bones I'd thrown away, and when I shared some of my catch with him, he started following me everywhere, helping me to flush birds and such."

Summer started on the other leg. "Had me two coatis who learned to hunt with me too."

"What are coatis?"

"They're like dogs, but with long snouts and tails that stick straight up, like they're always surprised about something."

"They don't have animals like that around here. Are you really from America?"

Summer started to stitch again. "Haven't you met any Americans? There's plenty in London."

"My father doesn't take me to the city. Is it true he helped you rescue animals?"

"'Course it is. Why do you find that so hard to believe?"

Cook quietly left the room to dispose of the pieces that Summer had handed her, and she silently thanked the woman for being so stoic. She hadn't expected it from the talkative woman and felt an even greater fondness for her. Bernard didn't say a word, actually seemed to be holding his breath while he listened to her and Lionel talk.

The boy shrugged. "He doesn't like animals."

Summer wrapped the cat's tiny stumps in clean strips of cloth and breathed a sigh of relief. "Now, all we can do is wait. Hunter's heartbeat is still strong, and if he makes it through the night, he should recover." She stepped over to the basin of water and washed her hands and face, trying to stop the tremor of reaction that started to take hold of her. Her words were said for the boy's benefit, for she didn't really think the poor critter would make it. The boy stood glued to his pet's side, and she knew he'd stay there the night.

"Lionel."

He looked at her with those startling blue eyes.

"Your father only pretends to dislike animals. There is a difference, you know."

He nodded, and she turned to leave the room, politely ignoring the tears that streaked down his freckled cheeks.

"Summer." She stopped when he called her name, her hand resting on the door frame. He made her name sound like a magic word.

"Would you really have done it?" he asked.

"Done what?"

"Chopped off James's legs."

Bernard choked from his corner. Summer tried to smile through the wave of exhaustion that threatened to overwhelm her. That doctoring had cost her more than she'd thought. "What do you think?"

Lionel looked at her, his head cocked to one side, smudges of black lining his cheeks where the tears had run. "I think... I think you've learned to look tough. And that you like animals more than you do people."

"Sometimes," she whispered as she left the room. "Just sometimes."

Over the next several days Summer went down to the kitchen to find the boy slumped over the table, sound asleep. This morning was no exception. She tiptoed over to the cat, breathed a sigh of relief when she saw the regular rise and fall of its furry chest. Chi-chi and the fox went over to the corner where they'd stashed their bone and began to worry it to death, and India clasped his hands at Cook with enough dramatic flair to earn him a slice of apple.

"We'll have to move the cat off the kitchen table," whispered Cook as she held up a padded basket. "Figured this would do for a bed."

Summer nodded, frowning in thought. With amazement she realized that the cat might survive his ordeal, and that created a whole new set of problems. "When Hunter wakes he'll be in awful pain. Maria and I always had a bit of laudanum on hand. I suppose brandy will have to do."

Cook tsked and waddled over to the herbs hanging at the edges of the room. "Didn't you wonder how I learned to be such a good helper? It's been a long time since I helped His Grace doctor his animals, but I still remember some things. He always used willow bark for pain… I put it in to soak when I got up this morning. I'll have it ready before the cat wakes." Cook handed her a plate of fried eggs and thick slabs of bacon and honey-smeared toast, before she set the pot of soaked bark on the stove. "I know how to cook, whether it's food or medicine, but never could do the doctoring. It's good to have another in the house."

"I'm not a doctor; I've just learned to fix things 'cause there was nobody else to do it," said Summer around a mouthful of egg. She thought of Monte, who'd be a real physician someday, and how he got to learn all kinds of fascinating things. But whenever she asked him to share what he knew, he'd told her that she didn't need to know such things, that after they were married she'd be too busy entertaining and raising their children to worry about anything else. At the time she'd felt warm at the thought that someone would finally be taking care of her, but now she wished he'd shared just a bit of what he learned. She could've used it.

Summer sighed and adjusted the plate of food on her lap, glancing over at the blond head still folded over the table. "The duke never mentioned he had a son." Bernard left the room to do his chores, and Summer looked over at Cook hopefully. "He looks a lot like his pa—father."

Cook opened the door of the old black stove and tossed in more coal, shaking her head. "How do I explain about the boy?" Her eyes rolled up to the ceiling as if she'd find some answers there. "His Grace was only a boy himself when Widow Plunk's loneliness got the best of her… or maybe she thought of it as an opportunity to better herself, who knows? But when His Grace confronted the old duke with the matter of his illegitimate son's birth, and that he wanted to marry such a low-born woman, he was sent off to school faster'n you could blink. So Widow Plunk raised Lionel in the village, and no one was allowed even to hint that the boy had aristocratic blood runnin' through his veins."

The pot steamed on the stove, and Cook hovered near it.

Summer couldn't understand how Byron could ignore his own son. "But when he became a man, didn't he still want to marry the widow and raise his son?"

"It was too late. She died, you see, and her mother took Lionel in, and His Grace quit doctoring animals after that, and stayed away from Cliffs Castle for a long time."

The boy murmured something in his sleep, and both women jumped.

Cook removed the boiling pot from the burner and waved at Summer to follow as she waddled outside, the sun highlighting her gray hair and making shadows in the hollows of her wrinkled face. The older woman began to weed a vegetable garden while Summer walked on toward a fence loaded with a profusion of white late-blooming flowers. She breathed in the sweet aroma, catching the faint salty tang of the sea and the rich mustiness of moist soil. India scampered through the grass, chasing bugs. "How far away is the sea?"

Cook grunted as she pulled out a long root. "About an hour's walk. Why?"

"There was coastline in New York, but nothing like the wild cliffs around here, and in Arizona there was very little water, even up in the mountains where my pa mined for ore. England is just so… wet, and green. I want to enjoy it while I'm here."

"But His Grace said you were to marry." She looked up at Summer with a frown. "You can enjoy it for the rest of your life."

Summer shook her head, began to pick flower after flower. That ridiculous man! Telling everyone that they'd marry.

Summer sighed. "Can't he adopt Lionel?"

Cook didn't bat an eye at the change of subject, being a master at it herself. "The boy would still be illegitimate and could never inherit the title or the estates. And he was happy in the village and wouldn't leave his grandmother, so I guess His Grace thought it best that Lionel stay there. There's some things even I don't ask him about."

Summer smiled, her arms now filled with flowers, so that she could barely see over the mound. She wondered if flowers always bloomed this late in the season, or if this was an unusual garden. She started toward the kitchen door when Cook's voice stopped her again. "Miss Lee? Ah, I wonder if you could do me just a little favor?"

"Of course."

Cook breathed a sigh of relief. "I did something, you see, that maybe I had no right doing, but I sent His Grace a letter, and with him staying with one friend after another, sometimes they don't get to him for months, and when Lionel's grandmother died, well, I had to do something now, didn't I?"

Summer turned and squatted. "Of course you did."

"I knew you would help me. You're so different from the rest of the duke's visitors, with their airs and all. And I know my place, don't get me wrong; we're trained from the cradle to respect our proper position in society—"

"Cook, what did you do?"

Cook pulled out another weed and tossed it on her growing pile. "I couldn't let the boy stay in that cottage all by himself. So I fixed him up a room in the castle, and he's been here ever since. But I'm not sure what His Grace wanted to do about the boy, and I'm afraid he won't be pleased when he finds out."

"It's his own *son*, Cook."

Her pudgy hand reached out and patted Summer's shoulder. "I knew you'd think I'd done right, but as for His Grace…"

Summer's eyes flashed golden brown, and she rose with her usual unthinking grace. "Don't you worry about it. I'll tell Byron. *That*, and a few other things besides." The older woman grinned so wide that Summer noticed for the first time that her front tooth was chipped almost in half.

"I'd started to worry about that man," she replied. "What with all his gallivanting and partying and blunt mouth. But now that he's brought you home, I see he's still the same boy that I loved."

Summer shook her head and stepped over the curly leaves of a lettuce plant. "This isn't my home," she insisted again, still trying to make these deluded people understand that she had no intention of staying here and marrying their duke. She was getting used to her words having little effect, however, and didn't get too riled up when Cook just grinned knowingly at her. Well, let them think what they liked, because as soon as she made sure Byron would take care of his son, she would go back to London and hire someone else to sponsor her.

Summer blew a bee off one of the flowers in her arms. And darn her insatiable curiosity about the Duke of Monchester. She looked back at the bended figure of Cook. There was something about a garden…

"Cook, have only you and Bernard been taking care of the castle?"

"Yes." She took the hem of her apron and wiped sweat off her upper lip. "Why do you ask?"

"Byron once told me about a Chinese gardener who taught him how to fight. I'd like to meet him."

Cook frowned. "A Chinaman? Oh, I remember. A small, serene little man. Why, he passed on years ago. Whatever would you want to meet him for?"

Because he was so important to Byron, thought Summer, and then quickly dismissed such a ridiculous notion. "I thought he might teach me how to fight like Byron does." She sighed dejectedly and stepped into the dim coolness of the kitchen, unaware that Cook continued to stare after her, the old woman's mouth opening and closing like a fish out of water.

Summer tucked some flowers into a large crock and set the rest on a ledge, then noticed that the boy had woke and rubbed his fingers through the cat's fur. She walked over to the table and peered at her patient from over Lionel's shoulder. "He seems to be doing fine."

The boy spun. "How do you *do* that?"

She looked at him in confusion. "Do what?"

"Just suddenly appear, as if out of nowhere?"

"Oh." India pounced on her shoulder, and she patted the tiny head. "You mean because I fox-walk."

He looked over at the small fox pup in the corner. "Fox-walk?"

Summer looked at his pale face, and the sunshine streaming through the door. "My injun friend taught me. Do you want me to show you how?"

The worry lines smoothed from his face, and he looked like a boy again. "When?"

"How about now? Don't worry, Hunter will be fine. I'll go get Cook, and she'll watch over him."

Those vivid blue eyes clouded over, and he began to frown again. "No, I better not leave him."

Summer knew she couldn't argue with him; she'd felt the same way when she nursed one of her own critters. But he hadn't left Hunter's side for days… She picked up the crock and ran to her room, placing the flowers next to Meg's bed to brighten up the sickroom, and then rummaged through her trunk to the very bottom, and pulled out a package and carefully began to unwrap it. She rubbed the stiffness from the deerskin shirt and leggings, careful not to touch the intricate beadwork that Chatto's mother had so laboriously sewn onto them. Maria would have a fit if she knew that Summer had packed them.

She changed quickly, sighing with relief when she removed the dreadful corset, tears coming to her eyes when she stood before the mirror in her old hunting clothes. The moccasins slipped on her feet like a second skin, and her hands flew to her hair, pulling out the puffy bun and quickly braiding it into two plaits.

Over the past few days she'd explored the forest, walked to the sea, and visited with the villagers who welcomed her as easily as Chatto's people had. She couldn't figure out why people of society were so much more difficult for her to fit into, and why she couldn't be as comfortable in London or New York as she was here. She sighed and pulled at the sleeves of the buckskin. They were shorter than she remembered, but she'd been a young girl and had grown a bit since then. But not much.

Grateful that Meg hadn't woken up to see her in her buckskins, she smiled a wicked grin as she slung the quiver of arrows over her back and looped her bow over her shoulder and flew down the stairs, the absence of swishing skirts and heeled boots allowing her to be as silent as a ghost. Summer stepped into the kitchen doorway. It took several minutes for them to notice her. Cook glanced up and dropped the spoon in her hand, clutching at her chest. Bernard choked on his cup of tea. Lionel stared as if she were indeed a ghost.

Fourteen

"THESE WERE A GIFT FROM THE *BE-DON-KO-HE* Apache." The boy's mouth opened, and Summer could see all the questions in his eyes and suppressed a grin of triumph. "I'll bring home dinner, Cook. I haven't been hunting in ages."

The woman just nodded.

"But," stammered Lionel, "you don't have a gun."

Summer padded to the open door. "I have other weapons."

"But, but how…"

Summer went out the door.

"Cook," asked Lionel, "can you watch over Hunter for me?"

"Of course, young master. He's on the mend now—no need for you to worry."

He stepped toward the sunshine, then turned back. "You'll call me if he wakes? I want to be with him when he wakes up."

Cook and Bernard glanced at each other with a knowing grin.

"I'll bang a spoon on the big kettle loud enough for the whole of Norfolk to hear," Cook assured him.

He sprinted out the door, catching up to Summer with a burst of questions. "Can you really hunt with a bow? Everybody uses guns. What are those clothes made of? Is that what real Indians wear? How did you…"

She held up a hand. "To learn the way of the *Be-don-ko-he*, you must first learn to be silent." Lionel snapped his mouth shut. They took a few steps when Summer sighed and turned to face him. "That means when you walk too. You sound like a bear crashing through the leaves."

His face fell, and she mentally kicked herself. Now she understood how Chatto had felt when he tried to teach her his ways.

"It's not your fault, Lionel. You walk like all white people do, like I used to. With your head down, leaning forward—like small falls. I'll teach you to fox-walk."

She placed her hands behind his knees and pushed them forward. "Keep them bent, yes, but keep your spine straight." Summer thought she could hear his back snap in his haste to obey her. "Good, now put your feet, toes forward, in the direction you're going; now lift your foot, lower it to the ground. No, Lionel, keep your weight back; there you go. Now touch the side of your foot to the ground and roll it in. *Enjuh!* Now do it again."

Lionel froze with his foot in the air. "What's 'in-juh'?"

Summer grinned, her mind alive with the memories of Chatto. "It means 'good' in Apache. It's a word I'd thought I'd forgotten."

And after Lionel practiced for days the art of walking like an Apache, she taught him how to see as well. He had just as difficult of a time as she did when she'd first learned it, trying to keep his eyes slightly unfocused so that he could see everything around him, instead of what lay directly ahead.

"I know it's hard, Lionel. But you're doing much better than I did at learning it."

He grinned at her. His days of learning the ways of the Apache had erased the dark circles around his eyes and turned his face pink with the outdoors and sunshine.

Hunter had woken today with a hunger that made her sure the cat would, amazingly, survive his injuries, and Lionel carried the animal with him in a sling around his neck, the cat riding along his hip. The boy helped the critter to eat and relieve himself, showing a devotion that made her heart ache.

Summer and the boy spent most of their days in the forest, making a game out of eluding the men who the duke had posted to watch over her. Summer didn't wear her buckskins again; Meg had fainted dead away when she'd seen her mistress in them. So she wore the riding habits His Grace had purchased for her. Even though they had an overskirt, they allowed her an ease of movement that her other dresses couldn't match.

She loved being with Lionel. She just wished that the memories he stirred with all his questions didn't remind her of who she'd been. She'd come to the understanding that if she wanted to be accepted by society, and by the man she'd promised herself to, she would have to leave that person behind. And she would, as soon as she left the estate. Meg had recovered enough to travel, but Summer still delayed. She had to make sure that Byron would accept his son.

"Tell me about the two coatis you raised," Lionel asked one rainy day as they huddled before the fire in the newly cleaned parlor.

Summer sighed and scratched beneath India's ear, the monkey smiling and pushing his head at her fingers. "I killed their ma—mother."

He raised an eyebrow, so very like his father, and waited for an explanation, his eyes telling her that he knew she'd never intentionally harm any animal, that after their weeks together, he knew her soul better than she did.

"It was a mistake," she began, the patter of rain at the window and the crackle of fire in the hearth making her drowsy, allowing her to remember that day with remarkable clarity. "I was cleaning the shack when I heard the growl of an animal behind me. I didn't stop to think, just took the heavy broom and whacked at a snarling pile of fur. At first I thought it was a stray dog, but my pa told me it was a coatimundi, and she only woke once, to give birth to her babies. Then she died."

Summer's eyes burned. "Pa didn't like it, but I was responsible for the death of their mother, so I took it upon myself to raise her pups."

Lionel grinned. "What did you call them?"

"Whiner and Fighter, 'cause that's what each one was born doing. And they became my best friends, and even started to hunt with me. After that day, Pa decided that even though I was a girl, he had to teach me how to shoot, 'cause maybe next time, it would be a bear sneaking up on me. But I was just happy to have fresh meat for dinner every night."

Summer paused. She'd thought she'd heard the jangle of harness, the clop of hooves on broken cobblestone, but it seemed that she thought she heard that every day since the duke had left; and her stomach would flop and she'd hold her breath to listen for the sound of an opening door, a deep voice full of amused scorn. But he never appeared, and then she'd sigh with either relief or regret; she wasn't sure which.

"So that's how a girl learned to use a gun so good," said Lionel.

Summer smiled at him, knowing her heart would miss him terribly when the duke returned and she left for London. "Yes, starvation teaches you to shoot straight. And that's how I met Chatto—because he thought I had some kind of animal spirit in me, the way the wild animals would come to my call. Even when I explained to him that the coatis listened to me because I had raised them since they were little, he still insisted that *Usen* had given me a gift." She held up a hand at his open lips. "And before you ask, *Usen* is the name they use for their god."

Lionel's forehead wrinkled. "I know, you told me before about their spirits and stuff. Summer, how come everybody says Indians are savages?"

"Because they just don't know any better. Oh, injuns are fierce all right; I taught you that too. But they're just different is all, with different beliefs."

Lionel nodded.

"Chatto gave me an abandoned eagle to raise because he thought I carried animal spirits inside me.

I named the eagle Talon, and he grew strong and beautiful." She sighed at the memory of spread wings soaring over rocky peaks. "Chatto said he wanted to see how I tamed animal spirits, but I think he wanted to make sure the eagle survived—they're precious creatures to the Apache. It doesn't matter; I was just lucky he did, 'cause he saved my life."

Lionel leaned forward, those pale eyes rounded in fascination. "How? What happened?"

Summer sighed, berating herself for that slip of her tongue, wishing the boy didn't have such a talent for listening. His loneliness touched her, and she couldn't help trying to fill his need for a friend. And friends shared with each other.

She bowed her head, the words coming out as a mumble. "It's something... It involves something I did that I vowed never to think of again. I've been trying to leave that person behind, to become someone else, you see?"

Lionel's face fell, and she could see in his eyes that he thought she didn't trust him, that just like everyone else, she didn't care enough about him to share her secrets. "Do you promise not to tell another soul?"

His face lit and he nodded.

Summer took a deep breath and lowered her voice. "A stranger came to our shack. Pa was down in the mine. The man said he'd kill me and Pa. So that he could steal our claim."

Lionel's eyes bugged.

"I reached for my gun, but I never would've shot him first if Chatto hadn't distracted him. He came hollering from out of some trees." The burning in her eyes had turned to tears, and Summer felt them hot on her cheeks.

Lionel's voice trembled with awe. "You really killed a man?"

"Yes, God save my soul. And then Chatto... He took the man's scalp..." Summer couldn't go on. The horror of that day wrapped her up in a black shroud of grief that threatened to overwhelm her once and for all. She remembered that moment when she'd realized that she couldn't count on anyone else to take care of her, that she could only rely on herself. And that when she'd asked Chatto to teach her to be Apache, he'd looked at her with newfound respect and had agreed to teach her how to be a warrior.

The fire popped, and Summer shivered as the memory of the body of the dead man superimposed itself over Lionel's avid face.

Then India gave a squeak of joy and hopped toward the open doorway, and Rosey and Chi-chi woke from where they'd been drowsing in front of the fire and bounded right after him, lapping at the boots of the Duke of Monchester. Summer's head snapped up, and she stared into his handsome face, the horrible memory of that day snuffed like a candle as a shiver of delight ran through her body. She *had* heard a carriage this time; he'd finally come home! She fought the urge to fling herself at him just like her critters and was horrified by her reaction.

His blue eyes smoldered as they raked hungrily over her, and she gasped at the peculiar expression on his face. She glanced at Lionel, and then back to his father. "How long have you been standing there listening?"

"Long enough to know that you've revealed more about yourself to my son than you ever have to me," replied the Duke of Monchester, as he tried to relieve himself of her animals and his sodden cloak. He pretended not to notice the look of surprise on her face, because he knew that he'd always been the one who'd set the rule that their relationship was strictly business. Didn't the woman realize everything had changed?

Evidently not, for she gawked at him as if he'd turned into a stranger. "What ever happened to our strictly business relationship?"

Byron rolled his eyes in answer—if she didn't know already, he certainly couldn't explain it to her—then tried to suppress a shiver. The rain had soaked his clothes thoroughly, but after he'd made his decision to return to her, nothing had stopped him. Not delayed trains, a broken carriage wheel, and certainly not the weather.

He'd spent a frustrating time with Scotland Yard inspectors, who'd interviewed everyone he'd ever insulted, and managed to come up with no suspects other than John Strolm, who Byron still believed incapable of plotting a murder. With little results from his efforts, and with images of Summer Wine pressed against a boulder, her mouth parted in a moan of ecstasy, the pull to return to Cliffs Castle had been irresistible.

And when he realized that there had been no further attempts on his life, and perhaps the true intended victim had been Summer, and perhaps even now she was being attacked and he wasn't there to save her, he'd made a reckless journey home.

To come into the house and see her calmly sitting by the fire, safe and sound, and more beautiful than he remembered, made him blink stinging eyes. He'd thought about nothing but her while he'd been gone, and had so much to tell her, that when he fully entered the parlor he at first didn't see the person she'd been telling her secrets to. He assumed it was her new companion, Meg, and then he saw the boy. His son. In his house.

"Lionel?" he asked. "What are you doing here?" He felt so shocked that he didn't realize he'd barked his question until he saw his son flinch.

He could see the shift of Summer's thoughts from her confusion about his attitude, to concern and anger for Lionel at the frightened look on the boy's face. His stomach twisted with another warmth of feeling toward her.

"Because this is where he belongs," she snapped.

Byron raised a golden brow at her but turned all his attention to his son. "What about your grandmother? Does she know you're here?"

Lionel laid a hand on the cat asleep in his lap, as if that furry body brought him reassurance. "She's dead."

Byron felt the blood drain from his face and sat on the velvet chaise, unmindful of his wet breeches. "When... Why wasn't I informed?"

His voice had risen on his last words, and Summer got up and stood between the two of them, partially shielding the boy with her body. Protecting his own son from him. "Cook told me she'd written you a letter telling you his grandmother had passed, but since you never seem to stay put in one place for very long, she thought it might not have reached you. And since she didn't know what else to do, she did the right thing and brought your son home."

Summer didn't even try to keep the accusatory tone out of her voice; she had narrowed her eyes at him and fisted her hands. Chi-chi growled, the look on his muzzle showing that he didn't know who or what he was growling at, but since his mistress was angry he had to back her up. India had scampered over to the boy's shoulder, wrapping a furry arm around his neck to stroke that blond hair.

If Byron hadn't been so happy, he might've resented the united attack against him. Instead, he just opened his arms to his son, letting his face reflect the joy he felt inside. It felt uncomfortable to let down his guard, to allow his real emotions to crack his carefully constructed mask of aloofness, but he hoped that in doing so, his son would respond.

Lionel blinked, as if he'd been slapped, then narrowed his eyes in suspicion and studied the face of the man before him. Byron kept his arms open. They stood frozen that way for some time, including Summer with her mouth open in shock, the angry words he'd felt her about to flay him with frozen on her tongue.

Byron's chest began to ache as he wondered if it was too late when the boy made no move to come to him. Had he destroyed any hope of a relationship with his son because of a foolish promise he'd made to the boy's grandmother?

Lionel made a choking sound, then lunged across the room, his small frame, so like a miniature of

Byron's own, filling his arms and heart with a warmth that he'd been lacking for so long that the shock of it set him to trembling again. And the boy seemed to be adding to the wetness of his shirt.

"What in tarnation?" mumbled Summer, the words she'd held for so long finally stumbling forth. "Here I was getting ready to tell you that the way you've neglected your son is shameful, especially after knowing how the treatment of your father affected you. And now you come in here like... like..."

Byron smiled against the softness of his son's hair, breathing in the smell of sunshine and the faint smokiness of the fire. He couldn't blame Summer for her feelings; he knew how it must seem to her. And answering her would help explain it to his son, who even now had stiffened a bit in his arms.

"It wasn't on purpose," he said, speaking to her but his awareness wholly focused on the young child in his arms. He still couldn't believe that the boy had come to him so willingly, after all these years. "After his mother died, I promised to allow Lionel to stay in her home, the only home he'd ever known, with his grandmother. My father"—and his voice hardened despite himself—"would not allow me to marry Lionel's mother, and I was too young to be able to defy him. And then when I was old enough to come for her, it was too late. I would've done anything for her, even if it meant giving up my son. I owed her that much."

Summer began to pace the room, that uncanny way she had of walking making it look as if she floated across the floor. "But why? Why would she ask you to do such a thing?"

"Lionel's grandmother," replied Byron, feeling the tension in his son's body, understanding that he needed the answer more than Summer, "said that her daughter's dying wish was that the boy stay with her. That since I didn't marry her daughter, and the boy would never be able to inherit, that it wouldn't be fair to expose him to my kind of life. That he would be happier in the village."

"So, his grandmother asked you to let him stay with her? But how could you know that's what his mother really wanted?"

Byron sighed. "I couldn't be sure. But when my father died, I was saddled with two decrepit estates and very little income. Would it have been fair for me to drag him from one weekend party to another? Would I have received invitations with my son in tow? Remember, I've supported myself off the hospitality of others. And my ability to be… entertaining."

Byron hadn't felt anything shameful in how he lived before, but saying those words in front of his son made him realize that he hated the life he'd been forced to lead. That there had to be another way to restore his estates and fortune, and maybe it was time to give up the life he'd been accustomed to. Maybe there was more honor in no longer being what society called a gentleman.

"I was hoping that someday I would have a business to give to my son. That it wouldn't matter when the estates went to my half brother, because they'd be dependent on the business I'd built for Lionel, and that would give him some kind of status. Because I couldn't give him what he was rightly entitled to."

He watched Summer's graceful turn about the room. She'd picked up some followers as well; both her dog and the fox trailed behind her. "But now that you have the income from the railroad, you don't need to live off of other people. And you have the funds to get this weaving business off the ground."

"I can only keep your payment if I've earned it, and so far I've failed to do so." He winced at the word "failed," knew that the only reason he could even use it now was because he'd finally realized that it didn't really apply... but he'd have to explain that to her later. Right now, he had to find out if his son forgave him.

"So," said Summer, as if she'd come to some final decision, "even if Lionel can't inherit your estates or a business, he still needs his father. And he needs to be acknowledged as your son, bastard or not. Are you going to do that? When I leave, can I be sure that Lionel will be properly cared for?"

Byron chose to ignore her comment about leaving. He'd set her straight as soon as he made sure that it wasn't too late for him and his son. She'd never realize how grateful he was that she'd asked him all the questions that his son needed answered. She'd made it so much easier for him. "What do you say, Lionel? Summer's right, you know, although I think I may need you more than you do me. Will you stay and live with me? Can I be a full-time father to you?"

Lionel gently disengaged himself from his father's arms, drawing himself to his full, if not very tall, height. "You have always been my father. But I would... I would like to live with you, if you're sure you want me."

Byron felt his guts twist in a way he hoped would never happen again. "I have always wanted you."

The boy nodded his head, and then turned and faced Summer. "What did you mean by saying that you're leaving? Didn't my father ask you to marry him?" He stressed the word "father," and this time Byron couldn't help but smile. He especially liked that the boy's tone implied that if he'd asked Summer to marry him, she certainly couldn't have refused.

Summer's eyes widened, and her steps slowed, staring from father to son. She looked astonished that their conversation included her. When would she realize that she was a part of his life? Byron wondered.

"Yes, he did, but Lionel, I've already given my word of honor to marry another."

"Ah."

Byron frowned. Why did the boy seem to understand that if she gave her word, she had to honor it? As if he knew her and accepted her odd ideas better than Byron himself did.

The boy turned and looked at him. "Then, Father, you'll have to do whatever you can to have this other man release her from her vow."

Cook appeared at the door as if she'd been listening and waiting for an opening to pop into the room. "Excuse me, sir, but it's far past the boy's bedtime. And if you don't mind my saying, sir, if you don't get out of them wet clothes you're liable to catch a terrible chill."

Byron looked down at the thoroughly soaked velvet of the settee. "As always, you're right, Cook. Good night, Lionel. We'll talk more in the morning." They stared at each other for a moment, unsure of quite what to do to say good night to each other, when Lionel stuck out his hand, and they shook manfully. The boy followed Cook from the room but paused a moment to ask, "Summer, whatever happened to Chatto?"

She blinked, caught off guard by the question, and Byron felt sure the pink in her cheeks wasn't due to the heat of the fire.

"He went to live on a reservation. Not by choice."

"I'm sorry."

"Me too."

An awkward silence fell over the room after Lionel left, as all Summer's pets followed Cook as well, looking for their nighttime snacks.

The fire popped and Summer jumped. "Well, I'll say good night as well. Cook's right; you'd better get out of those wet…"

"Not before we have a chance to talk." The duke strode to the door and locked it, knowing from the way her body had unconsciously reacted to him tonight that there would be more than talk. That even if she'd tried to forget it, her body remembered the pleasure he'd given to her at the pond.

"There's nothing to talk about."

"I disagree, madam. It's about time I set you straight on a few things." He stalked her, watching with amusement as she backed up until she hit the wall, afraid for him to get near her. Oh yes, she wanted him as badly as he wanted her. She was just too stubborn and misguided to know it. "First of all, thank you for your help with my son."

"Help? Oh, I thought you'd be mad at me for interfering."

"How can you interfere when you're a part of our lives? No, don't say it." He lifted a finger and set it against her lips, surprised by how hot they felt against his skin. "I had plenty of time to think about our business arrangement while I was away. You see, I'm not used to failing at anything. And I couldn't understand why I couldn't make you acceptable to society, until I realized something."

She was interested, he could tell, and just slightly annoyed by his assumption that he rarely failed. He smoothed his fingers across her mouth, and he felt them tremble, felt her trying to fight the urge to kiss them. He grinned.

"I realized," he murmured, his voice dropping to a husky whisper, "that I wanted to fail. That I didn't want you to change at all. And do you know why?"

He held her with the power of his gaze. He could feel the chemistry between them, had to fight the urge to replace his fingers with his mouth.

He had to talk to her first, even if it killed him.

Then he'd *show* her how he felt, as well.

The duke did permit himself to trail his hand down her cheek, to rest at the base of her throat, to feel the violent pounding of her heart. "Because I love you just the way you are. With your nutty animals, and the way you keep a knife under your skirts, and the way you make me look at the world differently. I don't want you to change, Summer Wine. And any man who does isn't worthy of you."

"But you know my secret now," she whispered. "You know the horrible thing I did. How can you even think about loving that kind of a woman?"

He studied her a moment, the shame in her eyes. Could he have been wrong? Could her pursuit of becoming a different person be because she wanted it herself, and not just for this Monte fellow? He suspected that might be the case and inwardly cursed. This was going to be a lot harder than he'd thought. Now he'd have to help her achieve her goal so that she'd realize that she didn't need to change, that she had a man who would accept everything about her. But first, she'd have to accept herself.

"I've killed more than one man for my country, Summer. I was an officer for a time. Does that change the way you think of me? Does that change who I really am?"

She pushed a wet tangle of hair off his forehead. "I don't know who you are. I thought I did, but now…"

Byron leaned into her touch, realized that words weren't going to change anything. She'd still go back to that man, thinking it was because of her honor, no matter what he said to her. But maybe, just maybe…

He put both of his hands flat against the wall, trapping her with his arms and body. She shivered, but those wide brown eyes snapped with excitement, as if being dominated by him enlivened her. With a groan he allowed his mouth to cover hers, tasting the flavor of his sweet Summer Wine, trying to show her with his body what she couldn't seem to understand with his words. Lightning flashed and thunder rolled, echoing the feeling of power that swept over him as he plunged his tongue into her mouth, swept his fingers through her hair, popping out the hairpins until the brown mass of it tumbled around her face.

His groin ground against hers, and she moaned low in her throat, the vibration of sound tingling across his tongue. Byron wanted to take her there, against the wall, with the wind and rain pounding on the other side. He wanted to shove himself deep inside that exquisite body, wanted to brand her as his own, and knew in that moment the depth of his love for her. He'd had sex with enough women to know that this was different, that his need for her had nothing to do with the pleasure of his body. That his drive to possess her had everything to do with making her his, by spilling a part of him into her and thereby claiming her forever.

He ripped his mouth away from hers, sucking her breath deep into his lungs as he did so, trying in that way, at least, to make her a part of him. The duke stared into her startled eyes, and he didn't know what his own reflected as he tried to devour her with his gaze; but it seemed to scare her. And she snaked her arm around the back of his neck, neither pulling him toward her or letting him go.

But she has to decide, he thought. Even if it took every ounce of his willpower not to rip the clothes from her body and take her as he'd done by the pond. She needed to realize that she wanted him as much as he wanted her. And maybe then she'd also understand that she didn't really want that Monte fellow.

He'd lit the fire, but she'd have to quench it herself.

"Byron?"

Her voice felt like a warm embrace, and he tried to harden himself against the faint tremor that made her sound like a confused child. She was a woman, and she wanted him. And she'd have to take him.

Byron pulled away from her, moving like an invalid, every muscle in his body screaming in protest as he increased the distance between them. He stood before the fire, staring at the bearskin rug lying before it, remembering that as a child he'd always hated the thing, with the poor animal's head still attached staring at him with sightless eyes every time he entered the room. He hoped that Summer would change his feelings toward it from now on.

Fifteen

HE KEPT HIS BACK TO HER, HEARING HER PANTING over the lash of the rain against the windows, and he steeled himself from his reaction to her excitement. She must come to him. He peeled the wet coat from his body, stripped off his cravat, and forced off the linen cloth of his shirt from where it stuck to his back. The fire warmed his face and chest, yet he barely felt the contrast of the coldness of the room behind him because of her gaze. She watched his every move, and he could feel the heat of her stare behind him.

He unbuttoned his trousers and rolled the wet cloth off his hips, bending over when it reached his knees, grinning when she gasped at the sight of his bare bottom. He stepped out of the wet puddle of cloth and clenched his fists, physically fighting the need to turn around, to hold out his arms to her in invitation. Instead he stepped onto the softness of the bearskin rug and lay down on his side, his bottom leg straight, the other bent upward, letting his shaft rest against his inner thigh, the hard weight of it throbbing against that sensitive skin. He held his head up with one hand

and let the fingers of his other stroke the fur while he stared into the fire, and waited.

She still panted. She moved about the room; he could hear the swish of her skirts even though the softness of her tread was, as usual, uncannily silent. She stopped at the locked door three times, spun, and crossed the room only to return to it again. His ears strained for the sound of the latch being turned, the click as she unlocked the door, and for one dreadful moment he thought she'd leave.

And then he felt the hem of her skirt brushing his bare back, and he started to breathe again.

"Byron?"

He clenched the fur in a sudden fist.

She fumbled at her buttons, he heard the rip of fabric, raised a brow at the creative American curses that issued from her sweet lips. He felt the slight breeze that her gown made as it landed on the floor. She stepped over his back, between him and the fire, and knelt. Again she questioned him with his name, and he fought not to look into her eyes.

She placed her hot little hand on his chest, and he obligingly rolled over, then laced his fingers behind his head with an air of nonchalance that felt difficult to maintain as he looked up at her, the swell of her breasts the most erotic thing he'd ever seen. His shaft jumped, and her eyes widened, her mouth parted, and she bent her head and molded her lips against his own.

When her tongue entered his mouth, he curled his own around it and she snapped her head back, her silky skin marred with a frown. Then her eyes lit, the corners of her mouth tilted upward in a wicked expression that barely resembled a grin, and she kissed him again.

He could feel his arms shake as he fought to keep them from wrapping around her. His fingers ached to touch the nipples that lightly brushed against his chest. Trying to teach her something about herself was painful for him. He had a hopeful thought that maybe he'd gone about this all wrong. After all, the girl had been a virgin when he'd taken her, she'd never had a man before, how would she even know what to do?

She looped her leg over his hips as if mounting a horse and rubbed the wetness of her opening up and down his shaft. When she scooted forward, his shaft sought her entry as surely as a bee sought honey, so that with barely a wiggle and a twist on her part, the head of his shaft was poised to enter her quicker than he would have thought possible.

"Say it." He meant it as a command. It sounded like a plea.

She bent and kissed him again, plunging her tongue deep inside his mouth, telling him without words what she wanted to do. She managed to bury the tip of him just inside her folds, forcing him to release his death grip on the back of his head to grab the cheeks of her bottom. His hands nearly encompassed all her flesh, and he held her still, turning his head to the side to break their kiss.

She bucked, and he held on.

"Tarnation, what do you want me to say?" she snapped.

"That you want me. That I'm not seducing you. That you've never wanted a man as much as you want me right now. This moment. And forever."

The glazed look faded from her eyes, and she seemed to be looking inside of herself. At least, he hoped so.

"Yes, I want you. Let me have you, Byron. Let me take you as you took me by the pond."

He wanted to hold out for the "forever" part. But he couldn't. The woman had broken his will, sitting astride him, her breasts a work of art, her opening wet and hot and teasing him past all endurance.

He dropped his hands.

Summer rose up on her knees, pulling his shaft straight up with her, still slightly surrounded by her folds, and he dropped his hands again to his side. She plunged herself down, the tight, perfect wetness surrounding and squeezing him until his mind went blank and he tore fistfuls of bear fur from the rug to stop from touching her. She continued to move up and down, pulling his shaft out of her and then plunging it in again, as if to repeat that first, pleasurable jolt of entry.

He had wanted her to take him, hadn't he? To prove to her how much she desired him?

The problem was that he desired her just as much, if not more. And her movements were slow and languid, driving him beyond any reasonable man's endurance. With a low growl, he grabbed her hips, his fingers pressed into the smooth cheeks of her bottom, and held himself deep inside of her, until she stopped fighting that slow torture of him.

They stared at each other, two people joined as one, and he hoped that she felt the same sense of completeness, the absolute rightness, that came from their loving. That she'd never want another man but him.

Still keeping himself deep inside, he began to move her hips back and forth, grinding her against him, until her eyes widened with surprise and she leaned her body slightly forward, causing her nub to stroke the skin of his pelvis as well.

"Oh," she murmured, straightening her legs a bit so that she half lay, half crouched atop him.

Byron could feel the muscles in his arms bulging as he took full control of her body, pulling her backward and forward, with an increased rhythm that had her breasts bouncing and rubbing across his chest, exciting him more, causing him to grit his teeth to hold back his own explosion of pleasure until Summer reached hers.

But he couldn't hold it back and he felt himself explode inside her, with only enough control over his brain to realize, with relief, that she'd stiffened with the pleasure of her own release at the same time. This made his own pleasure multiply tenfold, and he continued to experience waves of bliss longer than he would've thought possible.

Byron slid his arms up her bare back and enfolded her in his embrace with a tenderness that he'd never felt before. "Do you really think it's going to feel this way with that Monte fellow?" he whispered into her ear. "I've been with enough women, madam, to assure you it will not. What we've found within each other is rare and unique." He lovingly kissed the bottom of her earlobe and smiled when she shivered.

Byron continued to murmur nonsense words of love until the sleep that threatened to overwhelm him eventually did, and he wasn't aware that he'd drifted off until she started to wiggle out of his arms. Summer did it with a stealth that made him realize that she didn't want him to wake, so he pretended to be asleep until she'd dressed and left the room, the faint sound of the door closing behind her feeling like a slap in his face.

The Duke of Monchester sighed and rolled over, staring gloomily into the fire. He'd made her realize that she wanted him—physically, anyway—but it wouldn't be enough. If he hadn't overheard the conversation between her and his son, he wouldn't even know that she still wasn't his. But he had, and therein lay his problem... and his advantage. Even though she'd killed a man in self-defense, it was obvious to him that she'd never forgiven herself, to the point that she wanted to become another person entirely, in an attempt to leave that other Summer behind.

But he wanted that other Summer, and he lay awake for most of the night, planning on ways to make her his. After all, she'd never get presented to the Queen with the bumbling attempts he'd made to make her acceptable to society, and she wouldn't return to New York until she'd accomplished her goal. So he had plenty of time to make her realize that she didn't need to run away from herself, or her past. Just into his arms.

Summer woke the next morning with a sense of loss. India lay atop her head, Chi-chi and Rosey snuggled up to her side, and she frowned, trying to realize what she thought she was missing. And remembered Byron.

She rose with a curse and splashed her face with the frigid water laid out on the washstand, wincing a little when she wiped the cloth over the rest of her body. She encountered several tender places from her loving of the duke.

Oh yes, she thought to herself. He'd certainly taught her a lesson last night, one that she couldn't afford to ignore any longer. Her body wanted that man, even when her brain told her not to go anywhere near him. He was like having chocolate in the house; if it was there, she'd eat it.

A very grumpy Meg helped her to dress. Although her maid's head had healed, her humor had not, and she'd flatly refused to accompany Summer back to London; any penchant she'd had for adventure had been snuffed out of her by that drive over the cliff. She tended the animals with her usual kindness and helped Cook in the kitchen, but when Summer had written to Maria, Meg had sent her own letter to Sandringham requesting her former position back.

Meg took the animals and left the room to help Cook prepare breakfast, leaving Summer alone to stare at the little desk where the letter that Maria had written her still lay unopened. She'd been too afraid to read it yesterday, but took a deep breath and knew that she needed the answer even more today. The duke had made that apparent last night.

She tore it open and read the childish scrawl of Maria's answer to her and smiled with relief. Her friend had agreed to cut short her pleasant visit with the Baron of Hanover and accompany Summer back to London. And yes, she'd also help her find another sponsor. But once they'd achieved their goal of getting Summer presented to the Queen, Maria had every intention of accepting the proposal of Lord Balkett and would not be returning to New York with her.

Summer crumpled the letter in her hand and paced the room. So far, all she'd accomplished by coming to London was losing her best friend. And she couldn't blame the duke for failing at making her acceptable to society; too much of it had been her own fault. She'd come to England to become another person, and she hadn't even tried. She could've learned to ride that ridiculous sidesaddle, she should've ignored the suffering of those birds—just like the rest of the aristocrats. Foxes were to be hunted, not to be kept as pets, and a real lady would never carry a knife.

Before she could change her mind, she reached down and unstrapped the sheath from around her calf, only fondling the grip of the knife for a moment before tossing it into her trunk. With grim determination she began to pack her clothing, vowing to leave for London this morning, even if she had to walk. Even if the duke refused to let her go.

A little twist of fear knotted her belly. What if he didn't stop her from going?

Stop it, she told herself. Of course she didn't want him to stop her. He liked her just fine the way she was. To him, she'd always be that miner's girl who had shot a claim jumper. And she didn't want to be that girl anymore.

Summer swept down the stairs, her steps faltering as she reached the kitchen entryway, hearing the laughter of Lionel and Cook. And Byron. How could she go off and leave them? What would they do without her?

She fox-walked to the door and peeked around the corner, her brown eyes widening in surprise. The duke sat on the floor with Lionel, both of them wiping tears of laughter from their eyes, Cook beaming down, and even surly Meg grinning with delight.

Then Summer saw the cat and gasped. "What in tarnation…" she muttered as she entered the room.

"Oh, Summer," crowed Lionel. "See what my father made for Hunter? Now I don't have to carry him around anymore; he can get about all on his own."

"I see that," she replied, crouching to get a better look at the contraption that surrounded the cat. The critter's back end was strapped to a box with wheels; all he had to do was move his front legs, and the wheels turned and his back end followed. Hunter kept turning to sniff at the thing behind him. Summer felt surprised that the cat hadn't tried to twist out of the confining bindings, but the animal seemed to understand and even appreciate the contraption, making dashes across the room, and then stopping to lick at a paw as if nothing unusual hung from his rear.

"Very clever," remarked Summer, meeting Byron's eyes, and then wishing she hadn't.

"Lionel and I both worked on it," he replied, looking at his son with pride.

"But you thought of it, Father."

His lip quirked as he turned back to Summer. Her eyes hadn't left his face. She didn't know what amazed her more—the new softness to his features, or that he'd spent his energy creating something that would better the life of a mere critter. The man who sat on a kitchen floor without a neck cloth, his hair uncombed and the sprinkle of a beard across his chin, wasn't the same person who she'd met months ago in London. What had happened to him?

And even worse, what had happened to her? Summer rocked back on her heels. She couldn't ignore it any longer… She'd fallen in love with him! Not the physical loving that he'd helped her to discover. This was something deeper, something that sang in her soul and made the world brighten with a light that hadn't been there before.

Summer stared into the pale blue eyes of the duke, at the fall of blond hair across his forehead, the slight dent in the middle of his lower lip, and her pulse raced, and she knew Monte had never caused that reaction in her. But Byron knew who she really was. How could she live with the knowledge that he'd look at her every day, knowing what she'd done? When Monte looked at her he saw a different person, the person who she longed to be.

She felt so confused.

Then Summer realized that Byron had been gazing at her as well, that the entire room had fallen silent, as if the others had felt the chemistry between the two of them like it had actual substance.

Byron spoke to her in the injun way—with his heart in his eyes and his love showing nakedly on his face. He reached out and brushed her hair away from her face, leaving his hand on the back of her neck and pulling her toward him, as if he intended to kiss her right here, right now, in front of his son and Cook and Meg. If she allowed him to do it, it would be a public declaration that they'd been intimate with each other.

Summer leaned forward, ignoring the little voice in her head that told her she'd be a fool to kiss him, a fool even to consider loving a man whom she'd always feel inferior to. But it was so hard to resist the warmth in his eyes...

She'd gone loco, flipping back and forth like she didn't have a mind of her own.

And then she heard the rattle of horses' hooves on cobblestone.

Byron frowned, as if some important moment had passed, his hand locked behind her head as he turned to raise a questioning brow at Cook.

The old woman shrugged her shoulders and spun when Bernard popped his head in the door. "Who is it?" she asked her husband. The butler opened his mouth, glanced at Summer and Byron locked in an almost-embrace, and disappeared again.

Meg left and then returned to the kitchen, her mouth open to announce their visitor, when she was roughly elbowed aside and the lovely face of the Lady Banfour glared down at the two of them with disbelief.

Summer jumped to her feet, only slightly annoyed that Byron's grip on the back of her head had relaxed enough at the sight of the lady to allow her to move out of his hold. The woman's lavender eyes narrowed at her, and Summer resisted the urge to apologize. Tarnation, the lady should be apologizing to her for barging into her—the duke's—home.

With a sweep of satin skirts and a cloud of lavender perfume, the Lady Banfour dismissed Summer and advanced on Byron. "Your Grace, my word, when you go to the country you really get into the role, don't you?"

Byron rubbed a hand across his unshaven chin and rose from the floor, making a slight bow to the woman. Summer frowned at the sudden change in his demeanor, that mask of boredom she'd almost forgotten settling over his features, reminding her of that hard, rude man she'd first met. "Lady Banfour, for what reason do we have the slight pleasure of your company?"

The lady winced, and Summer rolled her eyes. His nasty tongue had returned as well.

"Why, Your Grace," stuttered the lady, "I have come with the best of news to share with you... and to fulfill our bargain."

Byron frowned in confusion. "Our bargain?"

She giggled and batted a hand at him, brushing his shoulder and making Summer narrow her eyes. At least she'd had the satisfaction of noticing that as soon as Byron had stood, the lady had hunched over, trying to diminish her height when she stood next to him. Summer didn't have to do that... nor would she have, if she'd been taller than the duke. It would be an insult to him.

"Oh, certainly you can't pretend to have forgotten, after all the trouble I've gone to!" She turned to

Summer with a determined look of delight pasted on her lovely features. "My dear, I've managed to get you an invitation to be presented to the Queen. Yes! You should look amazed. But it's true, I assure you."

Summer looked from her to Byron. What was going on? What was that about a bargain?

"It... You couldn't have," mumbled the duke.

"I assure you, sir, I accomplished the feat. And it took all the charm and persuasion that I possess, including using a family connection to the Queen's favorite lady-in-waiting, to squash the rumors of Summer's unusual behavior as nothing more than high spirits!"

Summer couldn't believe it. "I've really been invited to be presented to the Queen?" It had been her goal for so long that to have it actually realized left her slightly stunned. She couldn't help the joyful smile that crossed her face, and felt sorry for it only when she saw Byron scowling at her reaction. "Now you can keep the railroad interest and continue building your son's business."

"Son," asked the lady, glancing for the first time at the boy crawling across the floor. "Your Grace, you didn't tell me you were ever married."

"I wasn't."

"Oh. Oh, well, then, he really isn't your... My, it's terribly hot in here. Isn't there a place more... appropriate for us to talk? Cook, don't tell me you've let the parlor go to ruin as well? It was quite comfortable the last time I was here."

The old woman huffed. "I do what I can, Lady Banfour, and it's as tidy as you remember, I'm sure. I'd be happy to make the tea, if you'd all like to retire there."

Summer stood rooted to the spot as the lady grabbed her elbow and tried to steer her out of the kitchen. She'd just realized the full import of what this woman had said to Byron, and couldn't believe she'd heard right. "What bargain?"

Byron shrugged.

"He didn't tell you?" interrupted Lady Banfour. "How bad of you, Your Grace. Why, at the Sandringham party, he made it quite clear that he needed my assistance with your introduction into society, and that it would pave the way, well, shall we say, toward an arrangement of our own?"

Cook coughed and Meg gasped. Lionel continued to ignore all the adults as he checked the bindings to his cat's contraption.

Summer stared at Byron, and he stared back, his eyes glittering with hostility. Why? Because she'd been happy that her dream of presentation to the Queen had become reality, and he was afraid that she meant to return to Monte? Or because she'd caught him out in his scheme? That he'd been concerned only with their business arrangement, and the money it brought him, after all?

Summer looked into his eyes. Maybe he'd felt that way in the beginning, but not now. He loved her, and the hurt she saw on his face made her want to refuse Lady Banfour's sponsorship and stay at Cliffs Castle forever. But she couldn't. She couldn't just leave Monte. It wouldn't be fair to him. Nor could she give up her quest to become a lady. It wouldn't be fair to herself. Would Byron even understand?

"You still want to be someone else, don't you?" he asked her.

Summer nodded with relief. Maybe he understood, if only a little. She allowed her new sponsor to drag her from the sunny kitchen and into the stuffy parlor.

"We must leave for London immediately," said Lady Banfour, chatting on as if nothing were amiss. The woman had to be aware of the undercurrents around her, or could it be that she was just so very good at ignoring what she didn't want to see? "We must arrange a gown for you, and the feathers for your hair, and a hundred other little details. It's best if we leave today; can you manage?"

Summer nodded, collapsing onto the settee that still showed the water stain from the duke's clothes from the night before. She felt like she'd been in a dust devil of a storm, turned this way and that with indecision and emotions. In desperation she latched onto the one thing that she'd intended when she'd come to England, before His Grace had used his charm to confuse her.

"I'm already packed."

Byron had followed them into the parlor, with Lionel in tow, but he'd stopped dead at the doorway, when his eyes had followed hers to stare at the bearskin rug. When she uttered those three little words, his face turned into someone she didn't know, someone she'd never consider rolling in fur with.

"You can't leave!"

"Lionel," she said to the boy, "I told you about my vow."

"But Father said he'd fix it. He said that he'd make sure you wouldn't leave after all. That you'd stay here and be my mother—uh—friend. Why don't you let him fix it?"

Summer glanced up at him. Byron continued to stare at the rug.

"Children," laughed Lady Banfour, "are so darling, the way they get things confused. I'm sure you misunderstood your father, dear. Now run along and play with that... whatever it is, will you?"

Lionel looked up at his father, who continued to stare across the room as if he pondered some deep mystery. The boy grunted with frustration. "It's Hunter, my cat, and I'm not confused. I think all of you are!"

When he ran from the room, Byron finally glanced up. "You were already packed?"

Summer nodded.

"Lift up your skirts."

"What?"

"I said—"

Lady Banfour blinked at the both of them, her false smile faltering for just a moment.

Summer couldn't believe the woman could ignore the conversation between her and Byron this completely. Did she want the man so badly that she'd just pretend nothing was out of the ordinary? Or did a real lady just ignore whatever didn't suit her sensibilities? With hardly a glance at Byron, her eyes riveted to Lady Banfour's face, Summer pulled up her skirts.

The lady lifted her eyes to the ceiling, commenting on the sad disrepair of the exposed beams, and Byron snarled.

"Where's your knife?"

"Ladies don't carry knives," replied Summer, dropping her skirts and watching the other woman with awe. *So,* she thought, *that's what it's like to be a real lady.*

"You'd already decided this morning, then."

"Yes." Summer tried to sound flippant. If he knew how difficult it was for her to leave him, he wouldn't be angry, he'd be loving, and then she'd never be able to resist him.

"I hope"—he took a deep breath—"that you get what you really want."

He left the room then, and the light went a little darker, and the air smelled a bit mustier, and the furniture seemed a bit shabbier. Summer noticed that the bearskin rug had mats in the fur, and that one of the glass eyes in the head of it lay half out of the socket.

She sucked down a sob, and Lady Banfour patted her gently on the knee. "Don't worry, dear. You'll get over him. And it's for the best, you know. You're from a different world and would never quite fit in."

Summer goggled at the lovely woman who had certainly been aware of everything that had been going on between her and the duke, yet had chosen to ignore and dismiss it. If that's what it took to be a lady, she had a difficult time before her.

Before Summer knew it, her trunks had been taken to the lady's carriage, her traveling cloak had been wrapped over her shoulders, and she stood in the kitchen saying good-bye to Cook and Bernard.

Summer started to give Cook a hug when she caught the expression on Lady Banfour's face, and instead nodded with as much haughtiness as she could pretend at the old woman and her husband. "Where's Lionel? I'd like to say good-bye to him as well."

"I'm sorry, Miss," said Cook. "But he seems to be hiding somewhere. I sent Meg to find him as soon as I heard you were leaving... Are you sure you're doing the right thing, Miss Summer?"

Lady Banfour sniffed. "It's not your place to inquire, Cook. I know it's rather informal here in this country house, but please try to remember your station."

Cook lowered her eyes, and Bernard just continued to study a crack in the floor.

Summer watched the interaction between the two classes of people. Oh, she'd always known it existed, she just hadn't paid much attention to it. Another thing she'd have to watch if she were to become a real lady.

"I really wanted to see Lionel before I left," said Summer, "but perhaps it's for the best." She wasn't sure if she could bear saying good-bye to the boy and trying to answer his questions. How could she explain something that seemed so simple to him and yet was far more complicated than she could ever have believed?

Summer bent down and scooped up Chi-chi and Rosey and stuffed them into her pockets, and India obligingly hopped onto her shoulder.

"You can't possibly think to return to London with those animals?" asked Lady Banfour.

Summer's mouth opened, then closed. Would she have to give up her critters too? Yes, she decided. She'd have to give up everything in order to become a new person. Hadn't she told herself that this very morning? "I can't leave them here. My friend Maria will care for them for me. She's staying with the Baron of Hanover, and I thought if you'd be so kind, we could pick her up before catching the train to London and…"

"No, no, my dear. That simply will not do. You cannot have that gypsy woman tagging along with you in London again, much less with your stray animals too. There will be shopping to do, and fittings, and of course some visits, and even a few balls… We wouldn't want anything to go wrong before your presentation, now would we?"

Summer found herself shaking her head. This woman whom she'd always found herself at odds with was now taking control of her life. If she hadn't been convinced that Lady Banfour wanted Summer's presentation as badly as she did, she'd never have gone with her.

Cook had started to cry, and Bernard had silently slipped out of the room.

Summer ignored them. "But we can drop my critters off with Maria, can't we? I need to explain to her what's happened."

Lady Banfour graciously nodded her head. "We'd best be off, then."

"Cook," said Summer, "will you hug Lionel good-bye for me? And tell him… tell him I'll miss him. Very much."

Cook sobbed and hid her face in her apron. Lady Banfour sighed in exasperation and steered Summer out of the room, out of the house, and into her carriage. Summer kept hoping that Byron would reappear and at least bid her farewell, and craned her neck out of the carriage window. The Apache inside of her wanted to jump out that window and stride back into that dreary castle.

"Summer," chided Lady Banfour, "it's most unseemly for a lady to be hanging out a window."

Summer pulled back inside. It was time that the Apache inside of her disappeared.

"And for mercy's sake, will you get this monkey out of my hair?"

Sixteen

BY THE TIME THEY REACHED THE HOME OF LORD BALKETT, Summer felt ready to throttle Lady Banfour. She did nothing but complain about the bumps in the road, what a cold autumn they were having, and what a nuisance the animals were. Summer had to constantly remind herself that she had to emulate this woman, not choke her.

Summer stared out the window at the immaculately groomed estate of the Baron of Hanover. His country house was more of a mansion, and although it had beautiful marble columns and balconies trimmed with white scrolled iron and clean windows, Summer still thought the duke's decrepit castle far more impressive.

A black-haired girl in a gown colored a violent shade of green burst through the massive front doors as the carriage came to a stop in the circular drive. Summer threw open the carriage door, forgetting to let the footman lower the steps, and leaped to the cobblestones, flying into Maria's open arms.

They danced around each other until Summer heard Lady Banfour clear her throat in disdain, and she immediately stopped.

"Who's that?" asked Maria. "And where's Byron?"

Summer stepped away from her friend and folded her hands loosely in front of her. "You remember the Lady Banfour from the prince's party, don't you?"

Maria scowled and placed her hands on her hips. "Why are ya' acting so prissy? And where is he?"

"His Grace," interrupted Lady Banfour, stressing his formal title, "asked me to help him gain a presentation for Summer, which I have done. He didn't want me to think he was marrying me for my money, you see. And now he'll have the payment from his agreement with Summer. I'm sure he's still at Cliffs Castle, making the home suitable for us."

Maria's mouth fell open.

"Furthermore," the lady continued, "Summer will have no need of your... companionship in London. I will be fulfilling that role until her presentation. We have only stopped to deliver these abominable creatures to you."

Summer winced, but dug Chi-chi and Rosey from her pockets and handed them to Maria, trying not to feel envious when they licked Maria's face with joy. A weight lifted from her shoulder when India sprang from it to Maria's to join in the fun.

Maria spoke with her lips half-closed, trying to keep pink tongues out of her mouth. "Well, ya' can spend the night, at least, before going on yore way. I'm sure Lady Banfour's tuckered out."

"Ladies do find traveling to be trying on the nerves." Lady Banfour fanned her face, and Summer tried to look wilted as well.

They spent a lovely evening with Lord Balkett and his sister. Summer watched Lady Banfour with injun-eyes, emulating everything the woman did, realizing that there was more to being a lady than just having the right clothes. When the other woman picked up a glass with pinky finger outstretched, so did she. When she laughed with only a tinkle of sound, so did Summer. When she picked at her food, wrinkling her nose at game that Summer longed to dig into, she reluctantly did the same.

Summer charmed everyone but Maria; even Lady Banfour threw her glances of approval, especially when Summer ordered the critters out of the dining room.

When Summer crawled into bed that evening, and Maria barged into her room, she realized how opposite of being charmed her friend actually was.

"What'd ya' do with my friend Summer?" demanded Maria.

"She doesn't exist anymore."

Maria rolled her eyes. "Is that what ya' really believe? That posing as a lady will make ya' a different person? That it'll erase yore past as if it never were?"

"It's what Monte wants."

"So ya' keep saying." Maria sighed and sat on the silk spread next to Summer. "But I figured the duke to be smarter'n that. What happened?"

Summer laid back down on the feather pillows. "You heard Lady Banfour. He asked her to help him get my presentation so they could get married."

"Maybe he did," Maria said. "In the beginning, before he knew he was in love with ya'. But don't ya' see everything's changed now?"

Summer stroked India's head and widened the gap between her legs so that Chi-chi and Rosey would be more comfortable where they snuggled up between the warmth of her calves. Tonight would be her last night with them, and even though she could take Chi-chi with her back to London, the poor dog would be so miserable without her Rosey that Summer didn't have the heart to do it.

"Nothing has changed, Maria. I made a vow to Monte, and I have to honor it."

"Hogwash. Yore just using that as an excuse to run away from yoreself." She sighed and lifted the silk bedspread. "Scooch over."

Maria crawled into bed next to Summer, like they used to do when they were girls, whispering far into the night about their innermost thoughts. Summer smiled at the memory and breathed in the spicy, sweet smell that Maria's skin exuded. Her friend blew out the lantern, plunging the cheerful guest bedroom into half darkness, only the flickering light of the fire illuminating their faces.

"Do ya' think," whispered Maria, "that yore the only one who has something in their past they'd like to forget?"

Summer froze. "Are you going to tell me now?"

"Tell ya' what?"

"About whatever it is that makes your eyes cloud with some dark thought at times. Do you think I haven't noticed that you've kept a secret from me?"

"No," sighed Maria. "But I appreciate that ya' haven't nagged me about it."

Summer curled her fingers into Maria's hand. "I was waiting until you were ready to tell me."

"I won't ever be ready, but… I think it'll help ya' to know."

Maria squeezed her fingers, and Summer held her friend's hand even tighter.

"Mama liked to drink," started Maria. "No, I don't think she liked to... I think she had to. It made it easier for her... when the men... ya' know."

Summer nodded.

"Anyways, that's how she died, drinking whiskey; she fell down the stairs late one night. And I wasn't sorry, Summer. That woman never should've been a mama, and she reminded me every day that I was a mistake she wished she'd never made. If it weren't for the sweetness of the rest of the ladies..."

Summer couldn't ever remember seeing Maria cry, and she didn't want to now, so she stared at the ceiling, trying to ignore the tears that rolled down her friend's face.

"When I became a woman," continued Maria, "and I started the bleeding, Mama went into a rage. She took on twenty-two men that night—a record for Hafford's Saloon—and it still didn't quiet the rage in her. So she came after me."

Summer could hear Maria panting, could feel her body quiver next to her own. Tarnation, she didn't want her friend to be going through this, reliving something that's best forgotten. "Don't tell me. It hurts you too much."

"That's the point, Summer Wine. Unless ya' face yore fears, ya'll be running away from them forever."

Summer lay still for a moment, watching the fire making shadows on the walls, listening to the gentle snores of the critters snuggled up next to her. Lord Balkett's guest room was quite pleasant, as was the rest of his home. Maria would be happy here, and Summer felt a pang of loneliness at the thought. Whom would she share her soul with when she returned to New York?

When Maria spoke again, her voice shook. "Mama stood over my pallet for the longest time with a poker in her hand. I pretended to be asleep, 'cause it wasn't the first time she'd lit into me. I could smell the whiskey on her breath and the sweat of the men who'd been on her body, and prayed that she'd go away. But she started mumbling about not letting me make the same mistake she had. And she took my legs… I fought her Summer, but she was stronger'n a horse… and she took that poker… took it and made sure I'd never have any babies of my own."

Maria inhaled a great, shaky breath. "She passed out, and I would've bled to death if Lotty and Maisy hadn't heard my screams and torn down the door."

Summer's own tears now streamed down her cheeks. "I'm so sorry, Maria."

Her friend shrugged, as if now that she'd gotten the story out, she didn't hurt as much anymore. "Nothing to be sorry about. Bad things happen to good people, Summer. And sometimes even good people have to do bad things."

Summer tossed her head on the pillows. "I can't ever bring that man I killed back to life. I wonder sometimes if he had a family, and how they felt when he didn't come home."

Maria let out a great, long sigh. "That man would've killed ya' unless ya' shot him first. Ya' didn't have a choice."

"But I do now, and I choose to be a lady. Not a knife-toting, gun-shooting savage."

The fire popped in the silence that followed. "Well, I tried," muttered Maria.

Summer's eyes closed as sleep stole over her. She appreciated what Maria had tried to do, but there was no comparison between what had happened to herself and Maria. She had a choice, and Maria hadn't. But oh, how she was going to miss her friend. Would the people she loved always leave her?

Lady Banfour insisted on living in Summer's town house when they returned to London, to make sure "nothing went wrong," and Summer agreed, watching and copying the woman's every move. The days flew by with a flurry of shopping (which she learned was an art), visits to museums, afternoon calls (where she learned the trick of talking for hours and not saying anything at all), watching the opera (where she learned to sleep with her eyes open), and of course, the balls.

Summer had never been so completely bored, or miserable, in her entire life.

Tonight they attended a ball given by the Dowager Duchess of Monchester, and Summer couldn't help but remember that Byron had been with her the last time she'd been in this mansion. She missed the sight of him with a dull kind of ache, and the thought that she might see him tonight had her heart flipping over at the sight of any blond head.

Ridiculous, she scolded herself. Tomorrow she would be presented to the Queen, and thoughts of all the rules she must remember and her very real fear of tripping on the voluminous gown that Lady Banfour had picked out for her had to be the reason for her racing pulse.

A sharp elbow jabbed in her in the ribs, and Lady Banfour hissed in her ear, "Goodness, tomorrow is your presentation, and after all the work I've done, you will not ruin it at this late date."

Summer blinked, collected herself, while Lady Banfour's voice changed to that softly sweet timbre as she turned to the Dowager Duchess of Monchester—who had obviously asked Summer a question and awaited a reply—and complimented the stately woman on the color of her gown. Summer smiled weakly, but managed to nod and do a half curtsy without further embarrassing herself and wondered what the woman had asked her.

Then she stood before Lord Karlton, who smirked at her, the gaslight reflecting through his thinning hair to the shiny bald pate beneath, and he slobbered on her gloves again. Summer tried not to grimace but gracefully turned to extend her hand to Lady Karlton.

The lady took it as if it were a bug. "I'm surprised that my dear brother-in-law chose not to attend this evening."

"Oh," replied Summer, her heart plummeting, all the glamour of the evening fading at Lady Karlton's words. She twisted her hand slightly so that Lord Karlton's slobber stained his wife's gloves as well.

"I'm sure he's still at Cliffs Castle," interrupted Lady Banfour. "To prepare his home for our wedding."

Lady Karlton raised her brows, and the two women assessed each other with malicious eyes.

"I didn't credit the rumors," said Lady Karlton.

"Well, we've made no formal announcement, but one will be forthcoming very soon."

"Will it?" replied Lady Karlton, the tone of her voice suggesting the improbability of such an event.

Summer's brown eyes widened as she watched the interplay between the two women. It reminded her of two coyotes fighting over a dead carcass.

"Most assuredly," said Lady Banfour before she sailed away in her pink skirts. Summer started to follow her when a grip like talons curled over her arm.

Lady Karlton bent over to hiss into her ear. "Before you came, he was quite content to remain a bachelor. I'd return to New York at the earliest opportunity, if I were you."

Summer bridled. How dare she threaten her, and for no reason that she could see! But a true lady wouldn't respond to such a comment, nor would she use an Apache maneuver to use the woman's grip to toss her across the floor. With an inner sigh of remorse, she stared at the other woman's hand until she let her go, then sailed after Lady Banfour, swirling her coral skirts exactly as her companion had done.

Being a lady was killing her.

Summer smiled throughout the evening, danced with the men Lady Banfour pronounced suitable, and tried not to succumb to sheer boredom. She managed a bit of excitement when she encountered John Strolm, and lingered near his group to overhear their conversation, hoping to see if he mentioned the duke and if his feelings were still volatile toward His Grace.

But their heated discussion involved gaming wagers, so she drifted off to beg Lady Banfour to retire early.

"But you are such a success this evening, surely you don't want to cut it short."

Summer scowled.

"Then on the other hand," continued Lady Banfour, "we don't want to tempt the Fates, now, do we?"

Summer grinned and followed her out to the carriage, nodding at the sad regrets of the ladies and gentlemen at their early departure. Lady Banfour had spoken truly, for she'd been a great success. Summer remembered the ball she'd attended in New York, when Monte had attempted to introduce her to his family. How they'd looked down their noses at her, stepped on the hem of her dress, turned their backs whenever she approached.

But now, when she returned to America after being presented to the Queen, all of New York society would throw open their doors to her. She could imagine the apologies of those who had slighted her, and how she'd maybe let them squirm a little before she finally accepted their forgiveness. And how Monte would then be proud to walk with her on his arm, instead of always meeting her in out-of-the-way places so he wouldn't have to explain her to his cousins, the Astors.

As the carriage rumbled over the cobblestones to return to her rented town house, Summer felt herself deflate like an empty sack of horse feed. Why didn't she feel triumphant? Nervous about her presentation tomorrow, yes, but not giddy with longing.

"Gracious," snapped Lady Banfour as they reached their front door. "Whatever is that on the steps?"

Summer gave a cry and sprang from the carriage, pulling what appeared to be a shivering bundle of clothing into her arms. "Lionel, what are you doing here?"

The boy looked up at her, his eyelids swollen and red, his teeth chattering from the evening chill. "D-didn't know where else to go."

Summer nodded, to let him know he'd done the right thing. "Lady Banfour, ring the bell quickly; we need to get him to the fire."

"Who is it?"

"The duke's son—please hurry."

Lady Banfour sniffed but rang the bell, and as soon as the footman opened it, Summer ushered the boy inside, taking him to the nearest hearth that had a fire burning. She ordered tea and scanned Lionel from head to toe. He appeared uninjured, except for the terrified look in his eyes.

"I didn't know that you were in London, much less that you knew where I lived," said Summer.

He shook his head, but his teeth still chattered so that he spoke in spurts. "Father. Drives by h-here. Every day. Some... sometimes more."

Summer felt her heart lift until she heard Lady Banfour's remark. "I'm sure he comes by in hopes of seeing his *intended*." She stressed the last word.

Summer had done an exceptional job of containing her jealousy for this woman, especially given that the woman had to mention at least forty times a day the fact that she and the duke would soon wed. But even though they'd become reluctant allies, the smug assumption snapped Summer's resolve to appear indifferent.

"You told Lady Karlton that you thought he was still at Cliffs Castle. You didn't even know he was in London."

Lady Banfour curled her lips in a semblance of a smile. "But of course, my dear, he couldn't have knocked on your door and started up those nasty rumors again. It must be torture for him that he can't even visit me here."

Summer ignored her, turning back to what was important. Lionel. She held the hot tea to his mouth, and a few swallows did wonders to thaw him out the rest of the way.

"Where's your coat?" she asked him.

He shrugged. "Didn't remember to put it on. Didn't know I'd have to wait all night before you came home."

Summer felt guilty for no reason whatsoever. "Why are you here, Lionel? What's happened?" She couldn't imagine what had brought the boy to her door. Did he and Byron have a fight? After being instrumental in bringing them together, Summer felt responsible for their relationship.

"Father's gone," he replied, his voice still trembling from something other than the cold.

"Gone? Do you mean he left you alone? Where on earth did he go?"

The boy shrugged again, and for the first time Summer felt annoyance at the gesture. "I thought... I thought he might be with you."

Lady Banfour gasped, but Summer ignored her. "Why would you think such a thing?"

"Because he said he was going to this ball that his family was giving. He was going to introduce me to them, right there in front of everyone. He bought me a new suit." And he looked down at a dapper suit, slightly soiled now. "And just as we were about to leave, somebody came to the door and handed him a note. He looked surprised. Then he said he had to go somewhere, without me. That it was important, and that I'd meet his family some other time. That made me mad, because I thought he made an excuse... because he was ashamed of me."

Summer knew it would take a while for the boy to get over that feeling, and she wished she could help him. But not now. She still couldn't understand why he'd shown up on her doorstep. "Did you see what the note said, Lionel?"

"Not all of it, he said it was private." His eyes blazed. "But I snatched at it, and the bottom tore off." He dug into his new coat pocket and produced a ragged scrap of paper.

"It has your name on it, Summer. But it's not your writing, and I don't think Father's ever seen your writing before, or he would've known it was a fake."

Summer could hear Lady Banfour collapse on the settee, the whoosh of her skirts and the grunt of the cushions, while she read the bottom part of the message:

I will be waiting for you there, my love. Come to me now. Your adoring American, Summer Lee.

Summer wrote in a childish scrawl, for she'd never had much practice at it. This hand wrote with flourishes that she'd never managed to accomplish. She thought back and realized that Byron had never seen her writing, although Lionel had, when she'd given him the letters that she'd written to Maria to take to the village.

"I tried to tell him that you didn't write that." Fat tears ran down his flushed cheeks. "But he wasn't listening; he just ran out of the house like his pants were on fire. Why would someone pretend to send a letter from you?"

"I don't know, Lionel." Summer put her arms around him and gently squeezed. "But you did the right thing, coming to me, and none of this is your fault, all right?"

He nodded.

"You stay here. I'll be back as soon as I can."

Lady Banfour roused herself. "And just where do you think you're going? What was in that note, anyway?"

"I'm going to Scotland Yard. Someone impersonated me to get Byron to go… somewhere."

"Don't you think you're overreacting?"

Summer ran for the door, sighed with relief when she saw the carriage still out front, the driver flirting with one of the maids. "Take me to Scotland Yard. And be quick about it!"

She opened the door herself, lady's manners be hanged, and jumped through the carriage door without the aid of any steps. Summer felt a push from behind and turned an astonished gaze on Lady Banfour.

"I demand an explanation," she huffed while settling into a seat.

Summer tried not to grin at the picture of the elegant lady hiking her skirts into a carriage unassisted.

They both lurched when the carriage started to move, the coachman obviously following Summer's demands with serious intent. "I couldn't tell you in front of Lionel," she explained. "But Byron's life has been threatened before… Don't you remember the saddle incident at Sandringham?"

Lady Banfour waved a hand. "Everybody said it was some kind of joke."

"A joke doesn't get people killed. And there have been other attempts as well. And now this note… I just have a bad feeling about this."

"But what can we do?" Lady Banfour's lavender eyes looked black in the darkness of the carriage. "Ladies can't just go marching into Scotland Yard without an escort."

"Watch me."

But when they arrived Lady Banfour accompanied Summer, stating it would be better than her going in alone, insisting the whole time that there had to be a rational explanation for the note. That ladies didn't just go charging about London because of a bad feeling.

Summer ignored her, her footsteps never faltering as she marched through the paved alley, into the courtyard, past the policemen in helmets and greatcoats, and into the official-looking room, right up to the desk of a sergeant. She demanded to talk to an inspector. Within minutes, she'd told her story, showed them the note, and they politely tried to show her the door.

"Wait a minute," spat Summer. "Aren't you going to look for him now?"

The inspector yawned and scratched his stubble. "Wouldn't do no good, Miss. The note don't say where he was supposed to meet you—uh, I mean, whoever wrote it. Best we can do is notify all policemen to be on the lookout for him."

"No, that's not the best you can do. You need to start looking for him now, before the trail grows cold."

The inspector and the desk sergeant looked at each other with raised brows.

"Trail, ma'am? What possible trail could there be on cobbled streets?"

"They're dirty streets," snapped Summer, completely out of patience and no longer even trying to pretend to be a soft-spoken lady. "His carriage would leave tracks; they could be followed..."

The men looked even more astonished.

"She's American," interjected the Lady Banfour.

"Aaah," they sighed in unison.

Summer knew she'd lost after that and threw the lady a look of pure disgust.

"I told you," said Lady Banfour, practically pushing her out the door. "They won't take women seriously."

"But they remembered the duke coming to them; they knew that someone was trying to kill him."

"And they said they will look for him tomorrow. I still think there must be some other explanation, and I'm exhausted." Lady Banfour shook her head and ducked into the carriage, rapping the door smartly to awaken the sleeping coachman. "Home, Jeffries."

"No, Jeffries. To the house of the Dowager Duchess of Monchester."

Lady Banfour fluttered her hands. "Are you a fool? You can't go intruding on them at this time of night."

"Not even when it involves the safety of a family member?"

Lady Banfour huffed and sat back. "They're going to think you're mad."

"Then just remind them that I'm an American."

With her hair covered in an old-fashioned cap and her spectacles perched on the end of her nose, the dowager duchess blinked groggily at Summer. Lady and Lord Karlton could barely hold their eyes open and peered at Summer through slitted lids. Whenever she raised her voice, they both winced, so she surmised they'd had a bit too much to drink at the ball.

So Summer directed her arguments to the duchess. "Then you aren't concerned about His Grace's whereabouts?"

"Why should we be?" rasped the duchess. "He goes to whatever house will put him up. I gave up trying to keep track of him ages ago. He'll probably show up sooner or later."

"And the note?" insisted Summer. "It's obviously a fraud."

"Is it?"

"I can prove I never wrote it. My handwriting isn't even similar."

The old lady sank back into the cushions. "I still think you're making a row over nothing."

Lady Banfour tsked, and Summer knew it meant "I told you so." "All right, then, if you won't help me search for him, how about your servants?"

"The servants have jobs to do, my dear," answered the duchess. "How do you expect us to get dressed and fed tomorrow if they've been out all night on a wild-goose chase?"

Summer glanced around at these loco people and realized that, like so many other times in her life, she was on her own. They just didn't care about Byron. How had he managed to survive among such indifference?

"I apologize for disturbing you," she said, her brown eyes narrowed at them. "Lady Banfour, shall we leave?"

Summer turned toward the other woman and was surprised to find those lavender eyes narrowed in thought at the duke's family as well. They were halfway to the parlor door when Lord Karlton spoke up. "Mother, perhaps we can send a note to His Royal Highness? They are good friends after all… and even if Miss Lee is wrong, it wouldn't hurt to show our… concern."

"Yes… yes, of course we should. How would that suit you, Miss Lee?"

Summer didn't turn around. She no longer had any use for Byron's family. When they got in the carriage, Lady Banfour frowned at her. "She'll never forgive you, you know. You can't give a cut direct to a duchess."

"I've already wasted too much time." Summer felt on the verge of tears. "I can't believe they care so little for him. But it doesn't matter, I'll just have to go look for him myself."

"You have astonished me so much this evening, Summer Lee, that I'm afraid you're absolutely serious. A lady *cannot* go searching the streets of London in the wee hours of the morning."

"No, but an injun can."

Lady Banfour fiddled with the brooch at her throat. Her words of protest had sounded as if she spoke by rote, and she now considered the possibility that Summer would do as she said. "Can you really track him?"

Summer shrugged. "I can try. It depends on how much Lionel can tell me."

"But you don't even know where to look, or who might be trying to kill him."

"So you believe me now?"

The lady sat back with a sigh, her perfectly coiffed hair now dragging about her ears. "I didn't like the looks on their faces, that's all. And since I announced Byron's intentions toward me, their attitude is downright hostile."

"Do you mean they might have something to do with this?"

Lady Banfour shrugged.

"But why? What could they possibly gain? He has no money—other than the interest in the railroad, two fallen-down estates, and a new business that's surely in debt."

"The title," she replied. "Although Lord Karlton seems quite content with his situation, I know his mother has always wanted the title for her son. And then there's Lady Karlton… She wanted Byron, you know. When he wouldn't have her, she set her cap on the younger brother."

Summer's head spun as she remembered Cook's opinions of the family, and that she hadn't taken that conversation seriously. What had Lady Karlton said to her tonight—something about Byron wanting to stay a bachelor until he met her? "If Byron doesn't have any children, does the title go to his brother?"

Lady Banfour nodded.

Seventeen

Summer frowned. "They could have hired someone—"

"There's also the possibility of John Strolm," interrupted Lady Banfour. "He has an overdeveloped hatred of Byron. We can't rule him out either."

Summer couldn't believe she was sitting here with Lady Banfour discussing possible suspects. Then she realized that they both had something else in common after all. They both cared for the duke. "But Byron told me the police had ruled him out as a suspect."

"The police wouldn't think of questioning his family either. Not without direct evidence. It would be insulting… and you don't insult the aristocracy without good reason."

Summer nodded at her wisdom. She'd learned that the aristocracy held more power in England than the richest man in America. Class seemed to be inbred in the English people.

They had finally reached her home, and again she flew out the carriage door, the coachman not bothering to try to beat her to it this time, and ran up the stairs to her room, Lady Banfour on her heels.

"Really, Summer. What are you doing?"

She'd already stripped off her gown and fumbled with the ties of her corset. "Just help me, will you?"

Summer dug to the bottom of her traveling trunk and, with a sense of coming home, pulled out Chatto's knife and strapped the sheath around her calf. Lady Banfour gave a gasp of outrage when Summer stripped naked and dragged out her buckskins. She ignored the lady and pulled the pins from her hair and started to braid it.

Lady Banfour wrung her hands. "Even though I think you believe he's in danger—and that you're probably wrong—have you considered the presentation tomorrow? Even if you find him, the likelihood of you being able to attend... Well, I can guarantee that I would never be able to arrange another one for you."

Summer gathered up her bow and arrows and looked in the mirror. She scooped some ashes from the fireplace and rubbed them over her face.

Lady Banfour shivered. "A real lady could never do something like this. You look exactly like a savage."

"No, she couldn't," muttered Summer. "I'll go back to being a lady again tomorrow. I think Byron's life is a little more important right now, don't you?"

Lady Banfour's mouth opened slightly, then exhaled a resigned sigh.

Summer ran down the stairs and gently shook Lionel awake from where he slept on the settee. The boy blinked and smiled at the familiar costume.

"I need you to take me to your place," said Summer. "And to describe the duke's carriage to me and show me where it waited for you. Every detail you can remember, understand?"

Summer towed Lionel behind her out the front door and leaped onto the horse that the coachman had just finished unharnessing from the carriage. As soon as Jeffries put a bit in the horse's mouth, she gave Lionel an arm up and kicked her heels into the animal's flanks.

It seemed like years since she'd left the ball, although it had only been hours, but she felt the pressure of time running out as they galloped through the streets of London. Luckily, they missed any policemen who might be making their nightly rounds and reached Byron's rented home, on the very outskirts of the fashionable district, without incident.

Lionel's face shone with excitement when she helped him off the horse. "Can I come with you?"

Summer shook her head and pointed at the muddy tracks in the ground. Luckily, no cobblestones, but bare earth, making the impressions of horses' hooves and carriage wheels all the easier to distinguish. "Tell me what kind of carriage, how big were the wheels, where did it stand, exactly?"

Lionel answered as best he could, remembering the way Summer had taught him to pay attention to details, never to look just straight ahead. "You might need my help."

Summer frowned at the tracks, wishing she had Chatto's skill, hoping hers would be enough. "Are you sure this is the exact spot?"

"Yes."

She hugged the boy. "Then we're in luck… One of the wheels had a crack in it, which makes a large enough print—see here? Enough for me to tell it from all these other tracks. We're just lucky there's a full moon tonight, but it's still going to be hard to follow with any speed."

Summer gave the boy a gentle shove toward the door. She didn't have time to argue with him, and she understood that he wanted to help. But he'd only be in the way, and she couldn't say that to him. "You have to stay here, Lionel, in case your father returns. In case I'm wrong about this."

Lionel nodded his head, but she could tell by the look on his face he didn't think she was wrong. That he felt the same horrible wrenching in his own gut. The same one that told Summer that the Duke of Monchester was in terrible danger, and she was the only one who could save him.

Summer led the horse while she studied the tracks for that telltale mark. She lost it a few times, had to backtrack, cursed that she didn't have enough light, and in the next breath prayed for the sun not to come up, knowing that she'd wasted too much time and he might already be dead.

The streets lay empty, and the few people she ran into took one look at her and hastily scrambled in the other direction. When she reached the outskirts of the city, it became much easier; far fewer tracks overlaid the one she'd chosen to follow.

When only one road lay before her she leaped on her horse and galloped at a pace through the countryside that she hoped wouldn't kill her mount. Twice she had to dismount at a crossroads and check the trail; then she'd urge the horse on even faster.

When she reached a rise in the road, she could clearly make out the outline of a small building and the orange and yellow flames of a fire that licked along its walls.

Summer trusted her instincts and headed through the trees toward the fire. Halfway there she tethered her horse and silently crept through the underbrush, the thickness of it blocking her view of the flames. But the acrid smell of smoke made an even better guide.

She balanced along a fallen log to avoid the crackle of leaves along the forest floor, stopped on the balls of her feet at the edge of a clearing, the light of the fire illuminating the two men who stood several feet away from the building. Over the crackle of burning wood, she could hear only snatches of their conversation.

"… said to make sure the duke died this time…"

"As if we didn't know what we was doin'…"

"Told her… that carriage alive."

They handed a bottle back and forth, taking swallows between breaks in their conversation. Summer had pulled her bow and knocked an arrow after hearing their first words, then pulled back on the string to let fly. But she froze, unable to release it. She knew that Byron was in that building. That these were the men hired to kill him, and the only reason she'd found them was because she had trusted her instincts, the instincts that Chatto had honed to a fine edge.

So, he couldn't be dead yet… or maybe he was, and they just stayed to make sure any evidence burned with his body. Summer shivered. The only way she'd find out was to get into that building, and they weren't going to just let her walk right in. Of that, she could be sure.

She raised her bow and took aim. Then she remembered the man she'd killed, and the flat look in his eyes, and the way he'd haunted her life. She could hear Pa reading from the Bible, *Thou shalt not kill*. She felt that stain on her soul and knew she'd burn in hell.

A portion of the burning roof caved in, and the two men laughed.

Better her than Byron.

A real lady would never be able to take another man's life. But she hadn't been raised like a flower, cared for and cosseted from the evils of life. She'd had to take care of herself, and because of that she'd never be a proper lady. And so she had the skill and ability to help Byron. She really had no decision to make.

The arrow flew from her fingers and thudded into the wall in front of the men. Summer cursed and shot again, as low as she could, hoping not to kill them by shooting at their legs. Both of the men drew pistols and started to shoot blindly into the woods, one of the bullets kicking up bark from the log she stood on. She took a breath and aimed higher.

They went down one at a time, like two dominoes falling on each other, and Summer sprinted across the clearing, kicked the fallen men, and felt a bitter relief when she saw that they still breathed. Another sprint and she stood in front of the burning building's door, pulled up the beam that locked it from the outside, and kicked it in.

Heat hit her like a tangible wall, lashed across her cheeks, and made her gasp for air. The flames lit up the room, but the smoke obscured her view.

"Byron!"

Summer slung her bow over her shoulder and dropped to her stomach, crawling across the floor just the way Chatto had taught her when they scouted game. The smoke wasn't as thick; and she could see the leg bottoms of a couple of chairs, an old torn rug, scattered garbage across the floor, and what looked like a closed door across the room. Splinters dug into her palms, the sharp little pains almost distracting her from the heat that lashed at her face. She cried out when she reached the door and pushed. Darn splinters dug into her skin even deeper. Darn door must be locked, 'cause it wouldn't budge. She flipped around and spun onto her back, pushing at that barrier with her feet. It moved something behind it. Summer pushed harder, felt the blood rushing to her face from her exertion, even more heat flowing through the crack in the door.

The door opened farther, and she could glimpse his blond hair. He must've managed to crawl to the door before passing out. Summer coughed and blinked stinging tears from her eyes. Tarnation, the man may not be tall, but he was pure muscle. How was she ever going to move him?

"Byron!"

Had she imagined it, or had his head really moved? Summer pushed at the door again, gently this time, and suddenly it gave way. He'd spun out of the way and lay there looking at her as if he didn't know who she might be, those vivid blue eyes blinking above the gag around his mouth.

Summer pulled out her knife, and his eyes recognized her, the skin crinkling at the corners as if he smiled beneath the gag. But of course she had to be wrong. What crazy man would smile at a time like this? She cut away the cloth from that handsome face. He coughed and rolled again, revealing the bindings around his wrists, his swollen hands near purple from where the circulation had been cut off too long. She sawed through those, the ones around his ankles as well, and when she could be sure he followed her, turned to crawl back out of the house.

"Summer." His voice rasped. He'd half coughed her name. He'd crawled beside her, and she glanced at him, for just a second, just long enough to see… something in his eyes. Something that tugged at her insides and settled into her soul with a finality that she knew she'd never budge.

Something crashed behind her, made a burst of heat flare that had her and Byron scrambling across the wooden floor, splinters only a minor nuisance. Summer could feel the blessedly cool air from the open door and staggered to her feet, ready to plunge out of this inferno.

And stared into the barrel of a pistol. She'd forgotten about the men. Tarnation… but she still couldn't feel any regret for not killing them.

"I knew you'd look for him."

Summer blinked through the tears in her eyes, blinded by the smoke and the contrast of the dark night from the bright flames. That had been a woman's voice that had spoken. She tried to make out the identity of the woman who stood before her, but what little she could see kept centering on the pistol.

"I never underestimate my enemies," the woman continued. "Although I never would have imagined such a ridiculous outfit."

Summer inwardly groaned. It had to be a lady… with those cultured tones and a ridiculous concern about what she wore. If she didn't know better, she'd think it sounded just like Lady Banfour…

The barrel of the pistol moved. "Get back in the shack."

Summer felt the heat of the flames behind her like a wall of lava. She wasn't going back in there—this woman would have to shoot her first. Maybe if she kept her talking…

His Grace had the same idea. "Lady Karlton, I suggest you consider your actions. Your mantle of nobility will not protect you from murder charges."

"What nobility? I'm only a marchioness when I should have been a duchess, thanks to you. Even if I hang for this, the child I carry will become the next duke, and that will be enough for me."

One of the wounded men groaned, and the lady glanced over at him for just a moment. "I knew these idiots would mess this up again," she started.

Byron took advantage of her moment of distraction. With the same uncanny speed and agility Summer had seen when he'd fought before, his leg flew up, knocking the gun from Lady Karlton's hand. Byron spun and wrestled the woman to the ground, holding her still while she tried to bite and claw him. Summer sank to her knees, watching them tussle, trying to keep an eye on the two injured men in case they fully recovered. The fatigue of being up all night, the turmoil of her decisions tonight, and the smoke she'd inhaled all combined to make her head spin.

Byron pocketed the pistol, tied up Lady Karlton with strips of her own petticoat, and did likewise with the men. He put his arm around Summer, supporting her as if she needed it. She felt surprised to realize that she did, that it felt good to have someone else to lean on, and that reaction in her soul shivered again.

He had saved her life.

They rode back to London in the chilly darkness, and their mount spooked at every little shadow. Byron rode behind Summer, and the heat of his body, and the feel of his arms around her waist, made her wish that their ride would last forever. She felt so unsure of her future and what she really wanted. Summer decided to fish. "Lady Banfour was quite concerned for you."

"Was she?" His voice sounded tired and thick.

"She went with me to your family's home, and to Scotland Yard." The horse's hooves clopped loudly in the silent night.

"But she didn't come with you."

"No, she couldn't. She's a real lady."

His sigh stirred the hair against her ear. "That's still so important to you, isn't it?"

Summer opened her mouth and shut it again. After tonight, well, she realized that she'd never be a real lady. But if she had one wish, yes, she'd still want it.

His voice interrupted her thoughts. "It just occurred to me that you could have been killed tonight, and it would have been all my fault. Although I appreciate your assistance, it would be best if you let me handle my own problems from now on."

Tears stung Summer's eyes. He made it very clear that he didn't want to have anything to do with her anymore. He was still angry because she'd left Cliffs Castle, and she'd thought that he'd understood. But she couldn't blame him.

They rode the rest of the way into town in frigid silence.

Summer woke to late-afternoon sunshine streaming through her window and Lady Banfour scowling at her.

"I tried to wake you four times," she said. "You have missed your presentation!"

Summer groaned and clutched at her throat. Why did it burn so badly? The additional pain of the splinters that had gouged her hands made her remember the night before, and the fire, and how Byron had saved her life. He'd taken her home before fetching the police, telling her again that he'd take care of his own problems himself. She'd managed to do a quick wash, pull on a nightgown, and tumble into bed. But she couldn't sleep right away, remembering what he'd said. He could handle his own life, without her interference. It'd been a long time since Summer had cried herself to sleep, but last night she'd remembered how.

"What... what time is it? Have you heard from Byron?"

Lady Banfour's back went rigid, and she sighed with impatience. "I was right about that family, but I never would've guessed she'd go to such extreme measures." She tapped a finger against her pale cheek. "But Lady Karlton is an American too. So I shouldn't be surprised."

Summer ignored the remark. "Is the duke all right? And Lionel?"

"Of course they are. They came by earlier, and other than a few singe marks, Byron is fine. Lady Karlton has been quietly sent to an asylum for the insane to protect the family name from scandal. I thought it quite wise. You, however, have bigger things to worry about. Like your missed presentation. And this telegraph message."

Summer bolted out of bed, snatching the paper from the other woman's hands. She read it twice, feeling her heart sink further with each passing second. "Pa's sick," she whispered. "Maybe even dying. How can that be? He only had a little cough… I have to return to New York."

"But what about your presentation?"

"I thought you said if I missed it, there wouldn't be a chance of another one."

Lady Banfour fluttered her hands. "Well, under the circumstances, I might be able to arrange another."

Summer started pulling out clothes and stuffing them into her trunks. "You really want Byron badly, don't you? Are you afraid that he won't marry you unless you fulfill your end of the bargain?"

"Stop doing that—a lady has her maid pack her things. And yes, I really want to be a duchess, and don't tell me social position doesn't matter to you. You came all the way to England to get it."

Summer froze, her hands fisting around the silk fabric of a rose-print shawl. Could she be right? But she had loved Monte, and that's why she'd wanted social standing, not the other way around. Well, it didn't matter anyway, because she had failed to become a lady, and after last night she knew she never would. Even if Lady Banfour managed to get her another presentation, it wouldn't change a thing. She could never be the lady Monte had wanted for a wife, and she realized that the thought didn't bother her very much.

Because she was helplessly in love with Byron. But she could never be a proper wife to him either. Even though he said he loved her just the way she was, she knew that eventually he'd become ashamed of her, that even their children would have a difficult time becoming accepted among the aristocracy with her for a mother.

A tap at the door and the maid entered, bearing a tray of buttered scones, hot tea, and pudding. Summer's belly growled, and she realized she felt famished. So when Lady Banfour told the maid to take everything out of the trunks and pack it back in properly, Summer shrugged and attacked her breakfast.

She'd have to write Maria and tell her what happened of course, but she couldn't take the time to make the trip back to the Baron of Hanover's estate. It would be a lonesome voyage, but tarnation, that wasn't a new feeling for her, now was it?

The Duke of Monchester stared at the letter in his hand as if it were his worst enemy. She was gone. Just like that. And now Lady Banfour wanted to know if he intended to keep his promise, that it certainly wasn't her fault that Summer didn't attend her presentation.

He strode over to the hearth and threw the letter in the flames, the glow and smoke reminding him of when he'd been in that burning building, sure that his life was over. And then she'd pushed open the door. He'd never seen anything more beautiful in his life. With her hair braided and her face smudged with black, and in buckskins, no less. The memory of her backside wiggling across the floor made his pants feel uncomfortably tight, and he shifted to relieve the pressure. He'd never had just the thought of a woman affect him this way.

On their way back to London, he'd suddenly realized the danger that she'd put herself in, and he hoped he'd made it clear to her that he'd never allow her to do it again. He'd felt her small waist between his hands and realized how incredibly tiny she was, how infinitely precious to him she'd become. That he valued her existence over his own.

Byron shifted again. He should never have let her leave Cliffs Castle, shouldn't have given a whit about what she wanted. Should've married her first, then helped her to realize the wonderful person she was. The quicker he went to America to fetch her back, the better.

"Father?"

Byron glanced up from the fire. The worried face of his son peeked around the corner of his room.

He'd felt like that whenever he'd approached his own father, always unsure of his welcome. Byron erased the scowl from his face and smiled, a gesture he was trying to become accustomed to.

"Come in. What is it?"

"I was just wondering… When can we go see Summer? You said she was all right, but I'd like to see for myself."

Byron smoothed the hair back from his face. "That's going to be a bit of a problem. She went back to New York."

"Without saying good-bye?"

"Her father is sick. Don't be hurt, now. She didn't have time to see you before she left."

Hunter came rolling into the room, sniffed at the boy's leg, then started to prowl the corners of the walls, hunting for vermin. Lionel sat on the floor, in the injun style he said that Summer had taught him, and stared at Byron as if he seriously contemplated his father's intelligence level.

"She was the only one who would listen to me. The only one who would go help you."

Byron shrugged. "I know."

"When someone looks out for you," said Lionel, speaking slowly, as if to an idiot, "then that means they love you, right?"

He could feel the heat flare in his cheeks. "Usually."

"Then how could you let her go?"

"Yes, how could you?" boomed a voice from the open doorway. His son scrambled out of the way, and Byron bowed as Prince Albert Edward entered his dingy rented flat.

"Your Highness," growled Byron, deeply embarrassed to be caught by his friend in such lowly surroundings. But, he decided, he might as well get used to it. Instead of asking how HRH knew where he lived, for he knew the prince had more confidants than he'd ever know, he said instead, "To what do I owe the pleasure of this visit?"

Prince Albert puffed into the room and sat heavily on the largest chair. "I've been hearing rumors... What's that?"

Hunter had wheeled over to sniff the visitor.

"It's my cat, sir," said Lionel, scooping up his friend and cradling contraption and all in his arms. "He lost his legs, sir. And my father made this for him so he can get around. Sir."

Albert's eyes bulged, and he stared from the boy, to the cat, to the duke. "I see," he managed. "Your Grace, call for refreshments, will you? I think I need some nourishment."

Byron colored. "Forgive me, Your Highness, but I have no manservant. However, my son can fetch..."

"Yes, yes." He waved a pudgy, beringed hand impatiently. "Your son. One of many surprises I've learned of recently."

"The best surprise I could've received," replied Byron, lifting his chin a notch and giving his son a warm smile.

Lionel grew a couple of inches right before his eyes. "I can put together a tray, Father. Crackers and such."

Prince Albert coughed, and Byron ignored him. He knew what kind of "nourishment" HRH meant, and it wasn't crackers. "Take your time, son. His

Royal Highness seems to have a great deal to discuss with me."

Lionel's blue eyes lit up. "About getting Summer back? The prince can do anything, can't he, Father? Why, he can get her back for you!"

Byron shook his head, and Lionel's face fell. But Albert leaned forward in his chair and nodded at the boy. "I'll see what I can do."

"Thank you, sir!" cried Lionel as he ran from the room.

The fire crackled in the silence.

"Sit down, Byron; you're making me nervous."

He sat down in the chair across from the prince, and they both stared into the fire for a time.

Albert broke the silence first. "So, you've decided to acknowledge your son?"

"I should have done it long ago."

"Am I right in assuming that you wouldn't have, if it weren't for the American?"

Byron avoided the other man's gaze, hearing the note of triumph in his prince's voice. The niggling "I told you so." "What makes you think that?"

"Because the girl is good for you."

"I know."

A log popped on the fire. What was taking his son so long?

Albert crossed one royal ankle over another and changed the subject. "The dowager duchess came to see me. With her assurances that she had nothing whatso-ever to do with Lady Karlton's... actions. I believe her."

Byron nodded. The woman had come to him as well, not that it mattered. Lady Banfour had told him that she and Summer had appealed to his family to search for him. And how they'd responded. Whatever feelings he might have retained for his father's wife and son had withered in that moment. He had always thought that they'd cared for him. If only a little.

He looked at the prince, wondering why the other man looked so startled at whatever expression he wore on his face. In his eyes. "It doesn't matter."

"I think that's why I like you, Monchester. We are so much alike, you and I. Always careful to hold others at a distance, never sure of someone's motivations. Because of what we are."

Byron avoided his gaze again, afraid that he'd see the same barren look in his prince's eyes.

"But you," grunted the prince. "Now, you have a chance for something special, yes? Am I right in assuming that this American girl brought about your reconciliation with your son?"

"She brought it about, yes. She's changed my life in many ways... Is that what you wanted to hear?"

"Yes," laughed Prince Albert. "While you're at it, you can also admit that I was right. You're in love with the girl."

Byron sighed. "Yes. But I'm not sure if she'll have me."

Eighteen

"NONSENSE. YOU'RE A DUKE! I KNEW YOU *BOTH* WERE in love with each other the moment I laid eyes on you two. It's why I have squashed the rumors Lady Banfour has been spreading, that the two of you are going to be wed."

The prince's voice reeked with self-satisfaction, and Byron couldn't hold back the smile that tugged on the corners of his mouth. Well, at least that was one thing he wouldn't have to worry about. Without the prince's approval, Lady Banfour would never consider marriage with him. He'd been saved from a very messy confrontation with the woman. He should be grateful. But all he could think about was Summer.

"And it's why I had her investigated."

The duke's brow rose in surprise. "Summer? Why?"

"Oh, don't look at me like that," continued the prince. "Do you think I'd let one of my dukes, much less one who I consider a friend, marry someone who's unworthy?"

Byron blinked. He hadn't thought much about what his prince might think at all. Hadn't thought that the man considered him a true friend. A loyal companion, entertaining houseguest, and a source of excellent gossip to his prince, yes. But that the man considered him as more than that... it was more than he would've asked. More than he would have thought anyone capable of giving him.

Albert slapped his hands on the arms of the chair in satisfaction, the rings on his fingers glinting with the firelight. "You know I like these American heiresses, with all their new wealth and bold ways. I love the way they channel that money back to their homeland... For they were English once, weren't they? And it allows my noblemen to entertain me in style, and of course, to rebuild their crumbling estates. But a duke now, well, it's best I make sure of their bloodline, isn't it?"

Byron froze, casually leaned back in his seat, and steepled his fingers in front of his chin. It hadn't occurred to him that his prince would care one way or the other about who he married. Summer's lineage hadn't mattered to him; he'd even considered himself superior to this Monte fellow because the man couldn't see past that to the treasure beneath. But if his prince disapproved of the marriage...

Then he smiled behind his fingers, realizing that it wouldn't matter to him. Not a whit.

"Well, you may smile," said Prince Albert. "Did you know the girl's mother is distantly related to the Earl of Fenwich? My sources had an easy time of it, once they'd located the girl's mother's family."

"What? Are you sure?"

The prince snorted. "I brought the papers with me; they're out in the coach. You can study them later, but for now, I assure you, the girl comes from an excellent line of lords and ladies."

Byron stood and paced the room, the amused eyes of his prince following his progress. Could it be true? All this time Summer had been trying to be a lady, when she was actually descended from a line of them? Byron paused and snapped his fingers. He remembered, when they'd been trapped in the carriage, how he'd made her talk to keep her fear at bay. And how she'd mentioned that her mother had come from wealth, had given it up to marry her father, and that was why he was obsessed with finding gold. So that he could give Summer everything he felt he'd taken from her mother.

Of course, everyone in America was descended from the English in some way. But a traceable direct line!

He staggered with another sudden thought. He'd hoped that it would be an easy thing, to follow her to America and make her his, that this Monte fellow wouldn't want her, since she'd failed in her goal to be presented to the Queen.

And since he'd thoroughly ruined her reputation.

He didn't even try to suppress an arrogant smile at the thought.

But what the prince had discovered was worse than a presentation, which still might not have guaranteed Summer's acceptance into New York society. This certainly would. And then what were his chances of getting her back?

"I've located the girl's family as well."

He glanced up in horror at the prince's words, realizing that the man was enjoying himself immensely.

"It's in the papers I'll give you. She might want to meet them… but I'll leave that up to you." The prince eyed him shrewdly. "I'll leave it all up to you, whether to tell her or not. My goal in having her investigated is satisfied." He leaned back and crossed his hands over the bulge of his belly. "So, that's why I came today. To tell you that you have my royal permission to go after the girl and bring her back. And that I'll be looking forward to a party in my honor at your newly refurbished estate."

Lionel entered the room, carrying a tray covered with an odd assortment of snacks, but most importantly, a bottle of brandy and two glasses.

Byron ignored Albert's raised eyes at his rudeness and poured himself a drink and downed it in one swallow. What was he going to do now? If he showed Summer the papers, then this Monte fellow would happily marry her, regardless of her reputation.

If he didn't tell her, he'd take away her heart's desire of becoming a real lady… and deprive her of a family she'd never known.

He raked the hair off his face with a violent movement. Well, he'd have sufficient time to think about it on the journey to America. He turned to his son. "Lionel," he said. "We are going to America to fetch Miss Summer home."

The boy whooped, and Albert smiled with satisfaction, and Byron's next words went unheard by anyone but him.

"One way or another."

Summer stood by the newly dug grave, staring down at Pa's coffin, trying not to cry. She shivered in her heavy coat, unable to get used to New York's winters, still astonished at every fall of snow, the way it coated all the city's dirtiness and left it looking like sugar-coated candy.

Soft flakes fell on the coffin, a prelude to the dirt that would soon bury the only family she had left in the world.

She refused to look up at the few other people surrounding Pa's graveside, mostly business partners and solicitors whom she'd only met a few times. She refused to throw the obligatory flower on top of his coffin, signaling an end to the service and allowing the impatient diggers to begin throwing earth over it.

When she'd returned to New York, Pa had been beyond the help of the physicians who attended him. She'd written letters to Monte, begging him to look at Pa himself, hoping that there was something he could do. But Monte hadn't answered. In desperation, she'd even gone to his home, to be turned away at the door as if she were some beggar.

Summer fisted her gloved hands. News of her... adventures had reached New York faster than she had; the gossip columns had been full of headlines about "the social-climbing American heiress who showed her true colors." It had been foolish of her to think that Monte wouldn't realize that they were referring to her, foolish of her to think that she'd ever be accepted into society.

She hadn't expected Monte to flout his entire family and honor his proposal; she'd failed to live up to their agreement, after all. But she'd thought he'd come as a friend, to help her save Pa.

Summer blinked snowflakes from her lashes. She had only herself to think about now. Pa had been the one to bring her to New York, to insist that she lead the life that he'd deprived her mother of. He'd insisted on buying the fancy clothes and teaching her to talk right. And when she'd met Monte in the park and their relationship had blossomed, Pa had encouraged her, telling her how proud he'd be to have a man of such social standing in the family.

And when she'd told him of Maria's plan to go to London so that she could gain social acceptance among the New York elite, Pa had whooped for joy and bustled her off himself.

And now he was gone. Did anything really matter anymore?

"Pa," she whispered. "I can't be a lady, okay? I can only be me."

She felt him answer, a whisper of wind through the naked tree branches, a swirl of snow that lifted the hats of his business associates and sent them scrambling across the graveyard in pursuit.

If only she'd had the courage to tell him that while he was alive... but to Summer's surprise she felt this great weight being lifted from her shoulders. She'd failed at becoming a lady, but what did it matter now that Pa was gone? She could now do whatever she liked, be whatever she liked, and not have to worry about disappointing anyone.

She could... could buy herself a ranch... and raise cows! She could dress in pants every day, become a real cowgirl... and even if any of her new neighbors found out she'd killed a man, they wouldn't care. Because she wouldn't be pretending to be a lady.

But for some reason this beautiful fantasy seemed hollow and flat. And she realized that she wasn't used to being lonely anymore, not since she'd met Byron. He'd filled up this great empty space inside of her, and she hadn't realized it until she'd left London.

But the duke needed a lady for a wife, and she couldn't build a life by feeling inferior to anyone.

The diggers crunched their shovels into the frozen ground, and she glanced up to find them scowling at her with impatience. Summer dropped the flower onto the coffin and turned.

She thought for a moment that she saw a vision, like the ones Chatto had told her about, when she recognized Monte walking toward her, an elderly woman on his arm... and could it be? Mrs. Astor! With a gaggle of her followers, all dressed in black, to come and pay their respects... to her pa? Monte wouldn't come to save her pa, and now he had the nerve to show up at the funeral, with all his socially respectable family in tow.

Summer felt such a rush of anger that she couldn't breathe, couldn't speak.

"Miss Summer, I'm so terribly sorry," said Monte.

Something strangled in her throat. She hadn't seen him for over half a year, but he looked the same as she remembered, sounded the same as she remembered. Then why did he feel so different? She craned her head to look up at him, remembering the way her neck would get a crick in it when he kissed her. Remembering how perfectly she and Byron fit together when they kissed.

"Your letters just reached me," he continued, "and I was also informed of your visit of a few days ago. I've let go my footman for denying you entrance into my home. I must beg your forgiveness; if I had any idea that your father was ill…"

He's lying, thought Summer, seeing the sweat on his upper lip and the shiftiness of his eyes. But why? Why should he care to reconcile with her now? And who was the little old woman who kept staring at her with misty eyes?

Monte looked down on the gray head of the woman on his arm and smiled. "I see you're wondering who I brought to convey her respects? Miss Summer, I have the pleasure of introducing you to Gertrude Tarkington, your maternal grandmother."

Summer blinked.

"You look just like your mother, child," sniffed Mrs. Tarkington.

Monte patted her gloved hand. "You'll be astonished to know, as surely as I was, that your mother comes from one of the most respectable old New York families, with a heritage that traces back to English aristocracy."

Summer shook her head. Tarnation, was this some kind of joke? How could Monte just blurt something like this without any tact whatsoever, and at her father's funeral, no less? Lady Banfour had taught her that much about manners anyway.

"I don't understand." Summer couldn't help glancing at Monte's cousins, the Astor family, noticing the way they kept smiling at her with such friendliness. The last time she'd seen them was at the Astor ball, and they had pulled the hems of their skirts away from her as if she had a disease.

"Oh dear," said Mrs. Tarkington. "Monte, I told you this would be too sudden for the girl. Why, I've had days to get used to the idea, and it still seems like a miracle that we found each other." The old woman smiled, the wrinkles radiating from that expression all across her face. "You see, dear, when your mother married your father, well, needless to say your grandfather was quite upset."

Tarnation, thought Summer. *I have a grandfather too.*

"He swore," she continued, "that if she married that uncivilized mountain man he never wanted to have anything to do with her again. And then when he settled down and regretted his harsh words, they just seemed to have disappeared into the American wilderness."

"But Pa and I lived in New York for two years before I left for London. Why now?"

Mrs. Tarkington—Summer couldn't think of her as Grandmother yet—pulled a handkerchief from her pocket and dabbed at the tears in her eyes. "How were we supposed to know, dear? New York is a very large city. Why, if it weren't for that kind Englishman…"

Monte stepped between them. "Don't you realize what this means, my dear Summer? We can announce our engagement now, without fear of my family opposing the match." He glanced over his shoulder at Mrs. Astor, who nodded her head benignly at him in agreement.

But Summer had recovered from her shock and narrowed her eyes at him. "I'll get to you in a minute. Now, Mrs. Tarkington, what about this Englishman?"

Monte took a step back, his eyes looking almost fearful. The old woman smiled at Summer with a dreamy look on her face. "Why, he was the kindest man, very dignified and gracious! My neighbors are in a lather of jealousy that I had an actual duke in my parlor."

Summer felt as if she'd been punched in the gut. Byron was in New York? Why? And how would he know anything about her family? She still couldn't believe she had family... She thought she'd just buried the only family she had. She should be overjoyed, yet for some reason that weight that had lifted earlier settled back on her shoulders.

Summer interrupted the older woman's praise of Byron. "Why did he come to see you?"

"Well, he said that he'd come across some papers regarding a friend of his and felt it was his duty to let me know that my poor daughter had passed on, but left me a granddaughter—that's you, dear. And that this very girl lived right here in New York, and that he'd vouch for her character, and wouldn't we like to meet her? Of course, I was overjoyed at the news... It's almost as if our long-lost daughter has returned to us. Fortunately, you don't look anything like him"—and she nodded at the freshly dug grave—"so I'm sure Mr. Tarkington would have no reason to disapprove of you whatsoever."

Summer felt the blood rush to her face.

"Especially when you're the good friend of the Duke of Monchester. But, well, you come from royalty yourself, so it's not surprising."

"From royalty?" Summer couldn't decide whether to be angry or burst out laughing.

"Why, yes, dear. A fine line of lords and ladies are in your ancestral tree. And I must say, the name Tarkington is at the top of the social list here in New York—with or without that connection—but it's interesting nonetheless that the duke pointed this out."

Summer studied the wizened old woman. Her narrow shoulders barely held up an elegant, ermine-trimmed black wool cape, and next to Monte she appeared so tiny that from a distance she might be taken for a child. With a wealth of silver hair, a rather prominent nose, and eyes of brownish green, she didn't look anything like Ma. But then, memory of Ma was fuzzy anyway. She considered for a moment that Byron might have forged the documents to fulfill a sense of duty about their business arrangement. Family connections would gain her more social acceptability than meeting the Queen of England. She dismissed it with a shake of her brown hair. He was too honorable to do such a thing. Somehow he had tracked down her family for her, when she didn't even know she had any.

With a start, Summer realized that she believed all this... but why had Monte brought the old lady to her? Why not Byron? Maybe he still didn't want anything to do with her. Maybe she'd given up her only chance with him when she'd left Cliffs Castle.

But Monte wanted her. And the formidable Mrs. Astor obviously approved of the match now. They all kept staring at her as if they longed to welcome her back into the fold.

Byron had given Summer everything she'd ever wanted and then some. *No*, she reminded herself. Everything Pa had wanted. Time to stop lying to herself. She didn't want to live the rest of her life with this weight back on her shoulders. It was time she confessed what she was, what she'd done, and accepted it. Summer squared her shoulders, cocked her head sideways, staring up at Mrs. Astor and an even-taller Monte. She'd been trying to be a lady, and all along she'd already been one. Did that make any sense at all?

Snow swirled through the graveyard, the sound swishing in her ears, combining with the thunk of the dirt as it hit the coffin behind her in a sort of macabre melody. Summer refused to give herself time to think about what she was going to say. If she didn't have the courage now, she never would.

"I killed a man."

Old Lady Tarkington blinked, a smile still plastered on her face. Mrs. Astor and her nephew, and the girls who followed her about like ducks with their mother, gasped in unison. Monte just stared at her as if she'd grown two heads.

"I beg your pardon?" he managed.

"I told you that I grew up in a shack in the Arizona mountains and had an injun for my best friend. I had to learn to hunt and shoot and take care of myself, 'cause there wasn't anyone to do it for me. But… I never told you that I shot a man… a man who tried to shoot me 'cause he wanted our claim."

One of the younger girls made as if to faint, and Monte steadied her with an iron grip. "Why are you doing this?"

"Doing what? Telling you the truth about me? I'm tired of trying to be something I'm not, Monte. I won't do it anymore, not for you or anyone else."

To Summer's complete astonishment, Mrs. Astor stepped forward. "If you're trying to shock us, young lady, you have succeeded admirably. However, anything you might have been forced to do in your youth because you were unjustly deprived of your proper childhood can certainly be overlooked. With the guidance of your dear grandmother, I'm sure she can mold you into a proper lady."

Summer felt a noose tighten around her throat. Ever since she'd left Arizona, she'd felt like she'd stepped into a different world, into a role that she wasn't suited for. Into a life that shone on the surface with glitter and polish, but had no substance for her. Only with Byron had she felt like she'd become herself… when he was supposed to make her into something other than that.

Mrs. Tarkington kept smiling and nodding her head, Monte looked at her with relief, and Mrs. Astor held out a hand. Summer stepped back as if a snake had tried to bite her. The same woman who had scorned her for being nouveau riche now held her hand out in welcome. Now that she'd been proven to be one of "them," it didn't matter what she'd done.

Summer bit her lip. She'd been a complete fool. These people didn't care about what was inside a person, only what showed on the outside. How could she ever have desired to become one of them?

"From now on I will do as I wish, without thought of anyone else's ideas about what a lady is or isn't. Because... because"—Summer backed away from the group—"I happen to like myself just the way I am."

Summer turned and marched through the snow back to her waiting carriage, realizing that she'd spoken the truth, that somewhere along the way she'd come to accept herself. And she didn't really care whether she saw any one of those people ever again, even her newfound grandmother. If her family hadn't accepted her pa, well, then, they didn't need to accept her either. It would be their choice and their loss, but she wouldn't change herself to make them love her.

A grin started at the corners of Summer's mouth. Every third step, she gave a little skip. She was Summer Wine Lee... and she could shoot the spots off a card, ride like the wind, and walk like an injun. Her grin spread into a smile. She carried a knife under her skirts and rescued critters and loved a duke named Byron. She could never pour tea properly, or get her hair to stay up in a bun, or speak in a breathless whisper—and she didn't care!

She skipped all the way back to her carriage, the coachman giving her a frown of disapproval when she clambered up the steps laughing, because how could he understand that the saddest day of her life had turned into the happiest?

The carriage bounced along back to the hotel, Summer plotting madly inside, oblivious to the traffic surrounding them. Fine gentlemen dashed through the snow with their top hats tilted forward against the wind, snowflakes fell on the brownstone porches, ladies in their finest browsed the upscale shops. And Summer barely noticed any of them.

Because she had a duke to catch, and all she could see was fine gold hair, crystal blue eyes, and full lips with a small cleft in the bottom one. She'd been a fool not to realize that she could never feel inferior to him. How often had he told her that he liked her just the way she was? But she hadn't believed him, she couldn't, until she realized that she liked herself too. She was completely worthy of him... but how could she let him know that?

She jumped out of the carriage when they reached the hotel, the doorman near breaking his arm to get the door open for her. She ignored the lift as usual and ran up the stairs, her determination growing with each pounding step she took. When she entered her room, Lefty did his usual three-legged leap into the air, Moo-moo sprang to her skirts and stuck there, and pony-sized Sweetie slobbered all over her face. The poor critters had missed her when she went to London, and tried to never let her forget it.

It took a good twenty minutes of loving from her before Moo-moo launched herself to her usual perch on the draperies, and Lefty curled himself back up on her pillow, and Sweetie sprawled near her feet, seeming to take up half the room.

Summer stared at the stationery she'd lain out on the little writing desk, the hotel name engraved in gold along the top of it. What if he didn't come? What if he ignored her messages just as Monte had? She began to write hastily. Well, then, she'd just go after him herself.

When she delivered her envelope to the hotel clerk, he eyed it in consternation. "But, Miss, there's no address on it."

Summer threw up her hands. "Tarnation, he's the Duke of Monchester! Are you telling me that half of New York doesn't already know where he's staying?"

"Oh yes, of course. I... I'm sure we can locate him for you."

Summer felt sure of it. She had a feeling that the duke would not be hiding. She ran back up the stairs and had to go through another twenty minutes of loving before her critters would settle down and she could prepare for her seduction of the Duke of Monchester. She'd decided that seducing him would be the easiest way to show him he couldn't live without her. They always seemed to be in harmony with each other when... well, when they were loving each other.

Summer soaked in a bath until her skin wrinkled, washed her hair twice with rose-scented soap, used all the tricks that Lady Windolm had taught her, and stood in front of her wardrobe for hours, pondering her choices. The red silk would be too obvious, and the gold made her eyes look like amber but had a million tiny buttons. But the rose-printed tea gown would match her perfume, and best of all, she wouldn't need to wear a corset with it.

Having decided on the print, Summer pondered her underthings. She picked up the knee-length drawers that Byron had bought for her in Paris, the ones with the slit in the crotch that made going to the water closet much easier, but provided such a draft that

Summer had never worn them. Now, however, they seemed the perfect attire for what she had in mind.

She slipped the sheer silk over her legs and felt her face burn. She hadn't realized how difficult it would be to purposely seduce a man. Whenever she and Byron had come together it had just happened, as naturally as taking the next breath.

Summer stood before the full-length mirror and watched her face color again. No proper lady would invite a man to her hotel suite, dressed in an informal tea gown, with slits in her drawers. She grinned at her reflection.

It took a considerable amount of time to disengage Moo-moo's claws from the sitting room curtains and establish the cat a new perch on her bedroom ones. Thank goodness she had thought to have the hotel's walker take the dogs out; they should be fine for hours. Lefty had already fallen asleep on her pillow, his pink belly exposed, all three paws in the air. Sweetie had hidden under the bed as soon as he heard running water, afraid the bath might be for him, the big baby. Summer let out a nervous giggle at the sight of Sweetie's back end sticking out from under the bed. Too big to fit under it, he thought that as long as he hid his head, Summer couldn't see him.

She went into the sitting room and waited. And thought about how she might go about seducing a duke. And waited some more.

Nineteen

BYRON PACED THE FLOOR OF HIS HOTEL ROOM, glancing up at the ceiling every few minutes. Summer Wine Lee lived somewhere above him in one of the posher suites. His smaller room on the ground floor lacked a sitting room, so he continually bumped into the bed where Lionel sat reading.

"Father," said the boy in frustration. "I keep losing my place every time you jog the bed."

"Sorry."

"You should have let me deliver the note to Summer. Then she would have sent for you by now."

Byron swept the hair off his face. Lionel might be right; the boy he'd hired to deliver the message had looked scornfully at the few coins the duke had placed in his hands for payment, so how could he be sure his message had been delivered?

Bloody hell, how could he be sure of anything he'd done? He should have burned the papers his prince had given him, not handed them over to Mrs. Tarkington. And then, to compound his stupidity, he'd gone to that Monte fellow and told him as well.

The eager suitor had practically fled from the room to meet his "affianced family," as he called them.

The duke smacked his shin into the bed frame this time and suppressed a curse at the look on his son's face. He sat down hard and rubbed angrily at the bump. What had he been thinking? So what if the girl didn't realize what a wonderful treasure she was... Was that such a bad thing? Since when did his concern for someone else get in the way of what he wanted?

He should've married her first and then worried about her self-esteem. He should've controlled his anger about her stubborn insistence to change herself and told her that he had no intention of marrying Lady Banfour. Instead he'd let her leave Cliffs Castle without trying to stop her, trying to punish her for not seeing herself as he did.

And he'd handed Monte to her on a silver platter, without knowing if she'd realize that the man would never be good enough for her. The enormity of the risk he'd taken had finally occurred to him and shattered his resolve to let Summer find her way back to him. In a fit of panic he'd written a note asking to see her.

And then paced this room, considering several ways he could get her to commit to him. But he still couldn't decide what to do.

He glanced over at his son's bowed head. "You still think we should just kidnap her?"

Lionel nodded. "She loves us. She'll let us do it."

"What am I thinking?" Byron glared at the ceiling again. How could he even consider listening to a ten-year-old's suggestion? It stood testament to his rattled state of mind. Perhaps it hadn't been a good idea to stay in the same hotel that Summer did, because he'd almost bumped into her several times, and the sight of her weakened his resolve to let her come to him.

And then he'd seen her this morning, walking with that unusual grace of hers through the hotel lobby, on the way to her father's funeral. Her usually tan face had looked so pale in her black mourning clothes.

He'd had to physically stop himself from going to her.

Byron came to a decision. He'd always liked his first option, that of seducing her. If he were honest with her and told her how wonderful she was, she wouldn't believe him, unless she'd already come to that conclusion herself. And after all that he'd done so she could discover that, there was no guarantee that she had. And it was time he took what he wanted.

"Lionel," he announced. "I'm going to stick to my own plan."

His son looked up at him in disgust. "I don't think a bunch of kissing's going to solve anything."

Byron grinned. That was as close as he'd been able to get when explaining his plan to the boy. Actually, he'd been grateful that Lionel hadn't understood the full meaning of the word "seduction." He'd like to resolve his own women problems before facing any his son might have.

A rapid knock sounded at the door, and they both froze for a moment, then lunged at the handle.

Byron managed to grab the note out of the hotel messenger's hand only because he stood a bit taller. He tipped the uniformed lad and closed the door, his back flat against it, holding the note as if it carried the weight of the world upon it.

Which it did. His world, anyway.

"Father."

Byron shrugged and tore open the seal. He breathed a sigh of relief. She wanted to see him… and her room number was written next to the top of the hotel's letterhead.

"Er, this might take a while."

Lionel picked up his book. "I'll be fine… and don't worry, Father. She can't live without us."

Byron wished he felt half as confident as his son did while he took the lift up to Summer's room. But by the time he reached her door, he felt some of his old self-assurance returning. After all, he was exceptionally good at seducing women. Hadn't he lived on his charm for years? Didn't the finest homes in London open their doors and beg for a visit from him?

He pounded on her door.

Summer jumped a foot and clutched at her heart when she heard the knock. Tarnation, she looked just like Cook! She threw her hand down. He was here! He'd come, after hours of waiting… and she still didn't feel ready. She tiptoed to the door and grasped the brass doorknob, and then a cold wave of realization washed over her. She spun and looked wildly around the room. There was no place for them to… dadburn it! Why hadn't she thought of this earlier? Could she let the critters out of her room while she brought him to her bed? Oh, that would spoil his mood entirely, and her seduction would be a failure.

She studied her carved desk and its hardback chair, the tiny tea table with its cushioned seats, the small love seat with its upholstery buttons. She couldn't even imagine the possibility. She glanced at the fireplace, with its hearth of polished stone and its absence of a bear fur. Her eyes finally came to rest on the armless chaise near the window. Although very narrow, she thought it might be the only possible option she could imagine. They were likely to tumble off and break their necks.

Summer choked on a hysterical giggle.

Byron stood outside the door and unashamedly pressed his ear against the gilded surface. What was taking her so long? He swept the hair off his face and happened to glance down, noticing a white sliver of paper under her door. He snatched it up, realizing that it was his message to her, and it hadn't been opened. So, her note to him hadn't been in response to his. Now he couldn't be sure of why he was here. What did she want with him? How had she even known where to reach him, if she hadn't read his note?

His self-confidence started to quiver again, and he snapped his spine rigid. It didn't matter why she sent for him, whether to thank him for finding her family or to curse him for it. It didn't change his intentions for this meeting whatsoever.

He lifted his hand to pound the door again, when it opened.

It had been too long since her golden eyes had looked into his own; he felt the force of her gaze like a blow to his gut, and he could only stand there and stare at her like some love-struck ninny. Where had the charming seducer gone to? He tried to take control of the situation. "Aren't you going to invite me in?"

As soon as Summer saw him, she remembered the rock by the pond. Now, if they could make love on a rock, somehow they'd surely manage it on that narrow chaise, wouldn't they? She had to suppress another giggle. Tarnation, had he said something to her? Surely she'd seen his lips move.

"Won't you come in?" Her voice had a breathless quality that Lady Banfour would've been proud of.

She stepped to the side, and he brushed the front of her gown as he passed her, almost as if he'd done it on purpose. Her nipples tingled and she swallowed. How was she going to seduce him if she couldn't maintain her own composure? If she started falling all over him, how would she know when he fell on her? She knew she wanted him, but the point was to find out if he still wanted her.

Summer took a deep breath and closed the door firmly.

Byron's arm still tingled from where he'd brushed against her. He'd done it on purpose, of course, but his reaction to that brief contact unsettled him. Since when had the mere touch of a woman made him half-hard? He'd have to show more restraint. After all, his plan was to seduce her, and then once he had her in the palm of his hand, tell her that they would be married, and that she had no say in the matter. If he couldn't keep himself in control, he'd have her on that little chaise in seconds, and she'd be the one dictating to him.

Byron leaned a casual arm over the mantel, shook back his hair, and gave her his most disarming smile. Unfortunately, she smiled right back at him, lights sparkling in her eyes, that elfin nose upturned in such a look of mischief that he dropped his arm and took an involuntary step toward her.

"I, uh," said Summer, trying to recover from that smile he'd given her. "Ordered up tea… It's probably cold. But. Do you want some?" She wished her mind hadn't followed the feelings in her legs and turned to jelly. But, tarnation, that smile he'd given her could melt an iceberg.

"Yes. It doesn't matter." Byron ran his fingers through his hair in frustration. What had happened to the man who had the reputation for wielding his tongue like a sword? He could barely get two words out. "That it's cold, I mean." He strode over and slammed himself into a chair.

Summer blinked. Why would he be angry with her? This wasn't going as well as she'd hoped. It was time to be more direct. She flowed over to the table and picked up the porcelain teapot and leaned over to pour cold tea into his cup. She leaned very far over, farther than necessary. Far enough that the loose neckline of her tea gown dropped open, and if he would only glance up at her, he could see clear to China.

"You're much better at that," he murmured, his eyes never leaving the pot.

Summer's hand trembled. His voice had that husky quality to it, the same tone he used when he'd ask her if she wanted more… Yes. Oh yes. "Better at what?" she said aloud.

"The art of pouring tea," he replied. Byron had felt her reaction to his voice with a sense of triumph but made the mistake of looking up. Bloody hell. Her gown gaped open wide enough to reveal each rounded breast and, could it be? Yes, the rosy hue of taut nipples teased his eyes as well. Made his mouth water.

He jumped to his feet and held the back of her chair. "Forgive my bad manners, won't you sit down?"

Summer scowled and plopped down into the chair, letting him push it in for her. She'd thought he surely couldn't resist the temptation she'd hung right out in front of him. Maybe she needed to be more sensual? She reached up and patted at the strands of her hair bun. "Well," she breathed. "I may have improved at pouring tea, but my hair still won't stay up properly. I might as well let it down." She undid a few hairpins, knowing that ladies never let their hair down unless going to bed. The idiot man knew that—why, he's the one who'd taught it to her!

She felt the brown mass of her hair tumble down, caressing the sides of her face and pooling in the curve of her shoulders. She just wished the feel of it didn't remind her of the whisper of *his* hair across her face when he lay above her.

Summer shivered.

Byron stifled a groan. He knew she acted without thought, innocent of what such a simple action as letting her hair down might do to him. But it made her look wanton, brought up images of her mouth parted in ecstasy, that golden brown hair spread wildly around her face, until he couldn't resist the temptation of coiling it in his hands...

He shifted where he sat, trying to ease the pressure of his ever-hardening erection. He had to take control of the situation if it killed him. He reached across the small table, smoothing the hair off her shoulders, caressing it back off her face. "There. It looked a mess. Now, what did you want to see me about?"

Summer had to fight the urge to turn her face into his palm, and when one of his hands traced a path down her neck and stopped at the neckline of her gown, she had to force away the awareness of her body's reaction to the fire in his fingers. She stared fixedly at his other hand, which came to rest casually on the tabletop, and admired the strength of it, the length of his fingers.

And the fingers of his other hand, the hand she chose to ignore, curled over her neckline, the same way he would hook his thumbs into the pockets of his coat. She could detect no burning desire in his touch and silently cursed.

Hadn't he asked her a question? Oh yes… "I asked you here to, um… thank you." Summer breathed a sigh of relief. "That's right. Thank you for finding my mother's family. Um. How did you manage that, anyway?"

She couldn't help it. Her nipple seemed to have a mind of its own; she could actually feel it jumping at his fingers. It took just a twist of her body to brush it against them, and she almost groaned aloud in relief. When she glanced at his face, her heart plummeted. Those crystal blue eyes stared back at her with indifference, that handsome face gave no indication that he felt anything at all from the touch of her nipple against his fingers.

Summer narrowed her eyes and twisted again. A burst of wetness spread between her legs, but the man sat like a statue.

Byron couldn't move. The swelling in his pants had become quite uncomfortable. He'd swept his fingers across her breasts more than once, and the girl hadn't even blinked. She'd even had the presence of mind to ask him something, and it took his soggy brain several minutes to process it and come up with an answer.

"His Royal Highness had you investigated." There, he'd managed a reply. Byron scooted his chair closer into the table, until the edge of it creased the front of his silk vest. He brushed his leg between hers, slowly pushed outward, spreading her legs beneath the table. He took a sip of his tea to distract his body's response to the thought of what he was doing, and laid the cup in the saucer with careful precision.

Then he felt her bare toes against his calf and raised his eyebrows at her.

Summer couldn't look at him anymore. She kept thinking about how his lips tasted, how his tongue felt. She stared out the window and spread her legs as far apart as humanly possible beneath that table. Surely the accidental brush of his own leg made him aware that she'd spread open to him? While trying to ignore the jolt of fire that ripped through her body when her nipple brushed his fingers again, she wiggled out of her slippers and ran her foot up the leg of his pants.

"He didn't think I was good enough for you, did he?"

"What?" Byron couldn't remember what they'd been talking about. The feel of her toes against his leg occupied all his thought processes at the moment.

"Your prince. That's why he had me investigated."

"Oh, that. It wouldn't have mattered what he thought, anyway. I'm just glad he found your family for you."

"Are you?" Summer reached over and tugged at his cravat. "I'm just trying to make you more comfortable."

"Ah."

"Monte's family is overjoyed at the prospect of a marriage with me now." Summer slowly pulled the cloth away from his neck, wishing she were that piece of silk. The man acted as if undressing him at table were nothing out of the ordinary, that her toes curling into his calf had no effect on him whatsoever.

While she was being driven to distraction.

"So, are you?"

Summer reached across the table and ran her hands over the sides of his neck, curled her fingers into that soft blond hair. "Am I what?" She traced her fingertip over his lips, loving the feel of the tiny cleft in his lower one. He didn't move. Didn't blink. Just opened his mouth and captured her finger inside and suckled. She felt the pressure of it between her legs and snatched back her hand. The itch had become unbearable, and she squirmed against the seat cushion, no longer able to separate her mind from her body, because it had started to scream at her for relief. Seducing this man was hurting her.

Byron released his hold on her neckline and gripped both her shoulders. "Are you going to marry him?"

"Oh." Summer panted. "No, no. Who cares about him?"

Byron smiled. "Not I." He slid his hands down her shoulders, pulling at the light material, making the neckline of her gown sag even lower. He spread his fingers over her soft skin and realized through a fog that something hard had grazed his leg. Summer's knife. She wore her knife. The pressure of his erection was nothing compared to the throbbing he instantly felt. It was as if that part of him had a life of its own, and he'd never, ever, felt anything like that before.

"I'm just as good as you are," she blurted. "And I can't take it anymore!"

Byron looked up with alarm at the sudden anger in Summer's voice. What had he done? He was supposed to seduce her, not make her hate him. He'd made a mess of it, all because he couldn't control the reactions of his own body. Or the ignorant words out of his own mouth. "Huh?"

"I lied," snapped Summer, her itch now unbearable. "I didn't ask you here to th-thank you. I asked you here to… to…"

"To what?" he growled, more angry with himself than he could have ever imagined.

"To seduce you! And you don't even have the decency to… be seduced!"

Byron froze. He didn't know whether to laugh or shake her. "I also sent you a note. I found it still under your door."

Summer blinked at him.

"I asked to see you. So that *I* could seduce *you*." And he took his arm and swept it across the table, scattering dishes and tea and lace doilies across the floor. And he stood.

Summer gasped at the sight of him. His erection bulged through his pants; she could see it clearly outlined, even the curve where she knew he was most sensitive, where she'd run her tongue...

She opened her mouth, and something like a squeak came out of her throat.

Byron reached across the table and grabbed her shoulders, pulling her out of her chair, bringing his mouth to her own with a gentleness that belied his actions. He didn't so much kiss her as consume her, his lips hot and his tongue insistent. Summer let him swallow her whole and still longed for more.

Somehow the table was no longer between them.

He lifted her up and set her bottom on that small table, raking her skirts up around her waist, pushing down her neckline until her breasts sprang free. He gave them all the attention that Summer had craved, licking and suckling until she started to moan with the pleasure of it. He rested his hands on her silk drawers, and she could feel the heat of them branding her lower thighs, and then moving upward, until his thumbs brushed against the slit in the fabric, and he let out a groan of pure delight.

Summer reached forward and unbuttoned his pants, pulled him out none too gently, grateful that she no longer had to pretend indifference.

Byron pulled her bottom toward him, glad that the table was so low. He plunged inside of her and came with an explosion that rocked him to the soles of his feet. He hadn't done that since he was a boy, but no matter, for he knew it was just the beginning, that he'd stay rock-hard for a long, long time. So he didn't pause a beat but continued his rhythm, more aware of her pleasure now than his own. And completely unashamed of his initial selfishness, because the woman knew she'd driven him to it.

Summer held on to his shoulders and begged him for more. She wrapped her legs around his back and squeezed, drawing him deeper, filling her body and soul and heart with the strength of this man. And came with the sound of his name on her lips. She wrapped her arms around his neck and saw the chaise over his shoulder and smiled. She needn't have worried, not with Byron.

Byron held her in his arms, kept himself inside of her, a feeling unlike any he had ever known washing over him. This small, graceful woman had become his entire world, and he'd gladly give his life for her. It was frightening and empowering, all at the same time.

"Did you mean it, Summer? When you said you were worthy of me?"

She continued to hold him tightly to her, and her voice spoke at his ear. "Certainly. Now the question is whether you're worthy of *me*."

Byron frowned, gently pulled her away so he could look into her eyes. He refused to allow her to let anything come between them ever again. "Of course not. Will you marry me anyway?"

Summer felt herself drowning in the softness of his gaze. Where had that snobbish, arrogant man gone to? She watched the way one golden brow quirked upward, the curve of his lips that might be considered a sneer by someone who didn't know him as well as she did. Oh yes, the Duke of Monchester was still every bit as arrogant as he always appeared to be. But not to her, never again. All she had to do was look into his eyes to see beyond the surface to the real man inside.

"Of course I'll marry you."

Byron nodded, as if he never doubted her answer. Inwardly, he sighed with profound relief. "Then I'd prefer you to be on something softer."

She blinked those amber-colored eyes at him. "You mean… again?"

He swept her up into his arms and carried her to the other door in the room, which he assumed was her bedroom. Byron held her with one arm while he turned the door handle.

"I really should warn you…" started Summer. But she spoke too late. The door swung open, and the room erupted with flying fur. Moo-moo sprang from the bed back to her curtain when the cat caught sight of the stranger. Lefty barked furiously, jumping on the bedding in his lopsided way. Sweetie took one look at Byron and ducked his head back under the bed.

"What is that?"

Summer saw him staring at Sweetie's hind end.

"It's a dog."

"That's not a dog; it's a small pony."

Summer shushed her critters.

Byron sighed. "Lionel is going to be ecstatic. Don't you adopt any normal pets?"

"Only if they need me."

Byron set her down, watched her calm her animals,

his eyes glowing with love. Then he stepped forward and introduced himself to the rest of his new family.

The next morning, Byron shook his son awake.

Sleepy blue eyes blinked up at him. "Did she like your kisses, Father?"

"Yes. Now hurry and get up; we have a wedding to go to."

"Capital!" said Lionel, bouncing out of bed. "Can we take her home, then?"

Byron nodded, poured cold water into the basin, and slapped it on his face. He'd had very little sleep last night and couldn't help the grin of satisfaction that followed the thought. "Her and the rest of the family."

"Who, her new grandmother?"

"No, although I think with time they'll come to visit. I meant the rest of her 'critters.'"

"She's got more?" Lionel couldn't help but miss India, Chi-chi, and Rosey. And since he'd had to leave Hunter in London, he'd felt terribly lonely in America whenever his father couldn't be with him. The thought of new companions made him think that the voyage back home wouldn't be as awful.

Byron dried his face with a cloth and peered at his son from over the edge. "She's got a three-legged dog, another with four legs, but the size of a pony, and a mad cat that climbs curtains for comfort."

He watched his son's face light up with joy. "I'm dreadfully glad you got Summer back, Father! Our life will never be boring again, will it?"

"No, son, I'm afraid it won't," Byron replied, his own heart flooding with joy. *And it will never be lonely again,* he silently added as he brushed off his best top hat.

Acknowledgments

A special thank-you to Dominique Raccah and Deborah Werksman of Sourcebooks, whose enthusiasm and support put this book into reader's hands.

About the Author

Kathryne Kennedy is a multipublished, award-winning author of magical romances. She's lived in Guam, Okinawa, and several states in the U.S., and currently lives in Arizona with her wonderful family—which includes two very tiny Chihuahuas. She welcomes readers to visit her website, where she has ongoing contests, at www.KathryneKennedy.com.

Lessons in
French

BY LAURA KINSALE
New York Times bestselling author

"An exquisite romance and an instant classic."
—*Elizabeth Hoyt*

HE'S EXACTLY THE KIND OF TROUBLE SHE CAN'T RESIST…

Trevelyan and Callie were childhood sweethearts with a taste for adventure. Until the fateful day her father drove Trevelyan away in disgrace. Nine long, lonely years later, Trevelyan returns, determined to sweep Callie into one last, fateful adventure, just for the two of them…

"Kinsale's delightful characters and delicious wit enliven this poignant tale…It will charm your heart!" —*Sabrina Jeffries*

"Laura Kinsale creates magic. Her characters live, breathe, charm, and seduce, and her writing is as delicious and perfectly served as wine in a crystal glass. When you're reading Kinsale, as with all great indulgences, it feels too good to stop." —*Lisa Kleypas*

978-1-4022-3701-0 • $7.99 U.S./$8.99 CAN

MIDSUMMER MOON

BY LAURA KINSALE
New York Times bestselling author

"The acknowledged master."
—*Albany Times-Union*

IF HE REALLY LOVED HER,
WOULDN'T HE HELP HER REALIZE HER DREAM?

When inventor Merlin Lambourne is endangered by Napoleon's advancing forces, Lord Ransom Falconer, in service of his government, comes to her rescue and falls under the spell of her beauty and absent-minded brilliance. But he is horrified by her dream of building a flying machine—and not only because he is determined to keep her safe.

"Laura Kinsale writes the kind of works that live in your heart." —Elizabeth Grayson

"A true storyteller, Laura Kinsale has managed to break all the rules of standard romance writing and come away shining."
—*San Diego Union-Tribune*

978-1-4022-1398-4 • $7.99 U.S./$8.99 CAN

THE
PRINCE
OF
MIDNIGHT

BY LAURA KINSALE
New York Times bestselling author

"Readers should be enchanted."
—*Publishers Weekly*

INTENT ON REVENGE, ALL SHE WANTS FROM HIM IS TO LEARN HOW TO KILL

Lady Leigh Strachan has crossed all of France in search of S.T. Maitland, nobleman, highwayman, and legendary swordsman, once known as the Prince of Midnight. Now he's hiding out in a crumbing castle with a tame wolf as his only companion, trying to conceal his deafness and desperation. Leigh is terribly disappointed to find the man behind the legend doesn't meet her expectations. But when they're forced on a quest together, she discovers the dangerous and vital man behind the mask, and he finds a way to touch her ice cold heart.

"No one—repeat, no one—writes historical romance better." —Mary Jo Putney

978-1-4022-1397-7 • $7.99 U.S./$8.99 CAN

SEIZE THE FIRE

BY LAURA KINSALE
New York Times bestselling author

AN UNLIKELY PRINCESS SHIPWRECKED
WITH A WAR HERO WHO'S GOT HELL TO PAY

Her Serene Highness Olympia of Oriens—plump, demure, and idealistic—longs to return to her tiny, embattled land and lead her people to justice and freedom. Famous hero Captain Sheridan Drake, destitute and tormented by nightmares of the carnage he's seen, means only to rob and abandon her. What is Olympia to do with the tortured man behind the hero's façade? And how will they cope when their very survival depends on each other?

978-1-4022-1396-0 • $7.99 U.S./$8.99 CAN

A *Duke* TO *Die For*

BY AMELIA GREY

THE RAKISH FIFTH DUKE OF BLAKEWELL'S UNEXPECTED AND shockingly lovely new ward has just arrived, claiming to carry a curse that has brought each of her previous guardians to an untimely end...

Praise for Amelia Grey's Regency romances:

"This beguiling romance steals your heart, lifts your spirits and lights up the pages with humor and passion." —Romantic Times

"Each new Amelia Grey tale is a diamond. Ms. Grey...is a master storyteller." —Affaire de Coeur

"Readers will be quickly drawn in by the lively pace, the appealing protagonists, and the sexual chemistry that almost visibly shimmers between."
—Library Journal

978-1-4022-1767-8 • $6.99 U.S./$7.99 CAN

A Marquis TO Marry

BY AMELIA GREY

"A captivating mix of discreet intrigue
and potent passion." —*Booklist*

"A gripping plot, great love scenes, and well-drawn
characters make this book impossible to put down."
—*The Romance Studio*

The Marquis of Raceworth is shocked to find a young
and beautiful Duchess on his doorstep—especially when
she accuses him of stealing her family's priceless pearls!
Susannah, Duchess of Brookfield, refuses to be intimidated by
the Marquis's commanding presence and chiseled good looks.
And when the pearls disappear, Race and Susannah will have
to work together—and discover they can't live apart…

Praise for *A Duke to Die For:*

"A lusciously spicy romp." —*Library Journal*

"Deliciously sensual… storyteller extraordinaire Amelia Grey
grabs you by the heart, draws you in, and does not let go."
—*Romance Junkies*

"Intriguing danger, sharp humor, and plenty of simmering
sexual chemistry." —*Booklist*

978-1-4022-1760-9 • $6.99 U.S./$8.99 CAN

Highland Rebel

BY JUDITH JAMES

"An unforgettable tale." —*The Romance Studio*

RAISED TO RULE HER CLAN, SHE'LL STOP AT
NOTHING TO PROTECT HER OWN

Daughter of a Highland laird, Catherine Drummond
rebels against ladylike expectations and rides fearlessly
into battle against the English forces sent to quell the
Scots' rebellion. When Catherine falls into the hands
of vicious mercenaries, she is saved from a grim fate
by an unlikely hero. Jamie Sinclair only wants to finish
one last mission for his king and collect his reward. But
in a world where princes cannot be trusted and faith
fuels intolerance, hatred, and war, no good deed goes
unpunished...

"Complex, compelling characters and a good, galloping
plot... Upscale historical romance at its best!"
—*Historical Novel Review*

"The romance is tender, yet molten hot."
—*Wendy's Minding Spot*

"Wonderfully written. It's captivating and heart
wrenching." —*Anna's Book Blog*

978-1-4022-2433-1 • $6.99 U.S./$8.99 CAN

HUNDREDS OF YEARS TO REFORM A RAKE

BY LAURIE BROWN

HIS TOUCH PULLED HER IRRESISTIBLY
ACROSS THE MISTS OF TIME

Deverell Thornton, the ninth Earl of Waite, needs Josie Drummond to come back to his time and foil the plot that would destroy him. Josie is a modern career woman, thrust back in time to the sparkling Regency period, where she must contend with the complex manners and mores of the day, unmask a dangerous charlatan, and in the end, choose between the ghost who captivated her or the man himself—but can she give her heart to a notorious rake?

"A smart, amusing, and fun time travel/Regency tale."
—*All About Romance*

"Extremely well written…A great read from start to finish." —*Revisiting the Moon's Library*

"Blends Regency, contemporary and paranormal romance to a charming and very entertaining effect." —*Book Loons*

978-1-4022-1013-6 • $6.99 U.S./$8.99 CAN

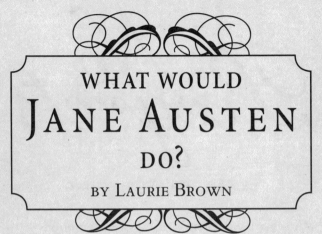

WHAT WOULD
JANE AUSTEN
DO?

BY LAURIE BROWN

Eleanor goes back in time to save a man's life, but could it be she's got the wrong villain?

Lord Shermont, renowned rake, feels an inexplicable bond to the mysterious woman with radical ideas who seems to know so much…but could she be a Napoleonic spy?

Thankfully, Jane Austen's sage advice prevents a fatal mistake…

At a country house party, Eleanor makes the acquaintance of Jane Austen, whose sharp wit can untangle the most complicated problem. With an international intrigue going on before her eyes, Eleanor must figure out which of two dueling gentlemen is the spy, and which is the man of her dreams.

978-1-4022-1831-6 • $6.99 U.S. / $7.99 CAN

No Regrets

BY MICHÈLE ANN YOUNG

"A remarkable talent that taps your emotions with each and every page." —Gerry Russel, award winning author of *The Warrior Trainer*

A MOST UNUSUAL HEROINE

Voluptuous and bespectacled, Caroline Torrington feels dowdy and unattractive beside the slim beauties of her day. Little does she know that Lord Lucas Foxhaven thinks her curves are breathtaking, and can barely keep his hands off her.

"The suspense and sexual tension accelerate throughout." —*Romance Reviews Today*

978-1-4022-1016-7 • $6.99 U.S./$8.99 CAN